**Barbara Metzger is the
"QUEEN OF THE REGENCY ROMP."***

Rave reviews for Barbara Metzger's romances

"Funny and touching . . . delicious, delightful!"
—Edith Layton

"A doyen of humorous, Regency-era romance writing . . .
Metzger's gift for re-creating the flavor and ambience of
the period shines here, and the antics of her dirty-dish
villains, near-villains, and starry-eyed lovers are certain
to entertain."   —*Publishers Weekly* (starred review)

"The complexities of both story and character contribute
much to its richness. Like life, this book is much more
exciting when the layers are peeled back and savored."
—*Affaire de Coeur*

"A true tour de force. . . . Only an author with Metzger's
deft skill could successfully mix a Regency tale of death,
ruined reputations, and scandal with humor for a fine
and ultimately satisfying broth. . . . A very satisfying
read."

—The Best Reviews

"[She] brings the Regency era vividly to life with deft
humor, sparkling dialogue, and witty descriptions."
—*Romance Reviews Today

"Metzger has penned another winning Regency tale.
Filled with her hallmark humor, distinctive wit, and entertaining style, this is one romance that will not fail
to enchant."

—*Booklist* (starred review)

The Duel

Barbara Metzger

A SIGNET ECLIPSE BOOK

SIGNET ECLIPSE
Published by New American Library, a division of
Penguin Group (USA) Inc., 375 Hudson Street,
New York, New York 10014, USA
Penguin Group (Canada), 10 Alcorn Avenue, Toronto,
Ontario M4V 3B2, Canada (a division of Pearson Penguin Canada Inc.)
Penguin Books Ltd., 80 Strand, London WC2R 0RL, England
Penguin Ireland, 25 St. Stephen's Green, Dublin 2,
Ireland (a division of Penguin Books Ltd.)
Penguin Group (Australia), 250 Camberwell Road, Camberwell, Victoria 3124,
Australia (a division of Pearson Australia Group Pty. Ltd.)
Penguin Books India Pvt. Ltd., 11 Community Centre, Panchsheel Park,
New Delhi - 110 017, India
Penguin Group (NZ), cnr Airborne and Rosedale Roads, Albany,
Auckland 1310, New Zealand (a division of Pearson New Zealand Ltd.)
Penguin Books (South Africa) (Pty.) Ltd., 24 Sturdee Avenue,
Rosebank, Johannesburg 2196, South Africa

Penguin Books Ltd., Registered Offices:
80 Strand, London WC2R 0RL, England

First published by Signet Eclipse, an imprint of New American Library,
a division of Penguin Group (USA) Inc.

First Printing, February 2005
10 9 8 7 6 5 4 3 2 1

Copyright © Barbara Metzger, 2005
All rights reserved

To peacekeepers and peacemakers

Chapter One

Honor is everything to a man.
          —Anonymous, *On the Nature of Marriage*

Pride is everything to a man. He is just too proud to admit that, so he calls it something finer.
                    —Anonymous's wife

Gray.

Everything was gray: the dawn, the day, the fog. The trees that appeared like ghostly soldiers in the mist were gray. So were the reasons for this blasted duel.

He was right. He was wrong. And neither made ha'penny's worth of difference this dreary morning. It was too damned late.

Hell, Ian thought as he walked the paces, his Manton pistol heavy in his hand, his footsteps on the damp grass sounding loud in the hushed clearing, nothing was black and white anymore. He had to defend his honor, didn't he? Yet Lord Paige had to avenge the insult to his marriage, didn't he? So which man had the right on his side?

Ian was wrong to have bedded the baron's wife, he readily admitted. But Paige was wrong to make an issue of it, choosing White's Club to issue his challenge, where Ian could not refuse and still consider himself a gentleman. Lud knew Ian had not been the woman's first lover, and the roomful of lords gathered at the card tables had known he would not be her last. Hell, half of them were hoping to take Ian's place in the lady's affections, he guessed, if they had not already enjoyed the lush beauty's favors. They were welcome to Lady Paige's perfumed embrace, Ian, Earl of Marden, decided, at least a week too late. She was the one who had broken her marriage vows, and she was the one who had sworn Paige was a complacent husband, content with his mistresses. Damnation, *she* should be the one out at Hampstead Heath at this ungodly hour, ruining her footwear in the wet grass.

Instead, Mona was likely curled in her warm bed, with a warm someone beside her. The devil take them both, and her loutish lord, too. Ian knew that, sooner or later, he himself was destined for hell, no matter the outcome of this morning's work. He prayed for later, of course.

Actually, Ian did not bother praying. Cursing, yes, praying, no, for this was not liable to be his day of reckoning. While an illegal duel might be brushed aside, a dead earl could not be as easily ignored. Paige knew it, so he was not likely to be aiming at anything vital. Even if he were, Paige was a notoriously bad shot. Besides, he was merely making a statement. His lusty young wife had cuckolded the fat old fool one time too many, and Paige had to protest before he became a laughingstock for all of London. Ian wished the beef-witted baron had not chosen to make his point by pointing his finger in Ian's direction, along with accusations of everything from seduction to wife-stealing.

It was too late now to wish he had simply bloodied the baron's nose. Hell, it was too late to wish he had never set eyes—or hands—on the buxom baroness. Never again, Ian vowed as he took another step. No more Lady Paige. No more married ladies, period. They were not worth the few moments of pleasure.

What if, Ian wondered as he felt the damp morning cold penetrate his shirt, Paige were a better shot? Mona Paige was hardly worth dying over. No woman was, except Ian's sister and his mother, of course, but that was different. A man had to defend his family— not that either of the earl's womenfolk would act the wanton, thank goodness.

The thought of his mother and sister chilled Ian worse than the fog. If he were to die today, they would be left at the untender mercies of his cousin Nigel and his shrewish wife, for Ian had not yet performed his duties of ensuring the succession. Damnation, there was another black mark in his book. A peer of the realm had one overriding obligation to his lands and titles: providing an heir and perpetuity. Ian's lands were all in good condition, the family coffers were full, but his nursery was empty. Here he was, thirty years of age, mucking about with other men's wives, without one of his own to bear the next Earl of Marden. His late father must be spinning in his grave that Ian might soon join him in the family plot before begetting a boy child. Lud, the old man had been a tyrant in life. The devil only knew how mean he would be in the afterlife. Ian did not fancy finding out. He could only hope that Paige's aim was not bad enough to kill him by accident. As for himself, he meant to fire in the air. He had trespassed on Paige's preserves, after all. In addition, while he had no respect for a man who could not control his wife, Ian had no wish to have to flee the country for killing an old goat whose worst offense seemed to be an aversion to soap and water.

Ian's friend Carswell was counting out the paces. Never had so few steps taken such an eternity. Ian felt as if he were walking under water, as if he were watching himself watching the fog roil across the clearing, as if time were standing still, waiting for two grown men to make imbeciles of each other.

Damn, he was too old for this claptrap. If he was too old, Paige was far past the age of hotspur and pistol, steel and sword. He should have known better. He should have known better than to take a wife twenty years his junior.

It all came back to the woman. It always did. A muddle-headed man committed any number of idiocies, all to have a woman warm his bed and no one else's. Warm? Bah. Ian wondered if he would ever feel warm again, or if his very bones would turn to blocks of ice, like Old Man Winter, with icicles dripping from his nose. The November morning was not all that cold, he told himself. The grave was.

Whose idea was it to remove one's coat during an affair of honor, anyway? Someone who thought jacket buttons made better targets than plain white shirts? Or someone who was such a slave to fashion that he had himself sewn into his coat, and could not lift his arm high enough to shoot? Ian would be deuced if he ever let his tailor fit him so tightly that he could not protect himself, and to hell with fashion. But Paige had shrugged out of his, with his second's assistance, like a fat snake shedding its skin, so Ian had done the same. Their white shirts—Paige's was slightly yellowed, and slightly spotted with yesterday's meals— billowed in the breeze.

Thinking of Paige's dinner made Ian's stomach growl. Most likely the same clunch who decreed gentlemen should remove their coats also decided they should meet at dawn, before breaking their fast. That lackwit must have possessed something smaller than Ian's six-foot one-inch, muscular frame, which needed hearty and frequent sustenance to maintain. The early hour might have been chosen for secrecy's sake, which was more of a fallacy than going to face one's enemy weak with hunger. Why, half of London knew Marden and Lord Paige were to meet this morning. They had changed the location of the duel at the last minute to avoid a public spectacle and to avoid running afoul of Bow Street. Otherwise the empty field would look like Epsom on race day, with odds-makers and ale-sellers amid the throngs of spectators.

Now the only witnesses to this madness would be Ian's second, Carswell, Paige's second, Philpott, and the surgeon, who was reading a journal. Perhaps they could all go to breakfast together when this was over. Ian would offer to pay.

Carswell was still counting. One would think Carswell was measuring his favorite blend of snuff, such precision Ian's fastidious friend was showing. Next time Ian would choose someone who counted faster.

No, there would not be a next time. Ian was not going to duel again, no matter the provocation. His right fist would have to be enough to settle any disagreements that calm, rational thought could not. He added affairs of honor to the list of activities he was swearing to forsake in the future. No more challenges given or accepted. No more dallying with married ladies. No more waiting for one more birthday, then one after that, before taking a wife. No more delaying his own dynasty.

He was going to be a changed man after this morning—a better man, by George. He'd begin right after breakfast.

Carswell was done counting the paces at last. Now Philpott took command. "Gentlemen," he began, "at the count of three, you will turn and fire. One. Two."

Boom.

Ian felt the pistol ball fly past his ear. Paige was as sorry a shot as he recalled. The baron was also a sorry excuse for a gentleman. Like a craven, like a cur, he'd shot early, aiming at Ian's broad back. Philpott was gasping. Carswell was so angry he looked as if he would have shot Paige himself, if he'd had a spare pistol in his hand. The surgeon was shaking his head in disgust.

Ian turned and raised his arm. No one could blame him for shooting now. He was defending himself, after all. He took careful aim at Paige, right at the man's heart. And Ian Maddox, Mad Dog Marden, never missed his target.

Paige knew it, too. He realized his days in London were finished either way. He would never be allowed into his clubs or invited to his friends' homes, for a back-shooting coward had no friends. He'd had one chance to avenge his honor and he'd botched it. Now he could only stand, waiting for the Earl of Marden's uncertain mercy. He was as good as dead to the life he knew, if he were not dead altogether.

Ian made him wait. And wait, while the earl's arm never wavered from pointing at the muckworm's heart, as small and shriveled as that organ might be. All color left Paige's flabby cheeks, and his jowls trembled. A tear started to trickle down his face; then a stain spread at the front of his trousers.

Philpott spit on the ground. "Demme if he ain't wet himself. I'm leaving. The dastard can walk back to town for all I care."

But he stayed on, to see what Ian would do.

The earl looked into Paige's eyes, willing the man

to acknowledge that his life was in Ian's hands, that he lived by Ian's philanthropy only, that he was not worth wasting a pistol ball on. Ian slowly raised his weapon up over Paige's head, then pointed to the left, toward the trees, and squeezed the trigger.

Whereas before everything moved as if embedded in amber, now time sped by, as if making up for the wasted minutes.

Boom, went Ian's pistol. Then *boom* again, as if the ball had ricocheted off one of the trees. Then almost at once, a cry. A shout. A thud. The squeal of a frightened horse, the gallop of hooves. Another shout and more hoofbeats. Then silence.

Ian was racing toward the trees. Philpott was standing, confused, and Paige was running toward his friend's carriage, fleeing. The surgeon picked up his bag and followed Carswell on Ian's heels.

As he ran, Ian could just make out two horses tearing off through the fog. One was riderless; the other had a brown-coated groom leaning over, trying to grasp the runaway's reins.

He put the horses out of his mind, intent on peering through the mist to the trees, to their bases, to what the knot in his stomach and the lump in his throat warned him he might find.

"There," he shouted to Carswell, pointing toward a darker form beside a thick oak's trunk. He reached the place first, and turned the inert body over.

Blood. There was blood everywhere, from the fellow's upper chest, from his head that had been lying next to a large, blood-stained rock. Ian could not tell if he breathed. He snatched off his cravat and pressed it to the head wound. Then Carswell was there, white-faced, holding out his monogrammed handkerchief. Ian wiped the sweat from his own suddenly overheated forehead.

Then the surgeon huffed up. "Let me see what this tomfoolery has wrought, then. Stand aside, my lords."

He pressed his head to the man's chest. "He lives. Not for long, on this damp ground, losing so much blood. Who knows which wound is worse, the one from the bullet or the one from the boulder. He needs treatment, on the instant. St. Jerome's Hospital is not too far away."

"We'll take him in my carriage," Ian stated. "To my home. He will get better care there."

Before anyone could argue, Ian picked up the limp body as gently as he could. Carswell stood ready to assist, but there was no need. The man weighed less than a sack of grain. The surgeon entered the carriage first, and Ian handed his burden in, then leaped in after, telling his driver to spring the horses. Carswell shouted that he would see about Philpott and the missing groom, and Paige, too. "Target practice, we'll say, Ian," he called after the rocking coach. "A shot gone amiss at target practice!"

Otherwise, one part of Ian's mind acknowledged, he had shot an innocent man in cold blood. If the man died, he was a murderer. No matter that it was an accident. Duels were illegal, so shooting bystanders had to be a worse crime. He doubted they would hang an earl, but he would have to leave the country for a while, anyway. Perhaps for good. Or the man's kin might want satisfaction. Heaven knew they were entitled to it. Not that his own blood—Lord, there was so much blood—could bring this man back to them. Ian's mind was racing, while his hand was pressed to the wound on the fellow's thin chest as the surgeon directed. With his other hand, he dabbed at the blood on the man's forehead and cheeks, praying for him to open his eyes, to live. The chap did not respond, but what Ian uncovered under the gore made his own blood grow cold: no whiskers, no beard, no wrinkled cheeks. He had shot a boy.

God, he had shot a boy. Ian almost gagged on the truth under his very hands and eyes. The lad could not be more than fifteen or sixteen, with wavy blond hair and a fine, straight nose. His coat was of good material, and his boots had a decent shine to them. Those facts, plus the groom who had been accompanying him, pointed to the boy being a gentleman's son, or the progeny of a wealthy cit. Not that it mattered, not that a well-born youth deserved to live more than a tinker's brat. No, it did not matter at all, except that Ian might have to tell someone he knew what had happened, instead of a stranger.

He had shot a boy. Someone's beloved son. Some mother's pride and joy. Some father's hope for the future.

He was almost tempted to reach for the pistol he kept under the carriage seat and shoot himself. But the surgeon was telling him to press on the wound with both hands now, to stop the bleeding. Killing himself would not bring the boy back, anyway. His prayers—to say nothing of the resources he commanded as a wealthy, powerful earl—might keep the youth alive, though. Ian swore he would do anything, move whatever mountains he had to, to get his victim the finest care, the most skilled physicians—anything it took to make him live, to make him forgive Ian.

He would never, ever forgive himself. He'd shot a boy.

"No smelling salts," the surgeon muttered.

"I do not need them," Ian replied. The sight of all the blood was making him sick at heart, not faint.

"For the boy, my lord. I will not try to rouse him until we have him settled. No need for him to suffer worse than he needs, in the transport."

"Of course," Ian said, even more ashamed.

The boy did not stir until the coach stopped outside Maddox House in Grosvenor Square. Jed Coachman jumped down as soon as a servant appeared to hold the winded horses, shouting to the groom that there had been an accident during a shooting match.

Loyal Jed, Ian thought, even as he held the lad steady. Jed reached in to take the boy, but Ian shook his head. He would carry his poor victim himself. It was the least he could do—and the most, at this time. The youngster opened his eyes—a clear turquoise blue, Ian noted—and tried to sit up.

The earl almost wept in relief that the lad had regained consciousness after the blow to his head. The surgeon had warned he might not, ever. "Can you walk, young sir?" Ian asked through dry lips.

The boy's brows knit in despair and a tear found a course through the bloodstains on his cheek. "No, my lord. I am sorry."

"Do not be foolish. I am the one who is sorry. More sorry than I can ever tell. Do not worry though, I will not let you fall. I swear."

"He's gone off again, my lord," the surgeon told Ian.

"Damn, and we did not find out his name or his address."

"But we did find that he recognized you, at least as a gentleman, and is in his right senses. An excellent sign, my lord. Excellent."

The whole household was tearing around, it seemed, fetching towels and sheets and hot water and hot tea and Ian's own family physician. Every servant who could find some reason to watch the earl's careful progress up the arched marble stairs did so, and if any of them noticed that their master's cheeks were wet, too, they ascribed that to the dampness of the day and the fog.

Ian's capable valet was waiting outside a guest chamber, the sheets already turned down, a fire hastily lit in the hearth by the time the sad cavalcade reached the upper story. As soon as the earl had set down his light burden, Hopkins handed him a glass of brandy before hurrying to assist the surgeon.

Ian set the glass down. "He is unconscious again, I am afraid, so this will not do any good."

"For you, my lord," Hopkins replied as he carefully, efficiently removed the boy's boots and produced a scissors to cut away the youngster's ruined coat while the surgeon wiped at the gash on his head.

Ian knew he would be no help until his hands stopped shaking, so he nodded and took a long swallow of the brandy, glad for its searing heat. It could not melt the icy grip on his innards, but it helped.

"What do you think?" he asked after what seemed an eternity. Hopkins had handed at least five basins of bloodied water to one of the footmen. Ian had finished his glass of brandy hours before, and had worn a track in the Aubusson carpet. He did not want more spirits, needing all his wits about him. But he poured a glass for the surgeon, and another for Hopkins.

The surgeon straightened up and accepted the brandy after wiping his hands on a clean towel. "I think he might live, my lord."

Ian's knees turned weak with relief. He sank onto the chair beside the bed, then jumped up to start pacing again when the surgeon continued.

"If, that is, he does not take a fever, has not lost too much blood, is not concussed, and the wound does not turn septic. The pistol ball appears to have made a neat exit, without damaging the lungs or heart that

I can tell. Of course, he might be bleeding inside. It is the head wound that worries me worse. No telling if his brain will swell, or if bits of the skull are—"

"Yes, I get the idea. How soon before you know?"

The surgeon shrugged. "Soon, if he dies. A week or so if he recovers. Yes, if he survives a sennight, he should make a full recovery. Unless his spine is damaged, or his lungs are weakened, or his wits are addled."

Good grief, if he lived, the boy could be an invalid or an idiot his entire life? Ian poured himself another drink. "I'll have to find his people."

Hopkins handed him a card case from the boy's pocket. Ian pulled one out. "Troy Renslow," he read. "Cameron Street." He did not recognize the family name, but the address was at the outskirts of Mayfair—respectable, but not on one of the fashionable squares inhabited by the wealthy and well-known. The fact that the lad had a calling card at all put him among the genteel, if not the *ton*. Whoever they were, his family would be frantic soon, when the groom returned without their son. Ian had to go, now that he had something to report to them.

Hopkins signaled for one of the footmen to stay with the patient while he repaired Lord Marden's appearance for such an important, disturbing visit.

Before he left, though, Ian stepped closer to the bed and touched the boy's hand. "I will be back soon, Master Renslow, after telling your family where you are." He spoke as if the youngster might hear him and be comforted. "Hold fast, Troy. You will be fine. I know it."

Hearing his name, or the voice of authority, Troy opened those startling turquoise eyes and looked into the earl's. He reached for Lord Marden's hand.

"My . . . sister," he struggled to whisper. "Attie . . . Can't leave her alone."

The boy and his sister were alone in London? "Of course not. I shall invite your sister to stay here at Maddox House."

"And Roma? Can't stay . . . by herself."

"However many sisters you have, they will all be welcome to come visit or stay here."

The boy looked confused and tried to speak more, but Ian hushed him. "Do not fret. I will take care of everything. You merely need to rest and recover your strength."

The boy's eyes were already drifting closed. The surgeon was packing his instruments and nodded. "Sleep is the best medicine. And he seems to be compos mentis—of sound mind—so at least you will have something positive to tell the boy's family."

What, he could tell Renslow's sisters that the lad could not walk, was in danger of contracting a fever, if he did not lapse into a coma, but that he recognized his own name and remembered theirs? That should reassure a loving family. Lud, Ian was going to have to lie through his teeth. He'd tell the women that their brother was going to be fine. Right after he told them the boy had taken a ricocheting bullet, fallen off his horse, and hit his head on a rock—at target practice.

For a man who took pride in his honor, Ian hated himself.

Chapter Two

To a man, honor is everything.

—Anonymous

To a woman, family is everything.

—Mrs. Anonymous

Ian hurried through his toilette as fast as he could, knowing the Renslow household must be in an uproar. In the back of his mind, placed there by the surgeon, was the worry that young Renslow might stick his spoon in the wall before his family had a chance to speak with him one last time.

He could not let that happen. His shirt and breeches were ripped off. They would be tossed out or burned, anyway. He never wanted to see the blood-soaked garments again, not even as rags. He could not make a call on the ladies unshaven, but was too anxious to suffer Hopkins's precise ministrations, and did the job himself. He did not shed quite as much blood as the boy, but almost. He was too impatient to be gone to fuss with a neckcloth, so had his valet find him a spotted kerchief to tie loosely at his throat. A swipe of the comb through his dark curls, a plain gray waistcoat, a loose-fitted blue superfine jacket, and he was bounding down the stairs just as the hall clock chimed.

Nine chimes? Could it be only nine in the morning? Ian reached for his watch on its fob chain. Nine o'clock. He felt as if he had lived through a whole day in Purgatory, yet it was far too early for fashionable London to be calling for morning chocolate. That was what happened, Ian supposed, when one started the day before dawn. Or when one had brandy for breakfast.

The boy's family had to be notified, even if they were still abed. Servants would be up and about, and that groom must have set up a cry when he returned to the clearing and did not find his fallen charge. Unless he was a casual acquaintance, along for the ride. Or unless he kept going, stealing the horse. That was too much for Ian to consider now. Facing . . . what were the names? Attie and Roma. That was it. Facing two sisters was going to be hard enough.

Ian's friend Carswell was waiting at the foot of the stairs, every hair on his head perfectly combed, not a wrinkle or a speck in sight on his clothes, despite the early hour and the events of the morning. "How is he?" Carswell asked without bothering with a greeting.

"He'll do, for now," Ian said, leading the other man to the library, out of earshot of the servants. "The physician and the surgeon are consulting about treatment. Hopkins and my housekeeper are positive they can keep him alive."

"Capital. But you look like hell."

Ian hunched his broad shoulders. "What do you expect? At least you look your usual elegant self, considering you were second to a possible murderer."

Carswell looked away and cleared his throat. "Yes, well, I thought you should know that Philpott won't say anything, not after his man turned craven. A shooting match gone bad is enough for him. He'll spread it through the clubs that you and Paige decided to settle your differences with a test of skill, but a shot went awry. Philpott swears he will make certain Paige leaves town, never to return. That dirty dish left before we discovered the lad, so he cannot refute the claim of a misfire. I know your driver will stand by the story, but what of the surgeon?"

Ian gave a rough laugh. "For the money he is making, the sawbones would say the boy shot himself. I am the one who cannot stomach the lies."

"It was an accident, man! You did not set out to shoot anyone. Why, you did not even try to shoot that dastard Paige. But you know what the scandal sheets and the gossip columns will make of it. You'll have days and weeks of explaining, with the rabble crying for your neck in a noose, as if they were Frenchies blindly attacking the aristocracy. The regent does not need such ill favor for one of his own, not now, when his own popularity is at so low an ebb."

"What, you think the truth of this morning's events can topple the government? If Prinny would spend the country's wealth feeding the poor instead of making a glutton of himself he could be a hero to the common man."

"We both know that is not going to happen. But think of what a scandal would do for the bill you are sponsoring next month in Parliament, if you are seen as considering yourself above the law. Think of your mother and sister. They will be devastated."

Ian was thinking of young Renslow's sisters, and his mother, if he had one. "Yes, I understand. Renslow knows the truth, of course. I shall wait to find out what he wishes said."

"Your butler told me he is just a boy. How can he understand the ramifications?"

"He is the one teetering at death's door, the only

one who is totally innocent. How can I not respect his wishes?"

Carswell kicked at a footstool. "What a muddle."

Ian seconded that, but turned for the door. "I have to go, to tell his family."

Carswell's already pale face whitened to the shade of his waterfall-tied neckcloth. He swallowed hard, but still offered to go in Ian's stead.

Ian clasped his old schoolmate's shoulder. "You are a true friend, but this is something I have to do myself."

"I understand," Carswell said, unable to disguise the relief he felt. "I'll look in at White's to make sure Philpott gets the story straight, but I'll stop by later, to see how the boy does. Renslow, you say? Someone at White's will know who his people are, I am sure."

"I have an address."

"Yes, well, I will leave you to it, then. Oh, I did bring back your coat and your Mantons. I left them with your man."

"You can have the pistols. Take them with you when you go."

"Really?" Carswell's eagerness was obvious, though he did say, "I cannot accept them. Much too valuable, of course."

"They are trash to me. I do not want them in my house."

"Well, if you are only going to toss them out, I will be delighted to own the things. A prize pair, of course."

Ian would not have purchased the deadly accurate set otherwise. He would never touch them again, never wanted to see them again. "Enjoy them. I will see you later."

Carswell walked Ian out the door and to the carriageway under the portico, where Ian's horse was waiting, along with a coach in case he had to carry the Renslow ladies back to Maddox House.

Carswell shook his hand and wished him luck, then pretended to polish his quizzing glass. "One more thing, old chap. My yacht is in the harbor, ready to sail, if . . . if the worst happens and you need to leave the country for a bit."

"You mean if the boy dies and I am charged with his murder and decide to flee rather than face the courts? I pray it will not come to that."

"Perhaps I'll stop by St. George's on my way to White's, what? Say a prayer and all that. Can't hurt, I always say."

"Say two, won't you? One for Renslow, one for me. Lord knows we both need it."

The Renslows' house was what Ian had expected: neat but not ostentatious, in a neighborhood whose residences were closer together, far less imposing than those nearer the fashionable districts. The carriages he passed were less highly polished, the horses less well bred.

The first passerby he asked had never heard of the Renslows. The second, an elderly nursemaid with two children in tow, directed him to a place a few doors away. "They'll be the captain's kin come to stay. And with himself out at sea." She clucked her tongue in disapproval. "Not that it is any of my affair, I am sure."

Ian was sure it was not, but he thanked her and made his way to the modest house she had pointed out. He waited for his carriage to pull up and one of his grooms jump down to hold his horse before walking up the short path to the door. Yes, a brass plate read: BARNABY BEECHAM, CAPTAIN, HIS MAJESTY'S

NAVY. Ian took a deep breath and rapped on the door. Then he rapped again when no one came.

"Hold on there, y'lubberkin, you know I can't do no jig to the door," he heard from within just as he was about to knock louder, or knock the door down altogether. "And it's about time you got back afore I had to tell—"

The door opened. So did a short old man's nearly toothless jaw. "You ain't young Renslow."

Ian surveyed the sorry excuse for a butler. The grizzled relic had a patch over one eye and a hook instead of a hand. Captain Beecham might be with the Navy, but this old salt looked like he'd been a pirate, pure and simple. All he lacked was a peg leg and a parrot on his shoulder. "No, I am most definitely not Mr. Renslow. I am here on his behalf, however."

"I told them he hadn't ought to be on a horse. Dangerous beasts, they are." The old sailor was eyeing the carriage in the nearby roadway. "Brung him home, did you? That Alfie Brown said he must've been fine, to walk away. Damn fool thing to do, if you ask me. Should of knowed Alfie'd come back for him with the horses. The nipper's all right, then?"

"He'll do." Ian was not about to discuss the situation with a toothless old tar, and certainly not out on the street where some raggedy mongrel was sniffing at his boots with who knew what intentions. "If you would take my card to the Misses Renslow, I will explain."

The seaman scratched his head. "Ain't no Mrs. Renslow. S'pose you ought to talk to Miss Attie, though."

"Or Miss Roma."

"You want to talk to Roma?"

"Whichever woman is in charge of the boy." He frowned and ordered, "Now. She will be worrying."

The sailor heard that tone of authority, and looked at the card in his hand. "Aye, milord. But she don't know the boy's gone missing. Seemed better that way."

And worse for Ian. What if she were the nervous kind? If there was no mother, the sister might have taken over the role—become doting or domineering, keeping the boy wrapped in cotton wool. After all, young Troy was here in London, tied to her leading strings, not away at school as a boy his age should have been. How could the earl tell a mother hen that her chick was pecking at death's door? Now Ian was glad for the battered old sailor, who gave his name as Macelmore, or Mack Elmore, and his slow gait down a narrow hall.

The earl would have been happier if the dog hadn't followed them, still snuffling at his boots and gnarling, making halfhearted attempts at the tassels dangling from Ian's Hessian boots—or Ian's legs. The ugly, unmannered beast must live here, then, which did not speak well for the place being a well-ordered gentleman's residence. Of course, no gentleman hired a one-eyed sea dog as his major domo, either. When the animal did not obey Ian's command to stop, to stay, to sit, or to go to the devil, Ian decided to ignore it, concentrating on what to say to Renslow's sister. "I am sorry" seemed pitifully, painfully inadequate.

He was rehearsing some way of gently informing the poor woman of her brother's plight, deciding to spare her the worst of it until she had seen the boy herself. If the servants had not told her about the duel—he would have to speak to that groom, Alfie Brown, and likely pay for his retirement to the West Indies—he would not mention anything but an accident. The longer he could put off telling a loving relation about her kin's condition, the better.

When they reached a door at the end of the corridor, Macelmore pushed it open without knocking.

The fair-haired woman seated at the narrow dining room table did not raise her head from the newspaper she was reading over her morning tea. "It is about time you returned home, Troy. Breakfast is cold and Mr. Wiggs will be here for lessons soon. Mac, will you bring a fresh pot of hot water?"

Macelmore said, "Don't need it. The boy ain't home. This here swell's come to tell you he's been shot off his horse. I told you no good would come of letting the sprat ride. Broke his neck asides, for all I know. That fishbait Alfie Brown left him."

So much for breaking the news gently.

The seafaring butler was going on: "The governor here came to bring the news. Earl of Marden, he calls hisself. Fancy coach outside. And he don't like dogs."

Ian liked dogs well enough, hounds and retrievers at the hunt, herders in the shepherds' fields. He did not like ugly, untrained mongrels of indeterminate ancestry who guarded their houses against gentlemen's footwear. At least the dog had stopped harrying Ian's boots to search for crumbs under the table. Macelmore did not stop his introduction, such as it was.

"His lordship ain't saying much about the nipper, which don't sound good to my ears."

Ian glared at the man to be quiet, but since Macelmore was headed toward the teapot on the sideboard, he could not see. The woman gasped and lowered her newspaper, half jumping to her feet, sending her chair clattering back. The dog growled at her, too.

She was small and slight, in a simple round gown, with blond hair trailing down her back. Good grief, Ian thought, clutching his hat and gloves, which Macelmore had never taken from him, the sister was no more than a little girl! Why, she had not yet put her hair up! No mother, an uncle at sea, her brother shot. No wonder young Renslow said she could not stay here by herself, not if Macelmore was any indication of the caliber of servants. But what the deuce was he going to do with a child? How much help or comfort could she be to the wounded boy, besides? And what if she became distraught or hysterical? Ian ran his hand through his dark curls, wondering how much worse this nightmare could get.

He grasped at straws. "Perhaps your other sister ought to be here?"

The young miss shook her head, sending long blond tresses flying, making her seem younger still. "I have no sister. Perhaps you have come to the wrong house," she said, sounding hopeful.

Her lips were white and her eyes were damp. They were that same turquoise you could see sometimes at the horizon over the ocean on a clear day, the same as Renslow's, so there was no mistake. Still, Ian asked, "Troy Renslow is your brother? You are Miss Attie?"

She nodded and gave a slight curtsy. "I am Troy's sister, Athena Renslow. Please forgive my manners, my lord. Won't you be seated and tell me about my brother. Mac, please bring coffee, and something stronger for his lordship."

Ian had to admire her fortitude. The chit had bottom, not flying into a pelter or collapsing into a swoon, thank goodness. Once the servant had left the room, she sat back in her chair and waited for him to be seated.

"Please, he is all right?" she asked.

"He is fine," he lied. "The surgeon has every expectation of a full recovery."

"Then why is he not here, where we can look after him?"

She was a clever little puss besides, Ian thought,

going straight to the heart of the matter. "Why, we did not know his direction at first, you see."

"He could not tell you?"

Too clever by half, Ian decided, wishing the uncle were home. "There was too much confusion at first, with his groom riding off and all, so it seemed wiser to bring him to my home. He did ask for you there, however, and I came as soon as I could."

"But you did not bring him home. Why?"

Ian recalled his cousin Nigel's two children from last Christmas. "Why can't we swim in the fountain? How come the munitions room is kept locked? Why? Why? Why?" He wanted to strangle Miss Athena Renslow as much now as he'd wanted to strangle the brats then. Why could children not simply accept his word without question? His servants did—his fellow members of Parliament did, by Zeus. He was not about to tell this half-grown female that her brother might die— not until he could place her in the capable hands of his housekeeper. Nor would he let the boy come here to be nursed by a mere slip of a girl and a hook-handed old man. He had not seen any other servants, although he still had hopes for Roma, whomever she might be, perhaps a cousin or a companion. He could only hope. He would get to that in a minute. For now he told Miss Renslow, "We decided that his rest should not be disturbed, once the surgeon cleaned the wound. At least five members of my staff are watching over him. And I brought a carriage to take you to him."

"I . . . see," she said, and Ian was afraid she did. She was making no move to hurry to her brother's bedside, though, so maybe his reassurances were adequate. She was too busy crumbling toast and tossing the pieces to the dog under the table, another sign of this household's lax standards. Nor had Ian been offered the dry, stale toast, which would have tasted like manna to his empty stomach. At least she was not asking about the duel.

His relief was short-lived. "Tell me," she ordered, as if he were not her elder, not a titled gentleman, not in a hurry to get home to the boy and his own breakfast. It would be nuncheon, by now, he supposed.

"He will be fine."

"No, tell me about how my brother came to be shot."

Lud, he could use that coffee. Or the something stronger Macelmore had gone to fetch. He owed her an explanation, though. Hell, he owed these children everything he owned and then some. So he began. "Some gentlemen were having a marksmanship contest out at Hampstead."

"No, my brother is not permitted to ride so far."

"I tell you, Miss Renslow, we were at Hampstead. How old is your brother, anyway?"

"Fifteen."

"That explains it. No lad of fifteen years is going to obey petticoat tyranny." Especially not when the petticoat wearer was hardly older than himself.

She frowned. "Go on."

"As I said, the gentlemen were firing their pistols and—"

"You were there?"

The chit definitely needed schooling in manners. Ian drummed his fingers on the table. "Yes. The grounds were very foggy."

"Not too foggy to shoot a target?"

He took a deep breath. "Not that foggy, no. But one of the shots went wide, into some trees. No one knew your brother was riding there. Perhaps he had halted to watch. I did not ask. The first we knew of his presence was when we heard him cry out."

"Someone shot him?"

"No! We think a ball ricocheted off one of the trees. No one shot him on purpose, you have to believe me."

"Of course I do. Why would anyone shoot a young boy?"

"Exactly. Anyway, his horse bolted at the sound and tossed him." Ian was not going to mention the rock that cracked the boy's skull, or the fall that might have left him paralyzed. Miss Renslow was holding up well for a girl. He would not press his luck. "The groom—Alfie, Macelmore called him—rode after the horse. We had coaches there, however, and a surgeon, so did not wait for his return."

"You had a surgeon at a shooting match?"

Ian ignored that question. "Your man says Alfie is out looking for Troy now, thinking he must have walked back to town."

"No, Troy would not have done that."

"No matter. He did not. I carried him to my house, where the surgeon could tend him, and a physician has been consulted. Everything possible is being done for his care and comfort."

"Thank you, my lord. I am sure you have been everything kind, opening your house to a stranger that way."

Ian had to clear his throat. "It was nothing. Anyone would have done the same. At any rate, he is there now, waiting for you. Will you come?"

"Of course. I was waiting for you to have refreshment, my lord. You look like you could use it. This morning must have been difficult for you."

Impertinent chit. Ian stood. "I am fine. But you might wish to pack a few things, in case you decide to stay a day or two, to keep your brother company. He did not want you to be alone, so he would rest easier knowing you were close by."

"That is very generous, Lord Marden, and I thank you again. I shall just be a minute, gathering some of Troy's schoolbooks and such, too."

"I will ride on and notify my household of your arrival, leaving the carriage for your convenience. You are, ah, welcome to bring your"—he almost said "nursemaid"—"companion with you."

"I have no companion."

"Your maid, then."

She shook those blond locks again. "The house-keeper helps with my wardrobe. Otherwise I can take care of my own needs."

"But Troy mentioned Roma. He did not think she should be left behind."

"How like him, and how very sweet of you, my lord. Roma is devoted to my brother and would pine dreadfully. My family is in your debt, dear sir." With that, she stood and bent down, lifting the mangy dog into her arms, then thrusting it into Ian's arms. "Will you place Roma in the carriage?"

Chapter Three

Men rely on reason; women rely on feelings.
> —Anonymous

What is truth? What your head tells you or what your heart tells you?
> —Anonymous's wife

Upstairs, Athena threw a nightgown and a robe, a change of clothes, and her hairbrush into a small satchel as quickly as she could. Then she took the brush out again. She could not leave the house this way, with her hair looking like a mouse nest. Her hands were shaking so badly, though, that she could not set the hairpins in properly. The gathered strands fell down her shoulders again as soon as she reached under the bed for her slippers.

She made herself take a deep breath before starting over again. Troy would be fine. Lord Marden had said so, and she had to believe him, for anything else was unthinkable. Of course, the earl did not know how frail Troy had been as a child, how they had fussed and fretted over him for years. Her brother was stronger now, Athena told herself, strong enough to ride such a distance. He was never going to be a big, broad tree trunk of a man like Lord Marden, but Troy was no puny sapling. They were all small in her family. Athena had rued her own lack of inches many a time, yet she had as much stamina as any of the housemaids back at home in Derby. They were wiry, the Renslows, not weak.

Was Troy strong enough to survive a gunshot? That was the question. No, it was only one of the questions rattling around her head, the earl's story having more holes than her silver tea strainer. It was the most important question, though. She knew such injuries often led to fevers. She knew wounds could fester and become gangrenous. Where was Troy shot anyway, and how had she neglected to ask?

She had to let her hair fall again, reaching for a stack of handkerchiefs. She used the top one to blot at her eyes and blow her nose, before packing the rest in with her clothes. At least she had not turned into a watering pot in front of his lordship. Bad enough she looked as if she'd been dragged through a hedge backward, without embarrassing the poor man with her tears, when he was being so solicitous. Athena knew how a weeping woman dismayed her brothers, so she had tried her hardest not to weep until she reached her own room.

Thinking of the earl reminded her again of his parting words, words she clasped to herself like a drowning man grabbed for a floating log. He'd sworn to her that Troy would be all right. He was no god, no fortune-teller, not even a trained medical doctor, to be making her that promise, yet she believed him. Lord Marden was so sure, so strong, so very kind, that she trusted him, as if his saying Troy would recover made it so.

Trusting his lordship did not stop her from sending for their own physician, of course, or scrambling to gather her brother's books and her belongings as fast as she could, to be on her way, to see for herself, to be with her brother.

She had to do something with her hair first. Athena dumped out a drawer, looking for a ribbon to tie it back. Botheration, she did not have time to braid the mess, or the patience. If she had a scissors, she would cut it all off and be done. Of all the stupid things, she thought, wiping at her eyes again, to be fussing with her unruly mop when her brother needed her. She reached for her bonnet, thinking to stuff the lot of it up inside and worry about fixing it later, but Troy would be upset. He hated that she took so little pains with her appearance, dressing as simply as one of the serving girls at home. Worse, he felt guilty that their meager funds were spent on doctors and books and sightseeing excursions instead of a fancy dresser and a fashionable wardrobe for his beloved sister. Dear Troy thought she should be trying to attract a wealthy beau while they were in London, so her future would be secured.

Goodness, what would Miss Athena Renslow of Derbyshire do with a town buck, a sophisticated man of refined tastes and experience? She was naught but a country girl, despite being the daughter of a titled gentleman. In all her nineteen years, this was her second visit to the metropolis, a green girl staring wide-eyed at the crowds, the cathedrals, the myriad attractions. Besides, they knew no one in the *ton,* had no established hostess to make introductions. Perhaps when their uncle returned to England . . . No, Athena was content with looking after her brother and letting the Reverend Mr. Wiggs escort her about town.

If, however, she had any ambitions of fixing the attentions of a gentleman of distinction, she would be tempted to set her sights on the Earl of Marden. Any woman with two eyes would, Athena decided. He had to be one of the most imposing men in all of London, tall and well muscled. He was certainly the most handsome, with his dark curls, strong jaw, and warm brown eyes. He looked comfortable in his clothes, not like the tulips she had seen on the strut in the park, too tightly garbed to move naturally. He was confident, courteous, and kind. What could be more appealing in a husband—if one were looking for a husband, of course.

Athena was not. That is, she was not shopping at London's rarefied Marriage Mart. Still, she collected her hairpins. Gracious, if Troy knew she had received no less a personage than Lord Marden in her oldest gown, her hair unbound, he would have a fit. She had planned on washing it this morning, and so had seen no reason to fix her hair for breakfast with her little brother.

She had to now, for Troy's sake, so he would not be embarrassed by her appearance at what was certain to be an elegant household. And Athena took the time to do the job properly for her own sake, too, because she was bound to have red, swollen eyes, and she still wore her oldest gown. At least her hair would be neat when she next saw the fine man who had rescued her brother.

He was as impressive as she recalled, standing in front of the open door of an enormous mansion facing the park, as if he had been awaiting her arrival. His bewigged butler was even grander, coming to hand her out of the coach with regal dignity that showed her mended gloves, shabby cloak, and limp bonnet to further disadvantage.

Athena would have turned tail and run home, but Troy was inside, and Mac was handing a waiting footman—one of two, in silver and gray livery—her meager baggage. Besides, Roma had already jumped out of the carriage and was racing up the steps to snap at the earl's boots.

Athena dashed ahead of the superior butler, who sniffed his disapproval, and leaped between the shouting earl and the ankle-biter. She tapped Roma on the nose to get her attention, then patted her own left thigh. Roma instantly ceased her attack and came to sit at Athena's feet, growling low in her throat, but not moving.

The earl was staring at them. "I do not believe it. I tried everything to get your stupid dog to obey my commands. It cost me five minutes and a perfectly good pair of gloves to get the creature into the carriage. I almost lost my—"

"She hates coach rides. That was why I asked you to put her in. Troy is the only one who can convince her to ride. Otherwise she is perfectly behaved."

Lord Marden looked at his once shiny, once perfect Hessians.

"Except for shoes. Her former owner used to kick her. We think he must have been wearing boots. Tasseled ones, I am afraid."

"Undoubtedly the fellow kicked her because she refused to listen."

Athena bent to scratch behind the dog's ears. "Yes, the cabbage-head never realized she was deaf."

"Oh. Deaf. Of course." He ignored the butler's cough. "Nevertheless, she shall have to stay in the stables. Maddox House contains far too many valuable—"

The mongrel was bounding up the stairs. Ian could not call back a deaf dog, and he was not about to chase after it the way the hoydenish girl had done before, skirts flying and ugly bonnet flapping around her face. Not in front of his waiting servants. Instead he bowed and said, "Welcome to Maddox House, Miss Renslow. If the dog has any kind of scent hound in that mixed ancestry, it will have discovered your brother's bedchamber. I am certain you wish to follow. My housekeeper, Mrs. Birchfield, will show you the way. We have prepared the adjoining room for you, and a maid will be assigned to serve your needs. Your man can—"

"Oh, Mac has already left. He needs to find Alfie, you see."

"Ah, I was hoping he would keep the dog with him." And Ian had been hoping to locate the missing Alfie Brown himself. "No matter. You have only to ask the maid or any of the footmen for whatever you require." He eyed the two small tapestry bags the footmen carried. She was going to require a great deal. That would be Mrs. Birchfield's problem, not his. The housekeeper was already nodding and smiling at the girl, eager to take the little chick under her wing. Ian said, "I shall see you after you visit with your brother and get settled."

"Thank you, my lord. Once again you have been everything kind."

Ian fled to the morning room and his long-delayed breakfast. Kind? All he could see in his mind's eye was the boy, as pale as the white bandage around his head, lost in one of Ian's own much larger nightshirts, lying still—too still—on the bed. He replaced that image with one of the girl, all splotch-faced from crying over her brother, he could tell, and intimidated by his household although she hid her anxiety by petting the dog instead of meeting his eyes. She did not come to his chin, and she still wore a frock his sister would have been embarrassed to put in the poor bag, topped now with a dreadful bonnet. At least she made him a creditable curtsy before she went off with Mrs. Birchfield, so someone was teaching the chit a few ladylike graces. Someone would have to see that she stopped chasing after dogs, stopped interrupting her elders, and stopped dressing like a ragamuffin. He could only pray that the uncle returned home soon. If not . . .

Lud, let the Renslow children not be his concern!

Ian's appetite was gone.

He was so pale, so quiet. But Troy was not fevered. Athena tore off her gloves to feel his cheeks. She dropped her bonnet on the floor so she could lean closer, listening to his breathing. "His lungs do not sound congested," she told the hovering Mrs. Birchfield. "That is a good sign, isn't it?"

"A fine sign, miss."

Roma was on the bed, licking Troy's face beneath the bandages on his head. "He was shot in the head?" That was the worst possible place.

"Oh, no, miss. He was shot in the chest."

Athena tapped the dog on the nose and pointed to the end of the bed. Roma went and curled up by Troy's feet, ready to stay until Doomsday, it appeared, or dinner. Athena pulled back the covers, and then the neck of a fine lawn nightshirt, but all she could see was more bandages. At least there was no blood seeping anywhere.

"His lordship never mentioned anything about a head wound," she said after replacing the blankets.

"He must not have wanted to worry you unnecessarily, Miss Renslow," a man who had introduced himself as Hopkins, Lord Marden's valet, answered before the housekeeper could reply. "It seems the young gentleman fell off his horse onto a large boulder."

"And his lordship did not think to tell me?" Athena's estimation of the earl slipped a notch. "I think it decidedly necessary." She would not have bothered

with her hair or packing at all if she knew how badly
her brother was injured. She would have run all the
way here, if she had to, or made his lordship take her
up on his horse. Why, she would have stolen his horse
and ridden it herself, if the man had not assured her
that Troy was simply resting after his ordeal.

"I suppose Lord Marden was merely being kind,"
she told the worried looking servants. But now she
had to worry about the earl's confidence in Troy's
recovery. If he could sugarcoat her brother's condition, what else was he not telling her? "My own physician will be calling shortly. Please have him brought
up at once. And I shall need a cot brought in here,
and the fire kept higher, so my brother does not take
a chill. He will require beef broth and lemonade. Troy
does not like barley water. No one has given him laudanum, have they? Not with a head injury, I hope. Or
spirits. He'll have enough of a headache as is. Did
your doctor leave anything for the pain or—"

"There's my Attie," Troy whispered hoarsely. His
eyes were open and his lips twitched. "Knew you'd
come, old girl. Knew you'd take over, too. No matter
if it is a nobleman's mansion. Suppose you'd try to
run Carlton House if the prince let you."

Athena started crying again. Troy was awake, and
he knew her. The housekeeper was mumbling a prayer
of thankfulness, while setting a glass—lemonade,
Athena noted—to Troy's dry lips. The valet handed
her a handkerchief, one with a coat of arms embroidered in the corner. Athena blew her nose on a different corner.

"Hush up, bantling," she chided. "You had me worried for nothing, it seems. We will speak of your being
so far from home later, after you have had a good
rest."

"Yes. . . . Need to rest." His eyes drifted closed.

Then they opened again, and Troy reached for her hand. "Not his fault."

Athena was dismayed at the weakness in his grip, but she said, "Alfie's? He should never have let you ride so long. And he certainly should not have left you there!"

"No. The earl's. Not his fault."

Athena patted his hand, and let Roma come up to lick it, so Troy would not notice the wetness from her falling tears. "Of course not. Why, I am beginning to think that he might have saved your life, you clunch. You might have bled to death if Lord Marden had not been there, and been so capable. We already owe him a vast debt of gratitude, so hurry and get well so that we can go home. His lordship has done enough."

Ian did not know what more he could do. If he could send for a magician or a witch doctor or a Hindi healer, he would do it. Anything. Now that he thought of it, hadn't Lord Abernathy called in an herbalist when his wife was ailing? Perhaps . . . No, Lady Abernathy had died. And if all the efforts of all the learned doctors in London could not cure the poor king, what good were they?

For that matter, what good was he, sitting in his morning room, contemplating uneaten platters of ham and kippers and kidneys? But he could not bear to see the boy lying so corpse-like on the bed, nor watch the girl trying to hold back her tears. He could not even look at the surly mongrel licking young Renslow's cheek to wake him up. Damnation, now he had to feel guilty over disturbing a deaf dog. Between his housekeeper, his valet, and scores of other servants, though, to say nothing of Miss Renslow and her own physician, everything that was possible to do was being done. Ian had nothing to do but wish the day undone.

Or wish he had never been born. No, that was going too far. If Ian had not been born, Paige would have chosen another of his wife's lovers to challenge, and that poor blighter might be dead now at the rotter's early-firing hand. Or else young Renslow might have bled to death, if the chap had an older carriage or slower horses.

If nothing else, Ian vehemently wished he had never met Lady Paige, or met her that time in the gazebo in her back garden. Or the maze at Richmond. The Dark Walk at Vauxhall. Lud, he'd lived a sorry life. And now he might have nipped a promising one in the bud.

Damnation, wallowing in guilt and self-pity was not going to help the boy. Ian gave himself a mental shake and then reached for a rasher of bacon. And a slice of toast, a dollop of jam, and a serving of his chef's excellent steak and kidney pie.

"Gads," his friend Carswell said as he strolled, unannounced, into the breakfast room, "how can you eat at such a time? All I could do was swallow a bite of eggs."

Ian put down his fork, no longer hungry. He gestured toward the pots of coffee and tea, and the decanters of more potent beverages. "Help yourself, and tell me your news. Am I to be taken up by the magistrate?"

"Not unless you've been tupping his wife, too." Carswell sat opposite Ian at the table and poured himself a cup of coffee. He added cream and sugar, then reached for a sweet roll, a lamb chop, and the plate of kippers.

Ian raised an eyebrow, but did not question his elegant friend's supposedly delicate constitution. He picked up his own fork again, like a good host.

"How is the boy, then?" Carswell asked between mouthfuls.

"As well as can be expected, they tell me, although it is too soon to be optimistic. The quacks warn of fevers and congestions and lasting debilities."

"Ah, but I have some welcome news. Paige has left town."

"What, already?"

Carswell nodded while he chewed. He swallowed and said, "He had a carriage waiting at his house, all packed and ready. It appears he always intended to shoot early, and shoot to kill. No other explanation for his confidence. Not with his aim."

"He hated me that much? Odd, I never did anything to him, except bed his wife, of course. More coffee?"

"Thank you. According to Philpott, the loose screw was awash in debts. Shooting you was a handy excuse for outrunning the moneylenders' heavy-handed collectors, without seeming to renege on his gambling obligations."

"He'd rather be known as a murderer than a shirker?"

"He was sailing down River Tick straight for debtor's prison, so he had no alternative but to flee. Since he was going to be leaving the country anyway, he must have decided to take a bit of satisfaction in his leaving. The family has holdings in Scotland, I understand."

"Mona will be distraught. She adores London, with all its, ah, diversions."

"Then Lady Paige should be delighted her husband did not take her along."

"You mean the nodcock fought a duel over her honor and then left her behind?" Ian added a dash of brandy to both his and his friend's coffee.

"With the bailiffs at the door. The jade will find

someone to keep her, never fear, but think what a good turn that rotter Paige did for you."

"I cannot think of any reason I should be grateful to that swine."

"Ah, but now if anyone hears of the misfortune with the youngster, they will place the blame on Paige, thinking that was the reason he left the country. Fleeing makes him appear guilty, don't you see."

"Yet you wanted me to sail off on your yacht."

"I was offering an option, nothing else."

They both considered the situation while they cut and chewed, ate and drank. After awhile, Ian said, "The sister arrived. A little dab of a thing, from a harum-scarum household. Young Renslow was right that she could not be left on her own."

"That reminds me of the other bit of news I discovered this morning. Are you going to eat that last bit of meat pie?"

Ian passed over the plate and waited. When Carswell finally wiped his beringed fingers on the linen napkin and delicately patted his mouth, Ian asked, "Your other news?"

"Oh, yes. I made a discreet inquiry about the Renslows of my cousin, who has his Debrett's memorized, I'd swear. Do you recall a Viscount Rensdale?"

"Runty fellow, some years our senior, sobersided and clutch-fisted? Had a limp, if I recall. I can't remember seeing him in town. Too frivolous and expensive, I'd guess."

"That's him. Spartacus Renslow, Viscount Rensdale of Derby. Your houseguest is his heir."

Spartacus, Athena, Troy . . . even the dog was named Roma. "Damnation." In a different world, a viscount's son would be no more important than a blacksmith's, but not in this world. Then Ian did the mental arithmetic and found it just barely possible, if

Rensdale had been a lusty youth. He could not imagine the dark-haired viscount begetting the turquoise-eyed pair upstairs, especially the little blonde with the flyaway hair. "You say Troy is his son?"

"No, a half-brother by his late father's second wife. She died in childbed."

Ian could not help feeling relieved. "Then Rensdale can beget his own heirs."

"Can't." Carswell offered Ian snuff from an enameled box, which matched his waistcoat, of course. Ian refused, but had to wait while his friend indulged in the revolting but fashionable habit of sneezing until his eyes watered. "Rensdale's wife never conceived after years of marriage. She was one of Harcourt's daughters."

Ian shuddered. "If she is anything like her sisters, I cannot imagine Rensdale trying very hard."

"According to my cousin, she was an antidote, and a shrew besides. Went through four Seasons without an offer, so Harcourt doubled the dowry. Rensdale jumped at the bargain."

"A fine bargain: a harridan for a wife and no heir. I hope that dowry was worth what he is paying now. No wonder the youngsters came to stay with their uncle, though, with that pair as guardians. Unfortunately the uncle is away, busy fighting a war. I shall have to write to Rensdale, I suppose."

"He won't be happy."

"Well, I am not happy, either. He should have taken better care of the lad then, instead of letting him run loose in London on his own."

"The thing is, the boy is sickly, my cousin says. He came to town to consult the physicians."

Ian remembered how light the boy had felt in his arms, and wondering why he was not at school. "Bloody hell. I shot an invalid."

Chapter Four

In adversity, a proud man stands tall, like an oak.
　　　　　　　　　　　　　　　　　—Anonymous

In adversity, a wise woman bends, like a willow.
Which one breaks first?

　　　　　　　　　　　　　　　　　—Anonymous's wife

The fevers started that night. Ian did not know until late, because Carswell urged him to attend the dinner party at Lady Waltham's, an invitation he had already accepted.

"Gossip thrives on bare ground," Carswell had told him. "If you are not there to refute the stories, they will grow like magic beanstalks, touching the sky. But if you act as if nothing is wrong, the seeds of doubt cannot take root."

"What, are you a farmer now?"

"And get my hands dirty? Never. I do know the *ton,* however, and the rumormongers. They will have it that you were wounded by the dastard, or that you killed him and shipped his body out of England. Heaven knows what story they will concoct, if they have nothing to grasp."

So Ian had gone out for the evening, after dispatching a note to Rensdale by one of his own footmen, rather than waiting for the post. After the dinner party, he had accompanied his friend to a ball and then a rout, where too many people gathered in too small a space.

He had danced and drunk and played a hand or two of cards. He had eaten lobster patties and paid false compliments to his hostesses. He'd held conversations about the weather, the war, and who were partners for the next waltz. If anyone mentioned Paige or the duel, he'd pulled out his quizzing glass, examined the questioner with aristocratic arrogance, and ignored the question altogether. He had smiled and nodded, and gone about his way.

He brushed aside sly winks and innuendoes from the port drinkers and the card players about Lady Paige's future with a wave of his manicured hand and a hint of censure. "A gentleman does not bandy a lady's name about."

And this gentleman swore he would have nothing to do with the female or any of her kind again. Lady Paige's affairs were, thankfully, no longer any of *his* affair. He'd broken off their relationship at the first sign of Paige's anger. That was, regrettably, when the dirty dish had issued his challenge, and far too late.

No matter. Ian was done with the woman who had never been more than a brief bit of gratification, anyway, a minor itch to scratch. Mona had made her own bed . . . and her bower in the gazebo, her bunk in the barn, and her berth behind the bushes. For certain, she would no longer be welcomed at the higher levels of polite society.

If Ian heard whispers of Mad Dog Marden, he ignored them, too. His friends knew that nickname referred to his daring steeplechase races, not a vicious temper. He was coolheaded, in control. He was the perfect gentleman of leisure, his slightly bored indif-

ference indicating nothing on his mind but the next
offering at Drury Lane Theatre.

Lud, the earl thought, he should be offered a role
in the coming play. His face ached from maintaining
the polite smile, his neck was growing stiff from holding his head so high, and his stomach was queasy from
all he had eaten or drunk this benighted day.

Finally, people stopped asking him questions or
whispering behind his back. They were all speculating
about the increasing Lady Ingersoll—and her handsome head gardener. Bless those who made things
grow—and who gave London something else to talk
about besides a duel gone bad.

Even Ian could almost believe that nothing was
wrong with his world but an upset stomach, until he
reached his front walk. He stepped out of the carriage
and into evidence of his unwelcome, unwanted, un-
avoidable guests and their ugly dog.

Barefoot and bilious, he stomped into his house and
immediately promoted one of the footmen to kennel
master, in charge of one stone-deaf, snappish dog and
its accompanying mess.

Then he went into his library, preceded by his butler, Hull, who made sure enough candles were lighted,
the decanters were full, the fire was burning warmly
for such a chill evening. All of which Ian correctly
interpreted as meaning that his major domo had something to say.

"How goes it with the boy?" he asked, afraid for
what he might hear. Thunderation, Carswell had been
wrong, Ian thought. He should have stayed home instead of going out and enjoying himself, or pretending
to be enjoying himself. What kind of cad goes dancing
when his houseguest—his victim—lay so perilously ill?

Hull answered, "The surgeon returned, and both of

the physicians. They disagree as to the treatment, but all concur that a fever was not unexpected."

Which meant there had been a contretemps between the quacks. Ian should have been here, instead of leaving the household to manage on its own. He hoped his man Hopkins and his housekeeper knew more about nursing than he did.

"And that Macelmore personage," Ian's superior butler was going on, "was here also. At the front door." Hull's nostrils flared in disapproval. "He visited the sickroom, then said he would return in the morning to speak with you, my lord. I did inform him that he should use the servant's entrance. What he said in return cannot be repeated in a gentleman's home."

Ian was positive that whatever the old sailor had said, it had been spoken previously, but perhaps not in such colorful terms. "I will see him, whichever door he chooses to use."

"Very good, my lord," Hull said with a sniff before turning to leave the room.

Fine, now his butler was offended. Ian called him back. "These are trying times, Hull. We must make do."

Hull tipped his powdered head. "Indeed, my lord. I made allowances for a loyal servant dismayed at his young master's pain."

"Pain? The boy is in pain and none of the medical morons can help him?"

"I believe the use of laudanum for a head wound was at the root of the physicians' disagreement. Too deep a sleep and he might not awaken."

Ian reached for a bottle. Any bottle. The ache in his gut felt permanent. Perhaps *he* should take the laudanum, if the liquor was not dulling his anguish. Then he could stop the clock from ticking, at least in his own mind. He could think of no other way to make the hours disappear, to get him through this night.

He did not want to forget; hell, he wanted the memories to disappear entirely.

How did one halt time, though, make the hands of the dial travel backward? How could a mortal man reclaim a moment, recall a hasty word, return a pistol ball to the gun barrel? There had to be a way, if only for an hour.

Athena had her Bible out, but she neither read nor prayed. She sang, instead. She was slightly off-key, but she crooned all of Troy's favorite songs, there by his bedside. When she forgot the words, she hummed, and when she ran out of popular tunes, she sang Christmas carols and hymns. She was hoarse, but her brother seemed to rest more easily when he heard her voice, so she sang. When she was quiet, he started to thrash around, crying out at the pain, sending himself deeper into the fevers.

She had run out of things to tell him hours ago. How many times could you tell a boy that you loved him, that you would be furious if he did not get better soon, that everything was going to be all right? She told him about the heroic earl who had rescued him, the magnificent horses who had carried her there, and the concerned servants who were helping care for Troy now.

They were as far from the sullen, uncooperative, and overworked staff at their half-brother's house as Derby was from London. Here, too, the Renslows were honored guests, not poor relations to be ignored and endured. The servants at home took their direction from their mistress, Veronica, Lady Rensdale, who saw Troy as a reminder of her barrenness. She saw Athena as a rival for the respect of their neighbors and tenants, although the viscountess made no effort to win anyone's affections, certainly not her younger, prettier sister-in-law's. The staff at Maddox House were eager to please, and obviously adored their generous, easygoing master. As Athena told her brother, one could tell a great deal about a gentleman by his servants.

Speaking of Spartacus and Veronica was too dreary, so Athena described for her brother the grandeurs of Maddox House that she had glimpsed. Why, the guest suite assigned to the Renslows was almost as large as the entire bedroom floor at their uncle's house, and all tastefully done in soft blues and greens.

Troy groaned. Of course. What boy was interested in household furnishings? So Athena told him tales of their mother, stories secretly gleaned from the servants when she and Troy were children. Their half-brother, Spartacus, had disliked his frivolous young stepmother, blaming her for his father's death of heart failure, and never wished her name spoken in his household. No matter to him that his orphaned, heartbroken little sister had cherished each memory of her beloved mama.

Later, the tales were often repeated in their nursery to comfort a poor, sickly, motherless boy. Athena told them again now, about the pretty woman Troy had never known.

"She wanted you so badly," Athena told her brother as he drifted in and out of consciousness. "Even though the doctors warned her of the danger after she lost two infants before. She wanted to make our father happy—as if anything could. He was just like Spartacus, you know." The former Viscount Rensdale had followed his second wife to the grave within two years, two years of never looking at his infant son.

"Mama was beautiful, you know. She had the same color eyes we have."

Troy mumbled something. Athena leaned closer to hear.

"I can . . . see them."

"No! No, you cannot! You see mine, Troy, my eyes, not Mama's. She is in heaven. You have to stay here, with me. And Roma. We need you, dearest! You cannot join our mother. She would be wretched if you went to her now. Besides, our father might be there, too. I doubt it, but you would not wish to encounter him. Believe me, dearest, our father would not be pleased that you have not finished your studies, not taken up a career, not provided heirs to his title, if Spartacus fails."

"Hurts."

"I know. But you are strong."

Troy tried to smile and Athena's heart almost broke into tiny pieces.

"Not . . . strong," he whispered.

She raised his head and held a glass of cool water to his lips. "You will be. I know it. Look how far you rode today."

"Not like Marden."

"Pooh. He is an ox," Athena lied for her brother's sake. The earl was a fine figure of a man, not a clumsy giant, but she said, "You would not want to be so big. Why, you'd hit your head constantly on the kitchen door. And you could never visit Uncle Barnaby on his ship. You know how low the ceilings are onboard. And . . . and we do not own a horse strong enough to carry that immense weight."

"Marden must. Neck or nothing rider, you know. Mad Dog Marden."

"No, he was not terribly angry when Roma scratched his boots."

"What they call him, silly." Troy's brow was starting to furrow as the pain washed over him. "That's . . . why I went to see."

Since she was already telling bouncers, Athena saw no reason not to tell a bigger one. "The earl offered us free use of his stables." He meant she could send riders and messengers, she understood, but Troy did not have to know that. "I am certain he would be grateful if you helped exercise his cattle when you recover. He might even take you to Tattersall's with him."

Troy lay back, a smile on his face. Athena went back to singing.

Enough. Ian was no nursemaid, and had no idea of what to do in a sickroom. He had never been sick a day in his life, and had been away at school when his sister contracted the smallpox. His father had broken his neck in a horse race, so he had been spared even that. Still, he had to go offer his assistance. He could not very well go to sleep in his comfortable bed and ignore the boy's struggle for life right down the other corridor. He had to check, at the very least, that his competent staff was managing the additional responsibility. He could offer to hire extra nurses, promise bonuses. Hell, he would carry coals and hot water, anything to feel that he was doing his share. He went upstairs.

Lud, the dog must be howling to get out. No, someone was singing, if you could call it that.

The guest room door was partially open, so he tiptoed in—easy enough, since he was still in his bare feet. By the firelight and the single candle left burning, he could see the girl curled in a chair at the bedside, her feet tucked under her, droning out a gloomy hymn, as if the poor boy did not have enough woes.

Ian had forgotten about the sister, or thought she'd
be asleep by now. He had not forgotten about the
dog, having come prepared with a slice of chicken
from the untouched platter his butler had brought to
the library. The cur was asleep, though, and had not
heard him enter, naturally. Lucky pup, Ian thought,
not to have to listen to the girl's ear-mangling music.
One of the maids was asleep in the corner, her mouth
open, snoring softly. The room was hot, the fireplace
piled high with coals. Attie, Miss Renslow, that is,
kept brushing damp tendrils of blond hair from her
cheeks, wisps that escaped the long braid that trailed
down her back. At least someone had gathered the
unruly mop into some semblance of order, he noted,
and found a ribbon for her. Her cheeks were flushed,
but he could not tell if that was from the heat or a
whole day of weeping, the poor puss.

Miss Renslow wore the same shapeless pastel gown
she'd had on this morning, and Ian had to wonder if
she had rested at all, if she had been offered a bath,
a meal, a drop of brandy. No, one did not offer a
young girl alcohol for fortification. And of course his
household had offered the female every amenity. He'd
have them tossed out in the street otherwise. She must
simply be afraid here by herself, and was staying at
her brother's bedside rather than sleep in a strange
bed.

He stepped closer and spoke softly. "You can go to
bed now, my dear. I will have a maid come to sleep in
your room with you. You should not be here alone."

Athena jumped to her feet and dropped a curtsy,
blushing that their handsome benefactor had seen her
sitting like a hoydenish schoolgirl. For that matter, she
had tugged her braided hair loose from the coronet
on top of her head and was looking frumpish again,

she had no doubt. Since it was too late to do anything about it, she merely gestured toward the maid in the corner, who was stirring at the sound of conversation. "I am not alone. Sophie rouses at my call and fetches anything I might want."

"Nevertheless, I'll stay to watch over your brother, and get another nurse to replace this sleepy one. You need your rest."

"I need to be with my brother."

Ian admired her loyalty, but could not approve of her recalcitrance to follow his suggestion. He was the earl. He knew better, of course. "Really, Miss Renslow, you are doing your brother no service." The singing alone would hasten anyone's demise.

"I am keeping my brother from reopening his wound or aggravating his fever, my lord, the best way I know how."

He could not argue with that, since the boy did seem to be lying peacefully. He was far too pale, with blue veins showing at his eyelids, but he was not thrashing about or drenched in sweat.

"How fares he, then?" he asked, his own stomach's discomfort quickly forgotten.

She turned back to the bed. "At times he is fine, speaking to me and sipping some water. Sometimes he sleeps. Then the pain grows too strong for him to sleep. He grows restive, which jars his head or the other wound, and his fever climbs. Then I awaken the maid to help me bathe him with cool cloths. Your Mr. Hopkins comes to help change his nightshirt—your nightshirt, my lord, thank you—when it is damp."

"And his legs?"

"His legs do not matter now."

They would to the boy, if he lived. But Ian saw no reason to mention that to the sister, who did seem to be competent in the sickroom, despite his misgivings: Hopkins and Mrs. Birchfield would never have left her on her own here otherwise, he was sure.

The heat in the room was stifling. "Did the physicians say he should be kept so warm?"

"The physicians said many things, all contradictory. I know the room should be kept hot, for chills are worse. Troy does not need pneumonia on top of everything else."

That made sense, Ian supposed. He'd talk to the doctors in the morning himself, which, he realized, he ought to have done before. He took off his jacket and loosened his cravat.

"My lord?" she asked with a gasp of surprise.

"Excuse me, but I would swelter in here otherwise."

Athena quickly averted her eyes from the earl's undress. She was well aware that polite manners did not matter one whit here at Troy's bedside, and she was relieved in a way that her own hurly-burly appearance was equaled by his lordship's casual dishabille, but she was still embarrassed to be noticing the breadth of his shoulders and the narrowness of his waist. She looked down—to see his bare feet. Goodness!

Her cheeks flooded with color, Athena said, "There is no need for you to stay."

"I am staying."

"But you have done so much already."

If only she knew. . . .

Ian supposed that he should have stayed and had dinner with the chit. Alone with strangers and servants, she had to be frightened. And worried about her brother, of course. "I have not done enough."

The girl and the maid were sitting on the two upholstered chairs in the room, and he was not about to sprawl on the low pallet in the far corner. Ian found a wooden chair at the desk in the sitting room. It was small and looked uncomfortable, but ought to hold his weight. He brought it back to the bedchamber and placed it next to Miss Renslow's. "I will just sit here, in case you need me."

So close? "No," Athena said. "Mr. Hopkins is waiting for you. He promised to return as soon as he had seen you to bed."

Ian was beginning to grow weary of having the chit contradict his every word. "I am staying. Hopkins has a cot in my dressing room. Let him sleep a bit longer."

Giving up in the face of his lordship's kindness and admirable sense of duty, Athena nodded and turned away, feeling her brother's skin.

"How does it feel?"

"Warm, but not burning." She wrung out a towel from the nearby basin and started to bathe the boy's face and neck.

"What can I do to help?" Ian felt foolish asking a little maiden.

"Help? Why, you can tell him about your horses, I suppose."

"But he is asleep."

"That is not really sleep, but a state halfway between sleeping and waking. He hears me, I know, and seems comforted by the familiar."

"But I am not familiar to him."

"Ah, but horses are. He adores highly bred cattle, and can recite the lineage of half the Thoroughbreds at every race."

"I would feel foolish telling an unconscious boy about my stables."

Athena clucked her tongue. "Would you rather I sing?"

"Diogenes Jim sired Lady Tiffany out of Sweet As Cocoa, who went on to win at Newmarket . . ."

Chapter Five

Women are weak. They need protecting.
                                    —Anonymous

Women need protection from arrogant, autocratic, overbearing men. A well-placed knee is usually sufficient.

                                    —Mrs. Anonymous

The boy grew warmer, weaker, then wilder, as he cried out and thrashed, as if trying to escape the pain that tormented him. Ian held him down so he did not injure himself worse. Athena spooned fever potions and herbal infusions into his unwilling mouth. They took turns wringing out sponges and towels and bathing his heated skin. If he had a minute to think about it, Ian might have been proud of himself, turning competent at this unfamiliar task.

He knew he was proud of Attie. The girl had bottom, all right. He could not imagine another female of his experience, no matter what age, who had the stamina and the stubbornness to keep going all through that long, long night. The well-bred women he knew had paid employees to perform such duties. They did not even feed their own infants, but hired wet nurses to do that job. Yet here was a slip of a girl, not even the boy's mother, working herself to exhaustion. Such devotion was inspiring to Ian.

It was also aggravating. His throat was sore, his head was aching, his eyes felt as if someone had kicked dirt in them, and he was about ready to fall onto that thin pallet next to Renslow's bed—but how could he? Worse, how could he seek his own vast feather bed while Miss Renslow worked and kept watch? She never rested, taking only moments for a cup of tea or a bite of a biscuit, half of which she fed to the dog.

Hopkins came to take his turn, but Ian could not let himself prove less stouthearted than a schoolgirl. The valet shook his head when Lord Marden refused to give up his place, and left to find his own bed. Mrs. Birchfield in her nightcap and robe came in, saw her master in his shirtsleeves, and almost dropped the candle she held. Maids and footmen toiled through the long hours, bearing more coal, more hot water, more fresh towels and linen.

"Make sure the staff is rewarded," Ian told his butler, once he recovered from seeing Hull without his wig for the first time in memory. "And let anyone who needs to, sleep in, in the morning. The dusting and the silver polishing can wait, or we can hire more people. We will not be receiving callers tomorrow, either."

"Very good, my lord," Hull replied and bowed himself out as if it were four in the afternoon instead of four in the morning.

"That was very kind of you, my lord," Athena said when the butler had gone.

"What, not mentioning that the fire's red glow was reflected on the top of his shiny bald skull?"

Athena's lips twitched, to Ian's satisfaction. The poor little puss needed a bit of silliness amid the frantic worry, and her brother seemed to be resting easier after the last bout of fever.

"No," she told him, "it was kind of you to remember that your servants have to arise early in the morning to get their assigned tasks done. Many employers simply expect their staff to be at their beck and call, day and night, without additional recompense, and without concern for their health and well-being. Not that I am surprised at your consideration, my lord. In the short time I have known you I have found you to be both generous and caring. Troy and I could not have found ourselves in better hands."

Embarrassed at the girl's praise, Ian changed the subject. "You sound as if you have experience with demanding masters. Is your brother's household one where the maids' hands are worked raw and the grooms have barely enough to eat?"

Now her lips turned down. "My brother and his wife are . . . difficult employers. Jobs are scarce in the country, so the workers cannot simply quit and move on. Which Lady Rensdale fully knows and takes advantage of."

"Does she also take advantage of having an unpaid servant to boss around—an unmarried sister-in-law, perhaps?"

Athena smiled. "She tries. But I do what I can to make the servants' lives easier, not to please Veronica."

Good for her for standing up for the less fortunate. Not so good for her, Ian thought, to be under the thumb of a mean-spirited, money-hoarding relation. "It sounds uncomfortable. Is that why you came to London?"

"Only partly. I love my life in the country, where I know everyone and feel useful. We came to visit our uncle and a physician I had heard highly recommended. Rensdale was opposed, of course."

"He does know you are here, doesn't he?" Ian asked, worried that this young pair might have slipped their leashes without permission. He could be charged with kidnapping, next.

"Of course he knows. Did you think Troy and I stole away in the middle of the night?" She carefully dribbled a spoonful of willow bark tea into her brother's mouth. "It was no such thing. Rensdale was happy enough to see us leave, as long as we took the Reverend Mr. Wiggs with us. As I said, Lady Rensdale and I do not agree on the proper management of Renslow Hall, although I am well aware that she is mistress. Not that Veronica would let anyone forget for an instant. Anyway, my older brother was not averse to our leaving, as long as it did not cost him anything."

Ian nodded. "I'd heard he was a squeeze-penny. But how did you finance the journey?"

"I had some monies put aside, gifts from my mother's family, mostly, and both Troy and I had been saving our allowances."

He could tell the frugal lass had not been spending her pin money on new gowns and fripperies, and he was disgusted that any man of means should keep his own kin in such straitened circumstances. Ian's own sister had never wanted for anything he could provide, and never would. "Your brother's care for his dependents leaves much to be desired," he noted.

Athena bit her lip. "Rensdale is my brother and I owe him my loyalty. Forgive me, my lord, I should never have spoken. Please excuse my mention of such personal matters as a product of the late hour."

"Nonsense—we have come to be friends, have we not?" To his own surprise, Ian found that to be true.

They had talked and worked together, and yes, they had sung together. He found the chit intelligent and interesting, when she was not being impertinent.

As for Athena, she was comfortable enough in his lordship's presence now that she was sitting cross-legged beside Troy on the bed, her feet tucked under her skirts, while the earl relaxed in the comfortable chair she had been using.

The idea that ordinary Attie Renslow could be friends with a London buck of the first water brought a smile to her lips. She liked the notion very well, and liked his lordship, when he was not trying to order her around. Then she grinned. "If we are friends, my lord, I am forced to admit that Rensdale does not know my uncle is not in town. The captain was supposed to take leave this month, but bad weather delayed his ship. We told Wiggy—Mr. Wiggs, that is—that dear Uncle Barnaby suffered a relapse of an old malady and is resting. Otherwise, Spartacus would have known as soon as the first post was delivered."

"He knows now."

She looked over at him through a curtain of damp curls that framed her face. "Pardon?"

"I say, your brother knows you and Troy are alone—were alone—here in London. I wrote to him."

Athena sucked in her breath and mumbled a word suspiciously like one no gently bred miss should know, much less say. Ian doubted she'd learned it at the Reverend Mr. Wiggs's side, and blamed the old sailor Macelmore. Now he said, "Pardon?"

She had the grace to blush. "Excuse me. But that was a remarkably forward, presumptuous, managing kind of action for you to take."

Ian did not like being called forward or presumptuous. As for managing, that was what a gentleman did.

He unrolled his shirtsleeves for a more dignified appearance, lest the chit forget that while they might be friends, he was still in charge. "How could I not write to Viscount Rensdale when his brother—his current heir, I understand—was injured and taken to my home? What if he heard gossip or such, from your Mr. Wiggs or another acquaintance? Do you not think he should know his brother is ill?"

"I do not think he will care much either way. He never did. If he cared, he should have been the one to bring Troy to town to visit the specialists."

"But if the injuries your brother suffered turn grave?"

"They are grave already. Do you mean if Troy dies? That would have been time enough to inform Rensdale, when he could not make matters worse. But do not even think that, my lord. My brother will live, and my half-brother need never have known. I think you have taken great liberties, my lord. You should have consulted me first."

"What, a mere girl? Do not be absurd."

She looked at him oddly but said nothing, so Ian went on: "And why should I not have told the head of your household? Are you worried that he is going to race to London to fetch you back? Rather than leave you in the keeping of strangers and absent seafarers?"

"He is Troy's guardian. If he wishes my brother home, he would have to hire extra servants, a comfortable traveling coach, and physicians to attend him— and that after staying in London at a hotel for weeks. Even he could see that Troy cannot be moved yet. As for me, Uncle Barnaby was designated my guardian, not Spartacus, thank goodness. Rensdale cannot order me to do anything."

"Except stay away from your brother?" he guessed, and knew he was right by the stricken look that crossed her face.

"Yes," she said with a hoarse whisper, "he can take Troy from me."

Only a monster would separate this devoted pair. "I will tell him how hard you are working to keep the boy alive. He will see."

"He will see an excuse to leave me in London, fixed in Uncle Barnaby's household instead of Renslow Hall."

"Nonsense. I will tell him—"

"You have already told him enough, thank you."

The angry voices, or the anguish in his sister's, disturbed Troy, who tried to say something. Both Athena and the earl leaned closer to him. "He'll say . . . told you so."

"Of course he will, the prig. But do not worry, dearest, by the time Rensdale arrives—if he bothers to come at all, and you know how Veronica hates to travel—you will be right as rain."

"Riding . . . Mad Dog's horses."

That was a surprise to Lord Marden, but he rose to the challenge. "Your pick of the stables, after you've proved yourself aboard Rita. She is a gentle mare I keep for my sister's use. Game, but not headstrong."

Troy smiled, swallowed another mouthful of the fever infusion, and shut his eyes.

The earl's startled promise redeemed him a bit in Athena's eyes, so she whispered a thank you. Then she muttered, half to herself, "We were doing so well that Rensdale could never have found fault. Troy was feeling a great deal better, until some idiot shot him."

"It was an accident."

"An accident that need not have happened if grown men were not out playing with guns."

The truth was painful. Ian broke off a piece of biscuit and handed it to the dog, seeking someone's approval, anyone's.

"Now Rensdale will have another excuse to keep Troy penned in at home until he does expire, from boredom. I was hoping Troy could attend university in a few years, and he has been working hard at his studies to be ready. Now our brother will claim he is too frail. The expense is too high, more likely."

"Surely he would not deny the lad an education if he is fit for it."

"More surely the gudgeon will not want it known that a Renslow is less than perfect. Troy's weakness has been a constant embarrassment to him and Veronica."

Ian understood that attitude, so prevalent in Polite Society that was anything but polite to its own cripples and invalids. "My own sister—"

She interrupted. "By Neptune's crown, you should have brought my brother home to Cameron Street, where he belongs!"

"What, with a pirate, a missing groom, and a cook to look after him?"

"We would have managed."

That was not worth a reply. Ian raised an eyebrow instead, but Miss Renslow was not looking. She was back to wiping her brother's brow, humming off-key, the ungrateful, unmusical wench.

She was an ungrateful wretch, Athena told herself. He was her host, her brother's rescuer, her companion through this darkest night of her life. Of course a gentleman would inform another gentleman of a catastrophe concerning his family. Lord Marden could not know the situation at Renslow Hall, and he was trying his honorable, noble best. Now he was trying his best to stay awake, the dear man. Any of the maids could have been as much assistance, but his fine sense of duty made him stay, just as it had made him write to her brother. She should respect a man who acted so conscientiously, not resent him.

Athena decided she would have to apologize when the earl woke up. For now she took an extra blanket and draped it over him, making sure to cover his bare toes. Without looking at them too much.

Ian awoke to his shoulder being shaken. "Please, my lord. I need help."

He was on his feet in an instant, but he needed a moment to reorient himself in the dimly lighted room. He heard a panting sound that was not coming from the dog. Oh, Lord. "What should I do?"

"We need to immerse him in a cool bath. The footmen are bringing it, but I cannot manage by myself."

"Of course not. Hopkins and I will handle the bath. Gently, I promise."

"No, I only need you to lift him. I helped bathe him for years when he had fevers as a child."

"He is not an infant now, and he will not welcome the ministrations of his sister, I guarantee you."

Athena almost argued, but knew his lordship was right, loath as she was to take her eyes off Troy, lest he slip away while she was not watching. Then the earl said, "I shall have a bath sent to your room at the same time, a hot bath, so you might relax for a bit."

The offer was too tempting. Athena felt as if she had been wearing the same gown for a week. She hurried, and then put on the other gown she had brought, thankfully pressed and hung up by one of the maids while she tended her brother. When she returned to the sickroom, Troy was back in bed in a fresh nightshirt, much cooler to her touch. The earl was back in the chair next to the bed, speaking softly to Troy, who did seem to be listening.

"Why do you not take a nap? Our patient seems much improved," Lord Marden said. "I am watching."

Troy added, " 'M fine, Attie."

Athena felt peculiar settling onto the pallet in Troy's room in front of the earl. On the other hand, she was afraid if she went to her own bed, no one would awaken her. His lordship was altogether too gentlemanly, too noble. She would have taken the other cushioned chair, but Roma was sleeping in it.

"Don't be a goose. Sleep on the cot here. Troy and I will try to keep our voices lowered, unless he knows some ribald sea chanteys I have not heard."

Athena smiled and lay on the narrow bed, careful to spread her skirts over her ankles. The earl came and placed a blanket over her. "I doubt I can manage two patients."

He really was the kindest man she had ever known, if a trifle overbearing, Athena thought, falling asleep almost the instant her head touched the pillow.

She did not know if the earl called to her or one of the maids came in with a clattering tray. She only knew Troy's breathing was harsh and ragged. She leaped to her feet. "You should have woken me!"

"He was fine a minute ago. What should I do?"

"Hold him up so I can try to get more of the medicine into him."

The medicine dribbled out of Troy's unresponsive mouth. He did not answer Athena's urgings, and his skin felt cold and clammy.

"I sent for the surgeon. Perhaps we should send for your Mr. Wiggs, too?"

"No! Troy does not like him. And he does not need a minister. He is not dying. He cannot be!"

Ian feared he was, though. And the sister was grasping the boy's hand, but looking at Ian, crying, "Do something!"

The dog was at the side of the bed, whining, looking up at him, too.

He wasn't God, although he had already done the Devil's work. What could he do? Attie was all red-faced again, tears streaming down her cheeks, staring at him as if he could put a broken doll back together. Ian had to do something. He could not let the boy die. He could not, for his sake, for her sake, for the sake of his own miserable soul.

So he prayed.

Ian prayed for the first time in more years than he could remember. He swore he would be a better man, if only the boy was saved. He'd do anything, give up women and become a monk if he had to—get married, even. May he be struck by lightning if he ever stepped off the straight and narrow path again, if the boy lived.

When he was done with his admittedly self-serving, once-in-a-blue-moon bargaining, Ian started to sing a hymn—all the while holding Troy, while Athena tried to get more medicine down his throat. More landed on Ian's sleeve. Athena's off-key voice, choked with tears, joined Ian's.

And Troy winced. He lowered his brows, opened his eyes, and said, "You . . . sing . . . almost as badly . . . as m'sister."

Athena grabbed for Ian's arm. "He is going to be all right!"

The earl felt as if his horse had won at the Derby, as if he'd been dealt four aces, as if . . . as if his prayers had been answered. He did remember to send a silent thank you heavenward. Then he felt obliged to remind the girl that her brother was not out of danger yet.

"Oh, but I know he will recover. He will! I knew he was much stronger than everyone said. And he never gives up, not my baby brother! He never did—not from the first time I held him, when our mother died and he was so sickly."

Athena was laughing and crying at the same time, with relief and exhaustion and enough overwrought emotion to level an elephant. Now that this latest crisis was over and she did not have to be strong anymore, she fell to pieces. She could not keep herself from great, gulping sobs and shaking shoulders.

The surgeon had not arrived and Mrs. Birchfield was asleep, so who could comfort the girl? There was nothing for Ian to do but gather her into his arms. She fit under his chin, wetting his chest through the thin fabric of his shirt. He awkwardly patted her back, thinking, Zeus, he hated a woman's tears, but this one deserved a good cry.

A woman's tears?

A woman?

Ian felt the dampness, but he also felt the unmistakable press of firm, tender, womanly flesh against his chest. For all her slight stature, Miss Renslow did not have a schoolgirl's figure under that loose-fitting gown. No, he was tired and imagining things that could not be there, like breasts. His mind was suddenly jarred into a frantic recollection of her earlier words, though, words he'd been too concentrated on Troy to absorb. She'd bathed Troy as a child. She'd held him when their mother died. She'd called him her baby brother.

Her fifteen-year-old baby brother. Which made Miss Athena Renslow older than that. How much older?

Surprised that his lips were able to move, considering he'd just been run over by a hay wain, Ian gasped, "Just how old are you, anyway?"

With her face still pressed to his chest, Athena sniffed and said, "Nineteen. Twenty next month. People think I am younger because I am small."

Nineteen.

The earl's arms dropped to his sides and his feet stepped back so fast he tripped over the dog, who snapped at his toes.

Nineteen.

And she was alone in this room with him. Alone at his home, except for a half-comatose brother and a handful of servants. Alone in the world, except for a missing uncle and two brothers, one a miser and one an underage invalid.

Nineteen. And alone in his arms while he wore no coat, no cravat. Bloody hell, he did not even have shoes on his feet.

Ian waited for the lightning to strike him.

Maybe no one knew. That was it. No one knew she was here except the servants, and they would not talk if instructed not to . . . unless they already had, at the pubs and the next door servants' halls. No, Ian hastily told himself, his mind in a maelstrom, his people did not gossip about him. He was not sure about hers. Or who had seen her arrive this morning. Or if Carswell had mentioned her to anyone. He started to pray again—but two prayers in an hour was too much to ask.

No one knew, he assured himself. They could squeak through this with her reputation intact. He'd write to his mother in Bath. And his sister in Richmond. No, he would send carriages for both of them. By the time anyone realized Attie—gads, he had to remember she was Miss Renslow—was here, at a notorious bachelor's establishment, his female relations would be at hand to lend respectability. Thank goodness.

Then he recalled his butler's parting words to her: "Your letters have been delivered, miss."

Letters. Which likely informed her friends, her uncle's staff, and that tutor cum clergyman where she was.

Nineteen.

He had stepped in more than dog droppings today.

Chapter Six

Women are fragile and flighty, like butterflies.
—Anonymous

Men are toads.
—Mrs. Anonymous

By midmorning of the following day, the seeds of Miss Renslow's letters brought their first fruit: a bitter lemon.

"The Reverend Mr. Wiggs, my lord, for Miss Renslow," Ian's butler announced, his nose slightly wrinkled as if from an offensive odor. The earl had learned to read a visitor's character by the flare of Hull's nostrils. "What shall I tell him?"

Hull could tell the tutor that the boy was a trifle better, having taken some beef broth this morning, and that Miss Renslow was resting in her own room. Ian had both bits of information from his valet, since he had fled to his own bedchamber early after his dire discovery. Once there, he had penned urgent missives to his mother and sister, then kicked himself nineteen ways to Sunday for being a fool.

He had not been back to the sickroom since. He made sure his housekeeper and two maids kept Miss Renslow company during her vigil, and a footman stood outside her door, but Ian was not going within nineteen yards of the chit.

He had slept for a few hours, then woke up with nineteen hammers pounding in his aching, brandy-soaked brain.

Nineteen. Hell.

After breakfast and a bath, he was still in a foul enough mood to welcome an interview with Troy's disapproving tutor, the minion of the miserly Lord Rensdale. He'd have preferred a session at Gentleman Jackson's boxing parlor, pounding something—a leather bag or a sparring partner—into the ground. Wiggy would do.

"Show him in."

Ian had expected an older man, a saintly graybeard mistakenly entrusted with the job of bearleading two children—no, a boy and a young lady—about London. Instead he saw a man younger than himself, of perhaps twenty-five summers, although one could not tell if the fellow had ever been out in the sun, he was so pale. Wiggs was nearly Ian's height, but half his weight, it seemed, with angular bones, a long nose, and a jutting Adam's apple. The man of the cloth was dressed head to toe in severe black, without a sop to style, comfort, or color. His straight mouse-brown hair was parted in the middle, and his mouth seemed permanently tilted downward. He stood stiffly erect, bowing at Ian's greeting as if his spine were made of steel.

Ian disliked him on sight. To be honest, he had disliked the man when Athena—Miss Renslow, dash it—had spoken of him. Now his assessment was proven correct as the man waved his bony fingers in the air and said, "This will not do."

Ian looked around his library, one of the finest in all of England, he believed, filled as it was with shelves of rare volumes, cases of priceless heirloom treasures,

walls of fine art representing centuries of his family's
collecting. It was a warm, inviting place, with soft
leather chairs and thick Aubusson rugs. He raised one
dark eyebrow. "I thought my library entirely
satisfactory."

"Not your library, my lord. Your house."

"You do not like the architecture? Or perhaps the
wall-hangings?"

"This is no time for levity, Lord Marden. I am, of
course, speaking of Miss Renslow. Your house is sin-
gularly unsuitable for a young, unmarried female. She
ought to have realized that, of course, and not trou-
bled your lordship."

"I assure you, the lady was no trouble at all." Ian
was going to hell, anyway; one more lie would not
matter.

"Of course not. Miss Renslow is the sister of a viscount, you know. Of course she is well-mannered. She
does, however, have a lamentable tendency toward
unthinking impetuosity. Especially where the lad is
concerned."

"She is certainly devoted to him," Ian agreed.

"But at what cost, I ask? She should never have
entered the portals of a bachelor's lodgings, much less
stayed the night. Forgive me, my lord, but that is especially true of your house, as pleasant as it might be.
Your reputation is not fit for innocent maidens."

"My reputation or my company? They are not the
same, I assure you."

"Tut." Wiggs actually said *tut*. Ian had never heard
anyone say it aloud before. "Tut, tut. Either way, Miss
Renslow will be ruined."

"Surely not, when no one has to know of her presence here."

"Tut, tut." One more *tut* and he'd find himself
tossed out the door. "I might have expected such a

response from Miss Renslow, who is a heedless green girl, but you have to know better, my lord. Nothing can be kept secret for long in London, and her presence here, without a chaperone, will be on everyone's lips by nightfall." Wiggs's own lips turned down even farther, until he looked like an anemic bulldog with a bellyache.

"Miss Renslow shall have a chaperone by nightfall." If Ian had to go to Richmond and drag his sister by her hair, he would have a duenna in the domicile.

"Tut, tut. Too late, with your reputation. Not that you are known as a rake leading innocent damsels to their downfall."

Ian sarcastically thanked Wiggs for acknowledging that saving grace.

"Think nothing of it."

Ian did not.

The vicar went on, oblivious to Ian's growing anger. "I do not know what that uncle was thinking, to let his niece leave the protection of his household for that of a known philanderer."

Ah, so Miss Renslow had not confessed about the absent uncle yet. Ian would not peach on her, not to this sanctimonious sprig. "The captain was undoubtedly thinking of his nephew's welfare, as were Miss Renslow and I. The lad is somewhat better this morning after a frightening night, although you have not asked."

That brought a hint of embarrassed color to the reverend's cheeks. "I was so wrought over Miss Renslow's condition, you see."

Ian saw that the prig did not care about the injured boy, although Athena's reputation seemed of paramount importance for some reason that Ian intended to discover. "The young lady is resting. She and I have been at Troy's bedside throughout the night."

Wiggs sucked in a breath of air. "That is entirely unseemly."

"But effective. I believe we might have saved the lad's life."

"But you say he is recovering now? Then Miss Renslow can return to her own lodgings."

"Aside from Troy's continued need for her, and Miss Renslow's dedication to him, I do not believe there is a respectable older female at the Cameron Street residence, either."

"Tut."

Ian did not like that affectation and he did not like the man, especially when Wiggs said, "But no ill can be spoken of her there as long as she does not go out and about by herself. Who could find fault with a female visiting her beloved uncle, a decorated military officer, versus . . ."

"Yes? You were saying?" Ian's raised eyebrow dared Wiggs to accuse him of being a rakehell, a here-and-thereian, a despoiler of virgins. Any of them might be true, but they were not for mushrooms like Wiggs to say.

The man had enough sense—or self-preservation—to keep his downturned lips closed. They were pursed as tight as a miser's purse strings, but he said nothing.

Ian did. "My thoroughly respectable housekeeper was in constant attendance, and Miss Renslow did not even join me for dinner. Or were you thinking that my unbridled passions would have me ravish the woman at her ailing brother's bedside?"

"It is not what *I* was thinking, my lord, but what others might say. I never—"

"And neither did I. Miss Renslow managed to survive the night at Maddox House with her virtue and reputation both intact. Small-minded persons might suggest otherwise, but no one of intelligence or compassion can doubt her honor."

The cleric tutted a few more times, headed for the door mumbling his intentions of calling later. Ian stopped him. "But you have not asked to see the boy. Your function was to tutor him, was it not? Was Miss Renslow also your student, that you made her reputation your concern?"

Wiggy wanted to reach for the doorknob and his escape, Ian could tell by the way his fingers twitched. He stayed, though, and admitted, "I did give Miss Renslow an occasional lesson, for she felt her education was inadequate. What use is geometry to a woman, I wondered, but since I was already there . . ."

"You took the opportunity to spend more time with the young lady."

Now Wiggs thrust out his lower jaw, making him seem more like a runty bulldog than ever. "Their brother entrusted both of his siblings into my care."

"How much of your care?"

"If you must know, Viscount Rensdale gave me permission to pay my addresses to the young lady."

Attie with her boundless love tied to this cold stick? Ian could not reconcile that in his head. "Has the lady agreed?"

It was none of Lord Marden's business and they both knew it. They also both knew he would have an answer, because he was Lord Marden.

Wiggs patted back his straight hair. "I have not asked her yet. I wished to see how she got on in London, for one thing. It would not do for a prelate's wife to have her head turned by the capital's frivolity. The shops and parties, you know."

"Might make a female resent the quieter, more frugal country life?"

"Exactly. For another thing, I was waiting to speak to Captain Beecham. Her uncle is Miss Renslow's legal guardian, you know, so it is only proper to seek his blessing, too."

"And perhaps discuss settlements?"

"Ah, I knew a man of the world such as yourself would understand. At the moment I am without a living of my own, although I am under consideration for a post of considerable authority and income. Lord Rensdale's influence would be welcome, as would a sizable dowry."

"In other words, a well-born, well-connected, well-dowered female would suit you very well?"

"To a cow's thumb."

"As long as her reputation is unblemished. Caesar's wife, and all that."

Wiggs looked uncertain, betraying his own ignorance.

"Caesar's wife, you know, had to be above suspicion."

"Quite. Who knows how high in the church an ambitious man might rise, with the proper wife?"

"Who knows, indeed? I regret that you will have to wait to find out, for the boy is too ill for Miss Renslow to consider her own future yet. I would hazard a few more weeks of recovery should see her in a more receptive frame of mind."

Wiggs looked disappointed at the delay in his plans for the archbishopric. "I knew this visit to London was ill-advised. And letting the boy ride an unpredictable mount was thoroughly irresponsible, and so I shall have to report to Lord Rensdale. Why, the whelp might have his wits permanently addled from the fall."

Ian gathered that Miss Renslow's letter had not informed Wiggs of the gunshot, only the mishap with the horse. He could not blame her, having met the preachy prelate.

"The doctors are hopeful of a full recovery."

"Until his next setback. All this is getting his hopes up for naught, and so I told Miss Renslow, but she would not heed my words—and see what happened. Telling the pup he can go to university. Tut."

The boy would have his education, Ian vowed, if he had to build a school of his own for invalids and asthmatics.

Wiggs was going on: "No, Miss Renslow requires a firmer hand than Viscount Rensdale sees fit. She must face the truth, and then secure her own future."

"As your wife?"

Wiggs puffed out his narrow chest. "I consider myself a suitable match."

"Unless she blots her copybook."

"Precisely."

"Or her dowry is very large."

"You jest, of course, but a female's dowry is no laughing matter to a gentleman without your lordship's advantages."

Ian bowed slightly and apologized. "As is a woman's reputation to any man considering matrimony."

"So you see why it is imperative for Miss Renslow to leave your residence immediately, my lord. I knew an eminent gentleman such as yourself would understand. One evening under a bachelor's roof might be forgiven, due to the emergency, of course. But any more and her good name is in jeopardy."

"You seem to be more concerned with her reputation than her virtue. Not that Miss Renslow's innocence is in doubt, of course, but I am curious."

"Tut, tut. You are known to be a connoisseur of women, enjoying the company of the most scintillating, sophisticated beauties of the *ton*. Little Miss Renslow cannot interest you, and her dowry means nothing to such a wealthy man." He waved his bony hand around the library once more, this time gesturing toward the paintings on the library's walls. "Would you hang an unknown country dauber's work among your masterpieces?"

If he liked it enough, yes.

And Ian liked Athena too much to see her shackled to this clod of a clergyman who could never come to appreciate her. The choice was not his to make, of course, so he suggested Wiggs visit with the boy. He knew that the chest wound would be covered by his nightshirt, and that Athena would hear the tuts from her own bedchamber. If she wished to see her erstwhile, ambitious suitor, so be it.

"I'll see if the boy is awake," he said, giving the tutor no choice.

When Hopkins reported back that the young gentleman was indeed awake, Ian went along with Wiggs up the stairs. He went half out of curiosity and half out of a sense of responsibility. Hell, he was entirely responsible. He could not throw his wounded lamb to this wolf in clergyman's clothes. One sneer at Troy, one start of a lecture, and the self-serving sapskull would be out on his arse.

Athena was in the boy's room, and Ian frowned. She should have been resting still. She did look refreshed, however, with her hair piled atop her head in a becoming fashion, a few fair curls left to frame her face. She was wearing a different gown; he'd sent a footman to fetch her trunks from her uncle's house, since she would not be leaving soon. He had also sent for the groom, Alfie Brown. Alfie had not arrived; the trunk had. This gown was of sunshine-yellow muslin with blue ribbons, and was more stylish than either of the previous. It was not up to London standards, of course, obviously being country made, but it did have the current fashion for high waist and low neckline.

What the gown left exposed also exposed Ian's stupidity. Miss Athena Renslow was a woman, by George—a lovely young woman with a lovely figure. She was petite but perfectly formed. If she was presented to society, dressed in silks and jewels, she'd be called a Pocket Venus. Such a little bit of perfection was never meant for a prig's pocket.

The dog leaped off Troy's bed and raced to the door. Ian stepped behind the reverend, who shouted at the dog to desist its attack on his boots.

Ian said, "The dog is deaf, sir."

"I know that, my lord." Wiggs shouted louder.

Having grown wise to Roma's ways, Ian tossed a macaroon in the dog's direction so they could enter the room.

"I always said that animal should be drowned," Wiggs muttered, waiting for Lord Marden to go first this time, too low for Athena to hear.

"Because she is deaf?"

"Because she is mean and a menace and no fit companion for a lady." With his next breath, Wiggs turned from ranter to Romeo. "How do you do, my dear Miss Renslow? I am appalled at the grievous shock you must have suffered, and I wish I had been nearby to comfort and console you. But you are looking lovely this morning, if I might say so. A breath of springtime in this darkest hour."

Athena tugged the covers higher on her brother's chest, so no hint of bandages showed at the neck of his nightshirt. Then she welcomed Wiggs as if she owned the house, offering him the most comfortable chair and a cup of tea.

"How kind of you to come, sir. And to worry about my welfare. Isn't Troy looking well?"

Wiggs must have expended his brief effort at wooing, for he said, "No, he is not, as a matter of fact. He is looking as if he'd been trampled by a horse, instead of merely falling off one."

"Tut, tut," Ian said, winning him a quick glance from Miss Renslow, whose lips twitched slightly upward. "The lad is vastly improved. With such a rapid recovery, he will be putting my jumpers through their paces in no time."

"Jumpers?" Athena clutched her brother's shoulder. "Jumpers? Ridiculous. The brat will kill himself for sure. Lord Rensdale will forbid such a thing, I daresay."

But Troy said, "Jumpers? Capital!"

The corners of Wiggs's lips almost touched his chin. "Acting in Lord Rensdale's stead, I cannot permit such dangerous activities, my lord. You have raised impossible expectations."

"Nothing is impossible with prayer, I have always heard. Is that not true, sir?" Ian said, challenging Wiggs.

Troy gave a weak smile, which angered the man more. "You, my lord, are precisely what I suspected: a bad influence. Miss Renslow, may we speak privately?"

"What, without a chaperone?" Ian countered. "Tut. That is not at all proper."

Before Wiggs could go on about how he was a man of the cloth, and acting as guardian for the young lady, besides, thus exempt from the conventions of Polite Society, Athena interrupted. "Whatever you wish to say, Mr. Wiggs, can be spoken in front of Lord Marden. No one could have been kinder or more generous, and it would be a poor repayment, indeed, to be telling secrets behind his back." Besides, she had no desire to be alone with the man, for another of his lectures.

Mr. Wiggs's protuberant Adam's apple bobbed a few times over his plain neckcloth as his narrow eyes shifted between his host and his hoped-for bride.

"And you are not my guardian, sir," Athena reminded him.

"Very well," the man said. "I shall be forced to speak bluntly. I was dismayed to learn how far my pupil was from your uncle's residence, and that he had to be transported to this gentleman's house. Lord Renslow will be upset when I tell him."

"Ah, but you need not bother." Athena smiled sweetly in Ian's direction—Thunderation, he thought, she was a beauty when she smiled—and explained, "His lordship has already informed my elder brother of Troy's mishap."

"He did? That is, of course he did. Correct thing for a gentleman to do. That is as may be, but I daresay he did not mention to Lord Rensdale that you are at Maddox House without adequate supervision."

Athena drew herself up to her less than imposing height, but she could have been a duchess for her dignity and the way she put down the prig's pretensions. "Young children and animals at the menagerie need supervision, sir. I assure you, I need no one to tell me how to go on."

Ian wanted to clap at the girl's show of spirit. He would not have to come to anyone's rescue, after all. He crossed his arms over his chest and leaned against the mantel, ready to enjoy this confrontation.

He did not have long to wait.

"You misunderstand, my dear. I do not mean that you require a nanny or a governess. I am merely concerned that you are without female companionship in a gentleman's residence."

Athena fingered the skirt of her freshly pressed

gown. "Mrs. Birchfield and the maids have been as attentive as one could wish. Far more so, I might add, than the female staff at my brother's home."

"And I daresay you have befriended them all. We shall not speak now on unsuitable associations, although I believe dear Lady Rensdale has tried to teach you the rudiments of ladylike conduct. What I am speaking of, of course, is the fact that you have no chaperone, here in a bachelor's dwelling. And not just any bachelor, either, I might add, but one whose reputation does not—"

Athena held her hand up. "I am lady enough to avoid gossiping about my host after I have eaten his food." She turned her eyes to the half-empty plate of poppyseed cake beside the tutor's chair. "And Lord Marden has shown himself the perfect gentleman, besides being the perfect host."

"Nevertheless, you are here. He is here. Tongues will wag."

"Only yours, sir."

"I did not take you for a fool, Miss Renslow. A headstrong young woman, perhaps, but not a fool. People will talk."

Athena snapped her fingers. "That is what I care about idle talk."

"And will you care when your reputation is destroyed and you are not accepted into Polite Society? Will you care when no decent gentleman makes you an offer? An honorable offer, that is. No gentleman will accept damaged goods, pardon the expression, for his wife."

"How dare you! I am not and never have been—"

"You will be, in the eyes of the world. That is why I must insist you come away from this place with me now. I shall return you to your uncle's care, and no one need be the wiser."

"What, and leave my brother?"

"You said he was improved. You also said his lordship's staff was attentive."

"I shall not leave my brother to servants, no matter how competent."

"Then I shall not be responsible for the outcome, madam. I shall have to reconsider my—"

Ian deemed it time to step in, before Miss Renslow burned her bridges. "The young lady's duenna will be here before nightfall."

Wiggs seemed more relieved than Athena. He needed Viscount Rensdale's patronage if he was to advance, *and* the chit's dowry. "On your honor, my lord?"

Ian held up an arm. "As God is my witness."

"God is *my* witness, heh heh. The word of a gentleman is ample enough."

It had not been, before, but Ian nodded. "I would invite you to take dinner with us, to see for yourself, but my mother will be fatigued after her journey from Bath." Ian would invite this insect to his table when donkeys donned tutus and danced at the Royal Ballet.

"Another time, perhaps." The promise of dinner with a countess—one who might sponsor Miss Renslow into society—was enough to make Wiggs smile. At least his lips turned up a bit, and his *tut*s turned to *heh*s. "Forgive my harsh words, my lord. But a woman cannot be too careful of her reputation, heh heh, especially if she hopes to attract a notable husband." He threw his puny chest out like a bantam cock, silently declaring that he was the best candidate for the position.

Heh heh.

Chapter Seven

A man looking for a wife has to be careful.
                                                    —Anonymous.

A woman looking for a husband has never had one.
                                                    —Mrs. Anonymous

"Do you mind?" Ian asked after Wiggs left. They had both accompanied him to the door, Athena out of courtesy, and Ian to make sure the clunch of a cleric really left. A maid and a footman were both watching Troy drift off to sleep, and the dog had found an old slipper of Ian's and was cheerfully shredding it to bits. Ian invited Athena to the morning room for a cup of tea, purposely leaving the door fully open.

Athena did not pretend to misunderstand, either his question or the open door. "What, do I mind that the rumormongers might slander my name if I stay and your mother does not arrive in time? I mind more that now I am imposing on your relations, too."

"My mother will be delighted to have a young lady to look after again. She is forever complaining of being bored to flinders in Bath, especially since my sister moved to Richmond. Dorothy decided that, having attained her majority and come into her inheritance, she could put on her spinster caps and set up her own establishment."

"You let her?"

He smiled. "You have not met my sister if you think I could have stopped her. The Richmond cottage is actually mine, although I seldom visit, so no one considers Dorothy an eccentric or a bluestocking. She does like to take in the occasional London play and visit the lending libraries, so she will not mind a visit to town, either. She refuses to attend the balls and breakfasts, considering them part of the Marriage Mart, which aggravates my mother to no end. They fare better apart."

"Yet you invited both?"

"Merely in case one or the other was indisposed."

"But you thought my being here without a chaperone was important enough to inconvenience both ladies?"

It was important enough that Ian was in a stew because neither one had yet reached his doorstep. Richmond was not that far away, and the messenger had left at dawn. "I think it is important to Mr. Wiggs."

Athena did not answer, but poured out the tea, as collected as a countess in her silence.

Did that mean that she did not care for her reputation, or did not care for Mr. Wiggs? As he accepted his cup, Ian asked, "Forgive me if I am intruding, but would you be distressed if you lost the reverend's regard? His, ah, calling requires extra attention to the conventions, I suppose."

"I should not wish to be thought fast, of course, but I will not sacrifice my brother to such a silly scruple, no matter what Mr. Wiggs says. And I believe that his narrow views have more to do with his ambition than his vocation. A true man of God would never condemn a person on hearsay or appearances."

"That was my impression also. And yet he is a close friend of the family."

"And wishing to be closer. Yes, I do know his intentions. Do not worry that he might not actually, ah, come up to scratch. I believe that is how my older brother put it. Despite what my brother thinks, the loss of Mr. Wiggs would not place me entirely on the shelf, you know. I am not at my last prayers."

Ian was. He was also curious. She had not told Wiggs about the missing uncle or the gunshot, and she had called him Wiggy in private. That did not betoken a fond regard, to Ian's thinking. A marriage was supposed to be based on trust and respect, was it not? Not that he had thought much about marriage, of course. On the other hand, if the young woman was promised to someone else . . .

Athena was not sure if she would mind the loss of Wiggy or not. Despite her brave words, she had no other suitor in sight, and none on the horizon. The few assemblies she'd attended in Derby had yielded nothing but youths and widowers, a few aged roués, and the occasional pinch from a married man. When her uncle eventually arrived in London, he could not introduce her to eligible *partis,* only naval men, and she did not want an absent husband, or one so liable to leave her a young widow. Her sister-in-law, Veronica, had no connections in town, having alienated the other women making their come-outs during her four Seasons, including her own sisters. She would not bestir herself on Athena's behalf, anyway, especially if Athena brought shame on the family name. That left Wiggy.

Athena wanted a husband and a family of her own. She wanted to be out from under Rensdale's roof, but still be near enough to nurture her little brother.

Wiggs seemed ideal. Until one considered spending the rest of one's life with the man.

She knew what Wiggs was planning. Her older brother had warned her. Actually Spartacus had congratulated her on finding such a suitable match, and without any effort or expense on his own part. Satisfied to see her suitably fixed, he would make no effort to find her another gentleman to wed.

Athena stared into her cup, as if trying to read the floating bits of tea leaves.

The earl interrupted her musings. "He is right, you know, that a decent gentleman would not offer marriage to a fallen woman, even if her fall from grace is only in the gossips' eyes."

"If he loved her, he would."

"Ah, does Mr. Wiggs hold you in such high esteem, then? He seemed quite determined that you not lose your good name."

"No, I doubt the man has any true affection for me. If I am ruined, I believe he would cast the first stone."

"Then what do you wish to do? Shall I call for a carriage to return you to your uncle's residence?"

"I will not leave my brother. I need to be here when he calls for me. He is better this morning, but I do not believe we have seen the last of the fevers, not at all. And the surgeon warned he is not to be moved."

"Zeus, no. Bound to open up the wound and cause him untold pain."

"So I have no choice, do I? With your permission, of course, I have to stay, and hope your family arrives in time to redeem my reputation. If not, I suppose I shall have one less choice in the future."

Everyone was entitled to choices—except Ian, who had given up his rights when he shot into those blasted trees. Now he vowed that Miss Renslow would have her options, Wiggy or whatever she wished. "You shall have your chaperone, I swear."

As Athena was finishing her tea and preparing to rejoin her brother, a caller walked into the morning room, unannounced as was his custom as an old friend of the family.

"Ah, Carswell," Ian said, "let me make you known to Miss Athena Renslow, who is sister to the young gentleman we assisted yesterday. Miss Renslow, I should like you to meet my friend, the Honorable Kenton Carswell."

Athena made a perfect curtsy. "If you helped bring my brother to Maddox House, you have my utmost appreciation, sir." She held out her hand.

Carswell was too stunned to take it. "This is the little sister you went to fetch?"

Athena blushed. Ian could feel the tips of his ears grow warm. "Miss Renslow is small in stature, not in age or dignity."

Carswell had his quizzing glass out and was inspecting the young woman.

"Please forgive my friend his affectations. He is truly the best of good fellows, under the guise of a coxcomb." Under cover of leading Carswell into the room, Ian put his hand around the slighter man's shoulder and squeezed, hard. He whispered in his ear, "Nineteen." Carswell dropped his quizzing glass, and said, "Gads."

"Precisely. Now make your leg to the young lady."

Carswell did, with all his polished elegance. "Forgive me, Miss Renslow, I was overcome by your age—ah, attractiveness. My friend did not see fit to mention that he hosted an angel at his table, or I would have arrived for breakfast. What need for food, though, when a man could feast on such a lovely sight? But how goes the young man? Your brother is a game one, Marden told me yesterday. Pluck to the backbone."

Athena blushed with pleasure. Mr. Carswell's non-sensical compliments meant little, but praise of her brother was music to her ears. She liked Lord Marden's friend already, despite his airs. Not that she had the least intention of becoming enamored of the handsome newcomer. Why, with his expensive apparel and suave manners, he was as above her touch as . . . as an earl. Shorter than the earl and slender, he was the elegant epitome of a fine London gentleman. With his neckcloth tied so intricately and so high, he could barely turn his head, yet he wore the fashion of the time with style and grace. He also wore a warm smile, which Athena appreciated more than his perfectly combed blond hair and refined features. He seemed to be forever smiling, half at the world, and half at himself.

"Thank you for asking, sir. My brother seems to be recovering. The doctors warn that it is far too soon to be certain, but I am optimistic. Now if you gentlemen will excuse me, I shall return to Troy's side and leave you to your conversation."

Both men bowed. When she left, Ian firmly shut the door behind her. He sank into his chair while Carswell reached for a decanter on the sideboard.

"Don't say anything. I have already endured a lecture from a jumped-up psalm-spouter."

"Nineteen?"

"I told you not to say anything, dash it!"

"Good grief, man, what are you going to do?"

"I have already sent for my mother and sister."

Carswell exhaled in relief. "That's all right and tight, then. Uh, what psalm-spouter?"

"The young lady's suitor, it appears, although he'd suit an old crow better." Ian proceeded to tell his friend about Wiggy, and Carswell related the latest news about town, which, happily, did not mention the Renslows, Lord Marden, or duels. Lord Paige's disappearance was mentioned in passing, but only when one of the patrons at White's recalled a gambling debt he would now never recover.

The two friends were about to discuss Ian's plans for the day, which included checking into the whereabouts of that missing groom, calling on the Admiralty for an expected arrival date for Captain Beecham's ship, and hanging himself if his mother did not arrive in time.

They were laughing, albeit Ian's merriment was forced, when the butler, Hull, entered the room. "The young gentleman is asking for your lordship," he intoned. "As soon as possible."

Ian was on his feet in a second. "Good grief, where is Attie? Should I send for the surgeon?"

"Miss Renslow is out walking the dog, I believe. And I do not consider a call from the surgeon necessary, or I would have sent for him previously."

"Quite, quite. I am not accusing you of dereliction of duty, man." Ian was already out the door and headed for the stairs. "Come on," the earl called to Carswell, "I might need help bathing him."

Carswell looked at his silk waistcoat with the delicate forget-me-nots embroidered on it, and his pale blue coat. "*Bathe,* did you say?" But he followed in the earl's footsteps, taking the marble stairs two at a time.

When they reached the boy's room, Troy's cheeks were flushed and his turquoise eyes had a glassy shine to them, but he did not seem hot to Ian's admittedly inexperienced touch. The maid put down her mending and curtsied to the two gentlemen, smiled and left. She would not have smiled if the boy was in peril, Ian told himself. She would have been rushing after Miss Renslow, yelling for assistance.

"I am sorry, my lord," Troy said when he noted that Lord Marden was out of breath. "I did not mean to worry you, but Attie will be back in a minute, and I needed to speak with you."

Ian let his shoulders sag in relief. Then he stepped aside to introduce Carswell.

"You were at the d—"

"The shooting match," Carswell put in. "Duels are illegal, you know."

"Of course," Troy said, proud to be part of this manly pretense. Then he forgot. "But that loose screw did shoot early."

"Yes, I saw him, too. It might be better for everyone if you forgot that, though."

Ian could not approve of asking the boy to lie. He would speak to Troy privately, when he was a bit stronger. Meanwhile, Carswell was going on: "I am delighted to see you in better curl than the last time, sir. You gave us all a scare."

"Me, too," Troy admitted. "But Lord Marden knew just what to do. That's why I had to speak to you while Attie is away, my lord." He glanced uncomfortably at the other gentleman.

"I'll station myself out in the hall, shall I, and whistle if she comes back too soon," Carswell offered.

Troy nodded gratefully, and Ian advised his friend to duck into the next room if he heard the scrabble of claws, if Carswell valued his boots.

"What, you are housing a vicious beast as well as a virgin?" Carswell quipped on his way out. Neither Ian nor Troy found his jest funny.

"That's what I wanted to talk about, my lord. You see, my sister has given up a great deal for me. Why, she could have had a London Season a few years ago.

One of her friends invited Attie to join her for her come-out, but Attie refused, on account of me. She might have been married and had babies by now. I wouldn't want her to go far away, but I don't think she ought to stay on at my brother's house either. It's not right, having the two women under one roof."

Ian remembered the rows between his mother and his sister. "No, it is not."

"And Wiggy wants to marry her, I know. He wouldn't be my first choice. Or tenth, if it came to that, but . . ."

"But the choice should be hers, correct?"

"I knew you would understand. You won't let her be ruined, will you?"

"Never."

The boy was not entirely convinced. "I know I asked you to look after my sister, my lord, and please do not think I am ungrateful. But maybe I asked too much?"

"I do not think that is too much to ask of any gentleman. I admire you for your care of her, in your own distress. You are a good brother, Renslow, and will make an honorable man."

Troy's fair cheeks grew red at the praise. "Well, it is nicer here than at our uncle's house, but if Attie's reputation is going to be hurt, and Wiggy backs out, and our brother hears of it—"

"Your sister's reputation will not be hurt. She will have a respectable chaperone at her side by dinnertime, I swear to you."

The problem was—well, one of the problems was—that Ian did not have a respectable chaperone to uphold the niceties of polite behavior, having neither mother nor sister on hand. He vowed he would disown both of them on the instant and declare himself an orphan without siblings.

His butler was waiting when Ian and Carswell returned below and repaired to the library. The messengers had returned, Hull reported, with winded horses but no ladies. The countess was indisposed with an ague in Bath. Lady Dorothy was away from her Richmond home inspecting cotton mills for a treatise she was preparing on child labor.

"My own sister cares more for those nameless children than she does for me!" Ian stormed as his friend poured them drinks. Of course, he had been the one to interest her in the issue of reform, and he did use her valuable research in his efforts in Parliament, but why the devil did she have to be out crusading now, when he needed her? As for his mother, she was always suffering from some ailment, especially when asked to forego her twice weekly card nights.

Ian threw his broad body into a leather chair and ran his hands through his hair. "Deuce take it, I need a respectable woman!"

"Not your usual style, old man."

"What, my hair?" Carswell's coiffeur was perfect, as always.

"No, your women. Never known you to get within ten feet of a virtuous female, other than your mother and sister, of course."

"Damnation, I am not speaking of dalliance now. I need a duenna for Miss Renslow. By dinnertime. Surely you must know a female who could come act as dogberry, just for a day or two until my sister returns to Richmond."

Carswell shrugged. "Sorry, but m'sisters are breeding in the country, my mother's been gone these fifteen years, one of my grandmothers is too old, and the other is too mean to put herself out for anyone. Besides, she hates you."

"You broke that blasted vase, not me!"

"Ah, but I looked innocent, a regular little gentleman. You were a big, clumsy oaf of a boy."

"And I am still a big, clumsy oaf, making a hash of other people's lives. But think, man. Surely between us we know some married woman I could ask to stay."

Carswell buffed his polished fingernails on his sleeve. "I hear that Lady Paige is seeking a change of address."

"Mona? I would not let that trollop near Miss Renslow! Gads, I ought to call you out for suggesting such a crime against innocence. I would, too, if I had not renounced duels. Mona Paige and Athena Renslow. That would be tossing mud into a clear well."

"Yes, but the neighbors and passersby would see a well-dressed woman getting out of a coach in front of your house. That's all it takes."

"You might be right about that, but who? Not a woman with a spotty reputation of her own. Think, man. Lives depend on it."

Carswell took a pinch of snuff, from an enameled box with blue flowers on it, while he thought. "I have it," he said between sneezes. "You need only dress one of your housemaids up in borrowed finery. Surely your sister and mother have left gowns here for the occasional visit."

"Wardrobes full. But—"

"It will work. Your maid hides the fancy dress under a plain cloak and heads for the stable mews, as if on an errand. Your carriage pulls out, with the curtains across the windows. An hour later it returns as if from a posting inn, windows uncovered, with your impeccably gowned chaperone inside. She steps down, you greet her outside as if she were your long lost

Aunt Ermentrude, veiled against the dust of the road, and, voilà, Miss Renslow's reputation is protected. The woman is not receiving, naturally, due to the illness in the house."

"But I do not have an Aunt Ermentrude, which everyone in London and everyone with a Debrett's knows."

"Hmm. There is that. Your pedigree must be as well documented as the Darby Arabian."

"And Wiggy is bound to know all of the Renslow kin. In fact, if there were any aunts or cousins in town, Miss Renslow would have been staying with them." Ian thought a moment, then snapped his fingers. "But I'd wager he does not know Captain Beecham's family. A cousin is possible, or perhaps the wife of a fellow officer. Yes, that just might do! You are a genius, Carswell."

"I always felt my talents were wasted being a wastrel. I should have taken up playwriting, don't you think?"

Ian was too busy thinking of possibilities. "There is a problem. No maid walks like a lady or sits like one. Besides, what if the chit thought it was such a lark she told her friends? I'd be in worse straits then, caught in a lie."

"You'd have to find an older, trustworthy one. What about your housekeeper, Mrs. Birchfield? She'd do anything for you."

"But she is short and as thin as a rail. My sister's clothes would never fit her."

"There is that. Lady Dorothy is a Long Meg. Decent sort, but larger than the average female."

"About your height, in fact. Dorothy does not have half your sense of style, of course, or your flair for the dramatic."

"No, she does not, and the answer is no."

"It would take a brilliant actor to carry this off."

"No."

"And a true friend."

"Impersonating the opposite gender is against the law."

"So is dueling. And I did take the blame for your grandmother's vase, you know."

"We were ten years old!"

"What about that monkey in Professor Dimsworth's bed? I got sent down for a month for that prank of yours. And that is not to mention the number of times you've borrowed my little house in Kensington for one of your opera dancers."

"They were actresses, not dancers."

His friend was weakening, Ian knew, so he pressed on. "And I did buy back those letters you were foolish enough to write to that harpy, Lady Caruthers."

"It's not as if I never pulled your irons out of the fire, you know."

"That's what friends are for, isn't it?"

Carswell thought a minute, then smiled. "You know that new chestnut you won off Graham?"

"The gelding? Damn, that is extortion."

"No, extortion is if I asked for your matched bays. A deal?"

"If you stay to have dinner with Miss Renslow and me, in costume, so she won't have to lie to Wiggy or the boy, the gelding is yours."

"Done."

They shook hands, sealing the bargain, but then Carswell grinned. "You will never make a good trader. I would have done it for nothing."

"That's all right," Ian said. "I would have given you the bays."

Chapter Eight

A woman needs a husband.

—Anonymous

*A woman needs a rich father, an honest banker,
and a good butler.*

—Mrs. Anonymous

"There you are, you dear, dear man," Lady Throckmorton Jones called out in a voice so loud and shrill it could be heard halfway across Grosvenor Square. Then she stepped down from a shiny coach with yellow wheels, the finest for hire in London. The lady herself was a vision in hyacinth satin, with furs adorning her somewhat broad chest, and a wide-brimmed bonnet trimmed with feathers and cherries and silk violets and a stuffed bird sitting upon her head. "How can I thank you enough for taking in the dear captain's poor orphaned kin?"

Then she grabbed Ian and pulled him forward, kissing first his right cheek, then his left.

"You are overplaying your role, dash it," the earl hissed in Lady Throckmorton-Jones's ear.

"And the gelding has a hitch in his gait," the lady whispered back, dabbing at her lips with a lace-edged handkerchief.

"You don't say," Ian replied, offering his arm.

"Besides, you want people to notice my arrival, don't you?"

By this time, Ian's footmen were unloading her ladyship's trunks—and bandboxes, tapestry bags and jewelry cases.

"Good idea," the earl admitted. "I should have thought of that. Now the servants will have more to report."

"Is it worth the bays?"

"Not quite, but I do have a spavined mare. What's in all those cases, anyway?"

"Books, rugs, the laundry. I thought that while I was here . . ."

They were passing through the portals of Maddox House. Whoever was going to report back to Lord Rensdale or Wiggy had seen enough. Now Lady Throckmorton-Jones had to pass muster with Ian's servants, and with the Renslows. The butler's disapproving nostrils were flared enough that a small coach could have driven inside his head, but Hull bowed and said, "Welcome, madam. I shall inform Miss Renslow that her, ah, cousin—did you say?—has arrived."

"Cousin to the dear captain, on the other side." The lady's piercing falsetto voice could be heard in the kitchens.

"Which side would that be?" Ian asked when Hull had left them in the drawing room.

"The right side, dear boy, starboard."

Lady Throckmorton-Jones gave Athena the same greeting she had bestowed on the earl, a hearty embrace and a salute on both cheeks. The embrace went on until Ian cleared his throat.

"How lovely to meet you, my dear, after hearing all about you from the dear captain."

"I am sorry, my lady, but Uncle never mentioned you."

"Isn't that just like Barnabas?"

"Barnaby," Ian whispered, pretending another cough.

"We call him Barnabas the Barnacle in jest, don't you know. And the silly man intended my presence to be a surprise for when you got to town, so you might have someone to guide you about the shops."

Athena looked askance at the lady's overembellished bonnet.

"Admire it, do you? I know where we can find one just like it for you, my dear. Wasn't it fortunate that I stopped by my cousin's house, today, dear girl, and discovered your direction?"

"Exceedingly fortunate, ma'am," Athena agreed, "and quite the coincidence."

"Yes, indeed. And to hear of the dreadful tragedy that had befallen the captain's nephew, why, how could I not write, offering my assistance? When the dear earl wrote back inviting me to stay at Maddox House to lend you countenance, how could I refuse such a generous offer?"

"How, indeed?" Ian muttered, putting a glass of ratafia in the lady's hand, so she had to release Miss Renslow's.

The lady took a fit of coughing when she took a swallow of the fruit-flavored liqueur. "What is this swi—? That is, what a delightfully sweet beverage."

"If you do not mind, I believe that young Renslow would like to make your acquaintance, Lady Throckmorton-Jones. He will rest easier knowing that his sister has such a charming, capable chaperone. If, that is, you feel up to the stairs?"

The lady patted her fur-covered chest. "A moment's

indisposition only. Of course I wish to meet the dear, brave lad. I brought him a book on horse racing from my library."

"How kind of you," Athena said, "and how peculiar for a lady to have such a volume on her shelves."

"Oh, I believe my late husband borrowed it from some ne'er-do-well or other, and forgot to return it."

Ian gritted his teeth. Now his prized tome would belong to the boy.

Athena was asking, "Was your late husband a naval officer like my uncle?"

"No, he was merely a gentleman of wealth and breeding. A girl should never settle for less, my dear."

Troy blinked at the bonnet, but he greeted the lady with grave courtesy. "Thank you for the book, my lady. All I have here are fusty old schoolbooks. And thank you for coming to look after my sister."

"Think nothing of it, my boy. It will be my pleasure."

Not if Ian had his way. He did not like how Lady Throckmorton-Jones was holding Miss Renslow's hand and leaning on her. He did not like the way the old lady was inhaling Attie's lilac scent, or how she reached out to tuck one of those wispy blond curls back behind Attie's ear. "I believe dinner will be served shortly."

He gave the chaperone the place of honor at the dining room table, across from him down the mahogany length. He seated Miss Renslow at his right hand.

"Oh, no, this will never do," Lady Throckmorton-Jones shrieked. "How can I get to know my dear young relative?" She directed the footmen to reset her place, at Lord Marden's left side. "That is much better, isn't it? Now we can have a comfortable coze and discuss your wardrobe, my dear cousin Athena."

Athena was wearing a sprigged muslin gown, cut simply but attractively. She had a few violets tucked in the ribbon holding her upswept hair and she looked exactly like what she was: a sweet country miss. Ian did not want to see her change. He glared at his latest guest and raised his glass in a toast to stop the conversation. "To Troy and his recovery."

After that, he made sure the footmen kept filling Lady Throckmorton-Jones's plate, so she was too busy chewing to natter on about fashions and furbelows. Then he realized that Athena was trying not to stare at the vast quantities of food her cousin was devouring. "I admire a woman who enjoys her food. You must agree, Lady Throckmorton-Jones."

The chewing stopped, and a blush suffused the lady's powdered cheeks. "Why, yes," she said, recalling the falsetto that had disappeared during one of her diatribes on the depth of a young female's décolletage. "I do appreciate fine cooking. My own cook is nowhere as talented as yours, Lord Marden. You must compliment the kitchens for me. And I did miss my nuncheon this afternoon, busy as I was with the packing and such."

"Of course. But do save some room for the syllabub."

"Ah, my favorite."

"Somehow I guessed it was, and had Cook prepare it specially."

"You dear, dear, boy," the lady said, patting Ian's hand. "Now about those pastels considered de rigeur for a young lady . . ."

After dinner, Athena stood to leave the room. Lady Throckmorton-Jones and Lord Marden got to their feet also, of course. "We ladies will leave you to your port, my lord, and repair to the drawing room," Athena said.

Ian bowed. "I'll just have a small glass and a brief smoke, then join you shortly."

Lady Throckmorton-Jones was eyeing the port decanter so longingly that Ian took pity on his friend, whose right bosom was sliding toward his waist. "On the other hand, I would not wish to forego a moment of the scintillating conversation. I believe I shall bring the port bottle into the drawing room with me, with your permission, Lady Throckmorton-Jones?"

"Granted, my dear boy. Too considerate. I do like a sip now and again. A taste I acquired from my dear late husband, may he rest in peace."

"Amen."

Athena smiled at both of them. "Since you have each other for company, I shall rejoin my brother above. I do not like to leave him too long. But thank you again for coming to my rescue, Lady Throckmorton-Jones, and thank you for being such a generous host, Lord Marden. I shall see you both at breakfast, shall I? At eight, I believe Hull mentioned."

"Eight . . . in the morning?" the older woman said with a gasp. "Hell, no. That is, Heavens above, a lady needs her beauty rest. And then I shall have to prepare for the calls I need to make, and a visit to my bank. And I do enjoy an afternoon nap. So I shall see you at dinner, my dear."

Athena curtsied. "I shall look forward to that. Good night."

"Attie, did you know that your chaperone smells of snuff?"

"Yes, and she needs a shave, too. Wasn't she wonderful, though?"

"Top of the trees," Troy said, looking over at the book at his bedside table. "Almost as nice as Mr. Carswell."

"That's what I thought."

"But not as nice as Lord Marden."

Athena doubted anyone could be as nice as their host, certainly not in Troy's idolizing eyes. Her brother ought to be sleeping, but he was too enthused for the rest he needed. At least his forehead felt cool to Athena's touch. She knew that could change in a minute, but for now she let him talk.

"You like him, don't you?" he asked.

"Lord Marden? Of course I do."

"No, I mean do you *like* him?"

"What maggot have you got in your brain now, my boy? Did your wits get scrambled in the fall?"

"Maybe I got smarter instead."

"And maybe you got too smart for your own good. My feelings for the earl make no matter. His lordship is far above our touch."

"I do not see why. Our father was a titled gentleman."

"A mere viscount with a meager holding. An earl can look as high as he wishes for a bride."

"But you have a substantial dowry. Wiggy would not be interested otherwise."

"My portion is a mere pittance compared to that of half the young ladies in his lordship's social circles. What might seem a fortune to a vicar is a farthing to a nabob. You have not seen much of Maddox House, but everything is of the finest. Masterpieces and treasures fill every niche. I do not doubt that Lord Marden's stables are better furnished than Renslow Hall."

"Well, you are pretty enough to please a duke."

"And I have the best, most loyal brother. But half the time the earl considers me a mere child."

"Not anymore. I saw how he looked at you tonight when you had on your nicest gown and did something fancy with your hair."

"He was merely surprised that I looked so well, I'd wager, for such a little dab of a chick."

"You are not that young, Attie," Troy said from his fifteen-year-old viewpoint. "Besides, our mother was a lot younger than our father when they married. I'd bet the earl is younger than our father was."

"However did we jump from liking the earl to marrying him, anyway? After two days' acquaintance? Do not start building air castles for us to live in, Troy, for his lordship will not settle for less than a Diamond for his countess. He'll pick a woman who is titled in her own right, wealthy beyond measure, educated at an exclusive seminary, if his family has not already selected the perfect bride. Her family will have political connections or land that borders the earl's. She will be part of his world, acquainted with his friends, the perfect, experienced hostess."

"She sounds dull as ditchwater. Or like Rensdale's wife, Veronica."

Athena ignored the slur to their wealthy, well-educated, and waspish sister-in-law. "You are assuming, my boy, that Lord Marden is looking for a wife, which is by no means certain. After all, what woman would turn him down if he offered? He has managed to stay a bachelor this long, seemingly enjoying his freedom, if half the gossip is true. I can guarantee you that he is not going to change his style for the likes of me."

Troy was not convinced. "But you like him?"

"Yes, silly. I like the earl. Very much."

Too much, she feared, for everything she'd told Troy was all too true. The Earl of Marden was not for the likes of Miss Athena Renslow.

"That went well, I thought." Ian was preparing for bed, his man Hopkins picking up the garments the earl haphazardly discarded.

"A noble effort, my lord," Hopkins agreed. The valet had necessarily been party to the performance, since they could not very well ask one of the maids to lace up Carswell's stays or stuff his bodice.

"Yet I detect some reservation in your tone."

Hopkins was inspecting his lordship's coat for lint or, worse, dog hairs, before hanging it up. He studied the coat, instead of replying.

"Out with it, man. You've been in the servants' hall. Were we successful or not?"

"I daresay we might have been, if Lady Throckmorton-Jones had not been seen outside by the footman whose job it is to walk the dog."

"What is wrong with that? She felt the need for some fresh air."

"She was in the garden, near the gate to the mews."

"Very well, she likes horses. She wished to see that they were well bedded down for the night."

"Forgive the vulgarity, my lord, but the footman reported that the lady pissed in the garden."

"Ah, she was outdoors seeking the necessary, but got lost, and the urge was too strong to wait. She is from the country, you know, without modern conveniences, and was too modest to ask anyone for a chamber pot."

"She hiked up her skirts to relieve herself."

"Of course she did. Nothing wrong there."

"Against a tree, standing up? Furthermore, that same footman told the others that, while Lady Throckmorton-Jones's skirts were raised, he saw boots. So did the dog, which is known to have an aversion to gentlemen's footwear."

"Damnation, I told Carswell to cram his toes into Dorothy's slippers, no matter how much they pinched. I suppose I owe him a new pair of boots?"

"I believe your debt is a shade more costly than that, my lord."

"The footman told the others?"

"It was too grand a joke, my lord."

Ian was not laughing. "I am sunk."

"Capsized, run aground, scuttled. Yes, I believe that sums up the situation, sir. Or if you were to pursue a different tack, you might consider yourself ditched, overturned, or splintered. In the ring, you might be—"

"Yes, I get the idea." Ian took his coat back from Hopkins, but he left his shoes off. "I will go check on the boy. With any luck, which has been sorely missing lately, no one has informed young Renslow of the masquerade. I'll have that footman's head if he did."

"The staff would not gossip with the young man. Amongst themselves, perhaps—no, positively—but not with a guest."

"Good. I would not want Troy to think I went back on my word."

"Even though you did?" Hopkins felt entitled to ask, after serving the earl since his university days. "Through no fault of your own, of course."

"This whole wretched mess is my fault! It feels as if the only disaster I am not responsible for is the army's last defeat on the Peninsula."

"And the fog, my lord. No one considers you quite that omnipotent."

"Thank you, Hopkins. That makes me feel so much better."

"My pleasure, my lord."

Athena was at the boy's bedside. Thunderation, he should have expected that. And she was weeping. The boy was still. Oh, no.

"Is he . . . ?" Ian could not say the word.

"Sleeping."

"But he is worse?" The earl touched the boy's hand, feeling skin that was neither hot nor cold nor clammy.

"No, he appears the same. The physicians are pleased with his progress. He has pain but no fever, and seems in his senses, so they decided he was not concussed. They are permitting him to have a small dose of laudanum. He will sleep better now, without that enervating restlessness."

"But you are crying?" It was not so much a question as a demand for an explanation.

Athena dabbed at her eyes with her handkerchief. "No, I am not. I never cry."

She had been crying last night, too. Besides, Ian knew what he saw, which was swollen eyes, blotches on her fair cheeks, and a red nose. Miss Renslow was not one of those women who looked attractive in distress. She looked wretched, precisely as he felt.

"If you are not crying, have you contracted a congestion?"

"No, I feel quite well. Thank you," she added with a sniffle.

"Then you are merely overtired and burdened with worry about your brother. The maids can sit with him through the night, if he is sleeping so soundly. I can stay up to make sure he has his next dose of the pain medicine."

"No, I am not tired. I rested this afternoon."

He gave up. "You are weeping because our miserable plan failed, then?"

"It was not a miserable plan. It was magnificent!"

"But it did not save your reputation, because the servants saw through the disguise. I am so sorry, my dear. My mother is ill, my sister is away from home, and neither I nor Carswell could think of one other female who was respectable enough—that is, one other female who could come on such short notice. I can hire a gentlewoman tomorrow from one of the agencies, but it was too late today. I could not think of anything else to do. I swear I never wished to see you distressed."

"I know. That's why I am crying."

"Not because of what Wiggy will say when he hears? Or your older brother?"

She shook her head, and more tears fell. "Because no one ever tried to rescue me before. You see, I was the one who fought for Troy, who insisted he get better care than those ignorant country doctors. I stood up to Veronica constantly, to make sure the servants were treated fairly, and to Rensdale, so he did not keep raising the tenants' rents. But no one ever fought for me. No one took my part when my brother's wife dismissed my beloved governess, or urged Veronica to introduce me to eligible gentlemen. My brother was too clutch-fisted, and too much under the cat's paw. My uncle was away at sea too long. And Troy is too young, of course."

"So there was no one to take your part?"

"No one until you and Mr. Carswell played knights-errant, trying to save this damsel in distress. You did your utmost to protect the useless reputation of a near stranger. I weep, not because my reputation is in tatters, but because it mattered to you."

"Of course it matters. I am the one who got you into this damnable coil."

"No, you care because you are the kindest man I have ever met."

Kind? Ian wanted to scream. She thought he was kind? He wanted to take her and shake her and shout at her that he was the dastard who had shot her brother. He was guilty, by Jupiter. He deserved to be hanged, and still might be. He was not kind. He was a cur, a cad, and too much the coward to tell her. She would despise him, and then where would he be? Where would they both be? Twice as miserable. "I—"

"I am sorry if I embarrassed you, my lord. Perhaps I am simply tired. I will rest for a few hours now."

If Ian feared Athena would cry alone in her room, for dreams that never could come true, he'd be right.

But the dream was wrong.

Chapter Nine

A man does not need a wife.

—Anonymous

A man does not need a wife if he has a cook, a butler, a valet, a housekeeper, a mistress, and a dog. Otherwise, he will be miserable.

—Mrs. Anonymous

Mr. Wiggs called early the next morning. Athena knew he would. The family was at breakfast, he was told by Lord Marden's butler. Wiggs was used to being invited to break his fast with Lord and Lady Rensdale, so he was doubly offended.

He called again late that morning. Athena knew he would, so she met him in the drawing room. As soon as he was seated, with a cup of tea and a plate of biscuits, he started lecturing. Athena knew he would.

She listened with only part of her attention, wondering if Troy should have another dose of laudanum, or if the earl's mother would ever arrive in London. She wondered if her Uncle Barnaby would let her stay on at his residence once Troy was recovered, if Spartacus refused to let a fallen woman come home. Or if she should simply seek a post as companion or governess.

"I am outraged, I say."

Athena was not happy about seeking a position, either. She did sit up straighter, though, and listened more carefully. Obviously, Wiggy had already bespoken his indignation. His bulldog face was turning purple with his anger. "Yes?"

"Any man of principle would be."

"I am sure he would."

"Deceit and lies and immodest behavior. I have never been so surprised at a person's behavior in my life. I expected far better of you, Miss Renslow."

"Of me? But I did not know they were going to— Ah, what behavior of mine are you referring to, Mr. Wiggs?"

"What, do you tell so many untruths that you cannot keep track?" He raised his voice in affront. "You are certainly not the woman I took you to be, and certainly not a suitable wife for a man of the cloth. Why, I do not believe you are a good example to young Renslow, and so I shall tell Lord Rensdale."

She knew he would.

With nothing to lose, Athena asked, "Just what would you have had me do, abandon my little brother?"

"Your brother? That young devil deserves to be whipped, and so I shall inform Rensdale as soon as the sprig is recovered. You have always pleaded for leniency, but this time you have both gone too far. And I might never have known, had I not gone to call on your uncle this morning."

"My uncle? Ah, that is what has you so riled."

"Riled? I am aghast and appalled. At least I made sure that you do indeed have such a relation. He was ailing, you told me. He was in bed, young Renslow told me. He is not even in London, by heaven, the next-door maidservant told me!"

"He will be soon. The Admiralty expects his ship—"

"Imagine my dismay when I called to consult with the captain about removing you and your brother from this house of tainted virtue. And, I must admit, I had intended to speak with him about a more personal matter. Thank goodness I did not!"

"You could not very well speak to Uncle Barnaby if he was not at home, could you?"

Her effort at levity made Wiggs even more furious. His Adam's apple bobbed and his mouth turned down and his voice rose louder, loud enough to be heard from a pulpit. He might never have that pulpit of his own without Lord Rensdale's backing, which he was losing, along with Miss Renslow's dowry. Of course he lost his temper. "The point is that he never was at home, by all that is holy! I might not have discovered that fact but for a servant sweeping the steps next door. You lied to me, Miss Renslow," he shouted, "an outright, immoral lie, so that you might stay on in London kicking up a lark."

"A lark? I stayed in London so that we could consult a learned physician about my brother's condition, and so Troy could see some of the sights while we were here. I knew you would not approve, so I chose to avoid an argument by neglecting to mention Uncle's delay. You make it sound as if I went strolling down the Dark Walk at Vauxhall, or tied my garters on Bond Street. I never even purchased a novel, for I knew your disdain for them. And yes, Troy lied along with me, because he did not wish to go home the day we arrived, not when he was finally free to experience something of the world. I do not consider that an immoral act, sir. And if you, Mr. Wiggs, had been more accommodating, more understanding, then we should not have needed to fabricate Uncle Barnaby's illness."

"What, now it is my fault that you betrayed my

authority, and that of Viscount Rensdale, who entrusted me with the care of his ward? Humph. That is just like a woman, to cast aspersions, rather than admit her failings."

"I admit many foolish traits, but loose conduct is not one of them."

"Yet you landed here, at the home of a known rake."

"Through no fault of my own, as even you must admit. Or do you think I planned my brother's injury so that I might bring myself to Lord Marden's attention, where I might join him in crude and lewd orgies, or whatever it is rakes do?"

"Never crude, my dear," the earl said from the doorway, strolling into the room. His clenched fists betrayed his anger as he bowed toward Miss Renslow, turning his back on the dastard who dared to shout at her in Ian's own drawing room. "A successful rake never gives offense."

Athena was mortified that his lordship had seen— or heard—her arguing like a fishwife. Her cheeks bloomed scarlet that she had called him a rake. "I beg your pardon, my lord. I should never have spoken so rudely."

"No, you should not be expected to know about rakes and orgies, thank heavens. Is there a problem?"

"*Humph.* I say there is a problem. Miss Renslow has shown herself to be less than honorable."

Ian turned to look at Wiggs, who had taken to snorting instead of clucking. Ian tugged on the ribbon of his quizzing glass and brought the lens to his eye. He slowly inspected the tutor from his center-parted hair, to his dusty footwear. Wiggs shifted his lean weight from foot to foot under the scrutiny. Without saying a word, Ian made his point: a female under his roof, under his protection, was above suspicion—

certainly above accusations from such a lowly speci-
men of humanity. "I have found Miss Renslow to be
admirable in every aspect, from her devotion to her
brother to her courtesy to my staff. A lady in such
circumstances should not be chastised for following
her own moral principles." Especially not in his house,
the earl's raised eyebrow emphasized.

"Even—*humph*—if they take to lying? What is
next, stealing?"

"I shall have to set a guard on the family silver,
I suppose."

"You might laugh now, my lord, but will you think
it amusing when the polite world turns its back on
Miss Renslow? As her family's spiritual advisor, I feel
it necessary to point out the error of her ways."

"Which you have done, at great length and volume.
Miss Renslow is not now and never shall be the butt
of Society's ridicule."

"What, protected by the presence of some woman
no one ever heard of? Lady Throckmorton-Jones?
Humph. For all I know, she is made up of whole cloth,
like the captain's presence in London."

"I assure you, the lady is quite real. And my mother
will be here as soon as possible."

"Then where is this connection of the captain's
now? If she is so careful of Miss Renslow's reputation,
I say she should be here, in this very room."

"What, when Miss Renslow entertains her
family's—what did you term it?—spiritual advisor?"

"When she is alone in the house with a known—"
Wiggs stopped one word short of insult. "Just what
kind of chaperone have you provided, anyway?"

One unlike any Mr. Wiggs had encountered, that
was for certain. "An acceptable duenna, who knows
her charge is safe from any dishonor in my home."

"I should like to meet this woman for myself, so I

might assure Lord Rensdale that his sister has not fallen into infamy."

Athena stepped between the two men. "You are the one who is being rude now, Mr. Wiggs. My host has gone out of his way to ensure my comfort. You must not harbor such vile suspicions. Perhaps my untruths concerning Uncle Barnaby have led you to mistrust me, but I assure you, his lordship does not deserve your lack of confidence."

Ian stepped toward the door, not so subtly indicating that Wiggs should precede him out of the room. "My dear Miss Renslow, thank you for the valiant effort, but I can fight my own battles." He winked at her and whispered, "And yours, too."

Wiggs *humph*ed, but held his ground. "You have not answered my question. Where is Lady Throckmorton-Jones? I should pay my respects."

"She is resting, after spending hours at young Renslow's bedside, which, I make note, you have not volunteered to do. Be sure to put that in your message to Viscount Rensdale, Wiggs."

Wiggs snorted and sputtered, but he did offer, belatedly, to visit with his charge in the sickroom. As Ian led him toward the stairs, after suggesting Miss Renslow join her chaperone in a nap—"No, I do not mean you should join the woman in her chamber, by George! Just that you should rest, yourself"—he wondered out loud why small minds were so quick to see something suspicious in the slightest irregular situation. "Why do some people delight in destroying another's reputation?"

"I am not delighted, I assure you," Wiggs said, and Ian did believe him. After all, a dowry and a living were at stake, to say nothing of Athena herself, not that this chawbacon in collars deserved such a wife.

Wiggs was out of breath, winded by the pace his

lordship set going up the marble steps. Between gasps he went on: "Nor is my own reputation so spotty that single females cannot be in my presence without suffering blemishes on their good names. However, I find Miss Renslow has lied in the past. What am I supposed to think?"

"Why, you are supposed to think of divine salvation, doing good works, bringing religion to the heathens. That is what I supposed a churchman did, not harangue innocent women."

And boys.

Ian declared Troy too weak to listen to more than three sentences of Wiggy's diatribe against telling untruths. The boy groaned a few times, smiled weakly in thanks, and let his eyes slowly close. Then as soon as they were out the door, he went back to studying the book on horse racing that Mr. Carswell had brought.

Athena had waited in the drawing room for his lordship's return, to ask his intentions. Not *those* intentions, which she knew to be nonexistent, but what he meant to do about Mr. Wiggs. She would have admitted the deceit and been done with it: that she was alone in a libertine's den with naught but a sick boy and a scamp in skirts. The earl had winked at her again, though, and piled fibs upon faradiddles for Wiggy's benefit. She waited to find out what rig he was running now, as the grooms would say, and what was her part in it. She heard the butler tell Mr. Wiggs good day, but Lord Marden never came. He'd left by the garden gate, in a hurry to find a horse, then find Carswell.

Ian tracked his friend to White's. "Is it cold in here, do you think?" he asked as he sat beside Carswell in a leather armchair, a wine glass in his hand.

Carswell offered him a cigar, which he refused.
"Cold? No, not at all."

"Then hell must be freezing over. I just invited that
maggot Mr. Wiggs to dinner."

"Good grief, why?"

"Because he came within an inch of accusing me of
seducing Miss Renslow. He'll make sure she is ruined
if I cannot convince him otherwise. I need to hold the
dinner so he sees she is not compromised."

Carswell blew a smoke ring over Ian's head. "Which
you intend to do by . . . ?"

"Sacrificing my bays."

"Ah. But you say the servants know."

"Christmas is coming early at Maddox House this
year."

"Blackmail, my, my."

"No, this is merely a reward for all the extra work
they are expending, with the extra guests. Attending
the sickroom is an onerous task, far above the call
of duty."

"And your staff is so shorthanded and overworked."

Ian was known to have twice as many servants as
necessary, just so they might have jobs. "Precisely. If
one treats one's retainers well, one gets better service."

"And loyalty."

"Lud, I hope so."

Athena was not certain why they were going
through this effort. Mr. Wiggs was sure to discover
the sham sooner or later. Sooner, he would be angry;
later, he would be beside himself. If the servants did
not give them away, Lady Throckmorton-Jones might
curse or belch or bow instead of curtsying. Heavens,
she might forget to shave again.

"Where is your gambling instinct, Miss Renslow? There is a chance Wiggy might never see through the pretense," Ian explained. "And we are reprising the performance so that when my mother finally arrives, he will not dare kick up a fuss."

"And because you should have gone to a hotel the moment Miss Renslow crossed your threshold, but you did not," Carswell added. Tonight he wore lime green satin with a matching turban that had false curls affixed in front, and a huge, also false, diamond brooch in the middle. The paste pin had formerly seen duty as a shoe buckle. The delicate shoes he wore had formerly belonged to Ian's sister, and pinched unmercifully, so Lady Throckmorton-Jones was in an irritable mood.

"But it is Lord Marden's house," Athena said, "and he was immeasurable help with my brother."

"And he was as blind as a bat," Carswell muttered.

No one could mistake Athena for a child tonight. The new maid assigned to help her had ambitions of becoming a lady's maid, so she was practicing her arts on Miss Renslow. Athena's blond hair was piled high on her head, braided through with a strand of pearls. Her loose ivory gown had been altered so that it hugged her slender figure. The gown's neckline was lowered, some of the lace edging removed to show more skin and less frill. When Athena worried about the immodesty, the girl assured her that a bit of bosom was all the rage. Athena felt she only had a bit of bosom, and most of it was on view. She also worried that Mr. Wiggs would assume she had joined the demi-monde in such a dashing style. Then again, he already assumed the worst of her, and why should she not look her best at the earl's table?

Lord Marden was certainly looking his finest, Hopkins having made an extra effort to see his master turned out in style. Ian's dark curls were carefully tamed and his neckcloth was tied in an Oriental knot. Athena had to force herself not to stare at his broad shoulders or, worse, at his well muscled thighs in the tight-fitting trousers. She licked her suddenly dry lips.

Ian groaned. Blind? He must have been deaf and dumb besides, not to recognize that little Attie Renslow was all woman. She might not be aware of her potent charms, but any man with blood pulsing through his veins was more than aware. Ian could feel every drop of his own blood coursing where it had no business going, and he was aggravated with himself. This was not how he should be thinking of the woman whose reputation and innocence he was determined to protect and preserve! He should not even be looking at those creamy mounds above the scant bodice of her gown. Or her tongue, darting out to lick her soft lips. Or the golden curl left to trail along her cheek. He groaned again.

Where his eyes focused or her eyes flitted made no difference. What mattered was where Mr. Wiggs's eyes went. He came into the drawing room where the others were waiting before dinner, bowed to his host and his erstwhile intended, then glared at the fluttering eyelashes and bead-bedecked bosom of Lady Throckmorton-Jones.

Athena and Ian exchanged glances, ready to admit defeat, ready for the coming explosion. Then Wiggs turned his back on the turbaned matron. He faced Ian, his eyes narrowed, his jaw jutting forward. Even the straight part down the center of his scalp seemed to point the finger of guilt at the earl. "I do not know what rig you are running, sir, or what you hope to accomplish by making me the butt of your humor, but you shall not succeed."

"I—"

Wiggs did not permit Lord Marden to continue. He

jerked his thumb at Athena's purported chaperone and snapped, "By Heaven, there is no Lady Throckmorton-Jones. There is no Throckmorton-Jones peerage in all of England, not listed in Debrett's, not known at the College of Arms. Is this female one of your mistresses, or a mere actress you have hired to perpetrate this fraud?"

"His mistress?" Athena asked, covering a startled giggle with her handkerchief.

"A mere actress?" Carswell demanded. "There is nothing mere about my performance."

But Ian held his hand up. "You have found us out, sir." He was about to take all the blame, make a full confession, but Athena's giggle stopped him. She was a game one, all right. And she would be ruined. So he layered flummery upon falsehood, and hoped for the best. "You are correct, and too clever by half, to discover our little deception."

Wiggs did not know whether to preen or to prate about the "little" ruse. He settled on a *humph*, so Ian went on.

"You see, I invented Lady Throckmorton-Jones to protect her identity."

"You did?" Athena asked.

Ian faced her and said, "I am sorry we could not tell you, either, my dear, but Her Highness worried you would show too much obeisance to her if you knew."

"Her Highness?" Mr. Wiggs's eyes bulged and his heavy jaw hung open.

"Her Highness?" Athena blinked.

"Her—?" Carswell began until Ian stepped on his already sore toes. "That is, you swore not to tell."

"But who can we trust if not Mr. Wiggs, a man of the cloth?"

"Who, indeed?" Lady Throckmorton-Jones asked

with a high-pitched titter. "I suppose you may as well tell him the rest now. I am sure you have whetted his curiosity enough." He murmured, "Mine, too," in an undertone meant only for Ian's ears.

The earl frowned, but bowed, low enough for royalty. "Miss Renslow, Mr. Wiggs, it is my great pleasure to make you known to Her Highness, Princess Hedwig of Ziftsweig, Austria. She is traveling incognita in England on a secret mission for her brother, who is deliberating his principality's allegiance during the confrontation with the Corsican. If word of her unofficial visit gets out, who knows what damage will be done to the foreign policies of both her country and ours."

"*Ach, Liebchen,* do not tell them more. It *ist* too dangerous for them to know."

Athena coughed, and Princess Hedwig slapped her on the back. "*Wunderbar,* yes?"

"*W-wunderbar.* Yes." Athena made a deep curtsy.

Wiggs made a hasty leg, then reached for the back of a chair to steady himself. "Do you mean that . . . that Miss Renslow's companion is a spy?"

"We do not use that word," Ian told him. "Her Highness is gathering information. She agreed to stay here as a favor to me."

"Why would a sp—Why would an Austrian princess play dogberry to a girl from the country?"

"As I said, as a favor. I have been friends with Her Highness's sisters for years, since they started to visit our fair shores."

"*Und* how better to hide than in the open, I alvays say. *Und* I felt sorry for the little *fraulein,* so alone, *ja?*"

"But wait, I have heard of the Ziftsweig princesses. If I recall, one of them had her name linked with yours in the *on dits* column, Marden." Princess or not, his belligerence seemed to say, Wiggs would not stand for Marden's mistress acting as mentor to Miss Renslow.

"The Hafkesprinke principality boasts a bounty of royal sisters. I had the pleasure of escorting Princess Helga on the occasion of her last visit to England, and of hosting a reception for Princess Hannah. I danced once with Princess Henricka before she married her Russian count."

Wiggs digested that, wondering if Marden had bedded all three of the illustrious light skirts. They were all accepted in the highest circles, of course. He nodded, without dislodging a single strand of hair. "But I never heard of Princess Hedwig."

Ian leaned closer to the curate. "Wrong side of the royal blanket, don't you know. Acknowledged, but not legitimate. That is why she was perfect for this delicate mission, which you must instantly pretend was never mentioned."

"My lips are sealed."

"Mine are not. Vere is *mein* dinner?" the princess demanded.

Chapter Ten

Tears are for cowards.

—Anonymous

Tears are for sorrow and joy and pain and panic . . . and cowards.

—Mrs. Anonymous

Troy laughed so hard he almost opened his stitches, then suffered with the pain so badly that Athena had to give him the laudanum an hour early. He fell asleep as soon as the drug started to act, but with a smile upon his pale face.

Athena went to her own bedroom and changed into her nightgown, intending to sleep, or nap, once more on the pallet beside his bed. Perhaps by tomorrow she could let one of the maids sleep there, but not yet. The housekeeper or his lordship's valet were willing to wake up for the next doses of fever powders and laudanum, but Athena was not ready for that yet, either. She had to see for herself that her brother had his medicine, that he was sleeping soundly, that he was not in a fever.

She had put on her night rail and her thick flannel robe, thinking that she was more covered now than she had been in her gown. She had the waiting maid

unpin her hair and weave the wavy length into a long
braid that she tossed over her shoulder, then she collected a book to read by the candle left burning at
her brother's bedside. Even if Troy awoke during the
night, she would rather read to him from Shakespeare
than from his horse racing encyclopedia.

When she returned to Troy's room, Lord Marden
was there, handing Roma a steak bone. He straightened up, his footwear safe for now, and studied Troy
for signs of fever or chill. "He seems to be sleeping
peacefully," he said, as she came near the bed.

"Yes, while the pain is held back. But his head
wound is already healing, and he seems to have taken
no lasting effects from that, thank goodness."

"But the fever? The surgeon warned that was the
worst, once the bleeding stopped. Do you think it
will return?"

"I pray not. Then the danger will be past and we
can go home. Troy can sleep as well at our uncle's
house as here, where we will not cause such a
commotion."

"I assure you, my household can withstand any in-
conveniences your brother's recovery might involve."

"But it is my presence that is causing the stir, isn't
it?"

Ian looked at her, taking in the schoolgirlish braid,
the faded flannel robe, the tiny flowers embroidered
on her delicate slippers. Oh, she had caused a stir, all
right. More like a whirlpool, in fact, than a current to
ruffle the waves of his placid existence. He was drowning, and she was not even aware that he was gasping
for his last breaths of air.

Let her keep her innocent ignorance, he decided.
There was no need for both of them to suffer, not yet.
The future would be misery enough.

Then he took a better look at Miss Renslow's face,

hoping to see the radiant turquoise light in her eyes that meant she still considered him a friend. What he saw instead was swollen eyes, color-stained cheeks, and tear tracks.

"You have not been crying again, have you?" he asked, ready to run from the room, before he remembered that he had already held her—a single woman of marriageable age—against his chest while she wept. They could not hang a man twice, could they?

But this time she did not fly into his embrace, and he was relieved. His arms, however, fell to his sides, feeling useless, empty, bereft.

"Oh, no, I never cry."

"Now that is a plumper if I ever heard one," Ian said, "and Jupiter knows, I should recognize a lie when I hear one."

She smiled, and he realized she had been laughing so hard that tears had fallen, the silly chit. Of course, he and Carswell had had a good chuckle over Princess Hedwig themselves, but they had managed to restrain themselves to a few hearty laughs and knee slaps, like the rational, reasonable beings they were.

"What possessed you to make up such an outrageous tale?" she asked now, wiping at the corners of her eyes with a handkerchief.

He did it for her sake, of course, but Ian did not want to say that. He was still hoping they could squeak through this mess unscathed, or at least leaving her with choices. What he said was, "I could not let that starched-up, strait-laced slug succeed. He is so sure he knows what is right, as if the Almighty himself whispers in the clunch's ears. He wants everyone else to be wrong, to be found wanting on the grand scales of life, so that he might weigh more, philosophically."

"In other words, he is a jackass?"

"Exactly."

"And you had to get the best of him, like boys taunting each other in a schoolyard."

"No, like rational, reasonable beings." Ian loosened his neckcloth. "He mangles the truth, anyway, so why not feed him a rasher of lies to chew on? Besides, what I told Wiggs was not entirely a fairy tale. I do know some of the Hafkesprinke heiresses."

Athena wanted to ask how well he knew them, but she could not, of course, being a lady.

He was going on: "Thank goodness none of them is in London now, but I'd wager Princess Helga would vouch for me."

Which answered Athena's question. At least one Austrian princess knew him very well, indeed. Wiggy might distort the truth, but he was liable to have his facts right concerning Lord Marden's mistresses. She sighed.

He mistook the sound for a yawn. "Why do you not go to sleep in your own bed? This has been an exhausting few days, and your brother will not benefit if you become ill. I shall sit up with him, if you think he needs someone, and promise to call you if there is any change."

"No, I am fine, really. I wish to be close to Troy. The laudanum makes him wake up disoriented, so he needs a familiar face."

Hers was a charming face, Ian thought, despite the reddened nose. He thought about waking up to that sweet, smiling mouth, the delicate eyebrows, the tiny blond curls that were always escaping their ribbons or hairpins to brush against her cheeks. A man could wake up to worse, a lot worse.

Ian liked to sleep alone. He had never spent the entire night with any of his lovers, although he had awoken from a nap more than once to find a strange woman sleeping with her mouth open next to him, or snoring, or stealing the blankets. He could sympathize with Troy.

He should not be thinking of waking up next to Miss Renslow under any circumstances, certainly not in the same breath as thinking of his former bedmates. And why was he, anyway? Lud, the robe she was wearing was about as appealing as yesterday's porridge. For an instant, he let his mind wander to what he knew was hidden by the thick flannel folds. That was why he was having unacceptable ideas about Miss Renslow: his memory was too good, and his imagination was too active, to say nothing of his warmer urges.

Luckily, his senses of honor and self-preservation were also on the boil. He knew he could not spend another night in this room alone with her and satisfy both. He should not stay here, anyway, no matter what lies he concocted, so Ian did not offer to keep Athena company during her vigil. He'd have to take himself to a hotel, in fact. Carswell's rooms at the Albany were too cramped, and the little house in Kensington was occupied by his last mistress and her new protector, until they could find a hideaway of their own. Now it was the earl's turn to sigh.

"You must be tired, my lord."

"No, making up Banbury tales is not hard work."

She smiled and said, "Do you think we will go to hell for all the deceptions?"

"You are far too innocent to go to hell. If the powers that be prove unforgiving, however, I will be there long before you, to welcome you."

"You are not all that much older, you know."

He knew. Eleven years. The same difference in age as between his parents. He sighed again and said, "Ah, but I am that much more wicked."

*   *   *

Wiggs returned the next morning at breakfast time. Lord Marden was not at home. Neither was Lady Throckmorton-Jones. Athena did not care that she would be meeting Wiggs by herself, unchaperoned and unprotected. She had been alone in his company any number of times during the past year and a half since he had come to tutor her brother. Her other brother certainly never worried that she might be endangering her good name. Athena doubted Spartacus remembered that she ought to have a spotless reputation. He never remembered that she ought to have a Season, a chance to meet other gentlemen.

Not even Athena's fault-finding sister-in-law had seen anything wrong with Athena and the reverend spending time like this, alone except for the servants who were bringing a fresh pot of chocolate and a plate of toast to the morning room, which was all Athena had requested for breakfast. Of course, Veronica had not forbidden Athena from private converse with the tutor. If they did make a match of it, Veronica would be rid of her pesky relation without any exertion on her part. Nor would she lose her precedence to the wife of a mere congregationless cleric, which mattered to Lady Rensdale.

If the conventions did not concern Athena, Wiggy's contentiousness did. The man was in another temper; she could tell as soon as he stomped into the drawing room. Perhaps it was the same temper as the previous evening, she decided: sour and sullen. Well, Athena was not in a sunny mood herself.

She had not slept well, and could blame neither Troy nor the thin mattress beside his bed. Her thoughts had kept her awake, and worries about the future. If she were labeled fast, who would marry her? If she were considered a fallen woman, who would hire her? If she went into service, who would look after Troy? Reason and logic told her that Wiggs was her best choice, which meant she was going to have to placate him—for the rest of her life. That thought gave her nightmares, and she had not even shut her eyes.

No, she was not in a comfortable frame of mind. In fact, after standing to greet her unwanted caller, Athena started to pace, rather than settling back onto her chair at the breakfast table.

Mr. Wiggs frowned at her, then frowned at the scant repast on the sideboard. He harumphed a few times to get her attention, then said, "If you are not going to sit, Miss Renslow, I cannot. Some of us remember our manners."

"I beg your pardon, sir. I am anxious to return to my brother." She did take a seat, however, and poured the scowling man a cup of chocolate. She would not encroach on the earl's generosity by asking his servants to fetch heartier fare, not when she herself was a guest in his home, but she did push the plate of toast toward Wiggy. Her own appetite had gone missing, anyway.

Wiggs reached for the jam and remembered his position, too, albeit somewhat late. "Oh, your brother. How fares the young man this morning?"

"Not as well as yesterday, although he does not appear feverish, merely lethargic. That might be due to the—"

"I am sure the physicians know best. Your situation, however, is of more immediate concern. I was hoping the boy would be well enough to move today, but you will have to leave without him."

"Leave?"

"You cannot stay here. I fear I have to insist."

"But why? You met Lady Throckmorton-Jones, or Her Highness, although I should not repeat her title."

"There is no title. No one seems to know of her existence."

"Of course not. You heard Lord Marden. She is here incognita, on a secret mission for her brother."

"Humph. I asked at the Austrian consulate. There is no Princess Hedwig."

"You asked? When we were told not to reveal her presence? Who knows what effect your prying will have on diplomatic relations between our two countries? Why, if an alliance cannot be formed, who knows what might be the outcome of the entire military campaign against France? England could lose the war without the support of the Ziftsweig armies, all because you have taken to being my watchdog. Without my permission, I must add."

"Tut, tut. I have your brother's permission."

"I shall not argue with you about my brother's authority over me. For now, it is enough that you have betrayed Lord Marden's trust after he has been so kind to Troy and me. You swore you would keep Lady Throckmorton-Jones's confidence."

"And you swore your uncle was ailing." Wiggs dabbed at his mouth with the corner of a napkin. He moved a spot of jam to his chin, and Athena did not bring it to his attention. "And you shall not think so highly of his lordship when you hear what I have discovered."

"Lord Marden has proven himself a true gentleman. I am sure nothing could make me respect him less, certainly not scurrilous gossip."

Wiggs drew himself up, looking as dignified as a man could with jam on his face. "I do not indulge in idle chitchat. I saw this with my own eyes. Well, I heard it with my own ears, at any rate."

"Whatever you believe you saw or heard is none of my concern. I am the earl's guest, not his censor."

"That is my point. You are his guest, and shall be tainted with the same red mark."

She was not the one with jam on her chin. She stood. "I will not listen to more of your carping about reputations and loose morals."

He stood too, looking at the last piece of toast with regret "You might be too innocent to see through the man's polished charm, and too trusting of his hospitality, but I am not, no longer. Mad Dog Marden is no fit companion for a lady, I say, and I can prove it. He was at a hotel last night."

"Yes, he felt he should sleep elsewhere, to protect that selfsame reputation of mine that has you so disturbed. You see, he is a considerate man, giving up his own comfort to satisfy your—"

"He was with a woman."

That gave Athena pause, and a sharp pain in the region of her heart, which she would never let Mr. Wiggs see. She pushed in her chair. "That is no business of mine. Or yours. And what were you doing, anyway, I should like to know, following the earl about like some sneak thief?"

"I was not following him. He chose my hotel for his scandalous tryst."

"Bosh, a coincidence only. Had his lordship known you were staying at McKinnon's Hotel, I am certain he would have gone anywhere else. I suppose he happened to select that one because he was less well-known there, and wanted to draw the least attention to his presence. Had he put up at the Clarendon or the Pulteney or the Grand, tongues would have wagged, asking the very questions he wished to avoid by leaving his home."

"So you say, persisting in believing the best of that libertine despite the indisputable evidence. I was in the very next private parlor, and I heard them, I say."

"You listened to a man and his . . . lady friend?" Athena found Wiggy's eavesdropping more appalling than the earl's philandering. She never expected Marden to be a monk; she never expected a would-be vicar to be a voyeur.

Wiggy's ears turned red, bringing attention to the fact that they stuck out slightly. "I could not help myself. They were in the adjoining room, with the windows open, you see."

"I see nothing but a gentleman being maligned for conversing with a woman, and another gentleman— one who ought to know better—being quick to cast the first stone. You saw nothing, and should have heard nothing."

"I do not call it nothing when I recognized the female's voice, even though she tried to disguise it with huskier tones. Come-hither tones, they were."

"Come-hither?"

Now Wiggs's whole face was the color of the jam smear. "They were trysting, I say. To say more would be indelicate in a lady's presence."

"Then perhaps you have said enough already."

"I have not said nearly enough. Your saintly earl was entertaining Lady Throckmorton-Jones in that private parlor, by Jupiter."

"His lordship was having supper with . . . Lady Throckmorton-Jones?" Athena repeated.

"Yes, and the woman had no German accent again. Your so-called chaperone is nothing but Marden's mistress after all, Miss Renslow. You have to come away this very morning, before they rouse from their foul love nest."

Athena sank back into her chair.

"You see, I knew you would be shocked. I regret having to sully your innocent ears with such lewdness, but my duty to your brother and my concern for your welfare forces me to speak."

Athena had heard enough. More than enough. She took a deep breath. "I am shocked. I am shocked at the lengths you will go to discredit the earl, who has been a godsend to me and my brother. No, there is no Princess Hedwig. And there is no Lady Throckmorton-Jones. Lord Marden and his friend Mr. Carswell were trying to shield me from gossip, because you seemed intent on stirring up the hornet's nest."

"There was no chaperone? Only another scoundrel in skirts?"

"There was no chaperone, and none was needed, except in your opinion. I have ceased caring about your estimation of my character, for I realize you will never understand that my reputation means nothing compared to Troy's welfare. I shall not lie anymore."

"There was no chaperone? Lady Throckmorton-Jones was a man?"

"That is correct. And I shall not force the poor earl into taking up residence at a second-class hotel."

"It is good enough for me."

"Exactly. I do not wish to hear any more on this matter. In fact, I do not wish to speak with you again, Mr. Wiggs." She stood beside the open door, waiting for him to exit through it. "And I do not care what you write to my older brother, either."

"You are wrong, Miss Renslow. You will care when I write the viscount to announce an end to our understanding."

"You might save your announcement, sir, for you are the one mistaken. We had no understanding. You shall never comprehend my devotion to my brother, nor, it seems, my gratitude to Lord Marden. And I shall never understand how you could care more for public opinion than for the person you wish to wed. For that matter, I cannot comprehend why you would wish to bind yourself to a woman you consider so lost to propriety, or how you think affection can grow from distrust and diatribes. I certainly do not wish to marry a martyr to manners. I bid you good day, sir."

After the butler handed her caller his hat and gloves, Athena said, "I shall not be at home to Mr. Wiggs in the future, Mr. Hull."

The butler bowed. "Very good, miss. Very, very good, if I might say so."

"But he is still my brother's temporary guardian, so he cannot be denied visiting Troy."

"More bad luck for the unfortunate young man."

"Of course, Troy is sleeping a great deal."

"As he must, to hasten his recovery. I shall be sure to inform the reverend gentleman of that when he calls. Master Renslow shall not be disturbed."

"Thank you. I knew I could count on you."

Ian bounded up the front steps. "Wiggs seemed more put out than usual when I passed him. Is everything all right?"

"Miss Renslow put him out," the butler replied for Athena. "Out of the door. Finally."

"Ah, then congratulations are in order."

"No," she said. "We have agreed that we do not suit."

He smiled. "Which is precisely why congratulations are called for. Champagne, I think, Hull. In the library."

As Ian led her down the hall, he asked, "By the way, did you hit him?"

"No, that was jam."

"Too bad."

Once they were alone in the library, Ian watched her staring out the window at the rear garden. He could not tell what she was thinking, so had to ask. "It is not every day a lady shows her suitor the door. Are you going to cry?"

"No, I think I am going to sing."

He remembered her lack of musical ability. "Gads, that is almost as bad."

Athena laughed. "I will not sing then, but I might dance." She twirled in a circle, her arms out. "I am free, free as a bird, at last. I might have thrown away my best chance, but I would rather have no choices than make one out of desperation."

"Wiggs was about as desperate as they come," he agreed. "He only wanted your money and your brother's influence, anyway."

"And I only wanted the security marriage to him could give, so my motives were not much better than his. Neither of us pretended to an affection we did not feel, although I had once hoped that tender feelings might develop. They never did, and never could. So now I am relieved."

Ian was, too, surprising himself. Wiggs had been the only thing standing between him and doom.

"Yes," she was going on in a happy, lilting voice, "now I do not have to marry without love."

Doom shook Ian's hand.

Chapter Eleven

A mistress is more fun than a wife.
—Anonymous

A mistress has more fun than a wife.
—Mrs. Anonymous

Time was a peculiar thing. First Ian wanted the hour hands to back up, to start over again before the duel. Now he wanted them to slow to a tick-tocking crawl, so slow that tomorrow was a week away. In fact, if tick never followed tock, that was too soon to face eternity.

He had a few days, Ian told himself. He had not yet heard from her older brother, and her uncle was not in town. With no male relation to consult, he was given a temporary reprieve. He did not count the captain's man Macelmore.

He called at Cameron Street to ask about the captain's arrival, and chanced on encountering Macelmore on his way out. The earl ended up promising that no harm had—or ever would—befall Miss Renslow. Thunderation, now he was near to pledging his troth to a one-eyed old pirate, in plain view of all of London! He changed the subject, and the direction of Macelmore's ire, to that groom, Alfie Brown.

The man had shown up, Macelmore told him, spitting on the ground not far enough from Ian's boots, looking for his back pay. He'd gone after the horse, Alfie said, because that was his job, and because he needed it to get the boy home, anyway. Once he found the nag, he'd lost the lad, so went out and got drunk, knowing he'd lost his post, too. He woke up robbed and beaten and ashamed, not remembering much else.

"Nothing about the accident that unhorsed Master Renslow?"

"Alfie allowed as how he were watching the nobs, not the nipper."

If the man had been watching the duel, he knew exactly what had happened. Why had Brown not mentioned it to Macelmore, Ian wondered. Even more curious, why had the groom not shown up on Ian's doorstep, demanding blood money for his silence? Something was wrong with the man's story, but Ian would not borrow trouble. Lord knew, he had enough of it on his plate now.

Meantime, Lady Throckmorton-Jones stayed gone. So did Princess Hedwig. Ian reclaimed his Kensington house so he had a private place to go to ponder his sins and his coming atonement.

His mother still claimed an ague; his sister was still not returned from her journey north; and the boy still frequently hovered in drugged stupor. He was no worse, but not much better that Ian could see. He could move his legs, Ian knew, which he took for a good sign. When Lord Marden suggested the cub might grow stronger with a bit of fresh air, a little exercise, though, Athena looked at him as if he'd proposed tossing her brother in the Thames to swim, naked.

Ian knew how he would feel, stuck in bed with no form of activity, with nothing but books to break the monotonous cycle of pain and sleep. He'd be throwing the volumes across the room, he would, even his favorite horse books. Ian admired the young man's fortitude, his stoic acceptance of the surgeon's orders, but he vowed to get Troy down the stairs and out of doors as soon as Miss Renslow's back was turned.

She never seemed to leave the sickroom long enough, however. In fact, other than the few minutes she walked the dog in the garden, the only time she could be counted on being apart from her brother was during dinner, which she took with Lord Marden. He feared she would not eat enough otherwise, or that she would sicken from being in that overwarm bedchamber so long, so he had insisted she join him in the dining room. He tried his best to make her feel at ease there, with the door always left open, and he left immediately after, making sure to be seen at his clubs and social engagements. Word was out that Miss Renslow and her injured brother were staying at his house. Word was also out that he was not.

He had managed to slow time, after all.

Athena was watching the clock, too. How long could she stay on here, enjoying the earl's hospitality? His lordship assured her she was welcome for as long as Troy's recuperation took, but she felt like an intruder, forcing him to leave his own house.

She did not have to seek a position yet, she had decided—not until she had spoken to her uncle. If he were willing to release the dowry he held in trust for her, a dowry she would never need now that she was declared unmarriageable by Mr. Wiggs, then she might be able to afford a tiny cottage somewhere, or genteel lodgings here in town, if Uncle Barnaby did not want her at his residence.

She was not going to go back to Derby and her

sister-in-law's carping—that, Athena vowed. She was
uncertain if Lady Rensdale would even permit her to
return, now that her reputation was in shreds. Mr.
Wiggs would have told his tale well, and Veronica
would make sure everyone in the neighborhood knew
of Miss Renslow's fall from grace, and wasn't she the
gracious one, allowing that baggage to sully her own
sterling name? If Veronica did allow her husband's
sister to come home, she would make Athena's life a
misery, more so than before. Veronica would expect
a fallen woman to hide away from country society, to
be grateful for whatever crumbs came her way. She
would expect Athena to tolerate any unkindness without complaint, for the sake of having a roof over her
head and Troy at her side.

Athena could not do it.

How she would manage without her brother to care
for, Athena did not know, and dreaded the idea. She
wished him a quick recovery, of course, but counted
the days until she had to send him home, without her.

Meanwhile she kept herself busy at Troy's bedside,
reading to him, playing cards and chess when he was
able, working at her embroidery when he slept. She
took Roma to the rear gardens but no farther, not
liking to leave the house. She did not want to be away
when Troy awoke, and she did not want to face the
earl's neighbors. The ladies might pull their skirts
aside when she passed. The gentlemen might turn
their backs or issue lewd suggestions. Even the neigh-
boring servants might show disrespect for a woman so
lost to propriety as to lodge alone under a bachelor's roof.

The earl's own servants were friendly and kind, with
not an ounce of insolence. Perhaps she was being
overcautious, or Mr. Wiggs was being overbearing in
his outrage, but Athena would not want to chance an

encounter with another stranger's scowls. Besides, she did not wish to make the earl more of a target for gossip than he already was.

At home she would have filled every hour with chores and tenant visits, with social calls and Troy's classes. There she took long walks, frequent carriage drives, almost daily rides on horseback. In fact, Athena spent as little time at Renslow Hall, under Veronica's narrowed eyes, as possible. Here at Maddox House, her daily life was the opposite, yet she was never bored. How could she be, when she was so busy falling in love?

She was, and she admitted it freely, to herself, at least. She loved the earl's house, with its endless treasures and countless masterpieces to be admired, its vast library of books and its well-kept gardens. She loved his staff, who were always offering to take her place at Troy's bedside, or to keep her company there. They made her feel as welcome in the kitchens and the butler's pantry as in the formal parlors. And she loved the earl.

She waited for the few hours a day she spent in his company, where she could watch smiles flash across his handsome face and watch his brown eyes turn thoughtful or inquisitive. She memorized his gentleness toward Troy, and his amused efforts to win Roma's affection. She studied his strong hands and fingers while he ate, admiring the breadth of his shoulders and the power in his horseman's legs as he walked beside her into the dining room. He was amazingly graceful for such a large man, guiding her to her chair with the effortless agility of a fencer, and he held the delicate china as one might cradle a baby bird.

She listened to his opinions about books they had both read and plays she had not seen, about the state of the government, the progress of the war, and why people acted as they did. Then she listened to him ask her own opinions, as no one else ever did. He did not treat her as the unwelcome responsibility she knew she was, but as a cherished guest, almost as a friend.

That such a man treated her with respect meant she was worthy. Athena felt bigger, better, stronger, more confident because of his regard. And she loved him for making her feel loveable.

This was not the unmitigated disaster it might have been, for Athena knew that her infatuation could bring nothing but some lovely daydreams. She was not about to have her heart broken or her hopes dashed, for she had no hopes whatsoever that the earl might come to care for her in a particular way, and she would not let her heart rule her head. She might be a silly chit, inexperienced and thus impressed by the nonpareil's manly attractions and his attention to her, but she was not stupid. He was a gentleman, and so was treating her with courtesy. He was a rake, and so was treating her with charm. Nothing else.

Nothing else could ever come of it, and Athena easily accepted that fact. She was too dull to interest him, too plain to attract him, too much a country nobody to suit him. Now she would not even be welcomed into Lord Marden's elite social circles. So be it. She could still admire him.

One could visit a great cathedral or view a masterpiece without having to own it. That was how Athena considered the earl: as something that was a pleasure to look at, that enriched one's life, that gave joy to one's existence—and that was as out of reach as a perfect, brilliant rainbow.

He was a memory she was going to cherish for the rest of her life. Whatever course that life took, whether keeping house for her uncle, going into service, or living the life of a recluse in some tiny lodging, she would have the images of her earl to take out and enjoy.

So Athena gathered memories, because she was going to need their company in the coming years. She stored the tales the servants proudly retold, of Lord Marden's childhood, and his boyhood pranks. They told her, too, of his position at court, of his place as one of the premier bachelors in all of London, of his openhanded generosity with the fortune at his fingertips.

Athena had to laugh at herself and her moonstruck madness. No, nothing could ever come of it. No matter—she could still enjoy her first, last, and only encounter with a storybook hero, outside of a novel.

Athena was ready to savor more of the experience, along with the French chef's delicacies, over dinner that evening. She dressed more carefully than usual, hoping to win his smile of approval with the white muslin gown that was trimmed in turquoise ribbons to match her eyes. The neck was too high and the waist too low for current fashion, but she thought it became her. Around her neck she wore her mother's pearls, one of the few items of family jewelry that Spartacus's wife had not been able to claim. Now she felt special, almost fit company for an elegant earl. If her style was dated, her sparkle compensated, for tonight she had wonderful news to impart.

"What, is Troy that much better? I looked in earlier when he was sleeping, and saw no change."

"Troy took less laudanum today, so that is a hopeful sign. But my news is still excellent. I have solved the problem of a chaperone, so you may move back into your own home!"

Ian was not concerned half as much with where he

laid his head as with what scandal was laid on his doorstep. His mother thought she would be feeling well enough for the jaunt to London soon, and his sister was expected back in Richmond any day. Neither was soon enough. With a respectable matron at her side, Athena could visit the shops, go for visits, meet other ladies of social standing. They would see in an instant that she was nothing but an innocent, a sweet young woman caught up in circumstances beyond her control. Just look at her now, grinning like a schoolgirl, her eyes twinkling like stars in an azure sky. No one could mistake her for his mistress in her virginal white frock and pearls. Her future depended on it. His was already decided.

He tried to smile, to share her enthusiasm. "Now that is fine news, indeed. Where did you find this manna—ah, matron? And more importantly, are you certain she is respectable?"

"Of course. She is a friend of your sister's. She had heard that Lady Dorothy would be coming to town and so stopped to leave her card. I happened to meet her on the doorstep when I was bringing Roma back from a walk."

"Some of Doro's friends are not up to snuff. This female is no spinster bluestocking, is she, or an old-maid reformer? They would do your reputation no good. And they are deuced uncomfortable to have around."

Athena would not have burdened Lord Marden with a dour, disapproving dowd, not even to rescue her reputation. Besides, that sort of woman would not approve of these dinners à deux, the hours spent at Troy's bedside. Athena was not about to give up her few pleasures for propriety's sake, especially since her name was already besmirched. "No, this woman is a married lady with a young son away at school. She dresses in the height of fashion, and seems to know everyone in London."

"Yet she would be willing to stay here?"

"Yes, she offered, even when I said that I would be staying at my brother's bedside, not going out or entertaining. She understood perfectly, and admitted that she was weary of the social rounds and could use a restful interlude herself. She had heard of our, ah, difficulty, and volunteered to act as my companion, as a friend of the family."

"What about her husband? Won't he mind his wife moving into someone else's home?"

"Oh, he is out of town on business, so the lady is lonely in her empty house. It is too far for Lady Paige to travel to her country place and—"

"Lady Paige?"

Athena smiled. "Why, yes. She did say you were acquainted."

"Mona, Baroness Paige?"

Athena's smile faded and she put down her fork. "Do you not like her? She seemed everything polite and charming."

Ian would wager she did. The *poisson* turned to poison on his plate. The asparagus spears pierced his innards. The mousse was a noose and the *bœuf* was a buffet to the head. "Lady Paige?" he choked out.

"Stop repeating the woman's name and tell me what is wrong with her?"

"Nothing is wrong with her!" Nothing was wrong with Lady Paige except that she had been the cause of the duel that shot the boy that brought the sister that he had ruined. His life was turned upside down by that lying, cheating Paige peeress. Oh, no, nothing was wrong with her except that she had been his mistress, and many other men's mistress. Now the husband-betraying bitch was going to befriend Athena? Hah!

She was going to create a worse scandal, that's what she was going to do. A ménage à trois, the *on dits* headline would read, spring and summer at Mad Dog Marden's garden of earthly delights. One more scandal would not bother Mona—not when she had a safe harbor from her husband's debtors. She would not care an iota about Miss Renslow's reputation, no more than she cared for Paige's jealousy. Look at how she cared for her son, Ian fumed. Away at school? The boy could not be more than seven—and Ian had not even known she had a child.

He pushed his plate away, half full. He was fully full of guilt and remorse and anger and despair. One more blighted mouthful of gloom would be more than he could chew.

Now Athena knew something was dreadfully wrong, as the earl was not finishing his dinner. "The lady is not a friend of your sister's?"

"The lady is a lady only in the formal sense, but yes, she did have her come-out the same year as Dorothy. I suppose they are acquaintances, but I would not call them friends. Nor would I consider Lady Paige a proper companion for an unmarried miss." Which had to be the biggest understatement of the day.

"Oh. I suppose that was why Mr. Hull took a coughing fit at the door when I invited her in for tea."

Hull would be sent packing. He should have slammed the door in the doxy's face. How could anyone let a light skirt like La Paige near an angel like Athena? Ian could imagine their conversations, and shuddered. Captain Beecham would have him keelhauled. Lord Rensdale would have him shot. Troy would stop looking at him like some kind of idol. And he would hate himself worse than he already did.

"No harm is done," he said around the lump in his throat. "You can just write and tell the woman that we have made other arrangements and that her generous"—Hah! Mona was not being generous; she had no one else to pay her bills—"offer is not needed."

Athena said nothing, wadding her napkin into a tight ball.

"You can write to her, can you not? I have her direction if you lost her card."

"I cannot." Her voice was a bare whisper.

"I know you can write. But if you are too embarrassed to retract an invitation, I can do it. Better yet, I will have Hull go explain to her." That ought to serve the bumbling butler right. If Ian went, he'd be tempted to strangle the jade.

Ian could barely hear Athena's murmured: "A letter is not necessary."

"No. Dear Heaven, no. Tell me that woman is not already installed in one of my guest rooms!"

"I cannot."

Ian was too angry to speak, thank goodness, or Athena would have heard words no gently bred female should ever encounter. He had to bite his tongue to keep them inside, but he did not sully the ears of the stupidest, most featherheaded, flea-brained, henwitted, sapskulled—

"How was I to know?" Athena demanded, when Lord Marden sat glaring at her, his jaw working but no words coming out. "And I did not invite her. I never would have taken it upon myself to ask a guest into your home, even though you told me to treat Maddox House as my own. I thanked Lady Paige for her kind offer and said I would discuss it with you. But she said I must not spend another night here alone, and that you would be sure to agree. You must admit you have been adamant about protecting my good name."

Ian still said nothing.

"Well, you have. You are almost as bad as Wiggy, staying at a hotel or some shabby lodgings instead of here."

There was nothing shabby about his Kensington cottage, but Ian still stayed mumchance, rather than mouth the obscenities he was reciting to himself.

"Then Lady Paige sent her footman for her trunks, which were already packed into her carriage," Athena continued. "She said she had intended to go visit elsewhere if Lady Dorothy was not at home. How could I tell Mr. Hull to order the boxes carried back to the coach? He was looking ill, anyway, so I sent him to rest in the butler's pantry. Lady Paige is in the rose bed chamber, taking dinner on a tray. She claimed a headache, and said that if you and I shared one more meal in private no one would comment—not with her in the house."

That was not what people would be commenting on, not by half.

Ian could not help himself. A foul term escaped his lips, and he did not even apologize when scarlet bloomed on Athena's cheeks. Once the floodgates were opened, there was no damming the *damn*s. "Of all the blasted, bloody, imbecilic, immature and I don't know what else, this is the worst! How in hell could you have been so—"

Athena stopped listening. She rose to her feet and left the room, left him to his swearing and his screaming. And she smiled.

Now she did not have to worry about loving the earl too much. He was not perfect after all.

Chapter Twelve

Any time a woman can put a man in the wrong, she will.

—Anonymous

Men are usually wrong.

—Mrs. Anonymous

The butler tendered his resignation. Ian offered Hull a raise if he got rid of the rodent in the rose bedroom. Hull said he'd rather quit; the earl could eradicate his own embarrassing vermin. The butler would be staying. Mona had to go.

Oh, for a rat trap big enough. Ian poured himself a glass of port. Oh, for a glass big enough to drown in. Oh, hell, the bitch wasn't going to leave without a scene. He had a second glass and wondered what he had ever found attractive in the rounded, round-heeled brunette.

Not the overripe curves or the pendulous breasts, the thick ankles or the thin eyebrows, tweezed to arch in perpetual surprise. But Mona was not surprised to see him, it appeared, despite the eyebrows. Ian had waited until he thought Athena would be safely at her brother's bedside, and until Hull took the bottle of port away. Then he'd rapped softly on the door of her bedchamber. The door was opened by the woman herself, in a nearly transparent nightgown of some pink gauzy stuff. She might have been part of the rose bedroom's decor, like the wall-covering, for all the interest Ian felt. No, compared to Athena's petite form, the baroness was more like a stuffed ottoman.

"What the hell are you doing here?" he asked in lieu of a greeting.

"Why, waiting for you, darling. I knew you would come as soon as the girl was asleep." She held her plump arms out to him. He handed her a robe from the end of the bed.

"The girl is a young lady, as you very well know, not a child."

Lady Paige tossed the robe over her shoulders and sat at the dressing table, taking the pins from her hair while she looked at his reflection in the mirror. "All the more reason for my presence."

"All the less reason for you to be here. Why the deuce did you come, anyway? You knew our affair was over. You yourself selected that extravagant diamond bracelet you are wearing as a parting gift."

"Ah, but I thought you might have missed me, as I did you, darling. You could have had second thoughts."

He did, and third and fourth ones, too, about what a fool he had been. "I would have come to you had I reconsidered. You know I never invited you to my home, even when we were, ah, friends." They had never been friends, never more than acquaintances. Ian could not, in fact, recall having a single weighty conversation with the overweight woman.

"Tish-tosh. Some foolish gentleman's scruple."

He said nothing.

"Yes, well, to be honest, I had nowhere else to go. I could not stay on at Paige House, not once all the servants left, the disloyal dastards."

"When had they been paid last?" he asked.

"That was Reginald's job." She shrugged her shoulders, sending the robe sliding to the floor, giving him what she obviously assumed was an enticing sight of bare shoulder. Then she shifted her position to make sure he could see her nipples through the thin fabric. Ian had seen enough. He turned. No, the bed was in that direction. He moved toward the open window, looking out on the gardens. The dark paths were illuminated by a single lantern on the rear gate.

"But what made you come here, of all places?" he wanted to know.

"Well, you were the one who was responsible for forcing Reginald to leave town. That makes you responsible for me."

"I do not see it that way at all. If I had made you a promise, or sworn eternal love or some such rot, then perhaps. But we had no such understanding. Whatever arrangement we had was ended before your husband challenged me. And while we are splitting hairs"—she was combing hers and it was not half as silky as Miss Renslow's—"you told me Paige never cared what you did."

She frowned as her comb snagged on a knot. She had been without a ladies' maid too long. "He didn't care until I told him what a good lover you were."

"Gads, you told your husband that? No wonder he did not take you along with him when he fled his debtors."

She got up and put her hands on his shoulders. "But it was true."

Ian moved farther away. He'd be falling out the window, next.

Mona went back to combing her hair. "Well, he was not a good provider, not paying my dressmakers' bills or the vintner. The least he could have done was provide a bit of excitement, and so I told him."

Paige had provided excitement, all right.

Mona went on: "Besides, you were younger and handsomer and had deeper pockets. Of course he hated you."

"You were his wife. And you still are," he reminded her.

"Oh, I am not asking you to help me get a divorce so we can marry."

Ian choked back the response he might have made, something about pigs and wings.

"All I want is a place to stay for a short while, without bailiffs at the door. Reggie will send for me eventually, you know. He really does love me."

So someone was a greater fool than Ian, he was happy to learn. "Well, you cannot stay here."

"Because of the Renslow chit?"

"Because I do not want you."

"Of course you do, darling." She puffed her chest out.

Ian shut the window so she did not catch cold. "No, I do not. And no, I do not want you anywhere near Miss Renslow."

"I do not see why not. It is not as if her reputation can be damaged more. And for all those vaunted scruples of yours, I am not the one who has had a marriageable miss under my roof for days."

"That is as may be. Even if her reputation cannot be salvaged, though, her morals can. You, madam, are no fit company for a lady. You are no fit company for a lapdog or a lamplighter. And I do not want you in my house."

That was when Ian's athletic ability came into play.

He ducked and dodged whatever flying objects he could not catch. Nothing hit him, and only one priceless pink jade figurine hit the wall. He made a point of picking up her hairbrush and putting it into her open, still packed trunk.

When Mona realized she could not move him with missiles, she resorted to tears. "I have no money in the bank and no place to go," she cried.

"Neither of which is of the least concern to me."

"And I am growing old and ugly and no one wants me."

She was growing fat, too, he thought, but he liked the other jade statues too much to say so.

When he did not immediately disagree with her effort to win his pity, she shrieked, "Then you do think I am old and ugly?"

This time Ian did not move fast enough. Her knotted fist caught him smack on the ear. At least he did not have to listen to her screeching for a while. Unfortunately, when the ringing stopped she was still nattering on about bounders who used women and then abandoned them.

"If you toss me out I shall tell everyone how heartless you are."

Ian rubbed his ear and gave a Wiggy *humph* of disinterested disdain.

"And how miserly."

Now he raised his eyebrow. They both knew no one would believe that, especially when she had that diamond bracelet weighting down her arm.

"And you are keeping Miss Renslow all snugged away here where no one can see her."

That caught his attention. "We shall leave the young lady out of this conversation, if you please."

"And her brother, so he does not tell anyone how he came to be shot."

"That, too, is not open for discussion."

"Or why Paige is being blamed."

"You can stay here tonight, but you leave in the morning, without speaking with Miss Renslow."

"Why, so I do not discuss the duel with your little chick? Or do you mean she does not know?" Mona made an unladylike noise. "Only a green cabbage head would believe that fustian of a gentlemanly competition of skill. Someone"—someone who was temporarily homeless and penniless—"is bound to tell her the truth."

"Very well, I shall pay your shot at a hotel."

Mona played her trump card, now that the game was almost won. "What, are you afraid the little peagoose will stop thinking you hung the moon and the stars?"

"I do not know what you mean."

She snorted again. "Come now, darling. I am not the one born yesterday. Your little virgin thinks you can walk on water. I should hate to be the one to disillusion her."

So he gave her the keys to his Kensington house. Ian would be the one to move to the hotel. "But this is not permanent, mind you. We had an affair, not an arrangement, and it is over. I am not taking you into my keeping, not paying your bills, not giving you an allowance. I will not be seen with you. In fact, I do not want to see you at all, and I particularly do not want to see you anywhere near Miss Renslow. Is that understood?"

She kissed his cheek, near where his ear was still red from the blow of her fist. "Perfectly, darling." Then she wrapped her arms around him in a grateful hug.

Ian was not cad enough to shove her away. Instead he vaguely patted her back and looked over her shoulder, out the window. Right into the upturned faces of Miss Athena Renslow and her deaf dog.

He should have jumped out the window when he had the chance.

It was a very good thing that Athena's heart was not irrevocably committed to Lord Marden. Otherwise she might have been upset. She was not—not in the least. She brushed a drop of evening mist off her cheeks and went inside. She brought Roma up to Troy's room and made sure that he was resting. She removed her cape and straightened her gown, and then she went back down the stairs, telling Hull she would wait for the earl's departure in the entry hall. The butler took one look at her militant crossed-arms stance, her flashing turquoise eyes, and found an errand in the wine cellar.

Lord Marden had said he was spending the night away again, to muzzle the rumormongers. She would give him ten minutes, no more, to come down the marble stairs. If he was not out of the house, out of that woman's room, in that time, she was going to start packing. She was not about to stay under the roof of a rutting rake and his rotund mistress. She could not, knowing they were in the pretty rose bedchamber, twining themselves together like rose vines on a trellis. The very image made her blush . . . and bristle like an irate hedgehog.

No matter that they were adults.

No matter that it was none of her business.

No matter that Lord Marden owned the house and had every right to behave as promiscuously as he wished here.

No. He had told her to consider Maddox House her own. Well, no lady put up with such goings-on while she was in residence. Athena's sister-in-law had dismissed a footman and a maid when they were found holding hands, nothing more. The earl had been holding a great deal more than Lady Paige's hand!

Why, Athena's brother could be corrupted. Yes, that was what Athena decided to say, that Troy was too young to be exposed to licentious behavior. He admired the earl, and so might come to believe that such lewd behavior was acceptable for a gentleman, even dashing.

It was not acceptable. Athena understood that bachelors—and too often married men—kept mistresses, but not in their own homes, and not when they had polite company, surely. Squire Dayton had been accused of dallying with his housekeeper, and it was the scandal of the countryside. No one accepted his invitations.

Besides, Lady Paige had a husband! Athena could not decide if an unwed mistress was better than a married one, although an adulterous married man was far more despicable than a carefree bachelor. Lady Paige might have lied about her missing spouse too, though, as she had lied about being a friend of the earl's sister.

No matter. Either Lady Paige or Athena had to go. Athena very much feared which of them Lord Marden would choose, the lush dark-haired beauty or her too thin, troublesome self. Athena could go to her uncle's house for the night, and pray that Troy was ready to be moved by morning. She could not like living at Uncle Barnaby's with no one but Macelmore for company, but that was better than the company here at Maddox House.

That was it: she would leave tonight, and take her pleasant memories with her. The silly infatuation could stay behind, over and done, finished, extinguished, erased, exterminated, out of existence. So there.

Her decision was the right one, Athena told herself when the earl eventually did come down the marble steps. His hair was mussed, his neckcloth was askew, and he had a red mark on the side of his face—from kisses, Athena supposed. Heavens, how had they grown so torrid, so fast? The ten minutes had not half elapsed. She would not permit herself to acknowledge that the man looked indecently attractive, in his indecency.

"I am leaving," she said.

"That is not necessary. I am going to Kensington." To pack yet again. "And Lady Paige will go there in the morning."

Athena made a strangled sound.

Now both his cheeks turned red. "That is, she will take up residence in the morning and I shall already be moved to a hotel."

Athena knew very well why the earl had a second London residence. It was not to store his snuffboxes or to write poetry in private. A gentleman kept a love nest to house his ladybirds, nothing else. She also knew that he could alight there any time. He could also lie to her about where he was staying.

"You said Lady Paige was no one I ought to know. You might have told me you and she were . . . close."

"We are not close, not by miles." He looked longingly at the front door, which also seemed miles away, with an angry little shrew standing between him and escape.

"She is your mistress."

He did not bother denying it. "Was. She was my mistress. At one time. One short time."

"How long ago?"

"Thunderation, one does not discuss such matters with innocent females."

"I am nearly twenty years of age, my lord, and have

an older brother. How innocent in the ways of the world do you think I could be? If I did not know about Susie at the Duck and Drake, and the Widow Johnstone and her gentlemen callers, then my sister-in-law's warnings about wicked London ways would have informed me. She said I could trust no man here except Mr. Wiggs. She was right."

"Deuce take it, she was not right. Furthermore, your sister-in-law should have taught you that ladies are not supposed to acknowledge the existence of these trifling affairs, anyway."

"Trifling? When they are on one's very doorstep? That is, I know this is your doorstep"—which Ian was inching closer to—"but you did say I should treat Maddox House as my home."

"As well you should. And will. This was an unfortunate set of circumstances which shall be corrected. You have my apologies for any insult to your sensibilities."

More than her sensibilities were hurt, but Athena knew she had no right to anything but an apology. After all, she had befriended the woman herself. "Does everyone know?" she asked.

Ian supposed there must be someone in all of London—someone isolated, illiterate, and as deaf as the dog—who did not know that he and Lady Paige had been lovers. "Of course not."

Athena did not believe him. The fact that he was twisting his leather gloves into corkscrews might have given away his lack of confidence in his answer. "What about the servants?"

"They are paid not to gossip about their employers."

"Which means they know. They all know. Mr. Hull is so embarrassed he cannot look me in the eye."

"The old fellow needs spectacles, that's all. And it does not matter who knows what, anyway."

"How can you say that? No one will hire me now."

"Hire you? What maggot has crawled into your brain box?" He tried to unwind the gloves and shove his hand into one at the same time. One of his fingers went right through the soft leather. "Blast. Now see what you have made me do with your nonsense about seeking a position."

"It is not nonsense. How did you think I was going to make my way in the world? Women have few enough options if no one will take them to wife. You heard Wiggy. I am firmly on the shelf."

"Blast Wiggy, too. You have a brother and an uncle. The men in your life will take care of you. That is their duty."

"What if I do not wish to be a duty, an obligation, a burden?"

"A woman has no choice. She is to be protected, and that is final." He examined the other glove, although one of a matched pair was useless.

"Your sister is independent. She travels and keeps her own household. You said so yourself."

"My sister has twelve years more in her dish than you do. She also has a fortune of her own, and other considerations. Besides, we are not speaking of my sister."

"I might have no choice but to be independent. My sister-in-law will not welcome my presence, now that I have been rejected by her favorite. She will likely wash her hands of me, and wash Rensdale's hands for him, too. And my uncle might not wish a permanent female tenant. He has been a bachelor all his life, after all, and obviously prefers things that way."

Ian was now shredding the ripped glove as well as its innocent partner. "Your future will be secured. You have nothing to fear."

Athena looked at him through narrowed eyes. "You

are not thinking that I will replace Lady Paige, are you?"

"As my mistress?" The pieces of leather fell from his lifeless fingers. "Good grief, that is the furthest thing from my mind!"

So he was not the least bit attracted to her, Athena understood by his appalled expression. He could not even bother to lie and say he had considered it, but knew she was too virtuous to offer carte blanche, after he had lied about everything else. Not that Athena would have accepted a slip on the shoulder, from the earl or any other gentleman, for that matter. But it might have been nice to be asked, to be wanted. She raised her chin and said, "In that case, my future is very much uncertain, now that my reputation must be shredded worse than your gloves."

He stooped to pick up the pieces, and looked up at her. "I will make it right. Can't you trust me?"

Trust a man whose mistress invites herself to stay at his house? Whose every other word was a lie? She would sooner trust her own battered and bruised and bleeding heart—which had lied to her, too.

Chapter Thirteen

To purchase a filly, check her stable, her pedigree, her conformation, her gait, and her temperament. Have her health looked at by your head stableman, and try her out so you know if she will suit. To find a wife, the first one to catch your fancy will do.

—Anonymous

To purchase a bonnet, try on a hundred that catch your fancy, but buy the one that suits you best. The same goes for finding a husband.

—Mrs. Anonymous

Lady Paige left in the morning, as she had promised. The earl's carriage was waiting to convey her and her baggage and a borrowed maid, as he had promised. The coach had been waiting since nine, however, and Mona was not ready until nearly noon. She had kept her word by ten minutes. Ian had kept his word by sending her off with the most hopeless scullery maid, the one who broke things, burned things, and became lost between the kitchen and the pantry.

He was not waiting to see Lady Paige's departure,

trusting in his repentant butler to see the deed done. Ian had ensured that Athena would not be present at the leave-taking, either, having his gardener ask her opinions of a new flower bed he was planning. The gardener's opinion was that Miss Renslow ought to walk the boot-biting dog elsewhere, but he tipped his hat and led her off, happy enough to find the young lady knowledgeable about plants and shrubbery.

Only the butler was in the hall, then, when Lady Paige glided down the marble stairs in her wide-brimmed bonnet and primrose gown, hoping to make a last, lasting impression on the earl. Disappointed, she sailed past Hull, who was also disappointed but not surprised that the baroness did not press a coin into his hand, for all the effort and aggravation her brief visit had entailed. The highborn high flyer did not so much as nod at the earl's senior servant, a far cry from the way Miss Renslow usually greeted Hull, with a smile and a friendly word. Now there was a true lady, Hull reflected, and so he'd tell the other butlers at the local pub.

He held the door for Lady Paige, but he did not offer to carry either her hatbox or her wooden jewelry case or the frilly parasol she had dangling from a string off her wrist, along with her reticule. Perhaps because her bonnet's brim was so weighed down with cherries and silk flowers that it obscured her view, or perhaps because she was carrying so much, or perhaps because her vanity would not permit her to wear her spectacles out in public—or in private where the earl might see them—Lady Paige did not watch where she was going. She collided with a gentleman just approaching from the other side of the earl's waiting carriage.

Mr. Wiggs bounced off the buxom lady, but got his

knee banged by the bandbox and his breath knocked out of him by the jewel case and his legs tangled in the parasol. He fell down, dazed, at the woman's feet.

"Oh, you poor, poor man," Lady Paige exclaimed, dropping the hatbox, but placing the jewelry case carefully on the ground before lowering herself to Wiggs's level. "And it was all my fault!"

Wiggy found himself well cushioned by a pillow of pulchritude, and he found the experience pleasant, indeed. He thought about sitting up, and then thought better of it. "Think nothing of it, madam. I was not watching my way."

The maid Lord Marden had assigned to Mona came and started to pick up the jewelry box, to load it in the coach. Mona grabbed up her parasol and swatted at the girl with it. "Not that, you goose. No one touches that but me."

The girl, Susie, leaped back, away from the point of the parasol, and dropped the case. It fell open, spilling Lady Paige's old-age pension onto the carriageway. Wiggy's eyes opened wide at the sight, and he scrambled to his feet, to assist the woman who was growing more attractive by the diamond—that is, by the moment.

"Please permit me to introduce myself, madam," he said. "I am Renfrew Wiggs, the Reverend Mr. Renfrew Wiggs, I should say, temporary guardian to Master Troy Renslow. I am calling to see how my charge fares this morning."

Wiggs was calling to see if he could mend his fences with Athena. A night's reflection had told him that he had scant other opportunities waiting. With few prospects and dwindling connections, he had no better chance at bettering his living. Besides, the wench ought to be grateful that he was willing to overlook her lapse in judgment, grateful enough to welcome him back. The silly chit had spoken in a moment of pique only. Not even the foggy-brained female could overlook her own best interests.

Now those mendable fences could stay so far fallen that a herd of cows could march through. "Please allow me to assist you," he told this new acquaintance, this bountiful benefactress-to-be. He handed her a diamond bracelet that could have fed a family of four for a year, at least.

"Why, how kind of you. And I suppose I must introduce myself, as well. No harm can come of such an informal introduction, I daresay, with you a reverend. I am delighted to make the acquaintance of such a courteous, kindly gentleman." She was, too. The man was a bit dour, and his mouth did turn down unbecomingly, but Mona saw a way to restore her own blemished reputation. What could be better than a Bible-bearer? He was smiling at her words, and staring at her sapphires, when his eyes raised past her bosom. "I am Mona, Lady Paige." She made a half curtsy, fluttering her eyelashes.

Lady Paige? The woman everyone knew to be Lord Marden's mistress? Wiggs almost fell back onto the driveway again. He staggered, but maintained enough balance to keep his grip on the ruby brooch he had picked out of the paving.

Mona took it from him, with more force than finesse. She clutched the wood jewel box tighter to her chest. "That is, Baroness Paige, Mr. Wiggs."

"Of course." Wiggy remembered his manners and made a half bow. "My, ah, pleasure. I must be going now, to see to young Renslow, don't you know."

Just then, the butler came down the steps to see why Lady Paige had not departed although her trunks had been loaded earlier. "Tut, tut," he said, noticing the dirt stains on the reverend's unmentionables. He did not offer to dust them off. "I regret that your visit has been in vain, Mr. Wiggs," Hull said, nodding to the waiting groom to assist the maid with getting Lady Paige's belongings onto the carriage. Susie had already restored the fallen contents of the hatbox, only dropping Lady Paige's best bonnet into the carriageway twice. She only stepped on one of the feathers. And let one of the ribbons trail against the coach's greased wheel axle.

"Master Renslow is sleeping," Hull continued. "He shall be for some hours, I understand."

"*Humph.* How can you know that?" Wiggs demanded.

"It is my job to know everything in the household, sir. Will that be all?" Hull turned to go back inside before receiving an answer, as if Wiggs had received all the attention he was going to get.

"What about Miss Renslow?" Wiggy called to the man's stiff back. "She cannot be sleeping at this hour."

Hull turned and looked past Wiggs, his long nose in the air. "I regret, sir, that the young lady is out."

Wiggs understood that Athena would be permanently out, to him, no matter where she was. Without an excuse to go in, he could only leave. He gave up.

Lady Paige did not. "La, sir, if you are free, perhaps you might do me a favor. I hate to travel through the streets of London with all my jewels, so unprotected."

So what if a groom sat up beside the driver, and another would ride at the back of the carriage once she was inside? "A woman cannot be too careful, you know."

Neither could a minister without a manse. "I am sorry, I have—*humph*—another appointment." Wiggs pulled out his pocket watch, as if he were in a hurry to return to that dreary hotel of his and another sparse tea.

"Then the carriage can take you there after. You would not wish to ride in a hired hackney, would you, rather than his lordship's finest vehicle? I am taking up residence in Kensington," she continued, "but there is no hurry for my arrival." She fluttered her handkerchief. "No one is waiting," she said with a sniffle, and with the intimation that his lordship would not be joining her there. "And I do hate to enter a strange house alone. Besides, you must let me offer you refreshments, after knocking you over that way, and for helping me gather my trinkets."

Since she had him by the sleeve and was tugging him toward the coach, Wiggy could not refuse. What harm could there be, anyway, in having a free ride at Marden's expense, and a free meal with a bounteous, bejeweled brunette?

The butler watched them go. *"Tut, tut,"* he repeated with a smile.

Athena told herself that it did not matter that Lord Marden was not at home for dinner that evening. She asked for a tray in her room rather than sitting in the dining parlor in silent solitude. Troy was asleep again, and the loneliness of her own chamber almost swallowed her up.

The earl did not owe her an explanation, Athena told herself. He did not owe her his company, either. He had done so much for her and her brother, she could not be greedy. He had done what he could to protect her from gossip, and she had to be satisfied with that.

His mistress was gone, thank goodness.

So was he.

It did not take a mathematician to complete the equation. One plus one equaled a full house in Kensington.

Athena sent the dinner tray back, nearly untouched.

Lord Marden was coming up empty, too. He had eaten. That was not the problem. He was not successful. That was.

He was in Bath, at his mother's bedside, begging.

"No, dear, I am too sick to return with you to London," his mother said, holding a cloth soaked in lavender water to her forehead. She had dismissed her maid so they might have a private conversation, but she would not leave her bed, or the stifling, overcrowded room. Vases of flowers covered every surface that was not filled with knickknacks or medications. There were roses on the chintz upholstery, and more roses on the wallpaper. Ian felt that he had walked into a conservatory.

"And I look too awful, besides." His mother did look dreadful, but her loving son lied and told her she was still one of the handsomest women he knew. On most days, she was, having the ageless, confident beauty a younger woman could not attain, with only a single, distinctive streak of gray in her dark hair. She was tall and stately, with a still-graceful figure, and her eyes had kept their brightness.

Today the countess looked more like a soggy biscuit than a former Toast. Her nose was red and raw, and her eyes were swollen nearly shut.

"Nonsense, Mother. You are as lovely as ever."

Lady Marden sneezed and blew her nose, then told him to go away. "I do have a mirror, you know, Ian." She sneezed again and lay back against her mound of pillows with a groan.

Ian touched her forehead with newly learned expertise. "Well, you do not seem to have a fever. What does the doctor say?"

"He says I should stay in bed and not exert myself. So do take yourself back to London or whatever brier patch you have fallen into this time. Really, Ian, you are too old to run to your mother when you find yourself in a minor difficulty."

The earl ground his teeth. This was not a minor difficulty; it was a thundering disaster. Did the woman have no maternal feelings? "Dorothy is away from home, or I would have asked her. That is, I did ask her first, knowing how you hate to travel. But she has not returned to Richmond, and I am desperate."

The countess barely waved one languid hand, as if the effort to hold up the four ornate rings and two heavy bracelets she wore was too much for her poor, frail constitution. "I am sorry, dear. I simply cannot be of any assistance." She draped the dampened cloth over her eyes and asked, "Will you pour me a bit of that restorative the physician prescribed?"

"Why? It does not seem to be working." He poured a glass anyway. The stuff smelled suspiciously like sherry to him. "I think you would do better with a walk in the fresh air."

"Oh, now you know more than the physician?"

"It is merely that the place is so warm, and so filled with flowers that you are in a veritable hothouse. Who could recover here?"

"My friends have been very kind and concerned, sending bouquets daily." As opposed to her son, her sigh seemed to be saying, who had brought no token of his affection—merely a selfish wish for her to ruin what little remained of her health.

"I am sure your friends mean well, but they are doing you no good."

"Fie. Flowers always make a female feel better."

She removed the cloth over her eyes so she could gaze fondly at the roses at her bedside, from one of her admirers' forcing houses. She reached out and brought one to her nose, forgetting it was too stuffed to smell that glorious aroma. She brushed the velvety petals against her cheek instead, and sighed in pleasure.

Then she moaned when she saw that Ian had cracked open the window of her bedroom. "What, are you trying to hasten my demise? I'll have you know that I have left all my worldly goods to Dorothy, so you shall not inherit a shilling. You are wasting your time here, torturing a sick old lady."

Ian ignored her pleas for pity and opened the window wider. "I thought you wrote Doro out of your will when she would not nurse you through last year's ague?"

The countess gave a whimper worthy of Drury Lane. "Ungrateful beasts, both of my children. Why, Lady Moncrieff's sons both visit her monthly, and on holidays, or if she feels ill, and her daughter keeps her constant company."

"Lady Moncrieff holds the family's purse strings, and a tight hold she has on them, too. Her sons have to travel to Bath simply to fetch their allowances, and the daughter stays on at her mother's because she has nowhere else to go, now that her husband has stuck his spoon in the wall. Their devotion is bought and paid for. Unlike mine and Dorothy's, which is sincere."

"More sincere the farther away you are! Why, I have not seen your sister since Christmas, and you never come to call except when you want something. How did I raise such unfeeling, unmannered brats?"

"Likely you hired the wrong nannies," Ian replied, for his beloved mama had never lifted a hand to her children's upbringing. "But come, you seem to be looking better already. Let me call your maid to help you dress so we might go for a walk to the Upper Rooms. Perhaps the waters will do you good."

"Nasty stuff, I never take it. I have missed my friends, though."

"And I am certain they miss you, too, especially whichever gentleman sent that entire potted rose bush. They will all be relieved to see you up and about."

"Not as much as you will, I'd wager. Ian, I am not going to London! I am ill, and this is my home, where I belong in my suffering. When I am not absolutely miserable, I am extremely happy here."

"Maddox House was your home for decades, and you have the same blasted—the same blooming roses painted all over your apartment there."

"Maddox House reminds me of your father. You would not wish to see me fall into the mopes, besides having this wretched contagion, would you?"

"You have managed to overcome your despondency well enough whenever you do visit, spending half my income at the dressmaker's, calling on every dowager in town, attending every ball and Venetian breakfast. You have not acted the grieving widow any time these past ten years."

"That is nine and a half years since my beloved was taken from me. And that is irrelevant. I am much too ill to enjoy myself in the least."

"Then you can come be as ill in town as you are here. You do not have to leave the house, just be there!"

"Do not shout, Ian. My head aches too badly. Besides, you do not truly need me. Your message said the girl was nursing her injured brother. No one can find fault with that."

"They can if she is nineteen and a Pocket Venus."

Lady Marden blew her nose and sat up, straightening the ribbons on the frilled cap she wore. "Nineteen, you say?"

Ian's jaw worked harder. "Nineteen."

"Hmm. Lady Moncrieff's sons have both done their duty and presented her with grandchildren."

This was not the non sequitur it seemed, Ian knew, nor his mother's usual complaint. "I am trying to avoid such drastic measures, Mama. That is why I require your presence in town."

"What, is the girl unworthy, then? The breeding is not of the highest, but not totally ineligible," she said, proving that she had looked into the matter.

"Miss Renslow is everything lovely." He could almost see his mother's ears perk up like a hound's on a scent, so he added, "That is, she is everything a young lady should be." He stressed the *young*. "Which is why I would see her extricated as quickly as possible from this embarrassment. The situation is entirely my fault, so I need to make amends."

"By doing what is necessary?"

"By doing what I have to," he agreed. "If it comes to that. I am hoping your presence will protect her."

"My coming to London will not help Miss Renslow if people know she has been alone in your house. I have not heard any such rumors, and I would, you know."

"I fear the tittle-tattle will be spreading soon, like a rash. Your residence at Maddox House can alleviate the worst of the gossip, however."

"Yes, I can see where you might need me. And I would not wish any aspersions cast on my grandchildren, either."

Ian's teeth would be ground to nubs soon, but his mother did seem to be weakening. Or strengthening, as the case may be, in light of the possibilities she foresaw. Ian foresaw more trouble, but he had no choice. "Then you will come?"

The countess blew her nose. "Tell me more about the young woman first. If she sounds nice, I suppose I can jeopardize my own health for her sake."

So Ian told her what a charmer Miss Renslow was, how caring of her brother, with a delightful sense of humor, intelligence, and kindness. He knew he was digging his own grave with every shovelful of praise he heaped on Athena, but he had to have his mother's cooperation. To ensure her leaving her sickbed, he described the petite beauty in glowing terms, from her golden locks to her dainty toes, with stops between that would not embarrass a fellow's mother. "She cannot sing worth a groat, though, and has a stubborn streak as wide as the Thames."

"She will need it," Lord Marden's mother said, even as she rang for her maid to begin packing.

"You will come?"

"How can I not? Besides, I believe that tonic has helped." Her eyes were less puffy and her nose not as stuffed.

"I believe it is the opened window that is doing you a world of good."

They both knew there was no tonic like matchmaking to cure a mother.

"But first," she said, "I need to know exactly what happened to bring the dear girl to such a pass."

So Ian told her, or as much as he thought she ought to know. When he finished, she wondered how she had raised such a lackwit.

"You must have hired the wrong tutors, too."

"You are insolent, Ian, and a fool."

"Yes, but I do not surround myself with roses when I know they make me sneeze."

Chapter Fourteen

Any husband is better than no husband at all.
                                    —Anonymous

Only a very good husband is better than none.
                                    —Mrs. Anonymous

If Ian had a farthing for every piece of unwanted advice he received, he would be rich. He was already rich. The advice was worthless.

Everyone he knew seemed to be telling him what to do, how to act. People who knew him well, people who had respected his judgment in the past, perfect strangers—all felt entitled to give their opinions. He expected the crossing sweep to offer suggestions next.

His mother, of course, was first.

"You'll have to marry her, you know," Lady Marden told Ian after her second day in London.

"What, is the gossip so vicious, then?"

"How should I know? I have not been out of the house since you dragged me here. The journey was so fatiguing, you know."

Ian had ridden, rather than spend the trip dealing with hot bricks, cool lemonade, dust, drafts, and *Oh, dears.* His mother had her maid, a groom, a driver, and two outriders to see to her needs. Ian had a good horse under him and the wind at his back. The ride had not been tiresome at all to him, just too long. He had been anxious to return to town, to make sure neither Troy nor Athena was suffering. Troy seemed better, with healthier color and more animation. He was having less pain, he said, so was taking less laudanum. Ian was pleased, although the boy had still not left his bed.

Athena had seemed different, more reserved, until he told her he had been to Bath to fetch his mother. Then it was as if the sun had come out, and he was basking in its warmth. Her smile could have brightened midnight. Lud, Ian thought, with that smile and those turquoise eyes, not to mention her slim but shapely figure, Miss Renslow would be the Toast of all of London, if she had the chance to shine in Society. He was hoping his mother could provide that opportunity, but now he had doubts.

"If the rumormongers have not been about their business, why does she need a husband so badly?"

"Because she is nearly twenty, you noddy. And she does not need a spouse as much as you do, to marry and set up your nursery. But I adore the darling girl."

Of course she did, Ian thought. Athena had insisted on helping the household get ready for the countess's arrival, offering to arrange a bouquet of flowers for Lady Marden's room, until he had vetoed that idea. Then she had greeted his mother with proper deference, catered to her every whim, listened to her complaints and her opinions on the best course of medicine for Troy, and kept her entertained and amused while the countess recovered from the rose fever and the carriage ride. Between her brother and his mother and the dog, Athena had no time for anything—or for Ian.

He should not regret her busyness, nor his mother's

approval of her. That was what he had been aiming at, so the countess would take Miss Renslow under her wing and help her soar. He should not regret how little he saw of her, but he did. He minded that she was at the beck and call of two invalids now, and not sharing minutes and thoughts and smiles with him.

Ian was not making sense, not even to himself. He wanted Athena to have the world at her pretty little feet—he owed it to her and the boy to see her happily settled, making her own choice—but he liked her at his side.

Before the earl could ponder that conundrum, his mother was going on. "Yes, you shall have to marry the precious girl. You'll never find a more promising bride, I'd swear, nor a better time for it. If you do not take that step now, who knows but that you would wait ten more years before you wed. I could be in my grave without having seen my grandchildren."

Ian had to wonder what had his mother so enamored of grandchildren. Her own offspring had not interested her in the least. He could not imagine what Lady Marden would do with a sticky, smelly, squalling infant—except take to her bed with a headache. What he said was, "You shall live far longer than another ten years, Mother."

"I should hope so, but with my frail constitution . . ." She let her voice fade away, but since she was wolfing down her third pastry from Ian's French chef's kitchen, he was not worried.

"You are the picture of health, now that you have stopped wearing live roses tucked in your bonnet's brim."

His mother ignored him. "Furthermore, in ten years, you will be forty, but the marriageable chits will still be close to twenty. They will seem even more harum-scarum, so you will choose the first one to hand

and be miserable for the rest of your life. And mine. I should not want a skitter-witted daughter-in-law. There is nothing flighty about Miss Renslow, for all her youth and inexperience."

"No, she is fairly sensible, for a female."

His mother ignored that, too. "I consider her charming. That is another reason you must marry her. If you do not wed the dear girl, my heart will be broken, not that you'll care, you ungrateful beast."

Ian did not wish to break his mother's selfish heart, any more than he wanted to ruin Miss Renslow. He did not want to hear any more about it, either.

He had no choice. His best friend, Carswell, was next, the disloyal dastard.

"You'll have to marry her, you know," that gentleman said as he sipped his cognac at White's. Carswell was looking so perfectly turned out, so elegant, that Ian felt like an unmade bed in his looser clothing, his spotless but simply tied neckcloth, and his tousled hair. He might make a better appearance, he knew, if he did not keep running his fingers through his curls, but he was a creature of habit—and of despair. What did it matter if he was disordered on the outside? He was a shambles on the inside, as well.

"Have the rumors been flying then?" he asked. "I thought my mother's presence would silence them. Heaven knows everyone in town must know of her arrival, the way cards and callers and invitations keep appearing." Flowers had been delivered, too, but he had ordered them sent to St. Cecilia's Home for Girls. He needed his mother out and about, not home with the sniffles.

Carswell nodded. "Everyone knows the countess has arrived, and that adds to the speculation instead of dampening it. If everything were aboveboard, there would be no need for her presence. Besides, you do not roll out the heavy cannon to shoot a mouse, do you? No, a fellow brings his mother to town to meet her future daughter-in-law, not to chaperone an unknown from the country. You could have married the young woman off to some needy second son, or shipped her back to her family without too much stir, I suppose. But to keep her here, with your mother? The scandal may have been averted, but now, expectations have been raised."

"Raised how high?"

"The betting books are three to one in your favor. In Miss Renslow's favor, that is, of having your ring on her finger before summer."

"Marriage would be doing neither one of us a favor, by Zeus!"

"But if you do not marry Miss Renslow after this, people will wonder what is wrong with her, you know. Ah, what *is* wrong with her, if I might be so rude to ask? Friends for ages, and all that."

"There is nothing wrong with her, dash it. You've met her, and seen her."

"A lovely little package, I'd say."

"You had better not say it, or that long friendship of ours is in doubt. That is no way to speak of a female in my care."

Carswell smiled. "Of course not. No disrespect intended to Miss Renslow. I found her everything charming, and as pretty as a rose."

"Lud, don't mention roses, either."

Carswell straightened his cuffs and brushed at a speck of lint on his sleeve. "I believe this affair has addled your wits, old man. But tell me, then, if you feel so protective of the lady, and are so aware of her excellence—upon which I shall not elaborate, lest you toss your wine in my face—why are you gnashing your teeth and pulling at your hair? To say nothing of that second bottle of wine you have started, which would leave a dreadful stain on my new waistcoat, so do not be offended. Do you like it, by the way? I cannot decide if the dragonflies are too large."

"Who can think of waistcoats at a time like this?"

Carswell took out his quizzing glass and inspected Ian's attire. The earl's waistcoat was a dark gray with a black stripe, like five others he owned. "Do you ever think of them? I wonder. But that is not the point. Marrying Miss Renslow is, or explaining why you do not wish to solve this dilemma to everyone's satisfaction."

"I told you, because it would not be satisfactory in the least. What, tell the poor girl she has no choice but to wed a man ten years her senior, one who has a rakish reputation, besides?"

"Your reputation is no worse than any other man's in town, and far better than some. And women seldom have choices, you know. Think on it, Miss Renslow might have been forced to take Wiggs."

"I would have shot him, first."

"So you do like the girl!"

"Too well to see her shackled to Wiggs, or to me."

"Ah, the poor lass, wed to a nobleman of ancient lineage, with four houses, more money than the prince—although everyone has more money than the prince, these days—and looks good enough to turn the eye of a blind woman. My, how she will suffer."

"She will if I am not what she wants."

"And I am a two-headed pig if you are not. I played Lady Throckmorton-Jones, recall. I saw how Miss Renslow acted toward you. In fact I had ought to place a wager in the betting book myself." He half rose from his comfortable leather chair, but a vise-like grip held onto his arm.

"Try to write there and your wrist will never work again."

"You *are* rattled, my friend. You must know I would never do anything to hurt the lady. I liked her very well."

Ian's eyes brightened and the creases on his forehead smoothed, leaving him the carefree, handsome gentleman he had been before Lady Paige and her loose-screw husband had entered his life. "You like her, and she likes you. You laughed together. Why don't *you* wed Miss Renslow?"

"Gads, I have laughed with any number of females, and at a few, too. That doesn't mean I want to marry them. Besides, I am not the one with entailed estates or a title that requires a succession of little Maddox heirs. I did not compromise the girl . . . and I am not the marrying kind."

Ian pulled at his hair. "Neither am I, and the devil take it."

Ian's butler commented that Miss Renslow was a welcome addition to the household. His remark would have been a subtle reminder of Ian's duties, except that Hull made his observation every time Ian handed him his hat, or took up his riding crop or looked through the pile of mail in the hall table. Subtlety was lost, the sixteenth time around.

"Yes, Hull," Ian said after yet another mention of Miss Renslow's fine qualities. "I do know that the young lady graces Maddox House, as she would any residence lucky enough to have her as a guest. A guest, Hull, do you hear me?"

Hull heard him as well as the dog did.

Roma was perfectly trained now. If Ian brought her a treat, she did not attack his footwear. Otherwise she growled when she saw him.

Ian's valet did not growl, but he was heard to mutter

that the sooner Lord Marden got on with the thing, the sooner the difficult and demanding countess would go back to Bath, and the house could stop being at sixes and sevens. "Although I must say, I have never seen Lady Marden so content at Maddox House," Hopkins said, "as now that Miss Renslow is here to keep her company."

"No, Hopkins, you must not say such things. Lady Marden is my mother, and Miss Renslow is . . . Miss Renslow."

Troy neither gave advice nor issued edicts. He wished. "I wish my sister could marry a man like you. You'd treat her right, and she would never have to worry about going out to work. I wish I were old enough to defend her reputation so no one could say she should not have come to take care of me. I wish we could stay here forever.

Now there was subtlety. The boy had not been taking lessons from Ian's mother, either, when he punctuated his wishes with a sigh and a weak smile. Ian would rather the lad snap and snarl, like his dog.

One person might—possibly—have had the right to criticize, condemn, or otherwise call the earl to account. That person walked into White's Club that evening.

"Been looking for you," Spartacus, Lord Rensdale, said as he spotted Ian sunk into his favorite leather chair.

"Been waiting for you," Ian answered. Carswell had departed for more congenial entertainment, and to show off his new waistcoat. Ian had stayed on at the club, contemplating his options and the level of wine left in the bottle at his side. Both were diminishing quickly.

Rensdale took a facing chair and signaled for a waiter to bring him a bottle and a glass. "Whatever he is drinking. On his account, too."

The waiter looked at Lord Marden. Ian nodded. He owed the viscount that, and more. Rensdale was older than he was, with thinning hair and a thickening waist. He had blue eyes, but a pale, ordinary blue, not the startling color Athena and Troy shared. He was short of stature, like both of them, and walked slowly, favoring one leg. He took a minute to settle himself comfortably, took a swallow of his wine, and said, "You'll have to marry her, you know."

"I already have the special license."

"Good. I'd hate to have to issue a challenge."

"I would not take it."

"Good. I'd lose, whichever weapon you chose. And my wife would likely kill me anyway."

"Devilish things, wives."

Rensdale raised his glass. "I'll drink to that." He did, copiously. Then he started to haul himself to his feet. "Glad we have that settled."

"That's all?" Ian wanted to know. "You aren't going to ask about the boy, or if your sister is dishonored? You do not want to discuss my prospects, or the marriage settlements? Hell, you have not even asked when the wedding is to be."

Rensdale sat back down and propped his bad leg on a footstool. "I've seen the sprat. He'll do. Until he finds another bit of tomfoolery to fall into. Always getting some contagion or other, anyway. Saw my sister. She doesn't look any different. Sings your praises, so she ain't in a pet over anything underhanded. She would be, too. Always been quick to tell a chap when he's done something she don't approve, our Attie. No pouting and sulking and giving a chap the silent treatment, at least." He drank to that, also. "As for your prospects, everyone knows you for a nabob. No business of mine, at any rate, nor the settlements, either. You'll have to talk to Captain Beecham's man of affairs, unless the captain shows up in time. And the wedding better take place as soon as possible, because I left my wife at home and need to get back."

Ian did not care on how short a leash Lady Rensdale kept the viscount. Ian had a glimmer of hope. "The captain! Seeing you, I forgot I'd need his permission. We cannot proceed until he comes home!" He would have stood and danced a jig right there, except the room seemed to be spinning.

"Not once I explain matters to his solicitor. Can't wait too long on these messy affairs, eh?"

Ian could have waited another five years.

"And what does a navy man know about girls and their reputations anyway? No, no reason to wait, that I can see. What does Attie say?"

"She, ah, has not said anything about the wedding date yet."

Rensdale nodded. "Too involved with the boy, as always. Loses sight of her own best interests, she does."

"She is devoted to the lad. In fact, she won't want to be apart from him. Will you object if he stays on here with us, even after his recuperation?"

"Hell, no. He's nothing but a worry. I'll be glad to let someone else pay for his lessons and doctors."

Ian had not offered to finance the boy, but he supposed he owed the viscount that, too. Rensdale was going on: "Likeable enough lad, but you never know if he is going to cock up his toes or not. He's weak. My wife calls him an embarrassment."

How could this pint-sized popinjay speak of his own brother that way? Troy was a fine young man, with more than his fair share of intelligence—and woes. Ian was outraged on his behalf. "He's your heir, Rensdale!"

Now the viscount grinned, and Ian could see a resemblance to Athena. Not her joyous smile, nor her expressive eyes, but a family resemblance, nevertheless. "Not any more, he isn't," Rensdale said, raising his glass again, "or not for long anyway. My wife is breeding, at last."

"My congratulations." Ian called for another bottle, since Rensdale's celebratory toasts were decimating this one. "You must be very pleased."

"That I am, that I am. A hell of a note when a chap weds to beget an heir and it doesn't happen. But now, now there is no reason not to hope for a whole parcel of them. An heir and a spare, at the minimum. Carthaginius, I thought, for the eldest."

"What if your firstborn is a daughter?"

"Faugh, I've waited too long for a son. So you see why I want to hurry home."

"The birth is imminent?" Ian asked. Athena had not mentioned such a momentous event.

"No, months away. But Lady Rensdale is suffering the morning sickness, and the afternoon one, too. And blaming me that she can't keep her food down. And crying all the time, when she is not shouting at the servants. On second thought, perhaps we ought to wait for Captain Beecham's return after all. A few more days can't matter, can they?"

"Not when you are seen to approve. Between your presence and my mother's, we shall weather the storm."

Rensdale laughed. "You think this is a storm? Hell, you ain't even married yet. You'll see what a real cyclone is, soon enough." He raised his glass again.

So did Ian, but to oblivion, not to matrimony.

Chapter Fifteen

A man can live without love. A woman cannot.
            —Anonymous

A man can live without love, but he'll get horses and dogs, so he doesn't know how wretched he is. A woman knows it every day.

            —Mrs. Anonymous

One voice was raised in dissent.

"No, she does not have to marry the clunch."

Ian would have rejoiced, but the voice was his sister's, who had finally arrived. Dorothy's happy declaration was unfortunately, to his ear, anyway, followed by, "She can come live with me."

What, send Athena off to the spinster realm of raising lapdogs and roses and money for charity? He could not do it. Athena was too loving, too lively, too . . . marriageable. She deserved a home of her own, turquoise-eyed angel babies in her arms, a doting husband at her side. She deserved a man who would cherish her and devote his life to making her happy, because only her happiness would make his world complete. Miss Renslow would not find any of that living in Richmond with Ian's sister.

She might find the life of a reformer interesting, and

the travel to coal mines and wool mills interesting, at first. She would cry to see the plight of the families, especially the children, and she would do her damnedest to see that their conditions were improved, like Dorothy did. But such a life was Doro's by choice, not by constraint.

Lady Dorothy Maddox could stay in London as hostess for her brother, perhaps making more of a difference in the government's policies by influencing those who voted in Parliament. A man was more inclined to listen to a female when his belly was pleasantly full, Ian had tried to tell her, than when he read her harangues in the newspapers before breakfast. But sweet persuasion was not in Doro's nature. She was fervid in her beliefs, and anyone who disagreed was simply stupid, stubborn, and wrong.

She did not like the social values that held sway in town, either, the extravagant waste of the *ton*, while children starved in the gutters five minutes from Mayfair. She could not enjoy the lavish dinners, Dorothy had said, loudly and often, knowing so many others were going hungry. The members of the beau monde had breathed a sigh of relief when she moved to Richmond.

She could have taken up residence in Bath, keeping her mother company—at least, until they strangled each other. They had both been relieved when Doro decided to live at the earl's Richmond estate.

Now, years later, and months since they had last seen each other, Ian's mother and sister had started brangling almost the instant Dorothy came through the door. Lady Marden thought her daughter's dress was unbecoming, out of fashion, and poorly constructed. Her hair was a mess, her posture was unladylike, and she had not been to visit in ages, while her poor mother was ailing.

Lady Dorothy thought her mother was dosing herself too heavily with that restorative, dressing like a woman half her age, and inflating her symptoms to make herself interesting and make her children feel guilty over their neglect.

"You see? You do admit you have neglected me shamelessly."

"Others needed my time far more than a self-indulgent woman who does nothing but gossip and play cards. I do not know how you bear life in Bath with all those old hags."

"They are not hags! And they are not old. Why, some of them are younger than I am."

"Precisely."

No, Lady Dorothy would not have been happy in Bath, either.

She could have married, Ian knew, for she had a handsome competence of her own, and a more than generous dowry, which Ian had handed into her keeping when she moved to Richmond. She had received several respectable offers that he was aware of, in the years closer to her come-out, and who knew how many since. Dorothy had claimed that the men who sought her hand in marriage sought that dowry more, and she had refused them all.

To Ian, his sister was a handsome female, tall like the rest of the family, but willowy instead of being a sturdy oak. She had fine brown eyes, chestnut hair, and a well-formed figure. She did, regrettably, have severe scars on her face from a childhood bout with the smallpox.

The fashionable world did not welcome imperfections. Lady Dorothy could not be excluded, of course, not when she was an earl's daughter and sister, but she could be ignored. Doro had sat on more spindly gilt chairs in her earlier years than most females see

in a lifetime. Her mother had kept dragging her to
party after party, urging her to smile, to sit up straight,
to add another ruffle to her hem, anything to see her
daughter wed. Ian had enlisted his friends to dance
with her when he was in town, but mostly she sat on
the sidelines of every ball. She was disfigured in the
eyes of her peers and, worse, opinionated. The other
girls were afraid of her and afraid to be seen with her,
lest anyone discover they had two thoughts to rub
together. Dorothy was a confirmed wallflower, to her
mother's dismay.

By the time Doro reached her twenty-fifth birthday,
Lady Marden had developed innumerable conditions
and Lady Dorothy had declared herself on the shelf.
She put on caps, moved to Richmond, and started
trying to change the world.

In Richmond, Ian's sister was a leading light of local
society. She held literary salons, fund-raising dinners,
and political debates, with at-home afternoons and
public days on the grounds. None of the neighbors
turned down her invitations, and she was a welcome
guest in every home in the area, from crofter's cottage
to squire's manor to the mansions of the nobility,
when the latter sought the peace of the countryside
after the hectic London Season.

She started a series of lectures to teach women how
to manage money, and she started a school for adults
who wished to learn to read and write. At Ian's urging,
she broadened her interests to conditions in the manu-
factories, which he was fighting to improve before the
ill-used workers started a civil war.

He was happy to have her eyes and ears in the
industrial regions, and Doro was happy to be useful—
but would that do for Miss Renslow? Not at all, in
Ian's mind.

Not in the minds of others, either, it seemed, for an

outcry went up in the drawing room when his sister offered to have Athena come stay with her.

They were waiting for Miss Renslow before dinner, with Lord Rensdale and Carswell invited, too, to make up the numbers and separate the sparring Marden ladies.

Predictably, Ian's mother was most vocal in her opposition. "Just because you have chosen to live like a nun," she told her daughter, "that does not mean every woman wants to forego the pleasure of matrimony and motherhood."

No one had the nerve to ask what pleasure Lady Marden had taken in motherhood, but Ian and his sister exchanged glances.

"Hear, hear," Rensdale seconded the countess's comment. "The gal's reputation is already dicey. Wouldn't want her known as an eccentric besides."

Ian wondered if he had to defend his sister's honor at that, but Carswell came to her rescue. He was dressed to the nines, as usual, even though they were mostly family and old friends. "I see nothing wrong with a strong woman living an independent life, but Miss Renslow's circumstances are different," he said, letting his quizzing glass dangle on a ribbon in his hand. "She would be your pensioner, Lady Dorothy, instead of mistress of her own home."

"A fine home," Viscount Rensdale added, looking around the vast chamber. "A countess. Can't sneeze at that."

Lady Marden could and did, until Ian moved the vase of flowers some idiot had placed on the mantel.

"So should a woman wed," Dorothy demanded, taking a sip of her wine, "for wealth and position? Will that make her happy?"

"Happier than a poor female going out to work would be, I'd wager," Carswell countered, bringing the quizzing glass to his eye to inspect a painting on the wall. "Men are married for their titles and women for their dowries every day."

Rensdale choked on his Madeira, having wed his wife for her father's money, as everyone in the room knew.

"And that is equally reprehensible. I would not wish my brother married to a fortune hunter."

Rensdale stopped coughing in time to say, "Here now, my sister is no such thing. Not her fault she landed in this bumblebroth. I say she needs a ring on her finger, not a poker up her—" He coughed again.

"And Ian needs a wife, anyway," his mother put in. "To ensure the succession. He knows his duty."

"Bah, what woman wishes to be wed out of duty?"

"A sensible one," her mother replied. "One who does not want to lead apes through Hell."

"And it's a wife's duty to give a man his heirs," Rensdale proudly added. "Attie knows the way of it."

"Don't you think we ought to let Miss Renslow speak for herself?" Ian asked when his mother and his sister appeared ready to unsheath their claws.

"Right, Marden. I'll put it to her as soon as she comes." Rensdale pulled out his pocket watch to check the time.

"No! That is, I will speak to her privately. This is, after all, between us."

Rensdale held the watch to his ear, then tapped on its face, to see if it was working properly. "Between you two and all of London, from what I heard in the clubs."

Carswell nodded in confirmation. "Which is precisely why we are here."

"No young girl can make such a decision on her own," Ian's mother informed the gathering. "She needs the guidance of her elders."

"I disagree. Miss Renslow seems a sensible sort, from the few moments I spoke with her. She can choose for herself," his sister insisted.

Rensdale started to turn red in the face. "Gals don't know their own minds. She'll do what she's told."

"A woman is not a servant to be ordered about."

"Servants do not wed without permission," Carswell reminded her.

"I say she has no choice!" Rensdale swore.

"The way you were ready to marry her off to that toad, Wiggs?" Carswell wanted to know. "Did she have any choice about that?"

"She isn't engaged to him, is she?" Rensdale answered, growing redder still, because she would have been, if he'd had his way. Or his wife's way. "Anyhow, Wiggs wasn't the one who ruined her."

No one had any replies to that.

Ian looked at the clock on the mantel and his mother started to grumble about setting dinner back. Carswell announced he was ready to lay odds that Miss Renslow would not come to dinner, not when she was being served up on a platter.

Lady Dorothy swatted him with her fan. "This is not a laughing matter, Mr. Carswell, nor a fit subject for a wager. A woman's future depends on this decision."

"And a man's," he reminded her. "If he marries the wrong female, he can wind up regretting it every day of his life."

No one looked at Rensdale, who blustered, "I still say Marden has no choice but to ask."

They all agreed on that. Even the butler, refilling the glasses, nodded his white-wigged head.

They were talking about her, and Athena knew it. She knew it before she reached the partway opened drawing room door and overheard them dissecting her future, carving up her past. The earl hadn't said much—not since she came to the door, anyway—and that made everything worse, somehow. He should have said she was not ruined, that he had not ruined her, that neither of them was under any obligation. On the other hand, he could have said that he would be delighted to have her as his bride. He hadn't said anything but that she was too full of pluck to miss dinner.

Athena was not full of anything but dismay. She did not want to go into that room, into dinner with the earl and his family and his best friend—and her brother, who only wanted to get rid of her. She wanted to run back up those marble stairs and sit at her other brother's bedside, where Troy thought she was just Attie, the same as always, no soiled goods to be wrapped in clean linen for a tidy disposal, or a ball of dust to be swept under the rug.

She was an adult, she wanted to shout, not a child, and not chattel to be handed from an uncaring man to an unwilling one.

Oh, she knew what they were saying, what they were planning, how they could resolve the messy problem that was Athena Renslow. Lady Marden had mentioned the word *grandchildren* with a fond smile, and the word *trousseau* with an even fonder one, showing that she preferred shopping to children, but was eager for both. Then she had turned the subject to her uncertain health, as usual, saying that Marden would do the right thing. He was Lord Marden, not some cabbage-headed caper-merchant, and could someone pass her the cordial?

Spartacus had said something, too, about his lordship being an honorable man. Athena had agreed wholeheartedly, that Marden was the perfect gentleman, until she realized what her brother meant by honorable. Spartacus was not referring to how the earl spoke up for reform in Parliament, how he treated his dependents, and paid his debts. Her brother was implying that he expected Lord Marden to sacrifice himself on the altar of propriety.

Even the maid assigned to help Athena dress spoke of how happy the staff was that Miss Renslow would be staying at Maddox House.

Athena was not. Not happy. Not staying. Not going to marry the earl. How dare they all, from scullery maid to countess, assume that she would accept Lord Marden's offer, when there was no need for it?

She would refuse, naturally. Of course, she could not refuse an offer that had not yet been made. She could not walk into that drawing room, announce she would rather wed Wiggy, who at least wanted her for her dowry and her connections, than a man who did not want her at all. She had landed on his lordship's doorstep by happenstance, she wanted to yell at all of them, like a stupid lost cow that wandered onto a neighbor's field. That did not mean he had to keep her! That did not even mean he *could* keep her.

She was a lady, though, and could not shout, could not stamp her feet, could not turn tail and run away. She stiffened her spine, raised her chin, and shoved the door open the rest of the way. The door bounced against the wall, she had pushed it so hard, and everyone jumped. The butler jostled the bottle of wine he was pouring, which dripped onto Mr. Carswell's trousers. That gentleman cursed, which caused Lady Dorothy to chide him for being so vain. That made Lady Marden groan, declaring it no wonder that her daughter was still unwed, for no man wanted a sharp-tongued wife. Which made Lord Rensdale, who had in fact married a shrew, take the wine bottle from the butler and pour himself another glass.

"I believe dinner is ready, Miss Renslow," Lord Marden said, coming forward to offer Athena his arm. He was looking elegant this evening, she thought, as if he had taken more care with his apparel now that his mother and sister were present, and she could not help comparing him to the other gentlemen present. He was larger, of course, but that was not the only reason her eyes kept returning to look at him, after the others managed to greet her.

The earl's indigo blue coat fit perfectly across his broad shoulders, with his black-striped gray waistcoat showing his flat abdomen, unlike her brother's waistcoat, which was puffed out and barely buttoned across his spreading paunch, or Mr. Carswell's, which was embroidered with silver hummingbirds. The earl's hair was neater than usual, too, she thought, with only one curl falling onto his forehead. Carswell's hair was pomaded in place and her brother's was . . . thinning.

Lord Marden was the only one of them who was not scowling, so Athena smiled at him. He thought she had pluck? She would not disappoint him. They could settle everything later. For now, it was enough that he smiled back at her. At least he did not hate her for placing him in this impossible situation. She did wish that she had fussed more with her hair, but she had lost track of the time, trying to keep Troy abreast of his lessons, for when Mr. Wiggs did come back. Her maid had only been able to gather it up with a ribbon and a few hairpins, which were already coming loose. At least she was wearing her favorite ivory gown and her mother's pearls, so she did not feel entirely like the country bumpkin she knew she was.

Athena expected the dinner to be awkward and uncomfortable, but everyone was too well-bred for that. Lady Marden, at the head of the table, informed Athena's brother of every complication she had suffered during her own pregnancies. Lady Dorothy and Carswell sat across from each other and disagreed at length and at volume about extending the vote, Sir Walter Scott's new work, and which were more clever, dogs or cats. They would have debated whether it was day or night, Athena thought, giving up trying to find a topic that was not controversial.

Lord Marden did not offer any conversation or attempt to mediate between his friend and his sister. Nor did he look at Athena. He only addressed his meal.

Oh, yes, they were all too well mannered to discuss the one subject on everyone's minds.

Finally Lady Marden rose, after finishing off a hearty meal for such an invalid. The ladies would leave the gentlemen to their port and cigars, she declared, while the women had a comfortable chat in the drawing room.

Athena did not see anything comfortable in listening to Lady Marden haranguing her daughter about failing once more to make herself agreeable to a gentleman, or Lady Dorothy's remonstrations that if her mother ate less, she would not suffer so many digestive complaints. Before they could turn their attention to her, Athena decided to excuse herself. Her brother—her younger brother—had been alone too long, she told the two older women. Troy was used to their reading together before bed, which helped him relax so he did not need as much laudanum.

Troy was also used to Lord Marden looking in on him before departing for the evening, but Athena did not mention that to the earl's family. They were too busy with their bickering to consider their chaperone responsibilities, anyway. She hoped to get the earl aside and settle this botheration about duty and honor and marriage once and for all. In no uncertain terms. Without sounding like a fishwife. Or weeping.

She found her brother sitting propped up in bed, not at all sleepy, and not interested in his books. "What do you think, Attie? Will the earl come up to scratch tonight? Spartacus says he can't wait too long or you won't be accepted at Almack's even after you get hitched, but it doesn't sound all that interesting, anyway. Lady Marden told me she'd take me with her to Bath and her physicians when you are on honeymoon. Do I have to go? Isn't Lady Doro the top of the trees? She says she has the map of the Richmond maze memorized and she'll take me if I don't go to Bath. And did you see Carswell's waistcoat? He offered to take me to his tailor while you are out of town. So what do you think?"

"I think you can read your own dratted book," she shouted, like a fishwife, dashing tears from her eyes before she rushed from Troy's bedchamber. She would settle with Lord Marden and everyone else . . . tomorrow.

Chapter Sixteen

A man gives up his freedom with marriage.
                                    —Anonymous

A woman gains freedom with marriage.
                                    —Mrs. Anonymous

Gads, she was beautiful, Ian thought as Athena ran past him. With her hair all wispy from her bath and her cheeks rosy, Miss Renslow was the prettiest girl Ian had ever seen, and he had seen every beauty to grace London for a decade, from debutante to Drury Lane actress to demimondaine. Others might disagree, but something about Athena simply struck Ian as exquisite, especially when she smiled—more so when she smiled at him.

This might not be such a bad bargain, after all, he decided . . . at least for him. He had to marry eventually, and here was a handy bride, one his family and staff already adored, one he knew to be capable and caring. He even liked her. More, he was coming to like looking at her, wondering how he had ever thought her child-like. She was all woman, without being blatant or blowsy. He wondered now how that small, perfect body would fit with his larger one.

Nicely, he thought. Very nicely, indeed, as long as he did not crush her.

He'd be careful, and she'd be strong, as always. He knew Athena was powerful for all her lack of inches, for he'd seen her help her brother sit up, and seen her carrying the dog. She was dainty, but graceful, lithesome. Yes, that was the word for her, lithesome. It flowed over his tongue like his tongue would flow over her smooth, white skin. He would be the first man to touch that skin, to taste her, to—

Damn, if the house was not on fire, he must have caught a fever from his mother. Ian offered Athena his arm for the walk to the dining room, hoping the stroll down the corridor would cool him off. Lord Rensdale brought Ian's mother along, while Carswell escorted Doro. The order of the procession might not be entirely according to correct protocol, but this was Ian's house. He was going to walk beside the woman of his choice—Lud, had he thought that? Had he conceded defeat, then?—and protocol be damned.

Now, though, he could smell her light floral perfume, mixed with a lemony scent from her hair. Instead of fanning his skin, the walk was fanning his desire, making him think of that golden hair spread out on his pillow, that perfume on his sheets. He used his free arm to tug at his neckcloth, hoping for a cooler breeze. Ian also hoped they reached the dining room before his appetite became obvious, and he did not mean his rumbling stomach. No, this might not be a bad bargain, after all.

But what about for Athena? Could he say she was getting a fair deal? She'd get a title and wealth and furs and jewels, things other women coveted. She'd get to have her brother with her until Troy went off to school. Ian was determined that the boy would have the best education the Maddox coffers could buy, and he would be healthy enough to go. Was that enough for Attie? What if she was one of those females with her head in the clouds, wanting True Love and a Grand Passion?

Judging from his body's awareness of her beside him, he might be able to provide the passion. Hell, Ian thought, he was going to provide a passionately embarrassing spectacle at the dinner table if he did not get his napkin over his lap soon. Once he'd started thinking of Athena in his bed, in his arms, out of her clothes, he could not get the idea out of his mind. The rest of him was proving just as difficult to control.

Watching her sip at her wine and then lick her lips was doing him no good, nor were the little bites of food she took, like delicate nips. From where he sat, he could almost look down the neck of her gown, if he craned his neck pretending to reach for the salt. His broth would taste like brine soon.

Thunderation, he was a grown man, not a randy boy. So he gathered what wits he had working at the moment, all three of them, it felt like, and concentrated on his meal—and how he was going to ask Athena to marry him.

He could not come out and say what he wanted: that he had shot her brother, possibly leaving him a permanent invalid, that he had dishonored her reputation by his paper-skulled presence, and that he would spend the rest of his life trying to make things better for both of them. No, he could not say that. What woman wanted to hear that her betrothed was her brother's near-murderer?

He could not offer her the words most females wanted to hear. Actually, most of the women with whom he usually associated wanted to hear that they could send him their bills, but the others wanted words of love. Hell, Athena would laugh if he professed an undying devotion. She'd likely feel his forehead for fever, as she did her brother's.

He certainly could not tell her that he lusted for her body. She was a lady, for heaven's sake. If she were not, he would not be in this fix. He'd satisfy his cravings, give her a parting gift, and go on to the next pretty face, the next inviting curves. Besides, they both knew that lust did not last. She might be an innocent— he was sure she was an innocent—but she had to realize that what attracted a man one day was of no interest the next. She'd met Lady Paige, after all.

So what could he tell her, to convince Athena that marriage to him would not be the end of the world? Could he tell her that she'd be free to fall in love with a gentleman of her choice? Not on his life. Could he swear fidelity? That was almost as far-fetched, although he did mean to try. For a while, anyway.

Ian chewed his meal and his options, and he enjoyed neither. Long before he had a satisfactory speech composed, his mother was standing, leading the ladies from the room. Athena was making her good nights, retiring, she said, with her younger brother as an excuse.

The boy would be Ian's brother soon enough, so he could leave soon, too. Gads, did that mean he would also have to claim Rensdale? The fellow was not impossible, merely harebrained, henpecked, and close as a clam when it came to parting with his blunt. Rensdale's sister seemed to have three decent gowns to her name, and nothing but the pearls on her neck for jewelry. That would change soon, starting with the diamond ring in Ian's pocket.

Rensdale's wife had chests full of fripperies, Ian guessed, deciding that he and Athena would not see much of the unpleasant pair. She might want to attend the christening for the couple's infant, though, which meant he would be forced into their company sooner than he wished. Why did no one mention that when a man took a wife, he also took on an entire family?

Perhaps Athena and the younger brother could go by themselves to Rensdale's seat in Derby. No, that would not do, not so soon after their marriage. People would talk worse than they were talking now, speculating on an estrangement. The idea of the old tabbies digging their claws into his wife did not sit well with Ian. Nor, now that he thought of it, did the idea of her going off with no one but the boy for protection. Lud, a wife was a lot of responsibility, it seemed.

On the other hand, if she were already breeding by the time the Rensdale infant was born, they could plead Athena's condition as a reason to miss the family celebration. Now that was an excellent notion, as was the picture in his mind of Athena growing large with child—his child—and bearing him an heir, or a tiny turquoise-eyed moppet.

The sooner Ian started on his fine new plan, the sooner he'd have that heir, and the delight of the begetting. He set down his glass of port, got to his feet, and begged the others' apologies. He left Carswell to entertain Rensdale while he went to bid Troy pleasant dreams, too. His own dreams were looking far rosier.

Carswell raised his glass—in commiseration or for luck, Ian did not know which—and Rensdale told him to get on with it, already, or Lady Rensdale was liable to descend on them all to see what was delaying the match and Rensdale's return.

That sent Ian up the stairs at a faster rate. He was still too late to catch Athena.

"She went to bed," Troy told him, sounding as suspicious as Spartacus. The dog was at his side on the bed, growling, too. Troy put his hand on the dog's collar, to keep her from launching an attack on Ian's shoes. "What did you say to upset her?"

"I did not say anything."

"Maybe that's what has her up in the boughs. I thought you would know better about how to turn a lady up sweet." Troy seemed disappointed in his hero, enough to let the dog loose.

Ian had a slice of chicken ready. While he wiped his hand on a towel he said, "I know more now than you will in your entire life, brat, so mind your manners. Besides, no man knows what goes on in a woman's mind. It's like quicksand. Stick to your Greek and Latin, for they are easier to master. Speaking of that"—and not Ian's marriage prospects—"I understand you are back to keeping pace with your studies."

Troy sighed and returned the horse book to the nightstand next to his bed. "Attie insists, even if Wiggy hasn't come by for a couple of days."

"She's right. Can't let your brain wither. Or your muscles. What say we go to Tattersall's tomorrow? I find that I need a new pair for my phaeton, and it would be good for you to get out. You seem healthy enough for a short excursion, and you must be bored to botheration stuck in this room. We can take blankets and hot bricks so your sister can't complain, and then stop at Gunter's for an ice, unless you'd prefer one of the coffeehouses. Or you could come to White's as my guest, and see what you have to look forward to in a few years."

Troy's smile faded, and he picked at the blanket with his hand, not meeting Ian's eyes.

"I cannot."

"What, afraid of what your sister will say? I'll talk to her. She has to stop keeping you wrapped in cotton wool or you will never get your strength back."

Troy looked down at his legs. "I . . . I cannot walk well enough."

"You've tried?"

"Oh, yes. Do you think I enjoy staying in bed?"

Ian could have kicked himself. "No, of course not. Jupiter, I did not mean to imply you were malingering. We'll wait until you are stronger."

"I am tired now," Troy said in a low voice. "I think I would like to go to sleep."

Ian left, knowing he would not sleep this night. All those sweet thoughts of an alluring bride and a comfortable marriage turned sour. He could taste the bitter bile of guilt, and nothing could destroy desire faster.

The boy might never be the same, thanks to him. How could Ian worry over which family ring best suited Athena, or how soon he could celebrate their wedding night, when he was responsible for maiming a youth, perhaps destroying a young man's life? Hell and damnation, if he sank any lower he'd be at the blasted dog's level. Unfortunately, unlike the dog, he thought he would always hear that doomed gunshot.

Morning had brought neither relief nor inspiration. It had brought Ian to the conclusion that he was a fool, a coward, and a craven for not bringing himself to the sticking point. Today he would do the necessary deed, perfect speech or not.

Breakfast time would be perfect, he decided. His mother never rose before noon, and his sister always took her morning chocolate and a sweet roll in her room, while she planned which peer to pester over her latest pet project. Ian believed she was going in the afternoon to visit one of the orphanages his family supported, with Carswell as escort, of all people. They had been arguing the issue of teaching street urchins to read, and Doro was determined to prove her point. Poor Carswell. If Ian could get this dreaded chore over with at breakfast, he thought, then he might enjoy the rest of his day. He needed a ride, a walk, a sparring match at Gentleman Jackson's. He did not need a visit to charity homes or a session of his sister's stridency. Perhaps Athena would like to go for a drive to celebrate—No, he had to get to Tattersall's first.

Resolved, his day and his life both planned, Ian had a cup of hot, dark coffee while he waited for Athena to come down.

"Miss Renslow has not broken her fast yet this morning, has she?" he asked Hull, as the butler carried in a tray.

Hull's nostrils flared in disapproval. "Since it has not gone seven yet, my lord, I do not expect to see the young lady for some time." He placed a pile of toast in front of the earl, arranging bowls of preserves, butter, and honey on the table. Then he removed a silver dome from another platter to reveal a mass of eggs for Ian's inspection.

"I thought it must be nine, at least," Ian said, shaking his head at the eggs. "I was, ah, hungry."

Hull looked at the unwanted eggs that Cook had hurried to make, hours before usual. "Yes, my lord." He placed the eggs on the sideboard and left to fetch a dish of kippers, also under a silver dome.

The earl turned that down, too. "The smell is turning my stomach."

Hull's next trip brought two covered dishes, one with kidneys, one with rashers of bacon. Ian sent both to the sideboard. One he rejected as too heavy; the other one was too greasy.

"Perhaps if your lordship would inform me for which item you are so hungry, the kitchens might not go into a frenzy of preparation. Kidneys? A sirloin?

Buttered rolls? Porridge? Ham?" If the butler's nostrils widened further, his sinuses might fall out. "Perhaps one of Lady Marden's digestive biscuits?"

Ian picked up a slice of toast in self-defense. Then he could not decide what to spread on it, so ate the bread plain. "Coffee, that's what I want. More coffee . . . and one of those silver dome things."

Hull moved the coffee pot closer to the earl. "You wish a plate cover for breakfast?"

"Yes, that is precisely what I want, and hurry, man, before Miss Renslow comes down."

The butler shook his head sadly. This whole marriage business had addled his lordship's wits. Soon the earl would be banging pots and pans together and marching around the dining room table. He would still be just as obliged to marry, of course. A plea of insanity might rescue a gentleman from the gibbet, but not from parson's noose.

Hull shortly presented the shining silver lid on a silver tray—surely one of the stranger requests he had fulfilled for his employer. So peculiar was the butler's errand that two footmen and the pastry cook crowded together just outside the dining room door to watch Lord Marden's next actions.

Ian set the silver dome next to a plate at his side, where Miss Renslow was used to sitting before the countess and Lady Dorothy had arrived. The plate was decorated with the Maddox coat of arms, which seemed fitting, to him. He removed the small velvet ring box from his pocket and placed it in the center of the plate, then placed the dome over it. One of the footmen sighed and the pastry cook wiped at her eyes. Hull scowled both of them back to their posts.

Oblivious to the witnesses, Ian scowled. He removed the dome, opened the ring box to show the large diamond surrounded by tiny emeralds, and replaced the cover on the plate. He took another bite of toast, staring at the dome. Then he removed it again, took the ring out of its box, set it so the diamond would face Athena when she raised the lid, and put the box back in his pocket.

Hull put the silver cover over the plate, giving it a swipe with a towel so it shone that much brighter. He moved the whole plate, ring, lid, and all, away from Lord Marden's reach. "Very good, my lord. Very good, indeed. Would you like your breakfast now, or shall you wait for the young lady?"

"I am famished. What do we have? Eggs sound good, and perhaps some bacon. Did you bring the kippers, too?"

Athena was not hungry, but she went down to the breakfast parlor anyway. She thought she could find the earl there, for the man always seemed to need sustenance for his large frame. She had spent most of the night rehearsing what she would say, once he had his say, so was as ready for the embarrassing conversation as she would ever be. Any longer wait would leave her stuttering and twitching, if she did not break out in a rash. Now she was calm and collected, with only a few butterflies in her stomach.

He was sitting at his ease, his coat left unbuttoned, his neckcloth a simple, loose knot. He was eating as if they had not had a meal in days, with enough food piled in front of him to feed the residents of that orphanage Lady Dorothy had mentioned last evening, for a week at least.

The sight of all that food plus the smells of fish and frying instantly turned the handful of butterflies in Athena's stomach into a herd of caterpillars, marching along on hundreds of heavy feet in her innards.

How could he be so hungry at a time like this? she

wondered. Most likely, Lord Marden could eat because the subject of marriage meant so little to him, she decided. Just another bit of estate business, some documents to sign, some words to speak, then his life would return to normal, while hers would be turned upside down. The horde of caterpillars were doing somersaults as he rose to greet her when she took another step farther into the room.

Athena hoped her voice did not waver too much as she bade him a good morning, while Hull seated her at the table, all too close to the earl's side.

Lord Marden went back to his breakfast as if his life depended on finishing every morsel. Athena pushed the covered plate at her setting away. "I'll just have tea," she told the butler.

Hull slid the plate back in front of her. "The kitchen went to extra effort this morning, miss."

She pushed it away again. "Perhaps later. I'll stop by and thank Cook myself. And share one of her raspberry tarts with Troy. No one makes them better, and they are his favorites, you know." Athena knew she was babbling but she could not stop herself, not when Lord Marden kept cutting and lifting his fork and chewing and staring at his plate as if it were a better breakfast companion than she was.

Hull brought her a cup of tea, and sighed. "Will that be all, then, miss?"

"Yes, thank you."

"My lord?"

"Unless you have some hemlock handy."

Athena glanced at the earl, but he ignored her, simply waving the butler out of the room.

"And do close the door behind you," he said, putting down his fork with seeming regret. He stared at her, making Athena wonder if her hair was coming undone again. Then he stared at the lidded dish Hull had been urging her to sample. He took a deep breath and said, "Open it."

"But I am not—"

"Just open it."

Athena took the cover off. "Oh." The ring was exquisite, the largest diamond she had seen since viewing the royal jewels in the Tower. She reached out one finger and gingerly touched it, turning the stone to catch the morning light through the window. "Oh, my." Then she pulled her finger back and clenched her fingers in her lap, over her roiling stomach. This could only mean one thing. A gentleman did not offer a lady baubles over breakfast unless his intentions were honorable. She dragged her eyes away from the beautiful ring and looked over at Lord Marden, who was watching her like a hawk watched a mouse. "Oh," she repeated. "I was afraid of this."

Chapter Seventeen

In a marriage, love is the frosting on the cake.
—Anonymous

In a marriage, love is the meat and potatoes, the bread and butter, plus dessert.
—Mrs. Anonymous

"Spiders and snakes, I might understand, but you are afraid of diamonds? Or is it rings you fear? Devilish things, I know, like manacles, or a hoop through one's nose."

"Do not be silly." Athena put the lid back on the ring's plate and pushed it in his direction. "We both know what this is."

"A very fine diamond that has been in the family for centuries, but I could purchase a modern ring if you wish. You seem fond of pearls."

"This is not a time for levity, my lord. The ring is simply a symbol."

"A symbol representing my affection? A pledge to look after you and your brother? A promise that you will never want for anything?"

"It is a proposal of marriage."

"Not a very effective one, it seems. I suppose I

should kneel on bended knee. The dog has not been in here, has she?"

Athena ignored his efforts to distract her. She pushed the ring and its plate farther away, as if their sight or smell was offensive. "The ring is a proposal I was afraid you would make."

"Ah, and I was beginning to worry that it was me you feared."

"I feared that your sense of duty would press you to ask for my hand."

"It did, of course."

"I will refuse, of course."

Ian was relieved at first, until he decided that he ought to be offended. "Since the proposal was unspoken, I suppose I cannot complain about your style of rejection, but I did understand that a gentlewoman was taught to thank a gentleman, to claim his offer as an honor."

"Very well, thank you. I am honored. Now your honor is satisfied. Is that enough?"

"Not quite. You said you would refuse, of course. I see no *of course* about it. A rational female would at least consider the offer carefully, for longer than one blink of an eye, especially when she has no other options."

"But I do have other choices."

"Wiggy? I believe he has taken up with Lady Paige. I suppose he thinks that her connections can find him a profitable parish. Either that or he intends to live off her money, the same as he was planning on living off yours."

"Mr. Wiggs . . . and Lady Paige?"

"I have seen stranger couples."

"Yes, like a green as grass country girl and a polished London gentleman."

Ian had retrieved the ring and turned it this way

and that to see the glimmers of light the stone cast. "There is nothing wrong with such a match. A man does not necessarily want a woman of experience for a wife."

"Can you honestly tell me that you have always wanted a rustic female with no style as your bride?"

"I can honestly swear to you that I have never considered brides at all, except to avoid them."

"You see? You do not wish to marry."

He held up the ring. "And yet, I have made the offer. Besides, style can be acquired. Character cannot. Only a fool marries for a pretty face."

Athena was silent, digesting that.

"Not that yours is not a pretty face," he quickly added. "But you have a great deal more to offer. Any man, be he duke or drayman, would be proud to call you his wife."

Athena blushed at the compliment, but she stayed quiet, as if expecting more.

Ian cleared his throat. More? All through the night, he had gone over the speeches that were not good enough. They sounded worse this morning. He supposed a woman deserved a better proposal than a diamond on a dish—or at least a better reason to wed where she was not inclined.

"I admire your sense of duty," he began, "which I believe will make you an estimable countess. You rub along well with my mother, which is no small accomplishment, and my employees adore you, which is a better testimony to a person's character. I have come to believe that we shall suit very well. We already seem to have an understanding, with interests in common."

"But you would not have offered for me if you did not feel obliged."

"I would not have met you if your brother was not

under my roof, no. But I do have to take a bride, as my mother keeps reminding me. My cousin Nigel is not an acceptable heir to the earldom. Featherbrained, he is, more interested in bird-watching than running an estate. And his sons are unmannered brats."

Athena was well aware that the first duty of a titled gentleman was to continue his dynasty. Hadn't her own father taken a young second wife to ensure his succession? "You would have chosen a woman from your own social circle, when you decided to start your nursery."

"Where else to look for a bride? Seven Dials? I would have picked a young lady from those presented to me, yes. But what is wrong with that? If you were in town, under your uncle's roof, who knows but that we might have met."

"Uncle has no *ton* connections."

"No matter. Your birth is better than that of half of the females who have their noses in the air at Almack's. Your father was a viscount, for heaven's sake."

"But my mother was merely of the gentry. And I have no lands or vast dowry to bring to a marriage."

"What do I need with more lands or money? Men like Wiggs have to consider such matters when taking a wife. I am fortunate to be able to choose for myself."

"But that is the point. You did not choose for yourself."

No, he did not. Ian had no answer. Athena pushed her chair back. "I will not accept a proposal made out of duty, my lord. I have honor, too."

Which was one of the things Ian liked best about Miss Renslow. She was no flibbertigibbet female only interested in her own best interests. The problem was, she did not know her own best interests. He did.

"What will you do?" he asked. "Go home with your

brother to become unpaid nursemaid to your new niece or nephew?"

She shuddered. "No, I shall not do that, even if my sister-in-law were to permit me to go home."

"Then what? Will you accept Wiggy's offer, if your brother can raise the ante enough to overcome your sojourn under my tainted roof? You do not even like the man. At least you do not run away from my presence."

"I had already decided not to wed Mr. Wiggs."

"Then what? No one will hire you, you know."

"I can keep house for my uncle."

"Who is a naval officer, in time of war. What if he does not return? Have you thought of that?"

"I pray for him every night."

"And that is sure to see him home safely."

"I could go live with your sister. She invited me."

"To be what, a permanent guest? What if Doro marries? She still might. Odder things have happened. And would you like being her companion, trekking across the country to visit coal mines and textile mills?"

"I could be doing something useful, the way your sister is. That ought to be satisfying."

"Cold water is satisfying, but you would not want to drink it every day for the rest of your life. Dash it, Attie, think! You do *not* have any other practical choice, none that I can accept."

"It is not for you to accept or reject, my lord."

"For heaven's sake, could you not 'my lord' me to death? I have just issued my first proposal of marriage—well, I put it on a platter, anyway—and I think I deserve to be on a more familiar footing. Ian. Call me Ian, deuce take it."

She nodded, with a slight lift of her lips. "Ian, who just proved what a tyrant of a husband he would be."

He slammed his fist onto the table top. "I would

not be!" Then he had to get up to retrieve the ring that had rolled off the table. While he was up he pulled his chair closer to hers, sat and took her hand. He liked how it felt in his clasp. "Miss Renslow, Athena, dear Attie, I would be a good husband, I promise. I would respect you, respect your wishes, let you go your own way as long as you were safe from harm. I would not insist on living in London year round if you prefer the country, and I would not force you to attend the tedious social rounds if you chose to live a quieter life. I promise you shall never be in want or in fear, not even from my foolish temper."

He brought her hand to his mouth and kissed her fingers. She did not pull away, so he continued: "Everything I have will be yours. You will have all the money you want, even if you spent it on . . . The devil, I do not know what you would spend my blunt on. Clothes, furs, jewels, carriages?"

"Books. I like books."

"I have an entire library of them, but I would build you another if that is what you want."

"And charities. I have always wanted to do more for the needy."

"I support schools and orphanages and homes for veterans that you can manage to your heart's content. Doro and Carswell are going to visit the orphanage this afternoon, and you can go with them to see how it can be improved. No, better not go with them or you will be refereeing all afternoon. I'll take you myself."

"I would like that, but—"

"But it will not change your mind about marrying me. Dash it, I am not such a bad bargain. Young ladies are constantly spraining their ankles outside my door, or swooning into my arms in overheated ballrooms. Everyone has always said I could have any woman I want."

"But you do not want me."

Now he leaned over and brought his lips to hers. He raised his hand to gently cup her cheek and kissed her softly, warmly, tasting the sweetness of her mouth. She responded as eagerly as he could have hoped, pressing closer, making tiny mews of pleasure.

"I want you," he said, when he needed to breathe.

Athena could not speak. Her lips were too tingled to talk, and her mind was muzzy with shock. Heavens, of course his lordship—Ian—could have any woman he wanted. One kiss and they would fall at his feet like flies in a frost storm. Athena was glad she was sitting, or she would have collapsed to the floor. No, she would have thrown herself into the earl's arms, like all those other betwattled belles.

Ian took a steadying breath, stunned by the desire that had blossomed with so little urging, like a wild-flower springing up after a shower. Lud, if one kiss could bloom like that, he could barely imagine the bouquet of delights marriage would bring.

"I promise we will be happy together," he told her.

"Can you promise to love me forever?"

He sat back, letting go of the hand he still held. "No one can promise that. I do believe that love will grow in time, especially with such a promising start."

"What about Lady Paige?"

"She is nothing. Gone, forgotten. Never to be a problem again, I promise."

Athena's hand felt cold now, without his fingers' touch. "What about others like her?" she asked. "Would you promise to be faithful, forevermore? Honestly?"

Ian picked up the ring again, looking for answers in

the diamond's depths. "I would try. I have every intention of honoring my wedding vows."

"That is not good enough. What if I merely said I would try to remain true to our marriage?"

Good grief, he'd have to kill her lover, despite his vow never to fight a duel again. "It is not the same."

"It is to me."

"No, Attie, think of the children that could come from such an affair. I would have to claim them as mine, even if one of your sons turned out to be my heir. That is intolerable. Every other wife understands and accepts this."

"Perhaps they do not care if their husbands stray. I would. Perhaps they do not care for their husbands at all, having made a convenient match without their affections being involved. I would care. It is no secret that I . . . admire you. Think then how I would feel, knowing that you were sharing your attentions with another woman, perhaps many other women, women who were not your wife, not me. I am horrified at the notion now, so imagine what I would feel once we were, ah, intimate. I think I would rather starve in the gutter than suffer that."

"So you would refuse me for crimes that I might commit in the future?"

"And for your past. You do not want to wed now, and you only asked me because it is the right thing to do, so why should you hold true to coerced vows?"

"Some men do." Not many that he knew of, but some, he was sure.

"When they love their wives."

There was that word again. Ian had been hoping Athena was too levelheaded to want flowers and poetry and all the folderol—like love—that went with courtship. "Love can grow, deuce take it."

"And it can die from neglect."

"Again, you are borrowing trouble. You cannot know what will happen in the future. No one can. I have seen marriages founded on nothing but love that go sour after a month. I have seen arranged matches turn into joyous unions, I have seen couples who swear they love each other, as long as they do not have to live together. I do not think anyone knows what makes a good marriage, any more than you know how you will feel in ten years." He reached for her hand again and pressed the ring into her palm, closing her fingers around it. "I do know that you were meant to wed, to have babies, not to live alone for the rest of your life as a disgraced spinster."

Athena let her hand stay closed, in his much larger hand, around his treasured heirloom. Everything he said made so much sense that she was swayed to consider his offer, to gamble that he might love her one day, to hope that, if she worked very hard at it, he might be content enough to be faithful. She was tempted by his words and his reasoning, and his wanting to convince her.

"You really wish to marry me?"

"I cannot be happy otherwise," Ian said, and meant it. He could never be at peace with himself if he let her go off alone. He would have ruined two lives then, not just the boy's.

"And you honestly think we will be happy together?"

"Why not? I like you, and you said you like me. You liked the kiss we shared, didn't you?"

If she'd liked it any better, Athena would have begged Ian to marry her, or take her on as a replacement for Lady Paige, or make love to her right here, sharing kisses amid the kippers, and caresses over the coffee cups. Now *that* would have been a disgrace! "Did you like it?"

He laughed. "I cannot tell you how much. In fact, I enjoyed that kiss enough to want more, and often. Let me show you."

This time the kiss was longer, deeper, more intense without being frightening, unless one counted being frightened of the butler's return. Athena forgot even that, transported by a heated excitement she had never known before. If this was why sinners roasted in hell, she was already burnt. She was alive and hungry and wanting more.

Ian opened his mouth on hers and urged her lips to part. His tongue met hers, tentatively at first, it seemed to her, giving her the chance to savor yet another new experience. When she did not pull away— or bite his tongue, she supposed—he brushed it against her teeth, her lips, while his hand—Good grief, he could do two things at once, when Athena could not even breathe and kiss at the same time, much less think. His hand was stroking her back, her arm, her neck, as if he wanted to touch every part of her. Her every part was straining forward, eager to join the celebration that was Ian's kiss.

Then his tongue pressed forward and back in a stirring rhythm recognizable to even the most innocent of misses, and his fingers touched her breast, where no man had ever dared. Athena grasped his head to pull him closer still. She needed more.

He needed a napkin to blot the blood on his cheek from the ring that had still been in her hand.

"Oh, I am so sorry!" she cried, dipping her handkerchief in the hot water not yet made into tea.

"I am not," Ian said, while he dabbed at his cheek. "Not in the least. You see, we do suit, in everything that matters. If I were not a gentleman, I would show you how much I enjoy kissing you and holding you and—Well, I am a gentleman, so that will wait until after the wedding."

Athena was sorely tempted, but not entirely lost to reason. She could not kiss his wound to make it better. She could not comb her fingers through his hair to set it to rights. She could not rub against him like a cat. She could not wed a man who was such a proficient seducer.

She set the ring back on the table and rose to leave the room before she was truly ruined, with her own cooperation. "I will consider your magnificent ring, your self-sacrificing offer, and all your promises, as well as the promises you could not make. But I will not decide until my uncle returns and I get to speak to him. He might have other plans for my future. Is that all right?"

"That is absurd, to think your seafaring uncle might have a better offer for you, one you never heard of. I cannot think you would wed a stranger over a man you already know, but I can accept the wait, if I must. Except for one thing," Ian added as Athena opened the breakfast room door. "You are wrong. Marriage to you would be no sacrifice."

Chapter Eighteen

Marriage is making love to the same woman for the rest of your life.

—Anonymous

Marriage is loving the same man for the rest of your life.

—Mrs. Anonymous

Ian stayed in the breakfast parlor for a while, not because he was still hungry, but because he was wondering what had just happened. He'd kissed Attie Renslow, twice. Good grief, he'd come close to tupping the mother of his future children between the toast and the teapot! If she had not held that ring, those scions might have arrived before he'd convinced the deuced woman to put the deuced diamond on her deuced finger. Damnation! The turquoise-eyed female had turned him into a rutting stag—something no other woman had accomplished since he'd turned eighteen. He did not like it. And he could not wait for it to happen again.

The butler came in with a fresh pot of coffee, saw the ring on the table, shook his head and left, taking the pot with him. Breakfast was over.

Ian tucked Athena's lace-edged handkerchief into his inside pocket, next to his heart. Then he took it out. The blasted thing was wet and blood-specked, and he was no moonstruck swain. He'd see that the scrap of linen was laundered and returned to Miss Renslow . . . tomorrow or the next day, when it no longer smelled of her.

He put the ring back in its box in his pocket before leaving the breakfast room. On his way up the stairs, he considered if he should find a different ring for his next proposal. Athena liked pearls. He'd have to see what else was in the vault. Or maybe he should buy a new one, with no history to it, for a fresh start.

His valet, affixing a sticking plaster to the cut on the earl's cheek, clucked his tongue, but he straightened his master's neckcloth with a smile. He had not sent the earl off this morning smelling of flowers. Now his lordship smelled of April and May.

It was Lord Marden's mother, though, who had the unkindest cut of all. Out of bed hours early, she was eager for news. Warned by her dresser, who had it from the upstairs maid, who heard from a footman, who had been in the kitchens when Cook started throwing pots and pans on the floor, she knew her son had broken his fast with Miss Renslow. Now he had broken skin.

"What did you do, frighten the girl into defending herself with a fork? I knew you would make a mull out of it, you chowderheaded clunch. Your father made a very pretty speech when he proposed, on his knees, of course. He did not attack me like a barbarian claiming his bride."

"I did not attack Miss Renslow. This"—he raised his hand to his cheek—"was an accident. A shaving accident."

"That is still bleeding hours later? Hah! Besides, I heard you were in perfect form this morning. The household thought you would do."

"Well, I did not. Miss Renslow turned me down."

"What? Are her attics to let, too? I thought the gal had something in her brainbox besides feathers and fluff, but perhaps she is not suitable to be your countess, after all. I should not want grandchildren who do not know their arses from their elbows. Pardon my language, but I am grievously disappointed in the chit. What could she be thinking, to refuse a rich man with a fine title?"

Ian did not tell his mother that Athena had been thinking of Lady Paige.

His mother had not really expected an answer, anyway. "Now that I think of it, you are better out of the match. Of course we shall have to find you a more suitable bride in a hurry, to still the wagging tongues. It is a good thing I am already in town to begin asking my friends for likely candidates."

Ian hurried to say, "Miss Renslow has agreed to consider my suit."

The countess sniffed. "I suppose that is something in her favor. Perhaps she is simply playing coy. Some chits do, you know, thinking they should not accept the first offer a man makes, lest he think they are too easy to please. Makes a man more eager, they feel."

Ian was as eager as a confirmed bachelor could be. "Miss Renslow is not coy, nor putting on airs. She wishes to consult her uncle."

"A man she has not seen in years? No, you went about it wrong, that's all. I knew you should have let me handle it. Woman to woman, we could have had the matter settled in minutes. I always said marriages were better left to lawyers and in-laws. Who knows better than older, wiser heads?"

"Who, indeed?" Ian echoed. "The prospective bride and groom cannot be expected to know what is best for themselves, can they?"

"Do not be sarcastic, Ian. It is not becoming. Besides, it is not as if this is a love match. The girl needs a husband, you need a wife. What could be simpler?"

Aristotle's metaphysics, for one.

Troy did not look at Athena's face. He looked at her hands, searching for a ring. When he did not see one, his welcoming smile faded, and he went back to his Latin translations. A fellow could learn a lot from the love poems of Catullus. Maybe he could give Lord Marden a few hints.

"I suppose I am to wish you congratulations." Lady Dorothy kissed Athena's cheek when they passed in the hall. "I cannot be more happy in my brother's choice of bride and am delighted to welcome you to the family."

"But . . . but I have not accepted your brother's noble offer."

"Gads, you really turned him down?" Lady Dorothy had to sit down on one of the chairs against the wall, despite her long list of errands. She was out and about early this morning, headed for the shops. She thought she might purchase a new bonnet for her ride in the afternoon with her brother's friend Carswell. He was such a handsome buck, elegant to a fault, that she felt dowdy next to him. They might merely be going to visit the orphanage, but she would not want such a fashionable gentleman to be ashamed of his passenger if they drove through the park to get there. Bad enough her skin was so marked; she could at least dress in style. Perhaps she would find a new parasol to match her favorite lilac gown she wore, or a Kashmir shawl.

While she was out, she just might stop in at the shop of a chemist her maid knew who specialized in cosmetics. He and his wife were experts in face paint for the theater and for masquerades and for women who could not accept the passing years.

In the ordinary way of things, Lady Dorothy did not try to cover up her ugly pox scars. She was who she was, and that was that. She had long since accepted the hand that fate had dealt her, and was content. Her pride was in her accomplishments, not in her face. She was on this earth to improve the conditions of the less fortunate, not to fill the coffers of storekeepers in trying to improve her own appearance. Lady Dorothy had stopped chasing futile dreams ages ago, and had vowed never to turn into an indolent, vain, self-centered woman like her mother.

But Mr. Carswell was who he was, too, a useless, frippery fellow—who was also intelligent company, a joy to argue with, and as good looking as the devil himself. What could be the harm in spending a handful of coins—she had far more than any woman needed, even after her charitable donations—on bettering her looks, so he might not be seen with such an antidote?

Dorothy could see nothing wrong with her plan. But she saw a great deal wrong with her would-be sister-in-law, now that she was sitting down, looking up at Athena. Miss Renslow had spots of color on her cheeks, swollen lips, and a dazed look. "It will not do. You cannot have it both ways, you know."

Athena barely knew her name. "Both . . . ?"

"You cannot let him kiss you without marrying him. My brother is a practiced seducer, I am sorry to say, but if you are not going to wear his ring, you must not wear that well-kissed look."

"I did not . . . that is, he did not . . ."

"Do you think I do not recognize the signs? Where

do all those orphans come from, then, if not from such illicit trysts? I do know what goes on between a man and a woman, despite my spinster status, and I am telling you, it will not do. With your upbringing, your conscience will bother you, for one thing, and your family will be ashamed, for another. You would not be welcome in any respectable house, and might be forbidden your brother's company. Worst of all, you will too quickly realize how soon the pleasure of being a rich man's ladybird flies away. Your protector will find a new interest and you will have to find another man, then another and another, until your looks are gone and none want you. Trust me, my dear Miss Renslow, the courtesan's life is not an easy one. I see too many former mistresses at the women's homes and hospitals."

"I am not a courtesan!"

"Then what do you call a woman who gives her favors without giving her hand, who shares a man's passions without sharing his name?" She waved her hand at the expanse of Maddox House. "A woman who repays a gentleman's generosity with her body, but not her bridal vows? What do you call that?"

Athena called it confused.

She went into her bedroom and dismissed her disappointed maid. She went to the window overlooking the gardens of Maddox House and tried to make sense of the turmoil she felt. Lady Dorothy was wrong. She was no light skirt, succumbing to a practiced flirt. She was a woman making a careful choice of her life's partner. No female should purchase a pig in a poke. Why, what if she found her suitor's kisses repulsive? Wouldn't it be better to know that before she accepted his proposal than after, when it was too late?

Hah! Who was she fooling, Athena asked herself. She adored Lord Marden's—Ian's—kisses. She was more than halfway in love with the man, anyway, and reveled in the passion he'd so effortlessly aroused. He was not unaffected, either, she knew. He'd been breathing just as hard, and his hand had been shaking when he held her dampened handkerchief to his cheek. So many sparks had flown between them, in fact, that Athena was surprised the breakfast parlor had not caught on fire. But was that good, as Ian seemed to think, boding well for a marriage of convenience, or bad, leading her to worse heartbreak?

Heavens, how was a girl to decide, with her head or her heart . . . or her instincts? Her heart wanted her to jump into his arms, into his bed, into the marriage. Her head told her wedding the earl was her wisest course. But her sense of self-preservation—that instinct that would not let her leap into unknown waters—was warning her that she would be in over her head, that she'd surely drown, reminding her that she had never learned to swim.

Ian was right, that her uncle could not have an answer to her dilemma, but Uncle Barnaby, or his absence, was a good excuse to delay her decision. Her reputation could not be ruined worse, not with his mother and sister in the house, and the rest of the gossip could be ignored, so there was no hurry. She needed time . . . to learn how to tread water.

Rensdale was angry, and let his half-sister know it in no uncertain terms. He was in a hurry to get home to his flocks and his fields, less so to his newly fecund wife. He berated Athena for being a dunderhead, a disgrace to the family name, and a drain on his purse. So what if she had only known the earl for less than a month? He was a gentleman, wasn't he? He was rich, wasn't he? What else mattered?

Troy tried to defend his sister, saying she was think-

ing about accepting Lord Marden, and it was her decision, after all. Not in Rensdale's book, it wasn't.
Marden was willing to take the cub along with the
chit, which suited Spartacus to a cow's thumb. He'd
be stuck with the boy otherwise, a sickly runt who
could not help on the estate, could not be shipped off
to the army or the clergy, and could only grow more
expensive to keep with his ailments and illnesses.

Rensdale's life would be a great deal easier without
both of his late father's progeny. His wife was jealous
of Athena, ashamed of Troy, and disdainful of Spartacus for keeping them around. If Lady Rensdale had
her way, Athena would be wed to Wiggs and the boy
sent off to an institution. His life would be hell if he
dragged them both home, one in worse condition than
when he left, the other a social outcast.

Rensdale huffed off to his hotel, muttering about
having a weakling for a brother and a wantwit for a
sister. He was ready to console himself with a fine
bottle of brandy and a fine-looking upstairs maid. No,
he did not want to see any wretched orphans. Attie
and Troy were enough. Let the others fend for themselves, was his opinion.

The rest of them—except Troy, of course—went to
the orphanage in the afternoon, even Lady Marden.
Despite her indolence and ailments, the countess did
take an interest in her children's philanthropy. More,
she wanted to decide for herself if Miss Renslow was
worthy of her son. If so, Lady Marden would put a
flea in the girl's ear about duty and destiny and the
value of a hefty bank balance.

She carried a lavender-soaked cloth over her nose
to avoid contagion, and stayed in the matron's office,
to avoid the orphans.

Lady Dorothy led the tour of the children's home,
with particular care to show Carswell the classrooms,

and then the records to show how many former charges had been apprenticed as clerks and shopkeepers and assistants. A few of the girls who could read had gone into service as governesses and two were acting as secretaries to ladies of letters. Literacy did not give the children grandiose notions above their humble stations, she declared to Mr. Carswell. It gave them opportunities to rise above those dismal beginnings. Learning to read gave them hope, she told him, which every child deserved.

Carswell had to admit that the orphans he saw here were a much cheerier group than the homeless urchins he saw on the street. But these had full bellies and a place to sleep at night other than the gutters. That was why they could laugh and play, not because their heads were full of useless learning.

"Useless? I'd wager the ability to read is more valuable to these waifs than it is to you. What do you read? The racing forms, your tailor's bills, the gossip columns?"

"And the occasional *billet-doux*. I was teasing, Lady Dorothy, to see your reaction. This home should be a model for all such institutions, and you and your brother are to be congratulated for such forward thinking." He tipped his hat in her direction. "And while I am singing your praises, may I say how delightful you look today?"

Dorothy had on so much paint and powder that she did not have to fret about Carswell seeing her blushes. His appearance still put them all in the shade, of course, but Dorothy was pleased she had taken the time—all morning, it turned out—to get fancified, as her maid said. Even her mother had something nice to say, if one considered "about time" to be a compliment. From the countess, it would have to do.

Doro felt better yet when Carswell took out his

quizzing glass and examined her more closely. "Yes, delightful, and not because of that fetching bonnet or the charming gown you wear. And no, not because of that hint of color so artfully applied to your cheeks, either."

A hint? Lady Dorothy's maid had emptied the chemist's shop, but Dorothy was not about to mention that, not when the most elegant gentleman in London was being so diplomatic, and so . . . so . . . Not kind, for Carswell did not have to say pretty things to his friend's sister. He was being honest, by George. He truly did find her delightful.

"That's it," he finally concluded. "That glow. Merely pretty chits can't hold a candle to your inner beauty when you let it shine out. Good works become you, Lady Dorothy. I can see where I shall have to follow you about to workhouses and insane asylums, to protect you from the inmates—and their keepers, their brothers, and every other gentleman who passes by."

No man had made improper attention to Lady Dorothy in her entire life, but she would not mention that, either. "I am quite capable of seeing to my own safety, you know. I have been doing it this past decade, and my servants are strong and capable."

"Yes, but I would feel better acting as your escort whilst you are in town. Do you object?"

Did the flowers resent the sun shining on them?

Athena was beginning to think that her brother was right. She truly was the stupidest female in all of London, maybe in all of England. Not only was Lord Marden titled and wealthy, handsome and intelligent, strong and well mannered, generous and kind, but he was genuinely nice. And he kissed like a dream.

And she had turned him down over a few silly scruples. The fact that he was honor-bound to offer for her still bothered, and the fact that he was a gazetted rake still rankled but, goodness, no one was perfect. His sister was lovely despite her imperfect complexion, and her own brother was no less dear for being sickly. Her other half-brother had a limp, and his wife was a shrew. She herself was hopelessly short. No one was perfect.

Ian was as close to perfect as a man could get.

He knew half the orphans by name, and all of the matrons and schoolteachers. He did not merely send a check to the home; he came in person to ensure that his money was being spent properly. When he saw a need, he filled it, like now, when he distributed a large sack of horehound drops to children who rarely had a treat. Other men of her acquaintance had to be bludgeoned into making charitable contributions, much less getting sticky at the same time. Yet here was Ian, a lump of candy in his cheek and a tiny girl in his arms. He was grinning at the orphans, seemingly happy amid the clamoring horde of them. He looked younger than his years, and looked at home holding a toddler. Athena could not imagine Spartacus holding an infant, nor could she picture Mr. Carswell, for one, laughing at the baby's drool on his coat sleeve. What a good father Ian would make.

And what a goose she was. She would tell him so tonight, accepting his offer without waiting for Uncle Barnaby's approval.

She felt a great deal better for the decision. Now she did not have to feel like a wanton, wanting more of his kisses, and what came after. What came after was a wedding night, and now she could look forward to it, wishing it were tomorrow. Her cheeks felt warm at the thought, at the wanting she had never felt before. She wanted to see what he looked like without his clothes on, and she could not wait to touch his skin, to feel the muscles she knew he possessed. Was his chest hairy, and how would that feel against her own bare breasts? Oh, my. She could feel her nipples tighten at the very idea, and pulled her shawl tighter, so no one would notice. She'd say she was cold, that was all, even though Lady Marden was fanning herself and Lady Dorothy had removed her wrap.

Then Athena had to worry that her figure was not adequate, certainly not compared to Lady Paige's amplitude. She would be mortified if Ian found her lacking. Bad enough he was getting an inexperienced lover. He should at least get a well-endowed wife.

"Are you ill?" he asked, hearing her sigh. "Or tired? Do you wish to go home?"

She wished her bosom was bigger. She sighed again and said, "No, not at all. I promised to tell the older girls a story and I was wondering which tale to tell. Perhaps we could purchase some books for them, next time we come. I saw a great many improving works on the shelves, but nothing simply entertaining."

"You see? You are finding ways to spend my blunt already. I promised you all the books you wanted, didn't I? We shall strip bare the shelves of the nearest bookstore, all right?"

Strip? Bare? Athena blushed so red, Ian asked if she was certain she was not coming down with a fever. "No, no. Simply growing warm."

"I thought you were cold."

"I was then. Now I am not." She turned to speak to the head matron about which books to purchase, to avoid his probing glance.

While the woman was discussing the dangers of letting girls fill their heads with fairy tales and such, Athena went back to building her own fairy castles in the air, or in the bedroom, filled with flowers and candlelight. She could not improve her bust, but perhaps she could borrow some of Lady Dorothy's new face paint to make herself appear older, more alluring, like the sophisticated women he was used to. That way, he might not miss his mistresses.

Then one of the younger instructors came by with a message for the head matron. She was tall and pretty and had red hair, green eyes, a lush bosom, and long, thick eyelashes that she batted fiercely enough in Ian's direction to cause a draft. She curtsied and simpered a greeting, the jade, and held her hand out.

Ian put down the child he was holding, handed Athena the sticky bag of sweets, and took the female's hand. He brought it to his lips with a smile that belonged in the bedroom Athena had been daydreaming about.

It seemed he was not going to miss his mistresses.

Athena would wait for her uncle's return, after all.

Chapter Nineteen

To make a good marriage, be good lovers.
                              —Anonymous

To make a good marriage, be good friends.
                              —Mrs. Anonymous

Ian would never understand women. He knew better
than to try, but now that he was contemplating—
nay, now that he was keeping that special license close
at hand—he wished he could make sense of one of
them.

Athena had started out the afternoon all smiles. She
had admired his carriage team, delighted in the drive,
when he pointed out landmarks and such, and seemed
pleased with his compliments on her simple bonnet,
with its one turquoise feather, which matched her
eyes. She approved of the orphanage and its management, and of him by association. She'd promised Matron to come again to bring the books in person, and
she'd promised to help some of the older girls find
employment.

Then her smiles evaporated. Her mouth took on a
closed, set look, as if she had eaten a sour grape, and
she stopped looking over at him, stopped asking him
questions, stopped walking by his side. She walked

with his mother instead, chatting about the family's other charitable works.

On the way home, she did not seem pleased with her ice at Gunter's, either, merely commenting that she wished she could bring one back to Troy. Then, when they strolled through the park before going back to Maddox House, she turned to stone, it seemed. Carswell and Doro had driven ahead in Carswell's curricle to try out the paces of his new—Ian's old—pair of bays. There would be a fight over who held the reins, unless the earl missed his guess, but that was not his concern. Athena's coolness was.

His mother told the driver to stop so often to greet old friends that Ian asked if Athena would like to get down for a walk. His mother almost shoved her out of the carriage, so she had no chance to refuse—or she might have, he thought.

It was not his fault that every female in the *ton* wanted to meet the young lady who was to become Countess of Marden one day. Her presence with him, with his mother close by, made her the odds-on favorite for the position. If she wished, his wife could be a leading light of society, with influence and opportunities at her fingertips. No one wanted to slight her now, so the ladies kept stopping them along the path, fawning at his sleeve for an introduction.

Athena was everything polite and well-bred, as he knew she would be, but she grew cooler and cooler toward him with every pause to present her to this patroness of Almack's, that political hostess, two young matrons who were starting a charitable fundraising circle, and one not-so-young widow, who invited them to a dinner she was hosting for some military friends of her late husband's.

The widow might have stood too close to Ian, and

she might have directed her invitation to him, but she had definitely included his mother and sister and Miss Renslow in the invite. That blown kiss when she walked off was a mere affectation, Ian knew. Did Athena?

She could not be jealous, could she? he wondered. Hell, no. They were not even formally engaged, and he had not engaged in any flirtations, besides. She must be unused to meeting so many strangers, he decided. Perhaps she was shy.

"You'll get used to the crush," he reassured her. "And we do not have to stay in London all the year, although I will have to be in town for Parliament's sessions. But you should know these women, as tedious as it all seems now. They are the ones who will make your entree into Society easier."

"I do not think I wish to enter their environment," she replied through closed lips.

"I doubt you shall have much choice. My mother is determined to see you take your rightful place in the beau monde. That is why she is chatting with every dowager in the park—other than to share with them her latest ailment, of course. I'd wager that cards of invitation will get to Maddox House before we do. You can argue with my mother about which to accept, but experience has taught me it is easier to agree than watch her go into a decline."

"But I—"

"No, you cannot claim your brother as an excuse to stay home. The boy is doing better, and he and the footman, Geoffrey, who attends him have become fast friends. Even that wretched dog has accepted the chap who walks her and takes her to the kitchens for supper. Geoffrey is teaching your brother how to swear and spit and play dice, I suppose, while Master Renslow is imparting his considerable knowledge of horses to the young man, who has aspirations of joining the stable crew."

"I see. Then I will be attending parties, willy-nilly? My life is out of my hands?"

"I would not have put it that way. But you will enjoy yourself, I promise."

"It seems to me you have been making a great many promises lately, my lord."

He noted the honorific, rather than the *Ian*. "But all for your—"

"While I have made none, except to wait for my uncle."

Any other female would have been pleased to find herself welcomed to the *ton*, to waltz and sip champagne, to go to five parties in a night. Any other female would have realized that, even if she retired to the country, her daughters—his daughters—would need these connections someday. Any other female would have smiled at him when he purchased a bouquet of violets from a street vendor for her. Not Athena Renslow.

Two hours ago she was as melting as honey, as warm as velvet, as willing a bride as Ian could hope for. Now she might have been carved out of cold, hard marble for all the friendliness he saw. She liked the orphans better than the beau monde, it seemed. And better than him.

Lud, he thought, the last thing he needed was a changeable bride with inexplicable moods and imagined complaints. A fellow had his mother for that.

No, he would never understand women.

He did far better with men.

Lord Rensdale was waiting at Maddox House when they returned home, in a pother. He did not have news of Athena's uncle, but he had had a letter from his wife. Lady Rensdale was not insisting he abandon his half-siblings and return to her side. Oh, no, she wanted a great deal more of him. Veronica wanted a new wardrobe, to be exact. Now that she was increasing, her clothes did not fit. The local seamstress was competent enough to make gowns that could be let out as the need arose, and Lady Rensdale would not be attending any truly fashionable functions, anyway, not in her condition. Rustic dressmaking could do, as long as she had the latest fashion plates from Paris and the finest quality yard goods from London, with bonnets and gloves and shoes and fans and shawls to match. Since her husband was in London anyway, he might as well make himself useful. Rather than devoting all his time to the unworthy brats he had inherited, he could be spending his time—and his brass—on the woman who was bearing—at no inconsiderable pain, discomfort, and nausea—his heir. Oh, and a few trinkets would not go amiss, she had written.

"What the deuce is a trinket?" Rensdale asked as he and Lord Marden retired to the library and the brandy.

"Jewels, man. Do not tell me you have been wed for all these years without learning that?"

"Devil take it, she has a box full of gold and gems from my mother, some older than time. Been in the family for generations. Besides, a man don't buy his wife baubles."

"He does if she is breeding," Ian told him. "Everyone knows women in her condition need special handling."

"Gads, what do I know about ladies' fashions?"

"Never fear, I know enough for both of us. Having a sister and a mother, of course." And a score of mistresses over the years whose bills he had paid, but that went unsaid. "What I don't know, Carswell will.

He has a good eye." Carswell's eyes had both better be on the bays and not on Doro, Ian thought, checking his watch for the time and wondering why the pair had not returned an hour ago. Carswell and his sister, not just the pair of bays, that was, although he worried about the horses, too. His friend was a dab-hand with a neckcloth, less proficient with the ribbons.

Rensdale was still in despair, and into his second glass of brandy. "But bonnets? Worse, she's making me go to a corset-maker."

"I think you can leave that up to my mother. There is nothing she likes better than shopping. My sister has also expressed an interest in expanding her wardrobe while she is in town—and in Carswell's company, I fear. Your sister will need additional gowns if she is to attend balls and the theater and such, so she can help, too."

"Gads, between them, Attie and my wife will bankrupt me."

Ian wound his watch. "Surely you are not suggesting that I pay for your half-sister's trousseau, are you?"

Rensdale choked on the too-large swallow he had taken. When he was done coughing, he gasped, "You said additional gowns, man, not an entire trousseau!"

"Isn't that what a bride buys, and doesn't her family pay for it?"

Rensdale mopped at his receding hairline. "Dash it, I thought her uncle would come down heavy for the bride clothes."

"But he is not here, and she needs new gowns now. I don't believe she has more than two for evening."

If Rensdale sensed the disapproval in Ian's tones, he disregarded it. "Well, I ain't buying the gal no 'trinkets.' "

"I would not think of letting you," Ian said. "That will be my pleasure. After we are wed, of course. It

would not do to shower her with jewels before, not
that she does not deserve them." Not even Rensdale
could be dense enough to miss the disdain. He chose
to scratch his protruding belly instead of looking at
Lord Marden.

"Your pleasure," Ian went on, "will be in seeing
Miss Renslow turned out as befits the sister of a gentleman, and in making your wife happy."

Rensdale brightened. "Veronica is a different
woman when she has a new bonnet to show off in the
neighborhood, the silly goose. They all are."

Ian drank to that.

"Do go, Attie. Spartacus owes you a new wardrobe
for all the years you helped keep the estate books and
looked after his tenants."

"I don't know, Troy. Why do I need so many new
gowns?"

"So you don't look like a dowd. No insult, of
course. I think you're the prettiest girl in the world—"

"Prettier than Squire's niece?" she teased.

Troy blushed, but he was not going to be distracted.
He went on with his exercises, saying, "But there is
no denying you don't dress as fashionably as the other
women. Even I can see that. Why, Lord Marden's
sister looks better than you sometimes, and she's old
and can't hold a candle to you."

"Troy! You must not say such things. Lady Dorothy
cannot help her scars."

"What scars?"

"Nothing, dear. But I have not had any use for the
latest styles, and do not know if I will in the future."

"Of course you will. Geoffrey says there's a pile of
invitations on the hall tray with your name on them
already. You can't go to all those fancy balls in the
same two gowns you've worn to all the assemblies

back home. People would say Rensdale is a skinflint, keeping you in rags. Well, he is, but the rest of the world doesn't need to know that. They'll say you have no taste, and you do, don't you, when you get the chance?"

"I like to think so."

"Besides, Marden might be embarrassed to be seen with you in your old frocks. He's used to regular dashers, Geoffrey says, prime articles."

"Geoffrey says a great deal too much. I do not know if I wish to be considered another of his lordship's dalliances."

"Well, you won't be if you look frumpish or like a schoolgirl. They'll say he is only being nice to you because he has to. But if you look like a Diamond, then they'll say he's smitten by your beauty. He will be, too. I just know it."

"You wouldn't be trying a little matchmaking, would you?"

"Gads, no. But what would be wrong with that? Marden is top of the trees. You couldn't find a better man, not if your dowry were ten times what it is. And I like it here. He says I can stay. Spartacus says I can, too. If you do, that is."

Athena could not discuss her doubts with her little brother. "I agree that Lord Marden is a fine gentleman. And attending one or two balls might be fun, so I think I will have a new gown made up, at our brother's expense. I said I would help select fabrics and such for Veronica, so I'll be in the shops anyway."

"Pick her an ugly bonnet, won't you? You can say it's all the crack in London and she won't know the difference."

"That's mean and unworthy. What do you think of puce with orange feathers?"

"Perfect," Troy said, grinning. "Especially if you add one of those stuffed birds on top. Oh, and Attie?"

She turned in the doorway. "Yes, dear. Was there something I could bring you from the shops?"

"No, I have everything I could need. But when you order your new gowns, could you make that part on top, the part that covers your, ah, you know."

"The bodice?"

"That's it. Could you make that part lower? A fellow likes to look at a woman's, ah . . . that is, Lady Paige's were half out of her gown."

"We shall not discuss Lady Paige, or my, ah, attributes. And wherever did you learn about such things? If Geoffrey has been filling your ears with such, I will have a talk with that young man."

"No, Geoffrey never said anything. Lord Marden did."

Athena squeaked. "The earl talked about my—"

"Gads no, not to a lady's brother. Don't you know anything about gentlemen? He said something about Lady Paige, was all, but he did not have to. I noticed myself. That's what I am trying to tell you. We men notice such things."

" 'We men' don't shave yet, bucko, so mind your tongue. You can go back to rebuilding your muscles, not planning my wardrobe, because I expect to dance with you sometime soon. Meantime, Lady Marden will advise me on the proper depth of my décolletage."

The earl's mother would have seen the neckline on Athena's new gowns dropped almost to her waist if she thought that might encourage this cabbage-headed courtship. But no, that might encourage other men to take a second or third look at the petite beauty. That would never do, the countess decided. Her slowtop son had enough trouble without competition.

Instead, she helped Athena select styles that were suitable for a young lady, but not the virginal white of a girl making her come-out, and not as modest as a very young miss's. While selecting fabrics for Lady Rensdale, they found a turquoise silk in the exact shade of Athena's eyes, and a sprigged muslin with tiny turquoise flowers. Then there was the pale rose satin that made her skin look like porcelain, the primrose sarcenet that complemented her blond curls, and a coral-colored velvet to match her cameo brooch. Of course, she needed shoes and gloves and petticoats and pelisses to match, studies of the fashion books, and fittings. A lot of fittings.

Not so amazingly, considering the countess's clout and the earl's income, the dressmakers often came to Maddox House for the pinning and basting and repinning. Otherwise, Athena might have cancelled half the orders.

She stopped feeling guilty about spending so much of her brother's money when she added up the purchases for Lady Rensdale's wardrobe, which would likely be given to the maids when her sister-in-law's confinement was finished. As a sop to her conscience, Athena did purchase lengths of the softest lawn fabric, to sew into tiny gowns and bonnets for her new niece or nephew while she sat by Troy's bedside, and more books to read to him there—on Rensdale's credit, naturally.

She would not have ten minutes with her brother if Lady Marden had her way. For a near-invalid, the countess had more energy for shopping than Athena, her maid, and Lady Dorothy combined.

The earl's sister was content with a few new purchases, and went back to her visits to the orphanage and other less wholesome institutions for the needy. She was educating Mr. Carswell on the plight of those less fortunate, she said. He said he needed no such lessons, for his own income barely covered his tailor's bills, but he went with her, and then helped her write down her observations, so she could report to various committees about passing legislation to improve conditions. She thought he ought to stand for office in the Commons. He thought she ought to come dancing with him at Vauxhall Gardens. She thought he was a fribble; he thought she frowned too much. They were both learning.

Ian did not abandon the ladies. He escorted them to every shop in London, it seemed to Athena. She had never before received such service, such attention, such choice materials from which to select. She did not consider this entirely a blessing, based as it was on Marden's money and his prior patronage of the modistes. Every dressmaker knew him, and so did every lady coming to window shop or have a new gown fitted. In addition, some of his greeters did not appear to be ladies at all.

Every time the earl polished his courtly image with his kindness in escorting them everywhere—his gentle humoring of his mother, his careful consideration of Athena's opinions—another female came along to tarnish his armor. Lady Marden assured Miss Renslow that she was a damsel in distress, about to be savaged by the social wolves, but Athena did not wish to be rescued by any knight who spent every night with a different female. She was no closer to accepting his offer than she was to enjoying greetings from his former flirts.

What she was closer to, gloriously so, were fabrics so soft and smooth against her skin that she felt almost indecent, as if she could be one of Ian's ladybirds after all. Her new gowns required new undergarments too, and she bought the silkiest, laciest, most frivolous she

could find. For the first time in her life, Athena did
not choose her intimate apparel for warmth or practi-
cality, or how long they would last. She chose them
for the sheer pleasure, and for their sheerness.

Ian did not go into those shops with her and his
mother, of course. But he did whisper to her as she
went into a corsetiere or a hosier, "Buy something
naughty, Attie, in case I convince you to marry me
soon."

She ought not consider a man's response to her
shifts and stockings, she told herself, holding up a pink
gossamer negligee that might have been sewn for seduction. She tried her best not to imagine what his
lordship would think of her in it . . . and thought of
nothing else, of course. The more she told herself to
ignore his possible reactions, the more she thought of
his laughing mouth, his gleaming, knowing eyes, and
his strong, gentle hands. On it, on her. On the bed.
Taking his time to take it off her.

"I'll take it," she told the storekeeper. That purchase she paid for herself, from her own money. Her
older brother would have apoplexy, paying for a
barque of frailty's bedgown. Athena adored it. She
came out of the shop with a smile that would have
stirred a septuagenarian.

Ian was already having a grand time spending Rensdale's money. When Athena would order one day
gown, the earl instructed the seamstress to make up
two or three. While she and his mother were selecting
lace caps for Lady Rensdale, he was picking out the
perfect bonnet for Attie, a chip straw one with silk
daisies and a blue bow. Her piles of packages grew
behind her back, and above Rensdale's figuring.

The nipcheese deserved to be pinched where it hurt,
in his pocketbook. Athena kept telling his mother that
she had never been treated so well, had never worn

such fine fabrics, had never owned so many clothes at one time. Well, she ought to have. She ought to have been treated like a princess, not a poor relation.

Rensdale complained when the bills started coming in, saying that the chit would grow spoiled. So what? Ian could afford to keep her in all the silks and satins she wanted. Besides, he told Rensdale, his own sister had never been denied anything, and she was no spendthrift.

Lud, if Rensdale could see the smile Athena wore coming out of that last emporium, he'd consider every shilling well spent. Rensdale might also consider that the wedding take place sooner, rather than later. Ian felt his pulse race just thinking about what she might have bought in that lace-shrouded store.

Ian had another reason for encouraging Miss Renslow to spend her brother's blunt: he wanted her to get a taste of being well-off, of being wealthy enough to have anything one wanted, and two of some of them. He did not think of Athena as mercenary, and he never wanted to be wed for his money or his title alone, but he was not above using every ace in the deck.

He wanted to marry her. It was that simple, and that complicated. He did not know how or when it happened, but he definitely wanted to marry the little lady. Well, maybe not definitely. He definitely wanted to make love to her, though, and he knew he could not have one without the other. Even if his sister had not taken him to task, he could not dishonor the moral Miss Renslow. He liked her too well.

Nothing could stop him from having decidedly immoral thoughts of her, meanwhile. All those silks and velvets and frothy laces, all those stockings and petticoats and nightgowns she was buying—he could not wait to see her out of them.

Chapter Twenty

Ah, the chase.

—Anonymous

Oh, the choice.

—Mrs. Anonymous

Ian brought Athena flowers and he brought her little gifts, none going beyond the line of what was proper. She was touched by his thoughtfulness, she said, but was embarrassed when he gave her a handkerchief to replace the one ruined with his blood from the cut on his cheek. A fan, a filigree bouquet holder, a box of bonbons, all met with pleased smiles, but no greater enthusiasm. The cartload of books for the orphans earned him a shy peck on the cheek, but nothing more. His offer to carry her brother out to the garden to sit in the sun was most gladly received of all, but then it rained for two days.

He was getting no closer to winning her favor, and he could not understand why. He could tell she was aware of him because of how she pretended not to notice him. He caught her staring at his doeskin breeches, and if her glance lingered any longer, he might give her something to stare at, indeed. She al-

ways looked away in time, thank goodness, hopefully
unaware of how her interest affected him. Hell, her
presence in the room was beginning to affect him,
whether she looked at him or not. Knowing that she
might be his—no, that she would be his—made his
every sense stand to attention, some more awkwardly
than others. The scent of her was enough to warm his
blood and make it flow southward, leaving his brain
as empty as his arms.

She never hid from his company, yet she never
sought it, either. She had not mentioned seeking employment in ages—but she had not mentioned marriage, either.

Ian had never tried to worm his way into a woman's
affections before. He'd never had to. His past amours
had all come to him, eager for pleasure and a bauble
or two. The idea of trying to buy the affections of the
female he wanted to wed was abhorrent, especially
when he was restricted to pennies'-worth presents.
The notion of letting Athena stay indifferent to him
was equally as unacceptable. She liked him, by
George, and she would grow to like him more if it
killed him trying. So he followed her from shop to
shop, and spent time with her brothers, for that
seemed to win her favor. He even befriended the dog,
sacrificing the tassels on his boots to do so.

If only he could hold her—in the patterns of a
dance, of course—he could fan those sparks that flew
between them. If only he could slip out to a secluded
balcony with her, he could remind her of the kisses
they had shared. She was not ready to attend any
social functions, however. Her new clothes were not
completed, and she was not convinced that she should
be paraded about like a pet pony. According to his
sister, Athena knew what people were saying, and re-

fused to encourage strangers to believe them promised. Going out and about with his mother was enough. Going to balls on his arm was too much.

If he could not entice her to the Dark Walk at Vauxhall, he would take her to his own gardens behind the house, by Jupiter, by lanterns' light and moon's shine, but his mother and sister were suddenly proving to be strict chaperones. His sister warned about playing with fire, and his mother declared that a man might not buy what he could get for free, mortifying both Athena and Ian in one sentence. He was not trying to seduce the female, damn it. He just wanted to convince her how compatible they were, show the inexperienced lass what enjoyments lay ahead once they were married. He was quickly losing confidence in winning her over with his wealth, his title or his charm, but his lovemaking ought to do the trick.

Very well, he wanted to seduce her—but not for base motives, he tried to convince himself. His intentions were strictly honorable, if not strictly proper. He was growing more and more frustrated both in his mind and in his body, and deuced impatient with this delay. Where was her blasted uncle, anyway?

He had a man stationed at the Cameron Street residence, and another at the harbor, listening for word of the captain's ship. He had suborned a clerk at the Admiralty with a check, to get soonest notice of changes in the captain's orders. And he had paid a fortune to that makebate Macelmore to see that the officer called on Ian before he spoke to his niece, whenever he did arrive.

The groom Alfie Brown seemed to have disappeared, which was still troublesome to Ian. He had not gone to the authorities, had not come to Ian for silence money, and had not reported to Rensdale, who had been his actual employer. Why would the man keep quiet about a possible crime? That made no sense to Ian, or to Macelmore, but it did not matter much now, for Troy seemed to be out of danger. He was no longer restricted to invalid fare, and was no longer taking laudanum, to Ian's relief. The earl had enough on his plate without the youngster becoming addicted to the drug. Bad enough Troy could not get out of bed without that young manservant Geoffrey's assistance. They told Ian he was exercising, though, which he took for a hopeful sign.

That was the only one he had that week. A few smiles from his would-be bride, and a list of how many sit-ups young Renslow could do. Botheration!

Lord Rensdale was despondent, too. He saw his cash flowing from his bank account like a waterfall, all downhill. His wife's letters were growing more strident and more demanding. Now she wanted new furniture, because her back ached too much for any of the hundreds of chairs at Rensdale Hall. She needed footstools, too, matching ones, because her ankles were swelling.

What did Rensdale know about buying furniture? Lady Marden and his sister were too busy, filling Veronica's other shopping list to be of help. Rensdale would rather visit cabinetmakers than ladies' clothiers, Lord knew, but he should be out with his hounds, riding his fields. He should be at the local tavern, trading tales with the squire and his cronies, playing a hand or two of whist, not staying in some expensive hotel, gambling for the outrageous sums they wagered at White's, and losing.

"Then stop playing," Ian told him when he and Carswell met up with his prospective brother-in-law at the gentlemen's club. "Half the chaps here are inveterate gamesters, and the other half have more blunt than they know what to do with."

Having played with Rensdale, Carswell added, "And they have far more skill than you do, for the most part."

With his losses proof of Carswell's words, Athena's brother could not take umbrage. He could take another swallow of his drink, but not offense. "Lud knows the luck ain't with me, either. But what's a fellow to do, then? I've never been one for the theater, and if I never sleep through another opera that's too soon." He sighed and ordered the waiter to bring another bottle.

What did Rensdale have to complain about? Ian wondered. He had a wife who was carrying his son at last, he was sure, and he had escaped her talons for once. The man ought to be rejoicing. Ian, on the other hand, was holding court at White's, fending off questions about his matrimonial plans, instead of holding a sweet armful of Athena. He was breathing smoke instead of her intoxicating floral scent, and hearing Lord Preakhurst belch instead of hearing her endearingly off-key humming. No, Rensdale had nothing to complain about. Still, he was going to be part of Ian's family. As distant a connection as possible, true, but a relation for all that. Ian ought to see to the man's entertainment.

The problem was how. They could not go to the less respectable gambling dens, where Ian sometimes spent hours at games of skill or chance. If Rensdale lost at White's, chances were he'd lose his last shilling to the ivory tuners and card sharps at the Green Door or the Black Dog. Ian saw no reason to partner him . and toss his own blunt away.

He had not accepted any invitations to dinners or

parties this evening, not knowing his mother's, his sister's, or Athena's plans, so could not drag Rensdale along for a free meal. His mother was resting after yet another strenuous day of shopping. His sister had found a new treatise on the rights of workers at the lending library. Athena was sewing baby clothes for Rensdale to take home, when her brother finally left.

Ian and Carswell would be welcome at whatever social gathering was being held this night, no matter if they had accepted or not. They were single gentlemen of utmost eligibility, especially since one of them, Lord Marden, was thought to be looking for a bride. Ian would eat a live eel before entering a ballroom full of hopeful mamas and their hopelessly homely daughters.

There was no fun in going to Vauxhall, not without a dasher on one's arm to show off, and with whom to view the fireworks from some secluded glen. Rensdale had no interest in opera or theater, so Ian supposed the lecture at the Philosophical Society would hold no appeal. The circus at Astley's Amphitheatre was too childish—and Ian was waiting to take Troy there—and Sadler's Wells was too common—and Athena would adore the pantomimes. The museums and galleries were closed by now, although Ian could not imagine Rensdale enjoying an art exhibit. The sporting venues were also shut for the evening. Jackson's boxing parlor, Manton's Gallery, and the Italian Fencing Academy would all be locked tight. Ian refused to attend a cockfight, bearbaiting, or dog pit, so blood sports were out.

So was the sport of skirt-raising.

"What say we go to Sukey Johnstone's?" Carswell asked. "I hear she has a new crop of—ooph."

Ian had kicked him.

Carswell brushed at his trouser leg. "I say, there

was no need for that, Marden. Oh, wouldn't want your bride's brother tattling? I see."

Rensdale had started on a description of his own crops, mangel-wurzels or some such, before realizing that was not the kind of bounty Carswell was proposing. He sat up, more interested than he'd been at the mention of boxing matches or a game of billiards. "A crop of Mother Carey's chickens, eh? I see." He started to rebutton his waistcoat across his paunch.

Neither one of them saw. Ian did not think visiting a bordello was fitting behavior for a nearly betrothed man. Whether Athena learned of it or not, he would know that he had forsworn his vow of fidelity before a week had passed, before the actual wedding vows were spoken. What way was that to begin a marriage? He thought of all the wives who had betrayed their husbands in his arms, and made those gentlemen a silent apology . . . except for ones who kept mistresses. They deserved straying wives.

In addition to an ethical issue he had never considered before, Ian was shocked to discover that he simply did not want any other woman. He wanted to know his wife's slender body and none else. He supposed Mrs. Johnstone could provide a slight young girl with blond curls, but his mind, and his body, he thought, would know the difference. "No," he told the other gentlemen. "Visiting a prostitute is disrespectful of one's wife."

Carswell almost fell out of his chair, and Rensdale almost cried.

"Gads, man, do you mean to be a benedict in truth?" Carswell asked.

Ian raised his glass. "I mean to show my bride that I am worthy of her, as any gentleman should to the mother of his unborn babes."

Now Rensdale sank lower in his seat, as if hoping the leather cushions would swallow him up.

Carswell stroked his chin, thinking. "You are right, of course. Tomcatting is for bachelors and unrepentant rakes. A decent fellow, wedding an esteemed wife, has to cease sowing his wild oats. A man with a dicey reputation might have to prove his honor beforehand by putting temptation aside."

"Exactly." Except that Ian was not tempted in the least. "But you two go on ahead, if you wish."

How could Rensdale visit a whore after Marden's moralizing? "No, no, got to think of my unborn son, too. Wouldn't want to pick up the pox or anything, either."

They both looked to Carswell. "No, I think I will forego the pleasure, too. Abstinence might be good for my soul. I'll try it for a fortnight or so and see. Perhaps a sennight. Maybe until week's end."

"It's all well and good to turn into monks, but what else is there to do?" Rensdale asked with a defeated whine in his voice.

"What do you do at home, then?" Ian wanted to know. "Are you at parties every night?"

"What, in the country? We attend the assemblies, and dine with Squire and his wife on Sundays. I visit the local, play a bit of cards, throw the darts some. But mostly we stay at home. Restful, you know. Not so costly. Veronica sews and I watch her."

"You watch your wife sew?" Carswell was horrified. "Gads, you might as well watch your sheep grow wool."

Rensdale's cheeks were flushed. "I like to watch her, when she's too busy with her needlework to carp and complain. Fond of the old girl, you know. And we talk of this and that."

"Gads," Carswell said again.

Ian could not tell if his friend's oath was for the watching of the harridan or for Rensdale's fondness for her. He understood, though. He thought he might enjoy watching Athena as she embroidered, chatting with her about their day, discussing his next speech in Parliament, speaking of all kinds of things. Her face held so many expressions, a man would not soon grow weary of watching her. Her opinions were usually well considered and reasonable. And when he did grow weary, he could go to bed, with her nestled against his side.

Maybe marriage was not all that bad. Ian hoped not, for celibacy was too uncomfortable without some reward. Hell, being hard without finding gratification was damned hard, indeed.

Carswell went off to find a card game, and Ian and Rensdale stayed where they were, talking. "Tell me about Athena then to pass the time, so I might understand her better," Ian requested.

"You'll never understand a one of them, but I can try." Rensdale went on to tell Ian about his father's young second wife. "A mere landowner's daughter, and nearly twenty years his junior, besides. Nothing like the ten years between you and Attie, of course. That's fine and dandy. My father made himself the laughingstock of the county, the old fool and his young filly."

He'd wanted another son, the former viscount had, and another wife to warm his bed. He must have loved the woman, Rensdale recounted, for he went into a decline when she died in childbirth, turning mean. The old viscount hated the boy who had caused her death, furious that the infant was sickly, imperfect, an insult to his virility. Only little Athena had loved the puny babe, and their father had hated her, too, for looking like her mother and for telling him how to raise his son. She'd been stubborn while still in pinafores and pigtails, and she was stubborn since. Proof of that was in her rejecting the earl out of hand, when he was the best match she could hope to make.

The staff kept treating her like mistress of the Hall, even after Rensdale brought his bride home, and she did nothing to change their attitude. She always thought she knew what was best, treating the servants like family, putting the tenants' welfare ahead of her own relatives'. Rensdale found her a nuisance, except that she had a good head for figures and the estate books. He could always hire a secretary who would not complain if he raised the rents.

Veronica found her young sister-in-law too harum-scarum to present to society. Athena was forward and fussy, strong-willed, disobliging, and altogether too immature to befriend. She had not the least understanding of a woman's place in the world, much less a female of modest means dependent on her half-brother. According to Lady Rensdale, Wiggs was good enough for the girl, and the least exertion on her own part.

They would both be glad to be rid of her.

The boy was simply an inconvenience, an embarrassing burden, like having a lunatic in the attics. Lady Rensdale did not like to speak of him at all. She could hardly bear to look at him, so having Troy stay on as Marden's ward would suit them perfectly. That was the only reason she was not calling her husband home to see to her comfort. She wanted him to get the job done.

"You can understand that, can't you?"

Ian thought he did understand Athena better after listening to her brother. Those who should have loved her and looked after her, putting her interests first, had all failed her. No wonder she did not want to entrust herself and her brother to yet another person who thought he knew what was best. If he had had to fight for every crumb of respect, every inch of independence, he doubted he'd want to give it up so easily, either. Hell, he had the world at his command, with no one to naysay him, and he was still worried about putting on leg-shackles.

He never meant to keep his wife on a tight rein, but how could he convince her of that? Athena did not trust him enough yet to believe his word, and he wondered if she ever would.

He'd try, he swore to himself. He'd try to make her understand that he was a man of honor . . . who only lied to her when he couldn't help it.

Some few hours later, Rensdale was ready to go home. Carswell was still playing cards, but Ian was happy to leave the smoke-filled room. With no carriage in town, Rensdale was about to have the doorman call him a hackney.

"I'll drop you off, Marden. On the way, don't you know."

"No, I'll walk home. It is not that far, and I need the exercise. It is not late enough to be dangerous, and the moon is full. I have my sword stick, besides."

Rensdale did not want to be thought less fit than the younger man, so he said, "Right. I'll walk with you." He patted his paunch. "I could use some activity, too."

"What about your, ah, disability?" It was not polite to mention another's infirmity, but the man had a limp. Ian wished he'd accepted the offer of a ride, after all.

Rensdale tapped his leg. "This? It's nothing. An old coaching accident, don't you know. Bothers my wife more than me."

So they stepped out into a clear night, for once,

with the stars out for the first time in days. Without the fog cover, the air was fresher, the streets seemed cleaner, and the ebony hush was a welcome contrast to the noise of the clubs. Ian did not keep his normal pace, and Rensdale did not huff and puff too much.

When they reached the corner where they had to take different directions, they shook hands, Rensdale wishing Ian luck, and Ian wishing Athena's brother a good night's rest.

Ian walked on, thinking about the woman, wondering if she was still awake, and if his sister and mother were not. The evening was still full of possibilities, and pleasures. He walked a little faster.

Then he heard a shout, a cry, a thud. "Rensdale?"

He heard no answer. He turned, pulled the sword out of his cane, and started to race back the way he had come. A man was loping off down an alley, lurching at an awkward gait. Why the deuce was Rensdale running away? Then he saw a lump on the ground at the same time he heard the moan. Rensdale had fallen, clutching his head. It was someone else who had fled.

"Good gods, what a brazen footpad! Did he get your purse?" Ian set his sword down and knelt by the man's side. Then he saw all the blood, ink black by the moon's light. "The devil!"

This was a lot worse than a stolen purse. A brick was nearby, also covered in blood. "Can you speak, man? Are you hurt badly? Where did the dastard hit you?"

Rensdale was trying to sit up. "M'head, I think. Can't see."

Ian had his neckcloth off, and Rensdale's own, trying to stop the bleeding. "You can't see because of the blood in your eyes. Head wounds do that, you know. Bleed a lot."

This much? Ian stood up and let out a piercing whistle, then shouted for the Watch as loudly as he could. He picked up his sword and slashed a circle, in case the thief was watching to see if he should make another try.

The Watch and two hackneys came at the same time. The first one drove off when he saw the blood. "Don't want 'is claret on me cushions, guv."

The second driver helped Ian haul the half-conscious Rensdale into his coach, while the Watchman took down his name and Ian's description of the limping felon.

"So where to, my lord? Yer friend needs stitches, less'n I miss my guess."

Where, indeed? Rensdale's hotel? Who knew what care he would receive there. Ian gave his own address and told the driver to hurry. He'd pay extra for the speed.

He got in the carriage, trying to cushion Rensdale so he did not bump his head on the side panels as the old coach rattled down the cobblestones at the fastest pace the old nag pulling it could go.

Rensdale groaned the whole time, but he stayed upright, which Ian took for a good sign. They were nearly to Maddox House when Ian realized he'd have to wake Athena if she were abed. No one could sleep through the stir his arrival was liable to cause, with messengers sent to surgeons and Bow Street, the servants roused to nurse another patient. Ian would have to tell her himself that he had dragged home another of her siblings, wounded. This time it was a half-dead half-brother. Lud, what the deuce could he say to the poor girl?

His mind went blank when he saw her face go as white as the marble stairs. Her hand clutched the bannister as if she would tumble down the steps other-

wise, which he did not have time for—not with
Rensdale leaning against him, held up only by Ian's
arms, blood dripping onto the tiles at their feet. He
looked at her and wanted to reassure her, wanted to
promise her things would be all right. All he found to
say, though, was: "I didn't do it."

Chapter Twenty-One

Marriage is endless.

—Anonymous

Marriage is endless possibilities.

—Mrs. Anonymous

What a popular man he was! No seafarer had ever been greeted so eagerly, or by so many, Captain Barnaby Beecham thought. No, not even Odysseus, home from the wars, after his dog pointed him out to the others. Captain Beecham wished he could have remained unrecognized for another day or so. All he'd been looking forward to was a long sleep uninterrupted by ship's bells, good English cooking, and clothes not permeated by dampness. The sail home had been nightmarish. His welcome to London was, too.

First, his man Macelmore met him at the dock and filled his ears with tidings that almost made the captain weigh anchor and head back to sea. Then a liveried footman asked if some nob could come alongside. Barnaby had no chance to regain his land legs before the Earl of Marden came calling at Cameron Street. The earl was impressive, for a civilian: big and strong and confident. Barnaby liked the cut of his sails, but he thought Marden's loose clothes could have a better fit. The man spoke briefly, eloquently, and to the point. Not tacking from side to side, the earl ran head on into the wind, and Barnaby liked that, too. He did not like what the man had to say, though.

Before the captain could look around for a belaying pin, which he would not have found, although an ugly vase was handy, Marden took full responsibility for the tangled rig. He meant to do right by both Athena and Troy, who was not the captain's ward. In Beecham's estimation, Marden did not have the desperate look of a man condemned to walk the gangplank, but seemed eager to wed the captain's niece. He did not care about her dowry, Marden said, trying to convince Barnaby of his bona fides, and would set it aside, whatever the sum was, for his and Athena's daughters. Marden meant to provide for his sons on his own, he said. The earl went on to state that he would be generous in the settlements, so Athena would be protected even if he died young and soon and without the heir his estate required.

What more could a bachelor uncle ask than to see his ward so fortuitously, fortunately, and fortune-filled wed—except a flea in the ear of the Navy brass about a promotion to admiral, with a fleet of ships of his own. It wouldn't have to be a large fleet, either.

Ian promised to see what he could do about convincing the Navy, and Captain Beecham promised to see what he could do about convincing Athena.

But first, the captain had to get past Lady Marden. The earl's mother waylaid him before he could send the niffy-naffy butler after his kin.

The countess was the kind of female the captain admired: full-bodied and full of spirit. She wouldn't blow over in a gale, and she wouldn't take sauce from anyone. She might hold a scrap of lace to her temple, and let out a sigh here and there, but she was as strong as the wooden figurehead on his ship, and just as bonny.

Where Marden went on about honor, his mother expounded on the social facts of London life. Honor had nothing to do with a gal's actions, she explained to the captain over a hearty tea and fancy cakes, and everything to do with her prospects. It was the *ton*'s perception of her conduct, not any wrong Athena had necessarily committed, that made marriage mandatory. Otherwise, his niece would be disgraced and his sickly nephew left to the Rensdales' begrudging care. The countess's son would be labeled a feckless flirt, and she herself would hang her head in shame that she had raised such an unconscionable cad. Why, she might go into a decline, her health being too uncertain for such . . . such anxiety-fraught events. Last night's happenings had sent her into a positive quake, although she had slept through Rensdale's actual arrival.

The woman was wolfing down every macaroon on the plate, having finished the cucumber sandwiches. Beecham did not think she would expire from a nervous disorder any time soon, but he did not wish to chance such a fine female's distress.

The captain decided to speak with Rensdale first. Athena's half-brother had never been one of his favorites, from when he was impolite to Barnaby's sister at her own wedding. Still, he was younger then, and in poor straits now. The captain decided not to tear a strip off him for taking such slipshod care of the younger Renslows. Not yet, anyway, if this argle-bargle could be resolved to the captain's satisfaction.

Rensdale gave his opinion as best he could, to both captains. The rudesby was still seeing double from getting concussed. He could not walk without falling over, and he could not touch his own nose. He could whimper and whine, though, blaming everything on Athena, because he'd have been safe back in Derby if she was not such a flighty, foolhardy female.

The captain left Rensdale's bedchamber, scratching his beard. The clunch had been hit on the head with a brick, and Troy had been shot and knocked off a horse. War was looking less dangerous.

Troy was thrilled to see his uncle, and the book on celestial navigation Barnaby had brought. The captain had given up plans for making the lad into a sailor, but still had hopes of expanding the boy's knowledge. He had certainly expanded Troy's vocabulary when he heard about Rensdale's plans to send him to a sanatorium if Athena did not wed the earl. Barnaby thought he might have Rensdale keelhauled after all. No one was going to cast his nephew overboard just because he could not walk right. The captain had a peg leg of his own, and that never kept him from the quarterdeck.

Then it was time to see his niece.

There were hugs and kisses and laughter and tears. Athena wept a little, too.

In the two years since the captain had been at sea this time, Athena had gone from a skinny little girl to a lovely young woman, the image of his beloved sister. No wonder Marden wanted to marry her.

"No, lassie, I can't keep you and your brother with me. Shipboard is no place for a gentle miss or a tender lad, if Rensdale let me take him. And I would not feel right, leaving you alone in London with only Macelmore to protect you. This place is worse than an unmarked channel for perils. Sharks and barracudas all over, whirlpools and riptides, and now you've run aground. Lord Marden told me everything."

"Everything?"

"Aye, how you came to be here and all."

"He told you about the kisses?" she asked, her voice rising to a squeal.

"No, the dastard didn't mention any blasted kisses! I'll have him flogged for that!"

"No, Uncle. It was nothing really. That is, they weren't."

"The devil you say! Now I see what Lady Marden meant about your needing to marry."

"But what if I don't want to?" she asked.

"Did you like his kisses?"

Athena studied the tortoiseshell combs her uncle had brought her. "Yes."

"Well, he is a braw lad, so his looks cannot be offensive to you. You don't mind that he's as big as a barge, do you?"

"Oh no, I find him quite attractive. And he is not fat at all, for all his size."

"And not too old?"

"Younger men seem shallow to me."

"Then, my girl, I see no reason why you shouldn't marry him. The chap is rich, but he is generous with his blunt. He's a powerful aristo, but using his authority to good effect. Says he'll see about sending more funds to the ships, for repairs and supplies. Seems good to his mother, keeps an excellent kitchen, and holds to his honor. Both of your brothers think he's top of the trees. What more do you want?"

Athena rubbed her finger along the toothed side of the comb, making it sing. "I want him to love me."

The captain was in over his head. He stroked his beard, then he stroked her hand. "Are you sure he doesn't? He seemed dead set on wedding you."

"Only because he is honorable and generous and cares about his family name. He doesn't want to marry me, he feels he has to."

"I wouldn't be so sure of that, missy. With his blunt

and influence, he could find another solution. Besides, a lot of marriages start off with less."

"And end with less. I could not bear years of seeing him leave me to spend time with his mistresses."

"I could threaten to have him impressed if he strays. Mac knows the crews who gather up new recruits."

She smiled. "You cannot kidnap an earl into the Navy."

"But I could have him beaten to an inch of his life if he makes you unhappy."

"I do not know if he can help himself." She lowered her voice as if imparting a great confidence. "He is a rake, you know."

The captain knew all about Marden, from his man Macelmore. In his opinion, a little experience made a man a better lover to a new bride, but Barnaby was used to rough-edged sailors onboard ship, not demure young ladies in a drawing room. "I don't think you can hold a man's past against him, from when you hadn't met," he said.

"That's what he said, too. That his past has no bearing on the future."

"There you go, then. Man's honest with you, which is better than most. The real question, though, is do you love him? Seems you've been doing the hornpipe around the mizzen, missy. If you hate him, I'll hire you a chaperone, or buy a place in the country for you and a paid companion. Not the life I'd have chosen for my only sister's gal, no husband, no babes of your own, but I cannot retire from the Navy now, not while we are at war."

"Oh, I would never ask that of you. The Navy is your life."

"No, I mean to hand in my papers as soon as we get the Corsican devil in chains. But till then, I'd rather see you in the hands of a gentleman than out on your own. What kind of guardian would I be, leaving you afloat in this sea of shoals?"

"You are an excellent guardian, Uncle. The best a girl could wish for."

"You could wish for one in town, or a gentleman with a wife who could introduce you to scores of bachelors to choose from, but the compass did not turn in that direction. None of which answers my question. Do you love the lubber or not?"

"I . . . I don't know. That is, I find him everything admirable, and I want to be with him, and I like how his mouth curves up on one side in a smile before the other. I enjoy his conversation, and think his brown eyes are like pools of chocolate that make me warm to my toes when he looks at me just so. He smells wondrously of lemon and spice, and he pretends my singing is not awful and he—"

The captain held up his hand. "But you don't know if you love him?"

Athena smiled. "I love him."

Her uncle let out a sigh and sat back in his chair, patting her hand. "Then marry him, lass. Nothing will make him love you more than your love for him, if he does not already. Besides, how will you know if you don't try? You know you'll be lonely without him, don't you?"

"So lonely I could die, if I never saw him again."

"Then take the chance, Attie. Hold your nose and jump in feet first, I always tell my sailors when we are in safe, shallow water. If you sink, I'll fish you out, but you just might touch bottom and float back up, or swim to some beautiful shore. You'll never know what you might miss if you don't take the leap."

"Will you marry me?"
"It would be my honor and my pleasure."

"Are you sure?" Athena asked.

Ian took her hand and brought it to his mouth to kiss her fingers. "I could not be more sure. Although I was hoping for flowers and a ring, perhaps a proposal from one knee. Of course I should not complain, since my own proposal was a great deal worse. Do you think I might do it over? After all, what will you tell our children about our engagement? That I offered you an omelette? Or that I was such a dimwit that you had to do the deed?"

Athena's heart felt warmed by his mention of their children. Her hand felt warm in his. She smiled and said, "They will think both of their parents are nodcocks if they learn that I refused you."

"Then I may do it again?"

"I think I would like that."

Still holding her hand, Ian stood up from the sofa and knelt at her feet. With his other hand he drew the ring box out of his coat pocket and held it out to her. "My very dear Miss Renslow, will you make me the happiest of men by accepting my ring? I shall do my best to make you happy, to keep you safe, to cherish you for all of our days and nights together. Will you do me the infinite honor of accepting my hand in marriage?"

Athena looked down at the face she was coming to adore. The foolish man was pretending her answer was uncertain, that it was not a foregone conclusion when she asked to see him alone, or when she asked him to marry her! He was still giving her the choice, giving her his respect. Her uncle was right. She was taking a chance, but the prize was well worth the dangers. She freed her hand to open the ring box.

Great gods, Ian fretted, what was taking her so long to answer? His knees were growing sore. What if she'd changed her mind already, and refused his offer again?

He'd go mad. No, he would not go anywhere. He would stay right here, on his aching knees, with the door locked so she could not escape. He'd spend the rest of the day—or the week if that was what it took—to change her mind back.

She was looking at the ring—pearls this time, to match the strand she wore around her neck, only the pearls on the ring were surrounding a heart-shaped ruby. She held it out, handing it back to him, with tears starting in her tropical-seas eyes.

"Don't you like it? I can get the diamond back if you'd prefer it. Or have a new ring made for you. I thought of a turquoise or an aquamarine to match your eyes, but this one seemed more special, with the weight of years behind it. It is in the portrait of the first countess, you know. You do not need to wear it for—"

"Hush, silly. It is beautiful, and I like it far more than the diamond. But it is your job to put it on me. That's part of the offer, isn't it?"

"How should I know? I've only done this once before, and made a hash of that. But does this mean you are going to accept this time?"

She raised her hand again. He slipped the ring on her finger. The fit was perfect, thank goodness. "With this ring—No, that is for the wedding ceremony. Deuce take it, I made the last speech. It is your turn."

"With this ring on my finger, with pride and with pleasure, and knowing what an honor you do me, I accept your kind offer. With this ring on my finger, I pledge myself to you and to being the best wife I know how, to cherish you and our children for every day of our lives."

"And the nights?

"Definitely the nights."

Then she slid to her knees on the carpet, facing him,

and they sealed their troth with a searing kiss that did
not end until he groaned.

"Oh, dear. Are you hurt? I did not mean to bite
down on your lip. I—"

"No, it is my knees. They have gone numb. But that
is easily fixed." He lowered himself onto his back, with
her atop him, and kissed her again, his hands pressing
her tight against his chest so their hearts beat next to
each other and their breaths were one breath. His
hand reached down to catch the hem of her gown,
and he drew it up, stroking her calf and the back of
her knee and her thigh as he went. Then he caressed
her derriere, making low hums of approval as he did.

Athena could feel his arousal beneath her, and
wanted to feel it closer, wanted, finally, to know what
it all meant. He groaned louder when she wriggled
closer still, trying to join her need to his.

His hands were on her back, her ribs, anything he
could reach with her on top of him, but that was not
enough, so he rolled over, pulling her with him onto
their sides, so he could touch her breasts, unfasten the
tapes of her gown, rip open his waistcoat and pull up
his shirt to feel her skin against his. Now they were
almost as close as a man and a woman could be with
most of their clothes on, and closer than they should
be, before the wedding. But there would be a wedding,
soon, as soon as possible. So he was not entirely beyond the pale, although he was almost beyond reasoning. One tiny corner of his mind reminded him that
there would be a wedding night, too, with a real bed.
His beautiful, inexperienced, but eager bride deserved
more than a quick tumble—Lud knew it was going to
be quick, at the rate they were going—on the floor
where anyone could walk in. He set her further away,
pulled down his shirt, and pulled up her gown. Tugging her skirts down over her shapely legs might have

been the hardest thing—no, not by half. "Oh, Lord," he moaned, "I think I am going to die."

"Not before signing those marriage settlements, you won't," Athena's uncle said from the doorway.

This was not going to be a long engagement, not if Ian or Captain Beecham had anything to say about it. Tomorrow was not soon enough.

Rensdale had little to say, still babbling after his concussion, but the physician assured Athena that it was a temporary condition. Her half-brother was almost back to his normal dull-witted self already.

Ian's mother wanted a huge wedding, a spectacle worthy of a Marden. She wanted St. George's in Hanover Square, not some hole-in-corner affair in their own drawing room. No one should be able to label them cheap, embarrassed at the choice of bride, or in a hurry.

"But we are in a hurry, Mother."

"So I heard from the captain. Such ungoverned passion is unbecoming in an earl." She scowled her disapproval at Ian, then turned her frown on a blushing Athena. "And unseemly in a countess."

"I meant that Rensdale needs to go home to his enceinte wife."

"He is in no condition to travel, as you well know. I should think such an injury would take months to heal. Yes, two months. Of course one with my delicate constitution would need longer."

"His wife would have the infant without him at that rate."

"No matter. He has already done his part. Your father was not present for either of my lying-ins. Speaking of which, your father and I were affianced for a full year."

"A year? That is preposterous."

"Furthermore, it would be far too fatiguing for me to make all the plans in less than two months. Why, the invitations alone take days to write out and deliver."

As if she had ever stirred herself to plan a family dinner party, much less a wedding breakfast. "We do not need an elaborate affair, and my staff can handle all the details. And Doro and Athena will help."

"Very well. A month."

"Two days. That's why I got the special license."

Athena cleared her throat to get the attention of the earl and his mother. "Forgive me, my lady, but I do not wish to be gawked at in a crowded church, or entertain a horde of strangers here. Neither can I bear to suffer more fittings for an extravagant wedding ensemble that I do not need. My new gowns are almost ready, and so are both of my brothers." Athena was ready, too, ready to pursue those unseemly passions she had glimpsed before her uncle arrived. The fact that Ian wanted her so badly—tomorrow—made her blood sing, slightly off-key, but with great enthusiasm. "And, my lord, not even your capable household should be asked to provide a wedding cake on a day's notice.

"One week is a good compromise," she concluded. When the countess moaned over the impropriety, and the earl started to curse, Athena put her foot down. She had to begin as she meant to go on, and that meant not being torn apart or trampled between these two strong characters. They'd swallow her whole if she let them, the way her sister-in-law had tried to. She raised her chin. "One week, and that is final. After all, whose wedding is it, anyway?"

Chapter Twenty-Two

Why do women cry at weddings? It's the groom who should be crying.

—Anonymous

Men cannot recognize Joy unless she's wearing a rumpled bed sheet.

—Mrs. Anonymous

Lady Marden looked at Miss Renslow with new respect. Ian, close to his betrothed on the sofa as if she might run away if he let go of her hand, said, "My lady goddess is as wise as the Greek Athena. And I told you she had bottom." He leaned over and kissed Athena on the cheek, whispering, "And a very nice bottom it is, too."

Athena's ears turned pink, but she was growing used to her new fiancé's suggestive remarks. In fact, she was looking forward to them. What a great relief to know he wanted her, and how much power that knowledge gave her. She used some of that authority now to state that the captain would give her away, Lady Dorothy, if she was willing, would be her witness and attendant, and Mr. Carswell could be Ian's groomsman. Mr. Wiggs could conduct the short service.

Ian dropped her hand. "Wiggy? The man is a sanctimonious sapskull, a rejected suitor, and you do not like him!"

"But he is an excellent teacher, and I know of no other London clergy. Wiggy—that is, Mr. Wiggs—is a friend of my family's, and I believe we owe him the courtesy of asking him to officiate and give his blessings."

She did not get to ask the Reverend Mr. Wiggs for two days, although she sent a message to the hotel where he was staying.

When he finally arrived at Maddox House for Troy's lessons, Mr. Wiggs went *tut, tut* over Lord Rensdale's condition, the sorry state of morals in the city where a man could not walk down the street without being accosted, and the depth of Athena's new gown's décolletage when she entered her older brother's sickroom. He tutted worse, almost sputtering, when she asked him to conduct her marriage ceremony at Maddox House at the end of the week.

"No, no. She cannot marry Marden now," Wiggs said to her brother, as if Athena were not two feet away.

" 'Course she can. He has a special license. No need to call the banns."

Wiggs started pacing. "But he is not fit for her."

"The earl seems fit to me. Works at it, don't you know."

Wiggs went as far as the hearth, then the window, and back to the hearth. "I mean his morals. They are not suitable for a young lady of gentle breeding."

"What's that? And stand still, dash it. There are two of you when you skitter about."

One of Wiggy was enough for Athena, who was sorry she did not let Lady Marden ask the bishop to officiate.

"I do not believe his lordship's morals are any concern of yours, Mr. Wiggs. I am the one marrying him."

"Humph. But you are an innocent miss. You need to be guided by older, wiser heads. After all, what do you know of rakes and reprobates?"

Enough to know they kissed very well. "Enough to decide for myself that Lord Marden and I shall suit."

"*Tut, tut,* you cannot know the depths of depravity if you think that."

"I think that you, sir, are no one to be speaking of morality. Where have you been these past few days, I wonder. You were not at your hotel."

Wiggs *humph*ed and *haw*ed, then finally fabricated, "I was about the Lord's business."

"You were at the lord's love nest, in fact, in Kensington."

"Gads," her brother put in, "the clunch is right. You cannot marry that loose screw, Marden. Not if he and Wiggs . . ."

"Do not be more foolish than your concussion warrants, Spartacus. Ian was here, Mr. Wiggs was there, with Lady Paige."

"Lady Paige, eh? No wonder we haven't seen hide nor hair of the man for days."

Wiggs was scraping his hands together in a washing motion. "She is his mistress, not mine. I was, ah, offering her counsel to mend her ways."

"Probably can't afford her, anyway, from what I hear," Rensdale told Athena. She pinched his arm.

"The lady *was* Lord Marden's companion. He was kind enough to offer her safe haven in her distress until she makes other arrangements."

What Athena was too much the lady to say was that Lady Paige was looking for a new protector. The woman had quickly realized that a parson with no parish could not fix her finances or her ill fame. She was not about to support Wiggs, not on her life.

While Lady Paige had enticements aplenty, Wiggs discovered, influence with the archbishop was not one of them. Nor was generosity. The woman was not going to part with a single one of her jewels, especially not after the poor showing Wiggs had made in Kensington. She said she hoped he was better at preaching than pleasuring a lady, and sent him off, looking for a fortune and a woman who would not know any better.

That woman—his Miss Renslow—seemed to be far more knowledgeable than she had been, and Wiggs did not like it. He began to chide her immodesty when Rensdale said, "Scruples aside, you wrote to me yourself saying that Attie had to get married posthaste."

Wiggs slicked back his hair from its center part and squared his narrow, sloping shoulders. "I shall marry her." He ignored Athena's gasp and continued: "I always intended to, you know. You and I and Lady Rensdale spoke of it before we left for London. You as near as promised the young lady to me. I believe I have a legal claim to her hand in marriage."

Lord Rensdale clutched his skull, claiming a headache. "Need my rest, don't you know."

"I know," Athena said, pinching him again, "that you had no right to bestow my hand anywhere." She turned to face Wiggs. "My uncle Barnaby is my guardian, not Rensdale. I am sorry if you were misled, but I believe things were made plain between us that we would not suit."

Wiggs started to make sounds that belonged more in a pigeon coop than a pulpit.

Seeing the man squirm, Rensdale grew braver. " 'Sides, if I had to choose between a minister with empty pockets and an earl with five houses and six kinds of fortune, which one do you think I'd pick? Think on it, man. I am the one with the cracked skull, not you."

"That is irrelevant," Athena told them both. "I am promised to Lord Marden, by my own choice, and with my guardian's blessings." And with Uncle Barnaby's threats to ship her to the Antipodes if she did not go through with the wedding. "I shall not renege on my promise to the earl. He is an honorable man who keeps his word, and I can be no less honorable."

"Honorable? What about the duel and your brother's injury? He lied to you about that!"

Rensdale made a rude noise. "Only a cabbagehead would have believed that claptrap about a target shoot."

Athena had believed it. Her younger brother had confirmed it.

Wiggs took a deep breath, his mouth puckered as if he were about to expel a grape seed. "I regret to say," he said with no regret whatsoever, "that the duel was over Lady Paige."

"Pshaw. Duels are always over some woman or other, unless a fellow's been caught marking the deck. And then he's doing it to support some ladybird, most likely. Paige fled, didn't he? None of it was Marden's fault."

"No fault?" Wiggs was shaking, he was so upset, or so disappointed. "No fault when he was fighting over a married woman? And this is the man you would let your sister marry?"

"Hmm. Attie, he's got a point. What do you think?"

She thought the handful of guests had already accepted, the cake was baked and awaiting decoration, the small orchestra hired. She thought she might be sick. "I'll speak to Troy."

*   *   *

Troy admitted going out to watch the duel the groom Alfie had mentioned. He didn't tell her, because he knew she'd be mad. He didn't know all the particulars, he swore, and had no memory of the final few minutes before he fell off his horse. He did know that Marden was the best of good fellows, and would never act dishonorably.

That had to be enough for Athena. She was too busy to fall into a panic.

Lady Marden was too fatigued to be of much assistance, but she did insist that her nearest and dearest friends—all twenty-five of them—be invited to the wedding breakfast, which was to be served late in the day. Lady Dorothy was solving some crisis at the orphanage, with Mr. Carswell's help, and swore she knew nothing of weddings and receptions anyway.

The staff was more than competent, but many of the decisions fell on Athena's slender, inexperienced shoulders. She did not want to commit any social gaffes, but neither did she wish to run to the earl with every question about precedence at the dining table or if his second cousin Spencer could share Rensdale's suite. Athena wanted Ian to think she was capable, mature, a suitable countess. She was none of those things, of course, but she could pretend for the rest of the week. Then it would be too late for him to cry off.

Ian had no intentions of backing out of the wedding, and no intentions of suffering through the rest of the week like a child at the sweetshop's window, looking at what he could not have. So he stayed away from his bride as much as possible, plotting the wedding night while she planned the wedding. He knew which one mattered more.

Meanwhile, he tried to use up some of the restless energy of enforced abstinence by sparring and fencing and trying out the paces of his new pair of chestnuts. He also attended several bachelor parties in his honor, hosted by those friends he had not battered, beaten, or bested at some feat of manliness. Ladies of the night were available at the parties, but he was not even tempted, waiting for the day when he could claim his own lady.

He was righteous, he was noble, he was frustrated as hell.

Maddox House might have been an infirmary, rather than the site of a wedding. One of the bride's brothers was in a wheelchair, crutches beside him. The other was being held up by Marden's valet and still seeing double. Her uncle was missing a limb, and the best man had a black eye, from connecting with Ian's punishing right fist at Gentleman Jackson's that morning.

The parlor was even filled with flowers like a sick-room, which had the mother of the groom wheezing and sneezing. Cousin Nigel was near to losing his breakfast on losing his position as heir, now that Marden had taken a bride and would begin filling his nursery. The butler swayed from exhaustion after the hurried preparations, and the earl's sister swayed toward the best man.

The cook, the housekeeper, and the maids crowded in the back of the parlor were all weeping as if a plague had struck the house. So was Mr. Wiggs.

Tears at a wedding were common, but from the officiator? Whoever heard of a minister growing maudlin at a marriage ceremony? He might have been conducting a funeral, for all the joy Wiggy showed.

His plum had landed in another's lap. His opportunities were clutching the arm of an earl. His ship had docked at the wrong pier. And the dog had bitten his ankle when he tried to kick it out of the room.

"Dearly beloved"—sniff—"we are gathered here"—snuffle—"to join this pair"—sob—"in holy matrimony."

At least the happy couple looked healthy. The groom was stalwart and superbly turned out; Miss Renslow was simply stunning. No wedding jitters for her, the witnesses decided. She appeared remarkably composed for such a young female—although not too young for the earl, of course—in good color, and altogether magnificent.

Of course she was composed. Her uncle had made her swallow a tot of rum. And of course her complexion had a rosy glow. Lady Dorothy had emptied her paint pots.

Miss Renslow was a vision in her rose satin gown with its lace overskirt and matching lace headdress, held with pink rosebuds. No one could tell that one of the thorns was digging into her scalp. No one could tell that her smile was frozen in place by fear, either, or that she stood perfectly erect to keep from falling over in a dead faint, or that she clutched the earl's arm in a vise-like grip to keep her hands from shaking.

Her throat might be constricted and her mouth as dry as the Sahara, but she spoke her vows in a clear, loud voice, to be heard over the reverend's weeping.

The consensus on the groom's side was that Miss Renslow was just right for their earl, and lucky to have him.

The bride's side, naturally, thought he was getting the better bargain.

The groom thought he had never seen anything so beautiful in his life as the woman at his side, her lips curved in a smile just for him. A perfect rosebud, she was, and his. This turquoise-eyed angel was going to be his wife. His. He almost staggered at the wonder of it all, but Carswell on his other side reached out a steadying hand. But Ian did not need his friend to keep him upright; he had Athena's hand on his arm. Her grip was so confident, so secure, she could not be having any last-minute doubts. He finally set aside worries that she had been trapped, that she was regretting her decision. She wore a smile, and so he was relieved and pleased and proud. His. By his side. He thought he might never again feel whole without her there. His.

Lud, Ian was so stupefied at his joy in getting wed that he could barely remember the order of his own names, to repeat them after Wiggs.

He got them out, got the wedding band on Athena's finger, said "I do" at all the appropriate places, he hoped. Then he got to kiss his bride. Her lips were cold, so he had to warm them. Hadn't he just promised something about that? He must have, he'd promised everything else.

The gathered guests started to applaud and laugh. Athena pushed at his chest, otherwise he might have stayed that way forever, he thought, a contented man. Now her lips were warm and rosy. So were his, from her lip rouge.

After the ceremony, the champagne flowed freely enough to wash away all the tears. The bumps and bruises and battered hopes abated with each merry toast and hearty congratulation. Even the newly titled dowager countess stopped sniffling, once the captain led her away from the flower-filled drawing room.

Having rested, Troy was jubilantly swinging around on his crutches, trying to avoid having his cheeks pinched by all of the dowager's friends who had nieces and granddaughters of suitable age for such a likely young man as Marden's protegé. Rensdale had taken over the wheeled Bath chair, and was holding forth on his attack, how he had saved his money and his watch from the footpad. Or had he fought off two of the dastards?

Wiggs decided to give Lady Dorothy the pleasure of his company, as soon as he could pry her away from that fop, Carswell. The female was looking better these days, and was independently wealthy, which was better still.

The newly married pair passed around the room for kisses and embraces and introductions. Ian never left Athena's side, and she never let go of his hand. She kept looking at the wedding band that had joined the pearl ring, thinking she would never take it off. He kept looking at the intricate fastenings on her gown, wondering how soon he could take it off.

Dinner was long and elaborate, the finest Ian's kitchens could provide. The wine was excellent, and plentiful. The toasts continued, or were repeated. As the meal progressed, the jokes became louder, a bit warmer. Ian was glad he had insisted that Athena be seated at his side, not at the foot of the table where her new position would have placed her. Here he could shield her from some of the more suggestive comments by whispering his own suggestions in her ear. She stopped blushing and started looking interested by the end of the fish course. If Ian were any more interested, they would be skipping the rest of the meal.

He ordered the butler to stop refilling his mother's wine glass when she started to recount her every ailment to the captain, and made a footman take away his sister's when she seemed to be sitting more in

Carswell's lap than in her own chair. He told Hull to stop serving Troy, for the boy was far too young and too recently near death to suffer a morning after.

Thinking of that, Ian set Athena's glass aside when she started to giggle at some of the ribald toasts. He wanted her relaxed, not tipsy, and not in a stupor. He did not want her to wake up in the morning with a headache, either, for he intended the wedding night to last well past tomorrow's dinner. Even that might not be time enough.

They would not be going away on a honeymoon, not with her brothers still ailing and her uncle so recently returned, but Ian had all of Athena's belongings moved to the countess's bedchamber attached to his, in a private wing of the huge house. His mother had relinquished the apartment ages ago, claiming the rooms were haunted by several former residents. Well, the ghosts would have a voyeur's picnic tonight, he swore.

Before then, he had to get through this interminable dinner. If he were a guest, he'd have left ages ago. His invitees seemed in no hurry, not even after the enormous wedding cake was trolleyed out.

Finally he noticed that Troy was half asleep in his chair, so mentioned to Athena that she should rise and lead the ladies out.

"Oh, dear, I forgot already. I was waiting for your mother to stand."

His mother could hardly get out of her seat, having imbibed so freely. Finally the women were gone and Ian offered to help young Renslow up the stairs.

Troy reached behind him where his man, Geoffrey, was waiting with the crutches. "Oh, no, I can do it myself," Troy said.

"I am delighted to see you up and about." Now Ian did not have to agonize that he had made the boy bedridden for life. "But I cannot help but notice that you seem frightfully proficient at those things." Ian glanced at the crutches.

"I ought to be, after all these years."

"Years? But you ride. That is, you were riding when I, ah, met you."

"Oh, my knees and thighs work fine. I need help mounting and dismounting, but then I can match anyone on horseback. Attie says I might go for a short ride soon, if you have a suitable mount in your stables."

"If I do not, I shall get one."

"I knew you were top drawer. Glad to have you for a brother." The boy held his hand out, and Ian shook it, thinking that there was more to this head of a family than he had reckoned. Now he had a new brother, who was not crippled by him. He watched, bemused, as Troy swung himself down the hall and up the stairs.

Then it was time to say farewell to the guests, and Ian forgot all about Troy, his responsibilities, his sister in the rear gardens with a bigger rake than Ian ever was, his mother batting her eyelashes at Athena's seafaring uncle, and Cousin Nigel inspecting the wedding gifts a shade too closely. All he could think about was his bride.

His Athena.

His.

Chapter Twenty-Three

A man teaches his wife about lovemaking.
                    —Anonymous

A woman teaches her husband about loving.
                    —Mrs. Anonymous

Mine, his body shouted. If the world and Athena did not hear, they could see his star performer ready to start the "Hallelujah" chorus. He pulled his paisley dressing gown into more careful folds as he walked through the connecting door between his chamber and his Attie's after she answered his knock. Most of the roses from the wedding had been brought here, so the room looked and smelled like a bower, with his wife the lucky gardener's champion bloom.

He was the gardener. He had a wife. He was a married man, by George. Ian wondered how long before he was used to that cataclysm in his life. Maybe a year or two. Or a night or two, with a wife like Attie.

If Attie was beautiful in rose satin and lace, there was no word in mortal man's vocabulary to describe her in the ivory film that called itself a robe. A spider web had more substance. Ian could not wait to see what was beneath the gauze, and then realized he did not have to wait at all. The candlelight on the side table limned Athena's perfect figure, showing him the dark area between her thighs, the dark area at her breasts. Unfortunately, it also showed him the dark shadows under her eyes.

"Are you tired, Attie? Should I let you sleep? This has been such a rush, I know, and you have done wonders. You deserve a rest if you want it." His body protested, but he was still a gentleman, not a rutting stallion. He kept his hand on the door, rather than reaching out to pull her into his embrace. He knew he would never let her go from there, not tonight.

Athena saw where his gaze wandered and quickly sat back at her dressing table. She picked up the brush her giggling maid had tossed there before leaving. She started to brush out her hair, then realized it was already smooth. Any more brushing and the ends would fly out like a corn-husk dolly's. She straightened the dish of hairpins instead, to avoid looking at his bare legs and velvet-slippered feet. "How kind of you. I am a bit tired. That is, I am not too tired, if you want—"

"Oh, I want. Do you?"

"I, ah. Oh, dear, I have spilled the pins."

He came fully into the room, bending at her feet to hand the fallen hairpins up to her. "Nervous?"

Nervous? Her fingers could barely hold the dish. "I—" She started to lie, then thought better of it, when he could see the falsehood in her trembling hands. "Yes, a little."

"Good. Me, too."

"You? What have you to be anxious over? You know how to do it, after all."

"Ah, but I do not know how to please you yet. I find that means more to me than I thought possible." He was still at her feet, his hands stroking her ankles, her calves, her bare skin.

"Oh, but I am sure you will figure it out. You are quite good at kissing, you know."

"Am I?" He raised her leg, letting the silken gown fall back, and kissed a trail up to her knee.

"Oh, yes." Her breaths were already coming faster, and all he had done was kiss her leg. Who would have thought that? "While I . . ."

"Hmm?" He was kissing a bit further up her thigh.

"I have no idea how to please a man."

"You please me very well, my dear." Now his hands stroked higher, and his kisses followed.

Athena leaped to her feet, almost toppling him over.

He stood and put the last of the hairpins on the table. "Do you wish me to wait? I will if I have to, but please don't say I have to."

She could see the need in his eyes—and in the protruding front of his robe. She licked her lips. "No, I do not want to put it off. Not when we would have to—"

"Do it another day? You've been speaking to my mother, haven't you?"

She nodded, staring at the pointing paisley.

He tried, futilely, to spread the folds more concealingly. "Well, ignore everything she told you about the pain and discomfort and thinking happy thoughts until it is over. And ignore this." He looked down. "It is only a sign of how much I want you and want to give you pleasure. I promise you will enjoy tonight. You trust me, don't you?"

She licked her lips again. "Yes."

"Good. That's all that matters."

Ian took her in his arms and began to kiss her as he had that time when her uncle had stopped them. Soon enough, Athena's fears were put on a back shelf of her mind, still there but gathering dust, while the

new sensations, the rising excitement, an unnamed
wanting took their place. After that, she stopped
thinking altogether, and simply felt. She felt his hands
and his lips and his tongue against hers. She felt her
robe slide to the floor, and her gown follow it. She
felt hot and damp, and she felt his heart beating
against hers. She felt as if her legs were made of maca-
roni, limp and only loosely connected to the rest of
her.

He knew. He carried her to the bed and placed
her between the turned-down sheets. "Shall I douse
the candles?"

"Yes, please." Although she did want to see him,
all of him, and she did not want him to leave her long
enough to blow out a single flame, she was not brave
enough to say so. Besides, the coals in the fireplace
still glowed enough that she could see his magnificent
shape when he untied his robe and let it fall to the
carpet beside the bed. Athena took a deep breath,
trying to remember her new husband's promise of
pleasure, and not the dowager's warning of pain.

Then he was beside her, face to face, skin to skin,
for their entire lengths.

"Your feet are cold," she complained.

"They will warm up." He started to kiss her again,
and the whole bed warmed up, it seemed. He kicked
off the blankets. She tossed back the sheet. It wasn't
enough, and it wasn't the coal embers that were causing the heat; it was their bodies rubbing together to
make a fire like some primitive, primordial feat of
magic.

Athena could barely think or breathe, lost in the
rapture of his arms, his touch, his caresses, his whispered endearments. She could stroke his hair finally,
the curls on his head, the coarser ones on his chest.
She reached to investigate the lower ones, but Ian

stayed her hand. "Not yet," he whispered, the words tickling her ear.

He felt free to go charting new territory, though, and Athena started to protest, until she realized where his hand was headed, what he intended to touch with his strong, knowing fingers. No one had ever—"Oh. Oh, my."

"Hush, sweetings. Hush and enjoy. I want to show you what your beautiful body can do. For you. For me."

She moved ·under his touch, crying out into his opened mouth, her fingers clutching at his shoulders, his neck, his back. Surely she would melt into a puddle beside him. She didn't, though, not even when his kisses followed the path of his hands. She could feel his warm breath and his tongue and—"Ian!"

"It's all right, my darling, we are married." He licked her there, where his touch had made her burn with some unknown need. "Climb, Attie. I'll catch you if you fall, but you won't. You'll soar to the sky and touch the moon, I promise. Then you'll float back to earth, to me."

He kept his promise.

"Oh," she said when she could speak again, when the earth and the stars had stopped spinning. "I never dreamed lovemaking could be so beautiful."

"And that's only the start."

"There's more?"

Now he guided her hand lower. "Much, much more. See?"

She could not see, but she could certainly feel. Still in the haze of her own rapture, she lost all fear, all shyness, and touched him. His little moans of pleasure must mean she was doing it right, so she grew bolder still, learning the silky parts and the soft parts, the ridged parts and the rigid parts. They were all exciting and enticing, thinking of what was to come. Finally she was brave enough to say, "I think I love you, Lord Marden."

He laughed, or moaned. It was hard to distinguish while they were kissing. He pulled back and stroked her cheek, forgiving her for wanting to speak at a time like this, with his soul ready to burst out of his skin. As long as she kept touching him, she could talk all she wanted. "No, Lady Marden. You love how I make you feel."

"I think I know my own heart, Ian, and, yes, I do love you."

He kissed her eyelids. "Thank you, my dear."

Her hand stopped moving. "Do you think you could love me in return?"

His heart stopped beating. "Honestly?"

She nodded, still not taking up where she had left off.

"I do not know, Attie. I don't know my heart the way you seem to. I did not know I had one, until today."

She patted where that organ would be, instead of the organ that was desperately straining toward her. "You do have a heart. A huge one. There is room for me in it, I swear. You will come to love me, Ian, I know it. I am going to make you so happy that you cannot help but love me."

"You could make me happy right now if you—"

"You'll see. You'll be so proud of me, so content, you won't want any other woman, ever."

He moved his hips against her, reminding her of his need. "Attie, I want you, now."

"I told everyone that Troy would walk one day, and he is close to it."

"What the deuce does Troy have to do with anything?"

"I am always right." She nodded again. "You'll love me."

"I'll love you sooner, and better, if I can make love to you now."

"Oh, I thought you were resting after . . ."

"After pleasuring you? That is an aphrodisiac, sweetheart, not an exertion. I could do that for the rest of my life, or until you were too exhausted to make those wonderful little sighs of satisfaction."

He started to prove his words. But this time he did not stop when she had reached fulfillment. This time he raised himself over her, and kissed her before she could decide on another friendly chat, and slowly, as gently as he could, savoring her gasps of surprise and pleasure, savoring her dewy, satiny smoothness, he began to make them man and wife, in truth.

He had not even entered the gates of Paradise when bells and whistles sounded. She was a marvel, his Attie. Never had the earth trembled before he had fully sheathed himself in a woman. Never had—

Bells? Whistles? Earth tremors?

"Bloody hell, that's the fire bell!"

He leaped up. The whistles were for the Watch, to call the fire company. The movement was feet pounding down the corridors, fists pounding on the door.

"Fire, my lord. The house is on fire! Get up! Get out!"

He leaped up and snatched his robe from the floor, racing toward the door. Then he remembered. He had a wife. "Oh, Lord!"

He ran back to the bed, where Athena was sitting up, blinking. He picked up her robe, then dropped it. All of London could have been burning, but no man was going to see his wife in that scrap of seduction. He tore the sheet off the bed and started to wrap her in it. She pushed him away.

"My brother! Troy can't get down the stairs on his own."

"I'll get your brother as soon as you are out."

Smoke was starting to filter into the room. Athena shoved Ian harder as she got off the bed. "I can get myself outside. Troy cannot. Go, by Heaven! Go."

His house, his people, his family, hers—Lord, so much was at stake. But he'd just sworn to protect this one, above all others. Hell, he couldn't stay to argue. "Move, damn it!" he shouted as he ran out, barefoot, and sped down the hall.

He opened doors as he tore past them. His mother's room was empty. His sister's, empty. Rensdale's, empty. Troy's, thank heaven, empty. The smoke was thicker, but Ian saw no flames and felt no heat beneath his bare feet. He still had time. He took the servants' stairs two at a time, shouting for everyone to get out.

The butler, Hull, was in his nightcap, tugging at a crouching maid. "Everyone else has gone, my lord."

The young female was huddled outside a door sobbing about her new gown. Ian cursed and said, "It is only a dress, deuce take it. Your life is far more important."

The girl was beyond reason, though, in her panic. Ian scooped her up and tossed her over his shoulder. She shrieked and sobbed and kicked the entire way down the stairs and out to the garden. He felt like smacking her bottom but was satisfied with dumping her in a flower bed.

He could see men forming a bucket brigade from the ornamental fountain, and he ran toward the head of the line. "Where's the fire, man?" he yelled over the commotion.

"The morning room. The draperies caught, and the wallpaper, but I think we have it contained."

Ian could hear more bells and whistles and shouts as the insurance company's fire truck arrived. Still barefooted, he ran toward the front of the house to make sure the firemen did not cause more damage in their zeal to win his largesse. They were already unrolling their hose near gray smoke billowing from one of the library windows. Ian's first thought was of his books. His second was: two fires?

He shouted at the men to carry on, carefully, then made a quick circuit around the house, looking for anything else suspicious. It was too dark to see footprints or lurkers—or sharp stones, for that matter—but Ian limped on, looking for smoke, smoldering rags, piles of leaves that might hide a lighted torch. He saw nothing, but yelled to one of the footmen to make a more careful search outside while he went back to the house.

Before he went inside, he made sure that Hull had everyone who was not fighting the fire gathered in the covered carriage drive. "The staff is all accounted for?"

"Everyone, my lord."

"And the family?" Ian could see his mother, seated on one of the chairs from the entry hall. Rensdale was in the wheeled chair, and Troy was on his crutches, with Athena at his side, thank goodness. She had on a thick flannel robe, he was happy to see, and had found a ribbon somewhere to tie back her hair.

"Where is Doro?" Ian would not put it past his sister to be pumping water or handing buckets to the men. "She was not in her room."

Hull's nostrils flared, and not from the stench of smoking draperies. "Lady Dorothy drove to Richmond after the wedding dinner."

"She left without saying good-bye? Deuce take it, I would have driven her in the morning."

"She did mention that she would likely return before you arose. She did not wish you or Lady Marden to be informed. Either Lady Marden," he added.

"I wonder what bee she could have in her bonnet to send her haring out of town in the dark without telling anyone?"

Hull's nose twitched. "I, ah, believe Mr. Carswell drove my lady."

"The devil you say." Ian had sworn off duels, but his philandering friend and his sister? "Damnation."

"Quite."

The head of the fire company came to speak to him, leaving Ian with a lot to think about: fires, flighty sisters, and his sore feet—to say nothing of his fardling frustration. He looked at the source of one of his aches and saw her arguing with her brother, then heading toward the front door. The fool was going back into the house, with who knew how much smoke or if more fires were still burning.

He intercepted her at the door. "Where the deuce do you think you are going?"

"Upstairs. Roma did not follow Troy out, it seems. She would not have heard the calls."

"The dog will be fine. The firemen are going through the house now, to check for any lingering sparks."

"Roma will not go to any of them. You know the dog is more likely to attack their boots."

"Then she can wait until we go in."

"She could die of the smoke."

"If she has half a brain she will hide under the bed. Smoke rises."

"Do you think a dog can know that? Besides, she'll be frightened."

"Well, I am sorry, but you cannot go into the house. It is too dangerous."

Troy had hobbled over. "Then I will go. She is my dog, after all."

Now that was ludicrous: a weak-chested boy on crutches, going upstairs into a burning building. It was almost as ridiculous as the notion of Ian letting his wife go after the mongrel. "Do not be absurd. I will go, dash it."

"You do not have any shoes on," Athena pointed out. "I at least had sense enough to find my slippers."

"You are not going, and that is final," he said as he turned and went in, taking a dampened cloth, to hold over his face, from one of the footmen.

The smoke was still thick. Maybe the dog would be having difficulty breathing, after all. He hurried on, then paused at the first landing to get his breath. A fireman was coming down, carrying a bucket of water and an axe.

"Don't go any higher, my lord," the man warned. "We found another blaze and a broken window in the kitchen. No telling but it might travel up the walls and ignite the wainscoting or wallpaper. Or the rugs."

Ian cursed, vowing that the villain who had done this damage would hang. Once for every fire he had set. And once for every member of Ian's family who could have been killed, or Athena's.

He went up. The hallway was so smoke-filled that he could barely see, not even with the candle he held. He was coughing, his eyes were burning, and his feet hurt. He stopped at his own room and located the pitcher and bowl on the washstand. He took a second to pour the water, sink his face and his handkerchief into it, and find a pair of shoes. He'd be no good to the dog if he could not see, or breathe, or walk.

He left his room, counting the doors down the halls to Troy's—and bumped into Athena.

"Thunderation, woman, I told you to stay outside! I will get your blasted dog."

"She does not like you."

"And I do not like her. I shall get her out, nevertheless."

"And I shall help."

Since she was already through the door, he could do nothing but follow her, then hand her his soaked cloth. "Put it over your face."

She did, and stopped coughing, although this room was smokier than the hall. It must be right above one of the fires, Ian thought, as he tried to find the dog in the dark. He caught himself from calling out to a deaf canine, but the blasted creature could be anywhere in this murk.

"She's under the bed, but she is not moving," Athena yelled up to him. "I cannot tell if she is alive or dead, and I cannot reach her."

"Move over." Ian did not have time to admire his wife's rear end in the air as he lowered himself to his belly next to her. He could not reach the mound he saw, but the air was clearer down here.

"Dear heaven," Athena was crying, "Troy will never forgive himself for leaving her if she does not survive."

Ian understood guilt all too well these days. The boy should not have to suffer such misery. Ian made a stronger effort to extend his arm.

"She's alive," he told Athena. Now his fingers were bleeding, as well as his toes. He drew back, grabbed a blanket from the bed and wrapped it around his hand, then he reached in and snagged the dog by her collar and pulled, while she snarled and snapped and tried to dig her claws into the carpet under the bed. "You stupid beast," Ian yelled, "if you bite me again, I swear I will leave you here to die."

"Oh don't, please. She is just frightened. She cannot recognize your smell in all this smoke."

He had Roma fully out from under the bed now, and she did seem to remember that he was the one who brought her treats, for she stopped growling and biting at the blanket on his arm. Then she tried to lick his face.

"That's worse than being bitten!" But he did not let go of the dog, picking her up, tossing the blanket over her head to protect her from the smoke, and carrying her out of the room with one hand. His other was firmly around his wife's thin wrist. He was not letting go until he knew Athena was safely outside, where he intended to strangle her.

He placed the dog at Troy's feet, telling himself that the moisture in his eyes at the joyful reunion was only from the smoke. He accepted the mug of ale someone placed in his hand, and saw that his housekeeper was bringing Athena a pitcher of lemonade. No, she was pouring water into a dish for the dog. But Athena seemed fine. She would live, at least until he got his hands on her.

"How could you be such a peagoose, woman?" he shouted when he had a good grip on her shoulders. "I swear the deaf dog is smarter than you are. At least she hid under the bed where the air was breathable. By all that's holy, we have not been wed one day and I am ready to commit murder. And it makes no matter to me that I might hang, for I am bound to have heart failure anyway. If I do, I vow I shall come back to haunt you for all of your days." He gave her shoulders a shake, not enough to hurt her, of course, just to tell her he was furious. "If you ever do that again, Attie, I swear I will throttle you."

"Do what?" she shouted right back, stomping on his sore toes. "Disobey you? You promised you were not going to be a despot, and here you are, already acting the bully when I don't follow your orders."

"Disobey me? Hell, no. You can take my orders and feed them to the blasted dog. But you put yourself in danger, that's what I mind. Do. Not. Do. That. Again. Not ever."

Athena threw herself into his arms, her own arms wrapped tightly around his chest as if she would keep him next to her forever. "You do love me! You do. I knew it!"

Chapter Twenty-Four

When a man decides to take a wife, he should find one he can trust.

—Anonymous

When a woman finds a man she can trust, she should marry him.

—Mrs. Anonymous

Maybe he did love her, Ian thought. If love meant putting her above all others, setting her welfare above every other concern, then yes, he thought he just might love his precious wife. If it meant wanting to celebrate their survival, and their wedding, in the most basic way he knew, then yes, he did love her.

He wanted her, he wanted to be with her. He wanted to keep her safe and happy, and he would want to die if he lost her in the smoke or the fire. Could love really be that simple? Why did those poets have to make such a deuced mystery of the thing, then? To sell more boring verses, he supposed, and to make lesser men think they were senseless clods for not going into raptures about a beloved's eyebrow. Athena did have a fine brow, now that Ian considered it, softly arched, the brown hairs tipped with gold, and two out of line with the others at the ends. He'd wanted to smooth them earlier, but had found too many other fascinating details of his bewitching bride.

He'd make sure to do it soon, tonight, right after he told her that he loved her. She would most likely cry, the silly goose, but he could dry her eyes with his kisses, and lick away her tears. No, that reminded him too much of the dog.

He'd bring an extra handkerchief, that's what he would do, after he had a bath to get rid of the smoke and some of Cook's ointment to get rid of the sting on his feet. The fires were all extinguished, but footmen were on watch to make sure they did not reignite. Others were patrolling the perimeter of the house, in case the arsonist decided to make another try. Bow Street had two of its Runners watching, too. In the morning they would look for clues, and Heaven help the gallows bait if Ian found him first.

Ian had thought of moving everyone to a hotel, but they were so many, and so tired. His mother was truly ill this time, pale and shaking, and Rensdale was seeing double again. The house did not appear to be heavily damaged, so it was safe, and the smoke had not reached every corner. With the windows open to the cool night air, the remnants of smoke were not pleasant, but they were not unbearable.

He would make a closer inspection in the morning, with architects and engineers called in to survey the soundness of the structure, and hire extra work crews to wash down the walls and air the rugs. That could all wait for morning, which was not so far distant by the time Ian had paid off the firemen, spoken to the Runners, and sent his servants—those not on watch— to their own well-deserved beds.

He deserved to finish what was left of the night in his wife's arms.

The problem was, Athena was fast asleep in the

countess's bedchamber. She slept on her side, he saw, curled over in the center of the bed. There would be room for him, he figured, if he slipped behind her— very close behind her.

But he might wake her. Hell, he intended to wake her, and that was not fair. She had been a trooper through the night, helping the maids serve refreshments to the workers, keeping her brothers from danger and his mother from apoplexy. She gave orders to the household staff as if she were born to the task, which she most likely was. Then she had gone with the butler and the housekeeper to inspect the sleeping quarters and direct the temporary locations of cots and pallets, the placement of fresh linens on the beds.

She'd had a bath, he could see from the damp, curling tendrils of hair that framed her face by his candle's light. She smelled of roses, despite the fires. Her room and his had been spared most of the damage, and the wedding flowers were trying their hardest to mask the traces of smoke.

Ian wanted to tell Athena that he was proud of her and grateful to her, but he would not. Not tonight. Tonight he'd let her sleep, like the gentleman he was—the tortured, tormented, and throbbing gentleman, that is.

He covered her with another blanket, for the open window was letting in the cold and the coals had all but gone out. She did not waken, not even when he kissed her cheek good night. He shoveled more coals onto the hearth and used the bellows to rekindle the embers, and she did not wake up at that, either.

Out of excuses, he had to leave, to seek his own cold, empty, most likely smoky bed, where no one complained if his feet were icy, and no one cared that they hurt.

Surely he must love her, to make such a sacrifice.

*   *   *

He was ready to tell her in the morning. Oh, he was ready for a lot of things in the morning. Athena was still sleeping, though. How noble could he be? Too noble to hurry through consummating his marriage while a Bow Street Runner, an architect, and a housepainter waited downstairs. Once he started, Ian knew, he was not going to stop making love to his wife, not if the regent, Christopher Wren, and Michelangelo himself were waiting downstairs.

He dealt with the household matters first, putting everything in his butler's capable hands, including a heavy purse to see the work done quickly, with the least disruption. Then he invited the Runner to take breakfast with him.

The Runner had eaten, but he followed Lord Marden to the dining parlor, since the morning room was damaged. He accepted a cup of coffee, then started with his questions. The first one was where Lord Paige had gone. Everyone knew the two men were enemies, he said, and Paige might have wanted revenge.

The cowardice of the arson attack might have been Paige's style, but Ian was certain Paige had left for Scotland. Carswell had checked, and Ian trusted his best friend. He had, anyway, before the cad seduced Ian's sister. Ian doubted that Paige had the funds to hire a ruffian to do his dirty deeds, but the Runner said he would ask around the gaming halls and the low dives Paige might have patronized. If he'd employed a torch man, someone would know about it. For a generous enough reward, that someone would talk. Ian emptied the household cash box, making a note to visit his bank.

If not Paige, the Runner asked, did Lord Marden think Lady Paige might have had anything to do with the fires?

Mona might be offended at his marriage, and insulted at the end of their affair, but she was living in his Kensington property, for heaven's sake, at his expense. Not even she could be moronic enough to think he would be more generous if his town house was burned to the ground. She was too lazy, anyway.

Did Lord Marden have any other idea of who might be behind the attempted homicides?

The very word sent chills down Ian's spine. The Runner thought someone had tried to kill him and his family, not simply tried to cause a mess and a commotion on his wedding night.

His wedding night. There was someone who might have felt he had a prior claim on Miss Renslow's hand and dowry. Wiggs might have decided that if he could not have Athena, no one should. Ian had a hard time envisioning the center-parted prelate as a creature of such burning, possessive passion, but he gave the Runner Wiggy's name.

"A man of the cloth, you say? Not your usual suspect. I'll look into it. Do you have his address?" He wrote down the location Ian gave him, then flipped back two pages in his occurrence book. Wiggs's address was indeed the same as Lady Paige's.

The Runner blinked twice. "Not your usual reverend, it seems. Can you think of any other enemies you might have? Gentlemen who lost to you at cards? Another irate husband? Someone you might have bested at fisticuffs or swords?"

"You might be speaking of half the gentlemen in London. I doubt my sins were so great to deserve roasting alive, however, and I have been a veritable saint recently. A married man, don't you know."

The Runner did not know if a wedding band was a cure for moral turpitude, but he kept flipping through his notes. "What about anyone else in the house? Might someone here have someone out to kill them?"

"Like my mother? Gads, I doubt whining and nagging are capital crimes. My sister offends everyone"—himself included, this morning—"but her reform movement does not have enough power to be a threat. My wife? Who could dislike that angel? Why, she is the most caring, loving soul who ever—"

The Runner coughed.

"Quite. Her little brother is hardly out of the house enough to annoy anyone. But now that I think on it, her other brother, Viscount Rensdale, was set upon by a thug a few days ago. I thought it odd at the time."

The Runner flipped through his occurrence book to last night's investigation. "Concussed, they said. A brick. Not your usual weapon."

"And not your usual robbery. Nothing was taken."

So they went to speak to Rensdale, who was still asleep after the excitement of the fires. Lord Marden had no compunction whatsoever about waking this guest, especially if he had been the target of the attacks, placing Ian's entire family at risk.

Rensdale knew of no one who hated him enough to light a match under his foot, much less a conflagration at his new brother-in-law's house. The attempted robbery could not have any connection. The pack of ruffians who set upon him must have been a street gang or some such.

"He limped," Ian interrupted Rensdale's tale of bravery. "The attacker ran away when I called out. I thought it might be you, because he limped."

Rensdale did not like speaking of his impairment. "A lot of fellows limp. They might have been returned soldiers, out of work and out of money."

"Do you know anyone else in London with a limp, my lord?" the Runner asked.

Rensdale thought a moment. "Only one of my grooms. I sent him to town with Attie and Troy. Haven't seen him, now that you mention it."

"Alfie Brown?" Ian asked.

"That's him. He must have found a better position. With my brother and sister staying here, I suppose he wasn't needed."

"Where did you find him? Who are his people? Where might he be, and why does he hate you?" Ian was sure Alfie was the culprit. He'd never trusted the man for leaving Troy in the field that day, and for not coming forth afterward. Any decent crook would have tried blackmail weeks ago.

Rensdale hemmed and hawed, then admitted that Alfie Brown's people were from his own neighborhood. His own house, in fact. Alfie was one of his father's by-blows, off a kitchen maid, Sally Brown. The former viscount had done the right thing, Rensdale told them proudly. He'd supported the maid and her son until the day he died.

"Alfie doesn't hate me. Gave him a job, I did, and he was grateful. Said he'd look after the nipper like his own brother. Well, stands to reason he would, since he was. A brother, that is, though no one spoke of the relation. Everyone in the neighborhood knew, of course. Family traits, don't you know. The limp, for one."

"The limp? You said yours was due to a carriage accident."

Rensdale tugged at his covers. "I didn't want my wife to think that our children might be clubfooted."

"And Troy?"

Rensdale nodded. "Him, too, but they tried to fix it when he was a babe. My father was so distraught over his young wife's death, he couldn't stand another deformed child. Some sawbones broke the infant's leg to set it straight. He was never the same after."

"Good gods, I should think not. No mother, and then they torture the babe? It's a wonder he survived at all."

Rensdale shrugged. "No one thought he would, except Attie."

The Runner cleared his throat. "You say this Alfie Brown is here in London? I'd like a word with him."

Ian wanted more than a word with the bastard, but he sent the Runner on to Cameron Street, to see if the captain's man, Macelmore, could help locate the missing groom.

He himself went to Kensington, in case he was wrong about Lady Paige and the Reverend Mr. Wiggs. The lady was still asleep, since it was not yet noon, and Mr. Wiggs had departed within the last half hour, for Lord Marden's house, the butler believed. Lord Marden did not care; it was the butler he wished to interrogate anyway. The man was in Ian's employ, after all, not Lady Paige's. His loyalties followed his pay to the bank. "The—*ahem*—lady and the—*ahem*—reverend gentleman were both in the house all night," the butler reported. Neither had left, for the doors and windows were still locked from the inside when the servants awoke.

That was the information Ian needed. He went on to the captain's house, to confer with the Runner and assure Athena's uncle that she and his nephew were unharmed by the fires. No one had seen hide nor hair of Alfie, but the Runner would put extra men on the search, now that the groom was the only suspect. Ian offered a reward, and the captain said he would double it, to protect his kin. In charity, they walked to their banks.

* * *

Wiggs had indeed called at Maddox House. He was convincingly appalled at the fire damage, more appalled that Lady Dorothy was out so early, and most appalled at the news he felt he had to impart to Athena.

"I warned you not to marry that libertine," he told her, puffing out his chest. "And I was right. Divorces are frowned upon, but I see no other hope of ending this disastrous misalliance. Annulments are near impossible, unless you gave false names, heh-heh. I know you did not, for I recited them myself. And I doubt you could prove him incapable of performing the—*humph*—marriage act, not with half of London swearing otherwise. Lunacy might be a legitimate cause. The man must be insane to think you would never find out."

"Find out what, for goodness sake?" Athena demanded. She was tired, peevish, and worried that someone was trying to harm them. She had a great deal to do, too, in seeing that Ian's house was restored to its former grandeur. "Just say what you are bursting to say, sir, so that I might get on with my day, and my marriage, which, I assure you, I shall not try to dissolve."

So Wiggs did, with more than reverendly relish. He'd had the entire tale from Lady Paige, who had it from her spouse before he fled without her.

"My husband was involved in that duel, you say? I assumed so, since Lady Paige's name was mentioned. I told you, that *affaire* is ended. It has nothing to do with me." She went back to her pad and her lists.

"Lord Paige fired early? No wonder the woman was unfaithful, if her husband was such a cad." Unlike Athena's wonderful husband. She could not imagine wanting or needing any other man in her bed or in her life. She smiled, inside and out. "I really am quite busy, as you can see." She held her pencil poised to add new slippers for Ian on her list. Roma had claimed the last pair, not to chew, but to carry around her rescuer's scent.

Wiggs wafted his final words.

The pad hit the ground. "My husband did what?" The pencil snapped in two. "He fired where?"

Athena was so mad, she marched into Troy's room and yelled at the boy. "What do you mean, you didn't see who hit you?"

"He was not aiming at me, I swear."

Then she yelled at her other brother. "You knew, and you let me marry that man?"

"Of course I knew. Marden's got honor, told me what happened straight out in his letter. Said he meant to take full responsibility, which included you. Only decent thing to do, of course."

Athena yelled at her new sister-in-law, who was aghast that she had not been at Maddox House for the fires, and aghast that she had been caught out.

"You warned me not to be seduced," Athena shouted, "and look at you. Coming home in the morning in the same gown you wore last night! And with Carswell, of all people. The man lies through his teeth. He is as big a scoundrel as your brother, and you are to have nothing more to do with him, do you hear me?"

Since Athena was nearly a foot shorter than Lady Dorothy, and since Doro fully intended to see more, a lot more, of Mr. Carswell, she merely patted Athena's cheek. "Whatever my brother has done to put you in such a pet, my dear, I am certain he will apologize nicely. If you play your cards right, you can snabble a new bracelet or a carriage of your own."

"I do not want anything from your brother! I do

not want your brother! The man is a liar and a fiend and a philanderer and . . . and a fiend," Athena repeated, because she could not think of anything worse.

Lady Marden chided her for shouting. The noise was giving the dowager a headache, for one, and such behavior was unladylike, for another, entirely unsuitable for a countess.

So Athena went upstairs and yelled at the deaf dog.

Ian expected his house to be a beehive of activity, with workers scrubbing walls and carrying out carpets. He expected his wife to be relieved that they had a name for the arsonist, and he expected them to spend the rest of the day in the hotel suite he had reserved.

No one was in the hallway, not a footman or a butler, although the doors and windows all stood open to allow the breeze to air the house of the lingering smoke. No one was in the drawing room, the library, or the dining parlor, although he knew his sister was back, having seen his former bay horses fly down the street ahead of Carswell's curricle when he approached the house. He knew his mother would be up, because the captain was to call in an hour. Rensdale was awake because he'd roused the man himself.

He knew something was wrong. Not a catastrophe, or someone would have sent for him or met him at the door. But something was wrong, all right, and he had a sinking suspicion he was it.

Young Renslow just shook his head. The dog cowered under the bed, not even offering a token growl. Ian loosened his suddenly tight shirt collar.

The walk to his bedroom might have been the march to the gallows. Every door on the corridor was closed; not a maid scurried past. The silence was worse than a death sentence.

A coward might have left. Ian thought about it, then

thought about the heart-shaped ruby pendant he carried in his hand, from the jewelry shop near his bank. He'd never given Athena a wedding present, and her wedding night had been ruined. Perhaps the necklace could make up for whatever sin he had unwittingly committed.

And perhaps pigs would fly.

"I trusted you!" his delicate, adoring little spouse screeched as Ian walked into his bedchamber. "If nothing else, I thought I could believe your word."

"I—"

"I thought you were a man of honor, despite your womanizing."

"I—"

"You lied to me!" she shouted, pummeling his last pair of slippers onto his desk.

He caught the ink bottle before it fell. "You—"

"Oh, no, you don't. You cannot make me responsible for your sins. You were the one who lied, who made me believe you wanted to marry me, when you and Rensdale had decided it days before, as a way to atone for your crime. You were the one who fired that pistol, not Lord Paige!"

"Yes, but—"

"You shot my baby brother!"

The best defense being a good offense, Ian launched his own attack. "Well, you lied about his injuries. I thought I had made him an invalid for life, and here he was already crippled. You let me go on feeling guilty for more than my fair share."

"How was I supposed to know you were feeling guilty when I did not know you had anything to feel guilty about? Furthermore, everyone knew about Troy and what they did to him as a baby. Rensdale must have told you when you discussed marriage, in case you were worried that your children might carry the

Renslow curse. I assumed it did not matter to you, since you love your sister despite her scars, and your mother, who goes into a sneezing fit at the first flower. I thought you could love our babies, no matter what."

"I can, and I will."

"How do you expect me to believe that, when you lied about so much else?"

"I did not lie, entirely, and I had good reasons."

"There is no good reason for this!"

"Of course there is. Be reasonable, Attie. You were here, and you were distraught. I did not want to add to your concerns thinking that you might be facing your brother's . . ." His voice trailed away.

"His murderer? Is that what you did not want to tell me? That I married the man who might have killed my brother, except for good doctoring and a lot of luck?"

"I did not want you to hate me."

"That's all you can say, for lying to me? For marrying me under false pretenses? For promising me that I could trust you. That's all you can say?"

No, it wasn't all.

He said, "I love you."

Chapter Twenty-Five

*Why does a woman marry a man and then expect
him to change?*

—Anonymous

*Why does a man not understand that marriage
changes everyone?*

—Mrs. Anonymous

The door connecting Ian's bedroom and Athena's
slammed shut, along with his hopes for a midday
romantic interlude. The clicking of the lock sounded
the death knell for his hopes for the night, too, it
appeared. Ian thought of shoving the ruby pendant
under the door, but he doubted Athena would be won
over by a bribe. Besides, the blasted thing would not
fit.

He sat at his desk, moving the slippers she had
thrown there, and composed a letter. In it he explained about the prevarications concerning the duel:
the ricocheted pistol ball, Paige's villainy and cowardice, his own decision to stay to look after Troy instead
of fleeing the country. He wrote that he was responsible, but never intended to harm the boy, or her. When
he realized that he had ruined her chances for making
a respectable marriage, he had decided to make

amends in the only gentlemanly way possible, so her good opinion of him mattered.

He continued to write, putting down things he had never truly thought, and had never spoken, how their marriage was not a mere matter of honor. He could have found another way to satisfy Rensdale and his own conscience if she had refused him. But, he wrote, he was glad she did not. He had married her gladly, with relief that she had agreed, with pride that she chose him, with joy that she would be his partner through life. He was a fool, he confessed, needing a fire to show him what any blind man could see, that he held a treasure in his hands, and would never be happy if he let it go. He loved her, he wrote, more than he thought possible, more than words could say, more than she loved him, if one small deception could so destroy her feelings for him.

His forehead was damp and his shirt was clinging to his skin, he was so overheated in his efforts to express himself. He took up the penknife to sharpen his point, while he wondered if he had left anything out, like his shock and horror at what he had done, like his vow never to hold a weapon on another person. He nicked his finger, thinking so hard instead of paying attention, and then wondered if Athena would be more likely to believe him if he signed the letter in blood.

No, she would think he was a clumsy idiot, which he was. He had bled out his soul in the deuced letter, anyway, and that had to be enough. He folded the page, affixed a wax seal, got up, and slid it under the connecting door.

A minute later, the letter came back under the door, the seal still intact. That was the only thing that was, for the page itself was in shreds, little scraps of unread remorse crammed under his door. He was reminded of a prisoner in a dungeon receiving his daily bread and water through a slot on the floor . . . a prisoner declared guilty, whether he was or was not.

Well, he had bled, and now he was empty. He could not beg at her feet—she would not open the door to his knock—and he would not shout like a fishwife (like his own wife) through the wood for all the servants and family to hear. Breaking her door down would be the act of a violent, threatening bully, which he had sworn not to be. He did not want her afraid of him, heaven knew. Her anger was bad enough.

He could always get the keys from the housekeeper, of course. That was cheating, though, taking unfair advantage of his superior position. Worse, his housekeeper might side with the new countess. Then he'd have no keys, no wife, no meals served on time and no clean linen. No, he would not ask for the keys.

Athena was as rational as a female could be; she'd come around. She'd see he had no choice, and she'd see that since they were already married, she might as well make the best of it. Then he could show her how good his best could be.

They could celebrate their marriage with wine and candles and flowers all over again, he decided, feeling his body stir at the thought. Perhaps at—No, Lady Paige was still at his Kensington place. The hotel, then, or a lovely inn outside of town. His mind drew air castles, and his imagination moved right in, with feather mattresses and fur rugs on the floor and hot, wet skin, glistening by the fire's glow.

Lud, he hoped Athena did not take long to get over her outrage. He needed her.

And he needed a bath. A cold one.

Afterward, when she still had not stirred from her room, he kidnapped her brother.

"What do you say we go for a ride, Troy, try out

your paces? I have a nice mare, sweet but with spirit. She won't toss you, but she does need a firm hand at the reins. The rain seems to have stopped and the sun is trying to come through. I need the exercise and would like the company."

Troy grabbed his crutches, then paused. "What about Attie? She said I could try to ride next week in the indoor ring at the riding school."

"She is not speaking to me right now, so I cannot ask. Do you wish to?"

"The mood she is in? Not on your life!"

Athena's mood was as black as her husband's heart. As black as his boots, which she heard when he walked down the hall. As black as sin, of which he had committed so many she stopped counting.

His final lie was the worst. He loved her? Hah! No one lied to one's beloved. Trust was part of loving, and he had not trusted her with the truth. At first, of course, he did not know her, much less hold her in affection. But when he proposed? When they were about to be married? Didn't he owe her the truth then?

More worrisome was the notion that if he could lie at that point, and after, when they were tangled in each other's arms, he could keep on lying. She could never trust him, never believe his promises, never accept his word. When he told her he loved her—if he ever did again, after her tantrum—she could not believe him.

What about later, when he was at his club, or visiting friends, or playing cards until dawn? Could she believe his promise of fidelity then, when he had been caught in a falsehood before? Would he bother to keep the promise, or simply tell her more lies?

He would tell her what he thought she wanted to

hear, and not tell her what he thought would upset her. She would be treated like a child, shielded from the truth and fed fairy stories instead.

What happened when a child realized that there were no ogres waiting in the woods to swallow up naughty boys and girls? He or she discovered that his parents did not always speak the truth, that's what. They were not all-knowing, all-powerful beings to be adored and blindly obeyed. They were human, and fallible, and the child learned to judge things for himself on the way to adulthood.

Athena was an adult, a mature woman, with her eyes open now. No more silly infatuation for her, no more thinking her husband could hang the moon, no more letting him treat her like a little girl. And no more tears.

They were married, yes, but on her terms now. Her door was going to stay locked until she could accept a lying, cheating, child-maiming churl in her bed. The fairy-tale ogre could stay in his own woods; he was not going to swallow her for lunch.

She did not come down for luncheon, and she did not come down for supper, pleading a lingering headache after the fire. She did keep busy, organizing the household to make necessary repairs and rearrangements while they were cleaning after the smoke. She woke in the morning and kept busy until dark, avoiding her relatives, including that traitor, Troy. She was polite to Ian's family, but distant. At night, her door stayed locked.

The dowager Lady Marden threw up her hands and threatened to return to Bath, until Captain Beecham begged her to stay.

Lord Rensdale would have gone home, but Lord Marden discouraged him from that. If that groom wanted to get rid of the entire Renslow family, Ian warned, he'd follow Rensdale back to Derby and kill him along the way, when he was unprotected and unsuspecting. Or else, the Runner put in, Alfie Brown might go after Lady Rensdale, when he discovered she was carrying another heir to the name and title. They sent an army of former soldiers to guard the estate, without telling Lady Rensdale, naturally.

Another troop circled Maddox House day and night. Troy could not set foot or crutch out of doors, not as far as the garden, not without an armed escort or footmen patrolling the vicinity. If he left the grounds, Lord Marden went with him. Rensdale refused to 'leave the house at all, lest he be set upon again. As for Athena, she seldom went farther than the park across the street with the dog, and never noticed how many veterans and servants were standing about. She had too much on her mind.

She missed him. She missed her brother, too, who was too busy with Ian and his lessons and his exercising to need her company. Lady Dorothy was also too busy, although Athena did not want to know precisely with what, or with whom, Doro was so occupied. Lady Marden was out with Uncle Barnaby, when she was not resting from her exertions. Describing the fire to all of her friends was almost as exhausting to the dowager as avoiding the workmen and extra maids.

Athena had all the organizing chores completed, and the house well on its way to being restored. She had her new clothes completed and in her wardrobe, and she had nowhere to go. She told Hull they were not receiving until the house was repaired, and she did not pay any calls. She was bored and she was lonely, and she was sick at heart that her lovely marriage had not lasted through an entire day. But she was right, she told herself. That had to count for something, although it did not warm her bed at night or send chills down her spine or make her toes tingle. Nothing but her husband had that power, which made her madder still, and sadder.

Ian was not by nature a patient man. He thought he was doing amazingly well not to hound Bow Street for news of the search, and he thought he was magnanimous to let his wife have her way while he slept in a monk's cell. He slept in the earl's bedchamber, of course, but it was getting smaller and colder and emptier every night he knew Athena was on the other side of that blasted door. He was married, by heaven, to a woman he loved and desired. Why was he sleeping alone?

His patience and passion warred for three whole nights. Pride won.

On the following day, Ian waited in the hall for his wife's maid to leave, then he stepped into the countess's chamber.

Athena had to catch herself before a welcoming smile burst across her face. Ian looked so handsome, so big and strong and determined. He carried a bouquet of violets.

"We are married," he said from the doorway.

"Yes."

"We have to come to some kind of terms."

"Yes."

"We cannot do that while you are avoiding me."

"No."

"Will you speak with me?"

"Yes."

"May I come in?"

"No. I doubt we would get much talking done."

She was right. Ian moved to his second plan. "I thought we might go on a picnic. The day is fine, your brother is well used to his new mare and itching for a longer ride, and I need to show you what happened the day of that duel. I need to see for myself, too. I was too concerned with getting Troy home then to make a careful look. Carswell and Doro have agreed to come, and your uncle and my mother said they would enjoy a carriage ride, although they do not know our direction. The fewer people who do, the better, so don't mention our destination to your maid. Not that I do not trust her, but discretion is called for until we know precisely what did happen. Will you come with us?"

She really wanted to go, to find out the truth, but agreeing might seem like forgiving, conceding, condoning his behavior. On the other hand, Athena had been cooped in the house for ages, it felt. Ian looked so hopeful, so eager, and the day was indeed perfect for a picnic: clear, but not hot. She was torn.

"If you don't come, how can you know I won't use your brother for target practice?" he asked, a smile on his face. It was the smile that convinced her. Goodness, how she loved his smile, so bright and endearing and slightly lopsided, that she had to smile back. "Yes, I would like to, but I shall travel with your mother and my uncle."

"They will not thank you, you know. I shall take my curricle if you would rather drive than ride."

"Will you let me take the ribbons?"

"Hell, no—That is, perhaps, after the pair has worked out the fidgets, and when the road is clear and we are out of London proper. Besides, that is blackmail."

"I was merely testing to see how much you wanted my company."

His smile turned into a grin that was half leer. "If you let me come in, I could show you."

She shut the door in his face. "I will be ready in half an hour."

Perhaps she should have ridden after all. She had not been on a horse in ages, though, and never on one of the caliber of Marden's stables. Furthermore, she had neglected to order a new habit, and did not want to embarrass herself or Ian on either count. Now she was sitting with her thigh pressed against his on the narrow driving seat, feeling his firm, hard muscles move with the coach's sway. Oh, dear. She had to fan herself, despite the cool breeze in her face. He shifted slightly closer, the cad, knowing how he was affecting her. He just grinned, enjoying the day and the ride and his horses—and her. She grinned back and held onto her bonnet as he set the pair to a ground-eating gallop.

When they reached a clearing, he had the footmen who had followed in another coach unload the picnic supplies and the growling dog, and take up positions surrounding the party, after they, the grooms, and the mounted guards were sure no one had followed, and the area was safe. The servants would eat later. The dog would eat when she wanted, as usual.

They set out blankets and baskets, and chairs for Lady Marden and Athena's uncle. They unpacked covered dishes kept warm with bricks, and bottles chilled with wet towels. Cook had prepared enough food for three times their number, and Athena had to laugh, recalling the picnics she was used to, with a blanket, a loaf of bread and some cheese in a sack. This was more of an al fresco feast.

The food, the day, the company, were all superb, and Athena could forget the real nature of the outing. She could forget her doubts about Ian, too, while he was letting Troy hold forth about his mare, laughing with his family and friends, feeding Roma the choicest bits of food, feeding Athena the plumpest strawberries. He insisted on putting them into her mouth, saying her gown was too pretty to chance stains, although she might have eaten more neatly without his nearness.

After the luncheon, Lady Marden declared herself in need of a nap under the nearby trees. The captain thought he might join her, to keep a watch, he said. Troy remounted, and the others walked behind his horse farther into the clearing.

"Here's the place," Carswell said when they had reached familiar level ground, with the trees bordering the field. "We were positioned about here."

Ian took his place, and Carswell took Paige's. Doro was sent to stand in the surgeon's stead, while Athena went with Troy and the dog to try to find where he had been watching atop his horse. While they waited for the Renslows to call out that they were ready, Ian raised his gun in Carswell's direction.

"About my sister . . ." he began.

Carswell laughed. "Good thing that pistol isn't loaded, eh?"

"Someone is trying to do away with my wife's family. Do you really think I would carry an unloaded weapon?"

Carswell stopped laughing on the instant. His face paled. "You wouldn't. You swore!"

"Oh, I would not aim to kill," Ian said, lowering the muzzle of the pistol. "I would just make sure you could not dishonor another respectable female."

Carswell threw his hands in the air. "Nothing dishonorable about my intentions, I swear. I asked her. She's thinking about it. You know how females are."

Ian did. He shouted to his sister: "If you don't marry him, I'll have to shoot the dastard."

"He wants a big, fancy wedding, one Mother would adore."

"What do you want?" he called over.

"Gretna Green, with no fuss."

Ian turned back to his friend. "You heard her. Scotland it is. Athena and I will go along as chaperones as soon as things arc safe. We never did have a honeymoon, you know, so I doubt you'll mind us, but the old tabbies would mind if we were not along. Then we can let Mother throw a ball in your honor at Maddox House, the biggest one the *ton* has ever seen. Does that satisfy everyone?"

"I'm game if you'll lower the gun," Carswell answered, and Doro nodded her agreement. "Unless you have any objections, Ian?"

"My only objection is the blasted delay to find a would-be killer. Troy, have you found the place yet?"

Troy wasn't sure, but the dog was snuffling around a trampled area under a tree. Too much time had gone by, and rain, for her to recognize her master's scent, but Athena thought dark patches on the bare dirt might be blood. "We think so," she yelled back across the clearing.

Ian raised his pistol again, as if he was going to fire in the sky, deloping. Then he moved the gun down, in a line with Carswell's head, and then to the left, toward the trees. "There. That would have been where the ball hit the tree. My Mantons aim true, without pulling to the right or the left."

"I see the spot," Athena called, headed in the direction of his aim.

They all followed. "What are we looking for?" Lady Dorothy wanted to know.

Ian was looking up at the trees. "There ought to be a mark on the trunk of one of them if the ball ricocheted into Troy."

There was a scar on one of the trees, but not from a passing blow. The trunk had a hole in it, with a lead ball still embedded in the bark.

"I didn't shoot him, Attie!" Ian yelled. "I did not shoot your brother!" He was so relieved and excited he picked her up, right off her feet, and twirled her around until she was dizzy. "I shot a tree!"

Athena was giddy from the spin and the kiss Ian had finished it with. He'd still lied to her, but that seemed irrelevant now. His happiness, and his arms around her were all that mattered . . . until she had a moment to think, while the others gathered around, watching Carswell extract the ball with his pocket-knife. She pushed Ian away. "If you didn't shoot him, then, by accident or mischance, who did?"

"Why, that groom of yours who ran off after the horses, of course. He told Macelmore some story of finding Troy gone when he got back, but likely he intended to keep going, until he realized the cub would live. Then he went after Rensdale. When that did not work, he tried to kill both of them at one time with the fires at Maddox House."

"Alfie Brown? My father's illegitimate son? Why?"

"We'll know that when we find him."

Athena looked around, at the secluded clearing and the thick stand of trees where any evildoer could be lurking. Then she kicked Ian in the shin. "You knew he shot Troy, and is out to kill all of us, yet you brought my brother out here, in the open?"

"With mounted guards and armed footmen. And I made certain we were not followed out of town."

She kicked him again.

"Ouch. What's that for?"

"For not telling me all three crimes were connected, or that you suspected Alfie. For not, by heaven, telling me the truth!"

Chapter Twenty-Six

Love conquers all. Doesn't it?

—Anonymous

*Love cannot tame a shark, soften a rock, or stop
the wind. It needs help.*

—Mrs. Anonymous

Athena came down to dinner and stayed afterward
to play a hand of cards. She beat Troy at chess,
and played to a draw with Ian. Her bedroom door,
however, stayed locked.

She came to breakfast, helped Ian's mother answer
her correspondence, and went shopping for bridal
clothes with Lady Dorothy. She visited a naval hospital with her uncle, a museum with Mr. Carswell, and
an at-home of two ladies who claimed to have known
her mother. She rode in the park early for practice,
and drove there late with Ian, at the fashionable hour.
But her door stayed locked.

They attended the theater, a dinner, and church.
He brought her flowers and books and a high-bred
mare. He tried apologizing again, only to be told that
he simply did not understand. She was right, he did
not understand, but he comprehended well enough
the fact that the blasted door was going to stay

locked. His patience had worn so thin you could see through it.

"How long, my lady? How long are you going to deny us both the pleasure we seek? You cannot deny you want to share my bed, for I have seen the way you blush when I brush against you, and the way your breathing comes faster if I sit too close. Why, every time I admire that ruby pendant between your breasts, I could swear I see them tightening for my touch. Your body remembers how good I made you feel, Attie, and it wants to join with mine."

She was blushing furiously now, happy they were at the opera where no one could see. Otherwise they would think she was wearing as much face paint as Lady Dorothy. She pretended to study the program, moving sideways in her seat so their shoulders could not touch, lest her traitorous body give away more of her secrets.

Ian took her hand before she moved so far that she fell off the chair. "We can overcome our differences between the sheets, for we had so much in common there, didn't we?"

"We would not talk."

"Of course we would, sooner or later. We are talking now, are we not?"

"No, you are trying to seduce me. That is not conversation."

He stroked her hand, his thumb making circles on her palm. She could feel the heat through her glove, and pulled her hand away.

"I would be within my prerogatives to claim my marital rights, you know."

"You would not. You promised."

"But if you already distrust me, if you do not believe my word, why should I bother to keep any of my promises?"

"Because you are a kind and honest man, a true gentleman."

He raised his voice in frustration. "Then why the devil won't you let me in your bedroom?"

His mother struck him on the shoulder with her opera glasses, but a woman in the next box giggled.

Mortified, Athena stared at the stage with a smile fixed on her face. So what if the hero of the opera was staggering around with a knife in his chest, singing his death throes? If she had a knife she might be tempted to use it, too, and smile while doing so.

"If you will not let me express my love for you in the best way I know, then tell me how. You owe me that, Attie, for being so patient. Tell me what I have to do to win back your favor. I swear I do not know."

"You have to start trusting me," she whispered as loudly as she dared.

Ian sat back and looked at her as if her peacock feather headdress had let out a squawk. "I let you go to the museum with Carswell, didn't I?"

"I do not mean that way. I swore to be faithful, and you must know I would never forsake my vows."

"Then how can I show I trust you?"

"By treating me as an adult, as an equal. I am not a child to be protected, or a dumb beast in your keeping. Nor am I a mistress in your keeping, wanting to be bought with jewels and honeyed words. I am your wife."

"No wonder there are so many estranged couples. I thought a wife could be a lover, too."

"Of course she can, but she has to be more than a bedmate. I want to be treated as your friend."

He jerked his head to where Carswell and Doro sat at the back of the box, in the shadows. "I already have a friend."

"As your partner, then, for that is what I am, your partner through the corridors of time."

"I'd wager none of the doors on that corridor are locked," he muttered as he escorted his wife out of the opera box. "Athena has a headache," he told the others as they left.

"I'll bet she does," Carswell snickered under his breath when they went past. "Every night."

Ian managed to step on his friend's toes before reaching the back of the box and leading Athena down the hall where they could have a modicum of privacy before the intermission.

Once he was positive no one could overhear, he told her his plan to trap the bastard, Brown. The earl had not considered doing so before, would never think of telling a delicate, sensitive woman his harsh plan now, but he saw no other way of winning back Athena's regard. Reluctantly, then, he described how they were going to bring the disgruntled groom out into the open where they could deal with him the way he deserved.

Too much time had been spent at this investigation, he told her, waiting for the villain to make another move. "But we have kept his targets so well protected that he could never get near enough to act, or for us to catch him."

Too much time had gone by, Ian had decided, with his wife in distress and his house full of guests. Rensdale could not go home while Brown was on the loose. His sister and Carswell could not go to Scotland without his and Athena's chaperonage. They had promised not to, although heaven knew they disappeared often enough to travel to India. His mother could not return to Bath, where the captain had offered to escort her. He could not send Troy off to school, not even as a day scholar—not when danger might be waiting at the next corner.

His home would know no peace while Alfie Brown was free, and he would know no conjugal bliss, it seemed.

"I am determined to catch Brown in the act, to prove his guilt. Troy cannot say for certain that Brown shot him, for he cannot remember what happened, and Rensdale did not identify his attacker. No one saw the cur lighting the fires. We have a good case against the man, but not good enough."

"What you are saying makes sense, but how do you intend to force him into sight of a score of armed guards and Bow Street Runners?"

"Well, I was not going to tell you because there is a mite of risk, but since we are partners, I will have to, I suppose. With a bit of skullduggery of our own, disguises and such, your brother will appear unprotected. He will walk in the park across the street daily, at fixed times, giving Brown confidence enough to make a plan. We will make it appear that we have stopped watching, or stopped caring."

Athena was thinking. She did not like the conclusion she drew. "You intend to use my brother as bait! You are going to tie Troy out like a lamb? Never! I will take his place, that is what we will do. I am near his height, and slender enough to fit his clothes. With my hair tucked under a cap, and using his crutches I can—"

"Never!" The idea of his bride in breeches sounded enticing, but her facing a bitter, vengeful, violent man was impossible. She was his wife, dash it! "Never," he repeated, louder.

"I thought it was safe?" she asked, looking around the deserted hallway to make sure no one could hear his angry voice.

"There is always some element of risk when dealing with the criminal mind."

She raised her chin. "I thought we were partners."

"Partners do not let their wives, ah, their partners go into danger."

"But you would send my little brother?"

"No, I would send Rensdale, as a matter of fact."

"Oh, that is all right then, I suppose." Her shoulders relaxed and her fists unclenched. "Ah, how much danger?"

"As little as possible while still letting Brown show his hand."

"And you persuaded Rensdale to agree to this? Why, he has hardly left the house since the fires."

"Oh, I told him I'd write to his wife about a certain housemaid he's been trying to meet in the broom closet. He'd rather face a would-be killer than Lady Rensdale."

She nodded. "Very well. When do we start?"

"We?"

She tapped her foot, not at all in time to the music. "Partners, remember? Besides, I know what Alfie Brown looks like. You do not."

He moaned, but agreed that she could help. Then he asked, "Do you still like me, a little?"

"I like you a lot, silly."

"Then you still love me?"

"I never stopped loving you, Ian. No matter how angry I might get, no matter how your high-handedness infuriates me, I doubt if I could ever stop."

"Good, because I think I love you more every day."

"Do you, truly?" She looked up into his eyes, seeking answers in their brown depths.

Ian gazed at her, then touched her lips with his gloved fingers. "I'll just have to spend the rest of my life proving it to you, won't I?"

He was ready to start that instant, replacing his fingers with his lips, but the audience burst into applause and people started to pour out of their boxes. "Botheration."

"You can start showing me tomorrow, when we catch the criminal."

Which meant her door was still locked. "Botheration" did not half describe his sentiments.

Athena took the dog out for a walk in the park at nine o'clock the next morning. She passed an ink-stained poet with his pad, a footman and a maid snuggling in the shrubbery, an old man asleep on one of the benches, and a tweed-capped bird-watcher, with his telescope trained on the trees. Two gentlemen walked past and tipped their hats, and three young men in evening dress staggered down the path, as if coming home from their nighttime revels. A bent old crone leaned on her cane near the ornamental fountain, and a bespectacled scholar sat beneath a tree, his book open on his knees. Half an hour later, Rensdale left Maddox House, looked furtively in both directions, scurried across the street, and took up a seat on an iron bench.

He opened the sack he carried and pulled out a nut, to feed the squirrels. He stared at it, wondering if he was supposed to open the cursed thing for the vermin, then tossed it as far from himself as he could.

Athena went past with the dog, who picked up the nut. Her brother looked at her sourly, liking the idea of her impersonating Troy far better. Both of them had been overruled by Marden.

Athena smiled, pulled Roma away from Rensdale's boots, and whispered, "Try to act as if you are enjoying yourself, for heaven's sake. The day is fine, the birds are singing, you are feeding your little furry friends. You are a nature lover, released from your sickbed at last."

"I am a sitting duck," he whispered back, kicking out at a sparrow who came to investigate. "And your husband is sick in the head if he thinks this is going to work."

"It will. Ian knows what he is doing."

"Hah, can't even bed his wife, I hear. At least I can do that!"

Athena tossed the dog's found nut right at her half-brother's feet, hoping a squirrel would come climb up his leg.

He was ignoring her indignation, complaining: "Leastways, I could bed my wife if I were home."

"Soon, Spartacus," she said, not looking at him, but at the curricle driving past the park's entrance for the third time.

No one threatened Rensdale, but a pigeon that landed on his hat. He shouted and jumped up as though he were shot. The old crone, the scholar and the bird-watcher rushed to his side. Two curricles outside the gates nearly collided, and the three inebriated young bloods nearly tipped over the bench where the old man was sleeping, in their hurry to get to Athena's brother. The whiskered old man muttered and shook his cane at them, then rolled over and went back to his nap.

After three days, Ian was disgusted. Rensdale was used to the pigeons and the squirrels by now. Ian was not used to sleeping alone. His wife let him kiss her good night, which only made things worse, and harder. She might have let him in her bedroom, but he would never know. The door was unlocked, although not open, but her maid reported to his valet that the mistress was "indisposed." That did not keep her from trotting out every morning with the dog, into the nearby park and into danger.

His heart was in his throat every morning she did, despite having taken every precaution he could. His men were growing weary and bored, especially the lad stationed up in the tree, and the one who was hidden in a privet hedge. A poodle on a jeweled lead had raised his leg on that hedge, and Ian almost had a mutiny on his hands. He almost had another one when Troy argued about taking his turn in the park. The only one who thought that was a good idea was Rensdale, who won frowns and jeers from everyone else.

Princess Hedwig Hafkesprinke made an appearance in the park with Lady Doro as attendant one morning, to brighten the wait. The three choice spirits were replaced by three barristers in white wigs arguing over a point of law, and the poet had become an artist with a sketchbook. The old man still slept on the bench with his cane beside him.

Ian circled the park on his horse, in his curricle, on foot. The pistol in his waistband and the knife in his boot gave him confidence, but the wait was making him doubt his strategy. What if Brown had left London after the fires, satisfied that he had wreaked enough havoc? They might never find him, and Rensdale and Troy might never be safe. Ian could only wonder if the man included Athena in his list of Renslows to be eliminated.

He found out the next morning.

His men were in their places, seemingly oblivious to Rensdale, who was taking aim at the squirrels with his nuts. Anyone could have approached him. No one did. From his place across the street, Ian gave the signal that Rensdale should go home, the guards should disperse, and Athena should stop letting the fool dog growl at the sleeping old man on his bench.

Athena tugged on Roma's leash. "Come on, then. Let us find you a bone in the kitchens," she said, even knowing that the dog could not hear.

"Not so fast, missy." The old man rolled over and grabbed at her arm. With his other hand he pulled at the handle of his cane. It opened to reveal a long blade, which was suddenly at Athena's throat. "One yell an' yer dead."

Athena was too stunned to scream. "Why, you're not—"

"On yer husband's payroll? I reckon I am now, Countess." Still holding her tightly, Alfie Brown reached with his knife hand to pull off the fake beard he wore. "I figure he'll pay me plenty to get you back. I was plannin' on runnin' you through next time that fleabag went after my boots, but this way is better. Gettin' even is all well and good, but it don't put food in yer belly. It don't get you passage out of the country, neither. With yer nob hirin' all them Runners and postin' a reward, I couldn't stay in England, now could I?"

Knowing that it was only a matter of time before someone noticed her plight, Athena stalled, rather than let Brown drag her out of the park. "I have no doubts that Lord Marden will be happy to purchase you a berth on a ship going somewhere. He will—"

"Oh, I figure he'll pay more'n that to get you back safe an' sound. I seen the way he keeps lookin' at you. Not now, o' course. He's takin' his horse back to the stables, he is. Prime bit of blood and bone it is, too. You landed in clover, missy, sure enough. Imagine, my little sister a countess."

Athena's arm was growing numb from his tight grip. She struggled anyway, saying, "I am not your sister."

"O' course you are. Same as yer Rensdale's, that

ass. Same father for all of us, him, me, you and the cripple."

"Troy is not a cripple!"

"He's not dead, neither. The horse moved, or I'd of had a clean shot."

"Why, Alfie? I cannot understand it. Why would you try to kill Troy? He never hurt you. He never hurt anyone. And Rensdale. He gave you a job, a place to stay."

"Crumbs, like he's been throwin' at the pigeons. Our da promised my mum an allowance an' a cottage. What did she get? The workhouse, that's what. Soon as the old man died, Rensdale had her tossed out without a shilling. You and the others had everything. We had nothing."

"That was wrong of Spartacus, I am sure. Perhaps he did not know of the arrangement our father made. When we explain to him—"

Brown laughed, an ugly sound near to Athena's ear. "He knew, all right. I should of been livin' at the Hall, wearin' fancy clothes, ridin' horses like your earl's."

"But you were . . . That is . . ."

"Illegitimate? A bastard? Go ahead an' say it. I've heard it my whole life, haven't I? An' I owe the old man for that, too. He could of married my mum when his first wife died. 'Stead he found a pretty young bride to take her place, yer mother, not the woman what gave birth to his second son. He gave me his bum leg, but not his name, the blighter. Now I aim to get what I have comin'."

Athena did not think there would be any reasoning with Alfie, not when he had a lifetime of resentment to avenge. She knew Ian would pay for her release, but she did not know if the money would satisfy the former groom. The glitter in his eye told her no, he wanted blood, besides the gold.

She dropped the dog's leash, hoping Roma would go home, alerting the household that Athena was missing. Instead the dog went after Brown's worn boots. He kicked out at the mongrel, connecting with her ribs. The dog yelped, which did get the attention of the artist, who had stayed to complete his drawing. That guard let out a shrill whistle, which made the Runner in the tree fall out. A nanny, not one of Ian's hirelings either, started screeching, running off with a little boy in tow.

The barristers turned, but they were at the other side of the park by now. One knocked the nanny over in his haste to get back, which made the woman scream louder, and the child start to bawl.

Alfie cursed, but dragged Athena over toward a large oak tree with a wide trunk. With the tree at his back and Athena in front of him, the knife to her throat, he waited.

Not for long.

Carswell and Marden came pelting through the park, pistols drawn. They pushed through the ring of Runners and guards who had gathered, uncertain of what to do. Neither one could chance a shot, not with Brown half-hidden behind Athena.

Brown said, "That'll be far enough, Marden," when they were close enough for Athena to see the beads of sweat on her husband's brow. "Put the guns down or yer lady starts bleedin'." He pressed the edge of his blade against her neck to make his point.

Ian stopped in his tracks and held out his hand to halt Carswell behind him, not taking chances with Athena's life. He carefully put down his pistol. So did his friend, cursing under his breath.

"Are you all right?" Ian asked, looking at his wife, inspecting her for injuries. The muscles of his jaw twitched, and his hands were in fists at his side.

She tried to smile, to wipe that look of helpless rage out of his eyes. "I am fine now that you are here. I knew you would come."

He looked at her, only slightly disheveled, and then he looked at the dirty, disreputable, knife-wielding maniac who had her in his clutches. "Damnation, woman, *now* you trust me?"

Chapter Twenty-Seven

Ah, love! What would I do without my wife?
                              —Anonymous

Ah, life! What would it be without love?
                              —Mrs. Anonymous

Brown gave him a gap-toothed grin. "O' course she trusts you, fer all the good it'll do her. An' I trust you, too, Marden, to see I gets my rightful share."

"I'll see you hang."

The knife pressed into Athena's neck. The drop of blood was as red as the ruby heart pendant she wore, the necklace he had given her. Ian sucked in a breath, trying to stay calm. Showing his emotion now would only get her hurt worse. He swallowed and said, "Think, man. You cannot get away with this."

"Why not? I got a carriage waitin' at the corner."

Ian waved his hand around to either side. "But there are ten men between you and there, and more on the way. They will be armed and mounted before you reach your vehicle."

"None of them will touch me, on yer say-so."

Ian was incredulous at the man's stupidity. "You think I am going to let you drive off with my wife?"

"You will, less'n you want to be a widower. If I'm

goin' to die, I ain't goin' alone. You let me take her now an' I'll keep her right an' tight 'til you get me a nice heavy purse. Then we'll trade. I'll have your word on it, o' course, that you an' yer men won't follow or shoot me in the back when I drive off. Gentlemen's agreement, don't you know." He smacked his lips at the humor of calling himself a gentleman.

"Don't do it, Ian," Athena told him, breathing in the stench of Brown's sweat. "You'll keep your word, but Brown won't."

Carswell agreed with her. "He'll kill her, either way," he said in a low tone, for Ian's ears alone.

"I have to try."

Athena understood their quiet dialogue. "No, Ian, even if he lets me go, we'll never be safe. He'll want more money, or more revenge. He told me. My father promised more than Alfie's mother ever got, and Spartacus took even that little bit away. He won't be satisfied with whatever you pay him."

"Ah, missy, you didn't used to think so bad of me." Brown gave her a shake. "But you better hope yer man has more confidence in my given word, else we're both dead."

Athena was beginning to realize that she might not survive, that Ian could not save her. Tears started to fill her eyes, but she shook them away. If she had minutes left on this earth, she did not want to miss an instant of seeing her beloved husband. Poor Ian, he would blame himself, when there was nothing he could have done.

Ian was not ready to concede. "If you would trust my honor if I promised not to follow you, why not trust me without frightening my wife? Let her go, and I will be much more generous. I'll get Rensdale to up the ante, too."

Brown snickered. "I'd only trust a swell when he

had somethin' to gain. Come on, now, Marden. Call off yer men and swear to let me pass with the gal. My knife hand is gettin' heavy."

Ian looked at Carswell, whose eyes flashed to Ian's boot, where his own knife reposed. He looked at the Runners who were poised to rush the bastard who was making Athena cry. Could they move fast enough? Could he take the chance? Then he noticed that Captain Beecham, Troy, and Wiggs had come out of the house and were hastening toward the park, the captain on his peg leg and the young man on his crutches.

Brown noticed them, too, and laughed again, spittle dribbling out of the side of his mouth. "Look at that, two cripples comin' to the rescue, along with the clergyman. Trust that coward Rensdale to stay safe by the fire an' let a boy an' an old man fight his battles, while the prig prays over it."

No one disagreed with his assessment of Rensdale, although the captain muttered about being called old by a piece of flotsam like Brown, and Wiggs said, *"Tut, tut."* He stopped before reaching the circle of men facing Athena and her captor, while her uncle and brother kept coming closer.

"Put yer sword down, Cap'n. You'd have to run yer own kin through afore you got to me."

Troy hobbled forward while his uncle set his sword back in the scabbard he'd hastily buckled on. Young Renslow did not stop until he was nearest to the oak tree, toward the side. His dog limped toward him and he knelt, dropping one of his crutches, to stroke her head. He glared at Alfie, but locked his gaze with his sister's, turquoise eyes to turquoise eyes, and for a moment, Ian felt jealous of the bond between them. Then he saw Athena nod slightly, and had to wonder what the two were planning in their silent communication. He jerked his head toward Carswell, to be ready to act, and took a step closer to the woman he wished with all his heart was in his arms, not in some scoundrel's.

"Very well," he said. "I give my word. I won't follow you, if you swear not to harm my wife. We will meet in one hour wherever you say. I'll be able to get to my bank by then to make the withdrawal."

Brown's eyes shifted from side to side. "An' yer men?"

"I'll vouch for them. They will let you go, if Lady Marden is safe."

"What about the uncle?" Brown asked, still ignoring Troy.

"What, do you think I can chase you down on one limb and a wooden peg?" Captain Beecham said. "Be happy I can't, you maggot, or you'd be shark bait for threatening my family."

Wiggs was tutting from behind one of the Runners. "This is not at all seemly, Brown. No, not seemly at all. Every act of evil we do comes back to haunt us, you know, in the afterlife. You will have to answer to the Almighty, after you answer to your own conscience. You will surely regret this day."

"I'll regret not havin' a knife at yer skinny throat, too, Wiggs, iffen you don't shut yer trap."

While Brown was concentrating on Wiggs, Troy inched forward. Ian's hand reached down. Carswell put his hand behind his back, where another pistol was tucked into his waistband, but Ian shook his head. Missing by a fraction of an inch meant hitting Athena. The risk was too great to take.

"So do we have a deal, Marden?" Brown wanted to know, before any more spectators arrived to get between him and his wagon, between him and freedom, him and a fortune.

"Yes, we have a deal," Ian said. "But know this: If one hair on my wife's head is disturbed, I will hunt you to the ends of the earth. When I find you, you won't have to wait for Judgment Day to suffer all the agonies of Hell."

Brown jerked his head in agreement and pulled Athena closer against his chest. He started to inch out from the tree. He was careful to keep her between him and the earl, his head tucked down so it did not present an easy target. As usual, he ignored Troy.

"You know I shall do everything I can to get you back, my love," Ian told Athena as he could only stand and watch her being hauled off like a sack of wheat.

"Of course I do, my love. You promised to keep me safe, didn't you? And you always keep your promises."

"Always," he said, for her benefit and Brown's.

"And I will always trust you." Athena was not exactly struggling, but she was digging her boot heels in the ground, making it harder for Brown to make any progress.

When they were the closest they were going to get to where Troy was leaning over, resting on one crutch, she raised her eyebrows to her brother. He shoved the dog in Brown's direction.

Roma was sore, but she needed no encouragement to go after the worn boots that had kicked her. Brown looked down to take aim for another thrust of his foot, and his knife hand relaxed a fraction. Athena sank her fingernails into his arm and kicked backward at the same time. Troy tossed his crutch at Brown's legs, the dog snarled, Brown shouted, the earl had his knife in his hand. Carswell fired his pistol over their heads at the oak tree, sending down a cascade of small branches and leaves. When Brown raised his hand to protect his head, Athena ducked to the side and yelled, "Now!"

Ian's knife flew straight toward Brown's shoulder. Athena pushed against his other arm, freeing herself, as Ian dove for the blade Brown still held. "No!" she cried, seeing her unarmed husband lunge at an enraged, pain-crazed, desperate man. She picked up Troy's crutch and started swinging it.

Carswell had to wrest the thing away from her before she knocked Ian unconscious. Two men had Brown pinioned between them, while a third man was fastening manacles on his wrists. Troy was on the ground, the dog in his arms, Uncle Barnaby proudly patting him on the back. Wiggs was at the other side of the wide oak, being sick, and Ian was shaking his head at Athena while he caught his breath.

"Too many risks, my girl. I thought you promised to be careful," he said in severe tones, but he held his arms out for her to rush into.

Brown was screaming. "I trusted you! You gave yer word! What kind of gentleman goes back on his promise?"

Ian held Athena close to him, so tightly her ribs might turn black and blue. Neither of them cared. "I am the kind of gentleman who puts his family ahead of scum like you. What good is honor if I lost my wife?"

"Oh, Ian!" Athena said with a sigh. "That is the nicest thing you have ever said to me. You really do love me."

"Of course I do, goose. I told you so, didn't I?"

Troy turned to his uncle. "I think I am going to be sick like Wiggy."

Carswell handed him his crutches and helped him to his feet. "You'll change your tune, my boy, in about ten years, I'd guess."

Brown was still screaming that he'd been robbed, that he was promised a fortune, that his mother was meant to be Lady Rensdale, that Lord Marden was a lying, cheating piece of—

His words ended abruptly as Captain Beecham yanked the knife out of his shoulder, none too gently. Brown slumped forward in the guards' arms, unconscious. They lowered him to the ground, also none too gently, and did not rush to press a cloth to his bleeding wound.

"What are you going to do with him?" Athena's uncle wanted to know.

Troy was all for pummeling the man to death with his crutch for shooting him and kicking his dog and scaring his sister.

"That's against the law," one of the Runners said, but turned his head when Troy accidentally placed his crutch's tip on Brown's foot.

"He ought to suffer for his crimes!" Lord Rensdale had finally arrived, now that the danger was over. "The bastard ought to be boiled in oil or be drawn and quartered."

"Tut, tut," Wiggs said, wiping his face. "Surely we are more civilized than that, my lord. Hanging is the proper punishment for evildoers like Brown."

Athena was too tenderhearted. "Half of this trouble was your own fault, Spartacus, with your clutch-fisted miserliness. If you had honored our father's promise and looked after Alfie's mother, he might not have turned so mean and vengeful."

"Bah, you can nag your husband into bankruptcy now if you want. I am well rid of you and Brown both. I am going home, that's what, as soon as I see this varlet taken away in chains."

"I say he ought to be given a purse and put on a

ship for the Americas, where he might make something of his life," Athena told anyone who was interested.

"Too chancy, my love," Ian said. "He might make enough to come back and have another try at revenge. I could not rest easy without knowing where he is. I think he should be sent to Botany Bay where he cannot bother anyone again."

"If he survives the journey there," Carswell added, earning him a frown from Marden, who did not think Athena needed to know the conditions on the transport ships.

Her uncle joined the discussion. "I say he ought to be taken up by the Navy. That's the only practical solution—get some use out of the slug. We need all the strong backs we can get, to defend and protect our country, and I can have an impressment crew here before you can say 'ship ahoy.' I'll see him put on a ship with a captain who knows how to deal with lawbreakers and hoodlums. He'll never set foot on shore again."

"Life in prison."

"A firing squad."

"The courts are too lenient these days."

"Want we should take care of it here, my lord, and save the Crown the bother?"

"*Tut, tut.*"

While they were discussing his future, Brown won the argument. Or he lost, depending on one's viewpoint. His heart gave out. At any rate, discussion turned to where to bury the bastard.

Athena insisted it be in the church graveyard next to Brown's mother's grave, with a monument. Rensdale owed him that.

Her brother finally agreed, when Ian glared him into

it. Lord Marden did have to offer to pay for carting the body, for Rensdale refused to ride home with his baseborn brute of a brother.

"There, my love. It is done. Now we can get on with our own lives." Then he noticed that his shirt was getting wet. "Damnation, woman, are you crying again?"

She shook her head no, with a sob and a sniffle.

"Yes, you are. You aren't hurt, are you?" He held her at arm's length, inspecting her for damage. Her hair was fallen down and her gown was torn at the shoulder, but the tiny nick at her throat had already stopped bleeding.

She shook her head again, taking the handkerchief he handed her.

"Never tell me you are crying for Brown, are you?"

"I cannot help but thinking how unhappy he was, and how I never knew."

"What could you have done for him if you had understood his resentment? Give him your pin money? Invite him to sit in at Troy's lessons? His raising and his education were up to his father. Your sire could never have made him legitimate, but he could have made Brown a gentleman of sorts. He chose not to. You are not responsible for Brown's sorry life, or his death."

She blew her nose, leaving it red. Her cheeks were splotched with color and her eyes were swollen. Ian thought she was the most beautiful woman he had ever seen. He supposed he would think that fifty years from now, when her hair was gray and her skin was wrinkled. She would still have eyes like summer skies, and she would still be his. "Do not weep, sweetheart. Brown was not worth it."

"But he was my brother, as much as Spartacus is."

"I can see you crying over the connection to Rensdale, but not the loss of Brown. He was nothing but a rabid dog, waiting to be put down."

"You would never do that, would you? Turn your back on one of your sons?"

Ian had to laugh. "Since I shall never have a son who is not also yours, sweetheart, you shall have to help see that our sons are raised as befits the children of an earl and a countess. We are partners in that, aren't we?"

She was back in his arms, smiling. "Partners."

They went to Vauxhall that night, not to celebrate Brown's death, but their own freedom and relief. The dowager had decreed that they should be seen about town to counteract the rumors that were bound to be flying through the *ton*. Captain Beecham was pleased they'd be going by boat.

Rensdale wanted to revel, he said, to erase the bad memories. What he really wanted was one night at the pleasure gardens before going home in the morning. They all knew his wife would never approve such frivolous entertainment as that found at Vauxhall, with its music, fireworks, and common performers, where the polite world mingled with the masses. She definitely would not approve of the Dark Walks, where females of opportunity awaited gentlemen of means. Rensdale meant to have a last lark away from his half-sister's censorious eyes and his new brother-in-law's sudden priggishness.

Lady Dorothy and Carswell were not concerned with propriety, either, only in having a few stolen moments alone. After legions of liaisons, Carswell knew every hidden rotunda and secluded clearing. Lady Dorothy was always eager to broaden her knowledge with new experiences. Carswell was simply eager.

Both Ian and Athena would have preferred a pri-

vate party—very private—but Troy had been caged in
the house too long now, Athena thought, not knowing
that Ian had been taking the youngster out and about
as much as he thought he could get away with. Troy
was thrilled to be going on an adult entertainment,
even if there were no horses. Wiggs decided he had
better go, too, to see that the boy did not fall into
bad company.

Once in the gardens, Lady Dorothy and Carswell
disappeared. The dowager, the captain, and Rensdale
went to find their reserved box and order the supper.
Athena, Ian, and Wiggs had to walk slowly because of
Troy, and because Troy wanted to watch the tightrope
walkers, the jugglers, and the Cascade. Wiggs clucked
his tongue, but Athena told him to go sit with the
others if he was going to ruin Troy's enjoyment.

Ian smiled. He could tell his wife was delighting in
the simple entertainments as much as her young
brother. As they made their slow way to the rotunda,
he was stopped by friends and acquaintances who
wanted to know the truth about the stories making the
rounds. They would have ignored Troy, not looking at
the imperfect youth, but Ian introduced him as the
hero of the day, making Athena swell with pride at
both of her escorts.

They had supper, listened to the music, and then
Ian and Athena had their first waltz together as man
and wife. The dance floor was crowded, however, and
Ian did not like how the men ogled his countess in
her low-cut silver gown—when he managed to raise
his own eyes from the delectable sight. He dragged
her back to the supper box and her shawl.

Rensdale was gone, and Wiggs was enjoying the fa-
mous arrack punch more than seemly for a man of
the cloth. The dowager was drowsing in her seat, while
Troy and his uncle were debating if Oxford or Cam-

bridge might offer the better education. Ian checked his watch and his wife's décolletage.

At last, it was time for the fireworks. They made their slow way to the viewing area. Troy was tired, but game. He leaned on his crutches and watched, entranced. Ian watched his wife, who was just as rapt in the spectacle. When it was over, he took her hand and whispered in her ear. "I know where we can make our own fireworks. Unless you are still, ah, indisposed?"

Athena was glad the darkness hid her blushes, and gladder that her husband was as anxious to resume their lovemaking as she was. "I don't want to go to your house in Kensington, though. I would keep thinking of the other women you have taken there."

Ian raised Athena's Kashmir shawl higher on her shoulders and said, "You do not have to worry I gave the house to Lady Paige. Good riddance to both of them, I say, the house and the woman. Even better if she keeps Wiggs there with her. I was thinking of a suite at the Clarendon for us."

"What about Troy?"

"He's not invited."

When she laughed he said, "We'll take him home first. He's half asleep as is. The others can get back themselves. Tonight, finally, is going to be ours."

The fireworks at Vauxhall could not hold a candle— or a shooting star—to the enchantment, the excitement, the ecstasy of the rose-strewn bedroom Ian had reserved. The night was indeed theirs, for no one else could have made such good use of it. The next morning and afternoon were theirs, too, because they had waited so long, and because they had so much to learn, so much to teach.

"Oh, dear. I forgot about my brother's leaving this morning."

"We'll see him again when his infant is born. That's soon enough."

Rensdale could survive without their farewells. Troy needed to learn to manage without his sister if he was going away to university. As for the others, well, if they were enjoying themselves half as much as Ian and Athena, they should consider themselves blessed. Ian certainly did.

The first time was awkward, like a firecracker that exploded before reaching great height, with more noise than color. At least it was not terribly painful. Ian was certain he suffered more than his delicate bride, trying not to overwhelm her.

The next time they made love was slower, with the stars sending spinning, shooting flames into the sky that lighted the universe, that made the universe shrink to this room, this bed, this instant.

The third time . . . Athena could understand why Lady Doro and Carswell kept slipping away. After that, they lost count.

When he could breathe again, Ian kissed Athena's half-closed eyelids and said, "Wait, my darling. It gets better."

Athena barely had energy enough to move her lips to speak. She was adrift on the sea of satiation, floating like a dust mote in the glory of utter fulfillment. She was also half asleep. "Impossible. I do not believe you."

Ian leaned on his elbow beside her, their bodies still one. "What's this? I thought you trusted me."

She smiled and brushed the damp, dark curls off his forehead, breathing in the smell of him and their lovemaking. "Yes, but you broke your promise to Alfie Brown. How do I know you are not lying about this, too?"

So he showed her, worshiping every inch of her

body, and Athena found that she was not sleepy after all. Ian kept his promise, like the man of honor he was, with occasional lapses.

"And it will be better tomorrow and the next day and the one after that, I swear to you. I love you, Lady Marden, and I will for all time."

"Promise?"

"Word of a gentleman."

"Good, because I love you, Lord Marden, even if you are not perfect."

He raised his eyebrow. "I'm not?"

"You did lie, you know. But I think I love you the better for not being quite so magnificent. Besides, no one is perfect. Look at Troy, your sister, and Uncle Barnaby. They are all well loved, despite their faults."

"What about Carswell?"

"Oh, he is too perfect. That leaves him lacking."

Ian tried to follow her reasoning. "Well, you are nearly perfect, sweetheart, except for that mole on your knee and those freckles I never noticed across your nose. I cannot think of one thing you arc lacking."

"Gammon. I am too short and my hair is too curly and—"

"Perfect," Ian declared. "Except you can't sing for a tinker's damn, of course. Not that I do not love your singing anyway," he hastily added.

"Oh, I do love you, Ian. And I will forever."

"Promise?"

"Word of a lady."

That was good enough for Lord Marden. It had to be, for his countess was fast asleep, a smile on her well-kissed lips.

Ian smiled, too. His wife. His partner. His, forever. "That just might be long enough," he whispered before he closed his eyes. "That just might be . . . perfect."

About the Author

The author of over thirty romance novels, **Barbara Metzger** is the proud recipient of two *Romantic Times* Career Achievement Awards for Regencies and a RITA award from the Romance Writers of America. When not writing romances or reading them, she paints, gardens, volunteers at the local library, and goes beachcombing on the beautiful Long Island shore with her little dog, Hero. She loves to hear from readers care of Signet or through her Web site, www.BarbaraMetzger.com.

BARBARA METZGER

"Barbara Metzger deliciously mixes love and laughter." —*Romantic Times*

Wedded Bliss
0-451-20859-5

A Perfect Gentelman
0-451-21041-7

Available wherever books are sold or at
www.penguin.com

All your favorite romance writers are coming together.

SIGNET ECLIPSE